Unmasking Ravel

Eastman Studies in Music

Ralph P. Locke, Senior Editor
Eastman School of Music

Additional Titles of Interest

Aspects of Unity in J. S. Bach's Partitas and Suites: An Analytical Study
David W. Beach

Beethoven's Century: Essays on Composers and Themes
Hugh Macdonald

Berlioz: Past, Present, Future
Edited by Peter Bloom

"Claude Debussy as I Knew Him" and Other Writings of Arthur Hartmann
Edited by Samuel Hsu, Sidney Grolnic, and Mark Peters

Debussy's Letters to Inghelbrecht: The Story of a Musical Friendship
Annotated by Margaret G. Cobb
Translated by Richard Miller

French Music, Culture, and National Identity, 1870–1939
Edited by Barbara L. Kelly

French Organ Music from the Revolution to Franck and Widor
Edited by Lawrence Archbold and William J. Peterson

In Search of New Scales: Prince Edmond de Polignac, Octatonic Explorer
Sylvia Kahan

Intimate Voices: The Twentieth-Century String Quartet
Edited by Evan Jones

Maurice Duruflé: The Man and His Music
James E. Frazier

Musical Encounters at the 1889 Paris World's Fair
Annegret Fauser

The Musical Madhouse (Les grotesques de la musique)
Hector Berlioz
Translated and edited by Alastair Bruce

Music's Modern Muse: A Life of Winnaretta Singer, Princesse de Polignac
Sylvia Kahan

Music Speaks: On the Language of Opera, Dance, and Song
Daniel Albright

Pentatonicism from the Eighteenth Century to Debussy
Jeremy Day-O'Connell

The Poetic Debussy: A Collection of His Song Texts and Selected Letters
Edited by Margaret G. Cobb

Schubert in the European Imagination
Scott Messing

The Sea on Fire: Jean Barraqué
Paul Griffiths

Variations on the Canon: Essays on Music from Bach to Boulez in Honor of Charles Rosen on His Eightieth Birthday
Edited by Robert Curry, David Gable, and Robert L. Marshall

A complete list of titles in the Eastman Studies in Music series may be found on the University of Rochester Press website, www.urpress.com.

Unmasking Ravel

New Perspectives on the Music

Edited by Peter Kaminsky

UNIVERSITY OF ROCHESTER PRESS

651916221

First published 2011

University of Rochester Press
668 Mt. Hope Avenue, Rochester, NY 14620, USA
www.urpress.com
and Boydell & Brewer Limited
PO Box 9, Woodbridge, Suffolk IP12 3DF, UK
www.boydellandbrewer.com

ISBN-13: 978-1-58046-337-9
ISSN: 1071-9989

Library of Congress Cataloging-in-Publication Data

Unmasking Ravel : new perspectives on the music / edited by Peter Kaminsky.
    p. cm.—(Eastman studies in music, 1071–9989 ; v. 84)
    Includes bibliographical references and index.
    ISBN 978–1-58046–337–9 (hardcover : alk. paper) 1. Ravel, Maurice, 1875–1937—Criticism and interpretation. I. Kaminsky, Peter.
    ML410.R23U56 2010
    780.92—dc22

                                                        2010049336

A catalogue record for this title is available from the British Library.
This publication is printed on acid-free paper.

Printed in the United States of America.

To Kim, Dave, and Matt

Contents

Acknowledgments

The publication of this book is due to the support, inspiration, and hard work of a number of individuals. First, I wish to thank all the contributors for providing the new perspectives on Ravel's music—historiographical, critical, analytical—alluded to in the volume's title. Suzanne Guiod and Professor Ralph P. Locke, editorial director and senior editor of the Eastman Studies in Music series for University of Rochester Press, respectively, were supportive of this project from its earliest stages. Leann Sanders provided expert assistance with all things editorial, as did Jennifer Wanner with graphics; their persistent good humor in the face of technical obstacles remains a small miracle. Nicholas Betson proved an able translator from German to English; thanks also to Peter Winslow for translation assistance. Generous and timely financial support was provided by Dr. David G. Woods, dean of the School of Fine Arts at the University of Connecticut, and by the Society for Music Theory.

Introduction

Peter Kaminsky

In a letter to critic Louis Laloy dated March 8, 1907, Claude Debussy, upon hearing the premier of Ravel's song cycle *Histoires naturelles,* writes:

> I agree with you in acknowledging that Ravel is exceptionally gifted, but what irritates me is his posture as a 'trickster,' or better yet, as an enchanting fakir, who can make flowers spring up around a chair. Unfortunately, a trick is always prepared, and it can astonish only once![1]

In a "Tribute" published in 1933, Ravel's friend and musicologist Michel Dimitri Calvocoressi notes:

> He had a marked taste for the recondite, which people who did not know him considered a sign of affectation. He was aware of this, but it did not worry him in the least. One day, however, he said to me, rather impatiently: *"Mais est-ce qu'il ne vient jamais à l'idée de ces gens-là que je peux être 'artificiel' par nature?"* (But doesn't it ever occur to those people that I can be "artificial" by nature?)[2]

The above statements are of course representative tropes in contemporary characterizations of Ravel's music. Significantly, both Debussy and Calvocoressi bring up the crucial idea of artifice. Without denying the grain of validity to their respective statements, it is fair to say that these and related tropes have had inordinate influence on the subsequent course of Ravel scholarship in its entirety and that for the most part, they have not been subject to a thoroughly critical interrogation.

Furthermore, one of the consequences of the pervasive concern with artifice in the characterization of Ravel's music is the relative dearth of analysis of his musical language. By way of comparison, there has been little question of Debussy's stature as a composer and clearly no lack of anaytical scholarship on his music. With Ravel, on the other hand, it seems that the perception of artifice in relation to his persona raises the broader critical issue of the full legitimacy of his music. More pointedly, the notion of artificiality brings with it the implication of lack of substance and depth, which traditionally is a distinct nonstarter in motivating analytical study. (How can you analyze what is not actually there?)

The present volume fills a unique place in Ravel scholarship to date in its balance of contextual, interpretive, and analytical focus. As a whole, the volume strives to balance aesthetic strands and critical modes of interpretation with in-depth analysis. It engages each of Ravel's major genres, including piano music, song, opera, chamber music and orchestral music, as well as the crucial topics of expression, virtuosity, melodic and motivic structure, form, and pitch organization; at the same time, individual chapters provide new insights into his development as a composer, as well as close readings of representative major works.

In part 1, Orientations and Influences, the opening chapters by Steven Huebner and Barbara L. Kelly serve a dual purpose: in engaging pre– and post–World War I aspects of Ravel's aesthetic and legacy, they also identify and examine historically and critically a number of the "master tropes" central to Ravel scholarship. A brief listing of these somewhat overlapping tropes will help provide an interpretive context for the essays in this volume. (Note that I have extrapolated these tropes from their chapters, where they may or may not be explicitly identified.) In no particular order, they are:

1. Ravel as classicist
2. Ravel's masks
3. Ravel as artisan
4. Ravel as "artificial"
5. Ravel and the aesthetic of imposture
6. Ravel as "cold"
7. Ravel as virtuoso
8. Ravel as "ornamentalist"

"Ravel as classicist" involves a broad range of issues, including his use of compositional models, the relationship between convention and subversion in his work, and the ever-problematic issue of influence. Regarding the latter, this trope may be thought of as spawning several important subtropes, including Steven Huebner's "influence without anxiety" (that of Poe, Mozart, Johann Strauss, and Chabrier) and "anxious influence" (that of Debussy, especially). "Ravel's masks" (the progenitor of this volume's title) represents arguably the most durable and pervasive of the tropes, implying qualities of deception, disguise, and mutability. "Ravel as artisan" cuts to the core of innumerable descriptions of the composer and his music: his self-professed obsessive perfectionism; Stravinsky's characterization of him as a "Swiss watchmaker"; Jankélévitch's as a "problem-solver"; and Roland-Manuel's application of the term *artisan*.[3] This too spawns a related series of important subtropes, e.g., "Ravel as copyist or imitator," which, as Barbara Kelly notes, represents a strategic branding more or less invented by Roland-Manuel to distance Ravel from the cult of originality associated with modernism.

The concept of "Ravel as artificial" has often been extended to include the ideas of fabrication and fakery (see Serge Diaghilev's reaction upon first hearing *La valse:* "Ravel, it is a masterpiece . . . but it is not a ballet. . . . It is the portrait of a ballet . . . the painting of a ballet").[4] The notion of "Ravel and the aesthetic of imposture," dating from 1925 with the publication of Roland-Manuel's article of the same name in *La Revue Musicale,* has exerted a mighty gravitational pull ever since. The conditions associated with artistic imposture—of difficulty, problem-solving, even impossibility, as goads to artistic creation—surface in Ravel's oeuvre in obvious ways such as making one hand sound like two in the Piano Concerto for the Left Hand, and less obviously, in the simultaneous empowering and disabling of the Child, the would-be knight-in-shining-armor, in *L'enfant et les sortilèges.*

"Ravel as 'cold,'" while inelegant terminologically, is intended to suggest the qualities so often associated with the composer—irony, distance, anti-romanticism, anti-sincerity, and objectivity; without such a trope, references to Ravel's intensity of musical expression (through his ties to his Basque origins, psychological acuity, etc.), such as the description by Alex Ross in reference to *Le tombeau de Couperin* ("emotion smolders under the exquisite surface"), lose their enabling source. Finally, both "Ravel as virtuoso" and "Ravel as 'ornamentalist,'" in their relative specificity, could be viewed as subtropes due to their close association with artisanship and artificiality, respectively. But their centrality to much of Ravel's music, in particular the piano works, and their deep interaction with what Michael J. Puri elegantly describes as his "valorizing the surface over the interior," warrant their inclusion with the master tropes.

On the one hand, the above list conveys the impression of a composer undoubtedly brilliant but in some fundamental way flawed and in need of defending—not quite eligible for entry into the "Hall of Fame" of high artistic masters, notwithstanding the popularity of most of his repertoire with audiences and performers. On the other hand, it is both possible and fruitful to interpret these tropes in positive ways, as enabling imaginative and novel approaches to Ravel's musical language. Indeed, the recent surge in Ravel scholarship bears witness to an ongoing reassessment that acknowledges the composer's idiosyncratic traits as crucial to an interpretive approach. In English alone, the work of Deborah Mawer, Michael Puri, Stephen Zank, Steven Huebner, and Carolyn Abbate (and my own modest contribution) affirms beyond any doubt Ravel's artistic stature.[5]

Within the context of current research on Ravel, this volume is unique in its combination of critical interpretation and strong analytical focus. The analyses cover a gamut of approaches: some focus on large-scale pitch and formal organization in their use of Schenkerian, sonata-theory, and pitch-collectional methodologies (Suurpää, Heinzelmann, and Antokoletz); some privilege the surface and more phenomenal features such as meter, embodiment, kinesthetic activity, and gesture (Bhogal, Leong and Korevaar, and Helbing); and some move between the two (Puri and Kaminsky). All of the analyses limn Ravel's creative and unique relation to stylistic convention and, whether explicitly or implicitly, interact suggestively with the multiple contexts suggested by the critical taxonomy sketched above.

Taken together, the essays by Huebner, Kelly, and Puri that compose part 1, Orientations and Influences, cover a large, colorful, and complex terrain that includes cultural and literary history, biography, influence, reception, branding (in the modern advertising sense), memory, and interpretive strategies. Our master tropes emerge and are interrogated via the examination of their sources and the agendas behind their creation. In chapter 1, Steven Huebner shows how Ravel's literary influences—including obvious figures such as Poe and less obvious ones such as Klingsor, Régnier, and Fargue—informed his conception of classicism; the author offers concrete structural analogues between literary and musical gestures, elucidating the inspirations for some of Ravel's compositions. Barbara Kelly's essay complements that of Huebner in its provocative assessment of the roles played by Ravel's critics and biographers, in particular Vladimir Jankélévitch and Ravel's student Alexis Roland-Manuel. Kelly's analysis not only enhances our understanding of Ravel's aesthetic vis-à-vis its "packaging" by Roland-Manuel and its association with the notion of "challenge" by Jankélévitch, but also helps illuminate the ingredients of his "Frenchness" and his influence on subsequent generations of composers. Michael Puri offers a critical interpretation of what at first glance appears a rather unlikely subject for Adorno to have engaged, the music of Ravel. However, in reading Adorno's short essays on Ravel with a positive spin, Puri offers insights into the composer's melancholic nostalgia in light of the philosopher's "prosthetics of memory" and the imminent demise of the Western European classical music tradition. Equally important, the author shows the relevance of an Adorno-inspired interpretive strategy for musical analysis in several passages from the *Valses nobles et sentimentales*.

Part 2, Analytical Case Studies, provides close readings of works representing the chronological boundaries of Ravel's mature work (from the 1899 *Pavane pour une infante défunte* to the 1931 *Concerto pour piano et orchestre*). The five essays that make up part 2 establish quite different but complementary analytical contexts, illuminating various aspects of structural process in Ravel's work. My essay extends Jankélévitch's assertion of an "aesthetics of challenge"—based on Roland-Manuel's "aesthetics of imposture"—to the domain of form; it provides a kind of introduction to the subsequent analyses by comparing formal process in three pairs of related works and assessing the resultant findings in relation to recent scholarship. As theorist-pianist and concert pianist, respectively, coauthors Daphne Leong and David Korevaar are well positioned to deal with virtuosity in Ravel's music. Taking the idea of conceptual blending as a point of departure, their analysis of selected works in terms of "mechanical motion" and "dance-like motion" shows how musical structure, physical gesture, and expressivity come together in ingenious ways. Sigrun Heinzelmann, in choosing the first movements of the String Quartet of 1903 and the Piano Trio composed eleven years later, covers the pre–World War I trajectory of Ravel's approach to sonata form from his first large-scale effort to full mastery. In her analysis, she enunciates a fundamental principle of Ravel's compositional approach to all works regardless of size and scope: the use of minimal material to maximal structural ends. Volker Helbing provides an anatomy of a specific historical model—the waltzes of Johann Strauss—and Ravel's creative use of the model. Observing the presence of repetition, circular movement, and dance in Ravel's early work, Helbing develops the notion of "spiral form" and its tendency toward self-destruction, focusing on its culmination in *La valse*. Elliott Antokoletz discusses Ravel's shift from extended tonality to his more modernist musical language of the 1920s, focusing on the elusive *Sonate pour violon et violoncelle*. As a prime example of the "stripped-down" style (*style dépouillé*—see Kelly's discussion in chapter 2), Ravel's turn toward a leaner, more linear, and less harmonic idiom in this work is shown to be influenced by Bartók's polymodal chromaticism.

The essays constituting part 3, Interdisciplinary Studies, take as their point of departure either a historical process or a contemporaneous aesthetic or sociological phenomenon, in combination with current analytical methodologies. The resultant effort elicits novel and illuminating perspectives on several important works. Lauri Suurpää draws on the work of semiotician A. J. Greimas as well as Heinrich Schenker in addressing text-music relations in two songs from the cycle *Histoires naturelles;* his approach provides insights into Ravel's "literalism" (a subtrope of "Ravel as artisan") by showing the depth and extent to which the musical and poetic settings correspond. Gurminder K. Bhogal complements the work of Leong and Korevaar in addressing selected virtuoso piano works. Focusing on the notion of the ornament and its potential priority over (or even displacement of) structure, she synthesizes aspects of the nineteenth-century art nouveau movement, pianistic pyrotechnics, current metrical theory, representation, and Ravel biography, bringing them to bear on her analysis. In the concluding essay, I begin by interrogating Freudian psychoanalyst Melanie Klein's well-known interpretation of Colette's libretto for the opera *L'enfant et les sortilèges* in light of alternative accounts of moral development in children. This provides the backdrop for exploring possible mappings between psychoanalytic theory and musical structure and applying these mappings to selected numbers as well as to the overall progress of the opera (over which both dramatic and musical imposture loom large).

In conclusion, let us return to Ravel's purported lack of depth. In a sense, the composer's own self-deprecating sense of irony helps foster this impression.

After all, any composer who heads a score with "the delicious and ever-novel pleasure of a useless occupation" (*le plaisir délicieux et toujours nouveau d'une occupation inutile*), as Ravel, quoting Régnier, does with *Valses nobles et sentimentales*, wittingly places that work within the domain of the divertissement. "I'm not to be taken too seriously," the music proclaims with a sly smile; but that is part of the seductive charm of Ravel's irony. Indeed, Roland-Manuel cites *Valses nobles et sentimentales* as marking a seismic shift in Ravel's harmonic and compositional conception.[6] (A glance at the voice leading of the opening two bars confirms this in spades.) Such a gap between the "face value" of a work and the depth of its technique, craft, and especially its expression manifests itself in virtually all of Ravel's major compositions. Perhaps more than any other factor, this argues for a reexamination of context, interpretation, perspective, style, and structure across his output. In this volume, complementary modes of critical exegesis and analysis not only provide a richer understanding of Ravel's work, but also help us to follow to its logical conclusion the suggestiveness of his irony.

Notes

1. Arbie Orenstein, ed., *A Ravel Reader: Correspondence, Articles, Interviews* (New York: Columbia University Press, 1990), 87.

2. Quoted in Roger Nichols, *Ravel Remembered* (London: Faber and Faber, 1987), 180.

3. See, respectively, Arbie Orenstein, *Ravel: Man and Musician* (New York: Columbia University Press, 1975), 118; Burnett James, *Ravel: His life and Times* (New York: Hippocrene Books, 1983), 11; Vladimir Jankélévitch, *Ravel* (New York: Grove Press, 1956), 69; and Alexis Roland-Manuel, "Maurice Ravel ou l'esthétique de l'imposture," *La Revue Musicale* (April 1925): 18–19.

4. Quoted in Deborah Mawer, "Ballet and the Apotheosis of the Dance," in *The Cambridge Companion to Ravel*, ed. Deborah Mawer (Cambridge: Cambridge University Press, 2000), 151.

5. See, respectively, Deborah Mawer, *The Ballets of Maurice Ravel: Creation and Interpretation* (Aldershot, England: Ashgate, 2006); Stephen Zank, *Irony and Sound: The Music of Maurice Ravel* (Rochester, NY: University of Rochester Press, 2009); Steven Huebner, "Laughter: In Ravel's Time," *Cambridge Opera Journal* 18, no. 3 (November 2006): 225–46; Huebner, "Maurice Ravel: Private Life, Public Works," in *Musical Biography: Towards New Paradigms*, ed. Jolanta T. Pekacz (Aldershot, England: Ashgate, 2006); Huebner, "Ravel's Child: Magic and Moral Development," in *Musical Childhoods and the Cultures of Youth*, ed. Susan Boynton and Roe-Min Kok (Middletown, CT: Wesleyan University Press, 2006); and Carolyn Abbate, "Outside Ravel's Tomb," *Journal of the American Musicological Society* 52, no. 3 (Fall 1999): 465–530.

6. See Alexis Roland-Manuel, *Maurice Ravel*, trans. Cynthia Jolly (London: Dennis Dobson, 1947), 60–61.

Part One

Orientations and Influences

Chapter One

Ravel's Poetics

Literary Currents, Classical Takes

Steven Huebner

In a panegyric published in *La Revue Musicale* (1921) that set the tone for much subsequent Ravel criticism, Alexis Roland-Manuel stated that if "the composer of the *Poèmes de Mallarmé* were ever asked to describe his poetics he would simply refer his interlocutor to Edgar Allan Poe's essay "The Philosophy of Composition."[1] There, famously, the American poet explained how "The Raven"—and by extension, all of his poetry—was conceived not in a state of "fine frenzy" but rather as an assembly of "wheels and pinions" and "with the precision and rigid consequence of a mathematical problem."[2] During the creative process, considerations of duration, tone, design, and phonetics preceded the invention of the poem's subject matter and matrix of metaphors. Four years later, Roland-Manuel reaffirmed Ravel's connection to the American writer in another *Revue Musicale* essay, this time by citing Charles Baudelaire's preamble to his translation of Poe's essay, including the memorable assertion that "accidents and the irrational were [Poe's] two great enemies."[3]

One of Roland-Manuel's objectives was to champion Poe in order to distinguish Ravel's art from that of his contemporaries. For example, long-standing aesthetic enmity against Vincent d'Indy emerges in his claim that Ravel's works do not adhere to the "religion of the *lied à cinq compartiments* or the cult of sonata form" (the choice of the word "religion" is a barb in this formulation).[4] Ravel's use of older forms, says Roland-Manuel, is inspired and free-spirited, not pedantic and wedded to preconceptions of Truth. In another phase of his argument, Roland-Manuel contrasts Ravel's harmonic and melodic language, as well as his attraction to classical forms, to Debussy's practice. But he also goes on to construct a more nuanced relationship between these two composers. He sees a deeper kinship between them in Ravel's commitment to a *musique plus nue*, that is, more transparent textures unencumbered by excessive counterpoint.

Thus a binary Ravel. On the one hand, he exhibits an aesthetic persona distinct from that of Debussy—Ravel's adherence to Poe's "The Philosophy of Composition" is implicitly part of that individuality. On the other, he is Debussy's "natural heir" to leadership in the French tradition. Roland-Manuel's agenda of establishing the "family history" of French music seems eminently amenable to Harold Bloom's Oedipal critical paradigm, in light of which one might reasonably suppose that Ravel's many expressions of admiration for Debussy's music coexisted with concern about his influence. Read retrospectively against such incidents as Ravel's insistence on his pianistic innovations in *Jeux d'eau* after claims for priority made by Debussy's acolyte Pierre Lalo,[5] the elevation of Ravel as predestined heir might credibly fuel biographical narratives that highlight Oedipal anxiety: Ravel as a young, independent voice seeking his own creative space within a national tradition strongly marked by a senior colleague he greatly respected. I want to suggest that literary affinities played an important role in defining that space, but that this was particularly delicate (and anxiety-provoking) in Ravel's relationship with Debussy, because the two shared many tastes, including one for Poe (albeit for different aspects of his work).

Continuing the nationalistic perspective, Roland-Manuel describes Ravel as a "sensual logician" (in contrast not only to Debussy but also to a Stravinsky who was dogged by an obsession with ends over means, a point Roland-Manuel elaborates in the second essay). Rather than dealing in cut-and-dry metaphors and obvious translations from music to image, Ravel subverts expectations, revels in antithesis and allusions, the equivocal, the ambiguous, and sudden shifts of balance. The prestidigitator implicitly rubs shoulders with the symbolist between the lines of Roland-Manuel's discussion. Ravel remains both grounded and difficult to pin down. Roland-Manuel exemplifies this by referring to the "magic of Ravel's harmonic combinations," sonorities that seduce the listener and blind unwary epigones to Ravel's commitment to the "golden thread of tonality."[6] Although Roland-Manuel is not explicit on this point, the shadow of Poe's theorizing seems unmistakable: to follow the charms of complex chords without the golden thread was to fall into "the bottomless pit of Chance"[7]—that corollary to the free play of uncontrolled passions. Whereas functional tonality was an article of religious faith (or, more broadly expressed, a core moral value) to a composer like d'Indy and a diminishing resource to one like Debussy, for Ravel it remained relevant as a parameter to test craft and "constructiveness" *tout court*.[8] To conclude the second essay, Roland-Manuel rearticulates the constructivist point (at least as the binary opposite to the chaos of Chance) by citing Paul Valéry's dialogue *L'âme et la danse:* Phèdre speaks of voluptuous dreams inspired by an intoxicating combination of music and dance, but Socrate warns his student not to let the sensuality of the dancers' movements blind him to the rational nature of gesture. Socrate suggests that sensuality is a mere sensory by-product and that reasoned apprehension of the inherent order of the spectacle regulates the real dream.[9]

Roland-Manuel does temper the constructivist perspective (in the first essay) by allowing that the "instinct and sensibility" of Ravel could scarcely be obliterated.[10] Nonetheless, the "quiet passion" of his music is not willed, but simply "is," and remains humbly subservient in the creative process. Roland-Manuel identifies the expurgation of "fine frenzy" (Poe's expression, it will be recalled) with "*hygiène classique*" (Roland-Manuel's emphasis), as if there were something undisciplined about more romantic orientations;[11] this takes on importance, I argue, in the entwinement of Ravel's aesthetic space and literary tastes with a network of critical categories associated with "classicism." The malleability of the latter emerges within both of these essays as Roland-Manuel proposes another take on classicism, that of the composer who installs himself "before a Mozart sonata or a Saint-Saëns concerto," like a painter before a clump of trees, and gets to work.[12] Thanks to the creator's originality and sensibilities, the finished composition shows no trace of the model, a process of sublimation unfathomable to rational apprehension. T. S. Eliot's celebration of the generosity of the past sits well with this paradigm of influence:

> What is to be insisted upon is that the poet must develop or procure the consciousness of the past and that he should continue to develop this consciousness throughout his career. What happens is a continual surrender of himself as he is at the moment to something which is more valuable.[13]

Roland-Manuel gives this perspective a nationalistic twist by observing that Ravel is, in this respect, "a descendant of the French classics" (presumably artists and writers of the *ancien régime*) and "following their example practices imitation of the ancients."[14] But nota bene: Roland-Manuel explicitly states that Debussy never furnished Ravel with a model in this sense. To speak of admired models who provoked little anxiety was one strategy that Roland-Manuel used to protect Ravel's aesthetic space from an admired predecessor who appeared to cause much anxiety: witness Roland-Manuel's singling out of a connection between Ravel and Saint-Saëns, a composer whom Debussy detested and Ravel regularly praised.

Two models for the creative procedure, two models of influence. I bring up different paradigms for understanding influence (inasmuch as they relate to compositional process) to suggest that one artist may experience both anxious and unclouded responses to his forebears and contemporaries. From one point of view, the two models of creative process that I have touched upon may seem distinct: Poe's process of creation *ex nihilo* (albeit with a basic syntax and materials that have been tested over time) appears to be quite different from that of positioning oneself before a model. Yet in the general aesthetic described by Roland-Manuel, the two approaches might be seen as connected. Both are compatible with Ravel's championing of order and discipline, and his disparagement of the play of chance, spontaneity, and impulsive inspiration in composition. As we have seen, Roland-Manuel attaches *both* models of compositional process to the word *classique*. His two uses of the word in these essays—*hygiène classique* and model—map onto the first two points in a typology of classicism that Paul Valéry recorded in his *Cahiers* at around the same time: "1. classic example—model—therefore Shakespeare and Dante are classics 2. idea of order—discipline—formal rules, conventions 3. a certain simplicity—economy of means 4. Completion—perfection of detail—polished *ad unguem*—finished."[15] Valéry's third and fourth points are also not without potential for critical application to Ravel: economy of means is synonymous with the *dépouillement* of some of the later compositions. And perfection is a critical trope often applied to his music. One might adduce further takes on classicism—for example, the idea of balancing form and content,[16] or a disciplined and rational approach to creation as a counterpoise to romantic ideals of natural genius.[17] The classical artist might thus champion the artisan's work ethic. Ravel once claimed that if he had any genius at all, it was in knowing how to work.[18] Another view might privilege top-down acts of choice among materials to fill frames as opposed to bottom-up nature-grounded metaphors of internal growth and necessity, metaphysical or otherwise. Or classicism might involve poetic reflections on a classical past (such as French culture in the seventeenth and eighteenth centuries) and the expression of different lyrical and affective relationships to it, from ironic distance to melancholic loss. In this view, classicism lies in ambience. But because stylistic emulation has often been used to create ambience, the border between these two aspects of composition can be vague, as in, say, an opera such as Massenet's *Chérubin* or any number of Verlaine settings by Debussy and Fauré. Classicism might also be pressed into various broader ideological categories as the product of universal or timeless values or, more narrowly, as the fruit of national temperament.[19]

In short, the "classical" is a notoriously broad concept. I have already noted how different perceptions of the classical might influence a composer such as Ravel in different ways: one response might be a warm embrace of a revered precursor; another might be an insistence upon rational rigor to clear a personal space in the shadow of the same. What mainly concerns me here is a *network* of aesthetic categories applicable to Ravel, where the classical plays an important role in opposition to romantic values of subjective immediacy and sincerity. Even more, I am interested in how this network circulated among writers Ravel admired or knew before he met Roland-Manuel. I develop these issues as they relate to a variegated group of Ravel's literary influences: Edgar Allan Poe, Léon-Paul Fargue, Tristan Klingsor, and Henri de Régnier. Baudelaire, Stéphane Mallarmé, and Valéry are obvious omissions from the list, with cultural significance and influence too broad to embrace systematically here— but ever-present nonetheless. In short, rather than look to Ravel's "classical" musical forebears—Couperin or Mozart or Haydn—I focus on Ravel's affinities with literary figures who shared his classical orientation—relationships and affinities that resulted in a musical poetics quite distinct from that of Debussy.

Edgar Allan Poe

So far, I have reported on two of Roland-Manuel's early attempts to communicate Ravel's aesthetics. How closely do these represent Ravel's own views? Did Roland-Manuel merely act as a spokesman for the polished ideas of his friend and mentor? Did he actually shape Ravel's more amorphous thinking into a coherent intellectual framework? Or did he operate independently? Roland-Manuel's postwar essays certainly provide a more extended and systematic approach to Ravel's art than his 1914 biography of the composer, although the seeds of several concepts (including the position that Ravel was certainly not a *debussyste*) are planted in the latter. Whatever the degree of intellectual symbiosis between Ravel and Roland-Manuel, just how Poe got woven in is particularly complicated, because the American writer's influence was varied and widely felt in French culture.

Through an early interest in symbolist poetry—and the fragments from the diaries of Ricardo Viñes make clear that Ravel shared this passion with his pianist friend—Ravel probably became aware of Baudelaire's and Mallarmé's admiration of Poe at a young age. Viñes wrote in 1892 that Ravel produced two drawings after Poe's short stories "Manuscript Found in a Bottle" and "A Descent into the Maelstrom."[20] But as literary scholars have often pointed out, Baudelaire's Poe is not Mallarmé's Poe, who in turn is not Valéry's Poe (just as, the musicologist might add, Debussy's Poe is not Ravel's Poe). James Lawler has written of Baudelaire's obsession with a demonic Poe and a "genre de beauté nouveau" infused with the terror of evil.[21] The image of the *poète maudit*—alcoholic, a misunderstood outcast—resonated with both Baudelaire and Mallarmé, the latter in his commemorative *tombeau* for Poe that speaks of "son siècle épouvanté"[22]—the fear of a voice where death emerged victorious. According to Lawler, Mallarmé's cultivation of analogies in which objects stand for one another in a vertiginous quest for primal unity owes much to the ghoulish uncanny recurrences found in Poe's stories. For Valéry, the attraction was, above all, to the rational Poe, whose rationality led inexorably to an obsession with the *process* of creation rather than with the finished work itself.[23]

Ravel inhabits this symbolist aesthetic field. His choice of Paul Verlaine's "Un grand sommeil noir" and Émile Verhaeren's "Si morne" (set in 1895 and 1898, respectively) for two early *mélodies* suggests his attraction to the *poète maudit* type. Verlaine wrote the first in a Belgian prison while serving time for having wounded Arthur Rimbaud with a revolver in a fit of rage; it is difficult to imagine that Ravel would have been unaware of the biographical circumstances surrounding Verlaine's dark text. The speaker balances on the edge of suicidal oblivion and moral relativism: "Je perds la mémoire / Du mal ou du bien." For Baudelaire, Poe's death was "almost a suicide" induced by alcoholism,[24] the subject of petty bourgeois condemnation but also the fount of his genius—an obvious parallel with the later Verlaine. Ravel's setting of "Un grand sommeil noir" becomes unhinged in dissonant octatonic vocabulary as the speaker drifts to his final invocation of deathly silence.

"Si Morne" also explores the dark side of creativity through a play on the homonyms *vers* (plural of *ver*, "worm") and *vers* (verse); worms/verses eat through the discarded "package" that stands for the introspective poet. Ravel's setting of 1898 has something of Baudelaire's Poe-inspired "genre de beauté nouveau," inasmuch as its highly dissonant vocabulary gives way to a glowing, and very beautiful, major-mode conclusion despite the rot described at the end of the poem. The dark Poe may also have informed *La valse*, as Deborah Mawer has recently shown by drawing attention to parallels between Poe's story "The Masque of the Red Death" and Ravel's ballet.[25] The ballet might, in turn, trigger a chain of morbid associations involving disquieting chimes and grotesque transformations, like those that populate Ravel's previous work from the *Sérénade grotesque* through to "Le gibet" and beyond. In *L'heure espagnole*, the poet Gonzalve (Ravel's autobiographical projection) even imagines his "entombment" within a clock as an ideal condition for literary creation.[26] In the context of the generic norms of comedy-as-fertility-rite, Gonzalve's symbolist-colored sexlessness makes for an especially morbid foil to the sex appeal of the muleteer Ramiro.

Acknowledgment from Ravel himself of another Poe—the constructivist Poe—came only after Roland-Manuel's first essay, which does not of course mean that Ravel was unimpressed by "The Philosophy of Composition" earlier. Indeed, in 1924 he told an interviewer from Spain:

> My teacher in composition was Edgar Allan Poe, because of his analysis of his wonderful poem "The Raven." Poe taught me that true art is a perfect balance between pure intellect and emotion. My early stage was a reaction against Debussy, against the abandonment of form, of structure, and of architecture.[27]

Here Ravel implies long-standing adherence to Poe the constructivist, and even cites him as a "teacher" by describing him as a binary opposite to Debussy—that is, as a model who enabled him to clear his own aesthetic space. The passage is not without an odd wrinkle, however, because it represents a truly idiosyncratic reading of "The Philosophy of Composition": on the side of compositional intent, Poe seeks less to achieve a "balance" between pure intellect and emotion than to show how the composition of "The Raven" was the product of rational calculation. Perhaps Ravel refers here to the effect produced upon the listener. Outright skepticism of Ravel's account of Poe-as-teacher is not called for, but, as I have intimated, neither is complete suppression of the possibility of postwar mythmaking.

Ravel's visit to America in 1927–28 provided an obvious occasion to be gracious with his hosts. To Olin Downes of the *New York Times* he revealed that, in addition to the factories he frequented as a youth and the Spanish songs his mother sang to him, his third teacher was Poe, "whom we were quicker to understand in France than you," and whose aesthetic was "extremely close and sympathetic with that of modern French art."[28] Baudelaire seems subliminally present here as the early Gallic torch-bearer for a Poe marginalized by an uncomprehending American public. Taking into account the reference to factories and songs, the word "teacher" seems more like a synecdoche for general aesthetic influence. During another visit with Downes, Ravel connected the dots between Poe and a classical ideal, if only in a cursory way: after explaining "The Philosophy of Composition" to the American critic, the composer claimed that Poe's treatise had influenced him more than anything else "in deciding to abandon the vagueness and formlessness of the early French impressionists in favor of a return to classic standards."[29] A short time later, at his lecture at the Rice Institute in Houston, Ravel observed:

> The aesthetic of Edgar Allan Poe, your great American, has been of singular importance to me, and also the immortal poetry of Mallarmé—unbounded visions, yet precise in design, enclosed in a mystery of sombre abstractions— an art where all the elements are so intimately bound up together that one cannot analyze, but only sense, its effect. Nevertheless I believe that I myself have always followed a direction opposite to that of Debussy's symbolism.[30]

Here the web of reference is explicitly wider, as Mallarmé becomes entwined in the familiar distancing from Debussy. Because Ravel and Debussy shared many of the same literary interests (including Poe, as I have already mentioned, and of course Mallarmé as well) such differences in orientation became decisive. What might well have attracted Ravel to Mallarmé is the counterpoint (in many of his poems) between conventional strophic structure and rhyme scheme and Lawler's "daemon of analogy" where fluid substitutions (Ravel's "elements . . . so intimately bound together") take on an abstract quality ("a mystery of sombre abstractions") by dint of the often arcane phonological, etymological, and symbolic criteria that govern them. Infatuation with "precise design" is the operative category that distinguishes Ravel's Mallarmé from Debussy's, and the important point here is that Ravel cites Poe—the constructivist Poe—to buttress his point of view. Not surprisingly, Ravel's attribution to Mallarmé of "unbounded visions, yet precise in design, enclosed in a mystery of sombre abstractions" strongly resembles Valéry's Poe-derived assessment of Mallarmé: "The more he moved forward in his reflections, the more his work gave evidence of the presence and solid design of abstract thought."[31]

In some ways Ravel positioned himself as even more extreme with regard to Poe's constructivist bent than Mallarmé himself. In 1931, in an interview with the provincial paper *La Petite Gironde,* Ravel described "The Philosophy of Composition" as "the best composition treatise." "Mallarmé," he continues, "might well have suggested that this was merely a myth [the account of how Poe actually wrote "The Raven"], but I remain convinced that Edgar Poe really did write his poem "The Raven" in the way he describes."[32] Poe came up once again in a conversation between Ravel and the violinist Joseph Szigeti about *Tzigane*. According to Szigeti's memoirs, Ravel sensed the violinist's discomfort with what he felt to be the inauthenticity of the work:

> I suppose my being Hungarian has something to do with it, but I never have been able to overcome the resistance I always felt and still feel toward this brilliant and (to my mind) synthetically produced pastiche of Ravel's. He must have sensed this, for I distinctly remember that his conversation swerved suddenly to Edgar Allan Poe's elaborate description of the genesis of *The Raven*. Then . . . taking Poe's essay as starting point he expounded some of his pet theories of conscious cerebration, which insure the mechanical excellence of whatever a composer sets out to do, in however remote a field, whatever idiom he chooses to write in. My somewhat chauvinistic 'hands-off' attitude when it came to Hungarian folklore may have nettled him, and may, too, have been the reason for the otherwise reticent master's going into such detailed theorizing.[33]

The implied binary in Szigeti's account opposes the sincerely felt to the "synthetically produced." Szigeti's concern about artifice, and perhaps even about pastiche that borders on cliché, seems especially germane to *Tzigane* because one might indeed make a compelling argument that, of all of Ravel's postwar compositions, this is the one in which the composer's personal musical style is the most difficult to discern. Szigeti's reminiscences emphasize Ravel's interest in a Poe-derived *ex nihilo* creation in which authenticity (or "sincérité," the word more often used by Ravel himself) is trumped by technical polish—or, in terms that Valéry used to define the "classic," by order and discipline.

Was Ravel's conviction that Poe actually wrote "The Raven" following the steps described in his "Philosophy of Composition" some sort of clue about his *own* method of composition? Édouard Ravel once discouraged such speculation by telling the American writer May Garrettson Evans that whereas his brother "had always greatly admired Edgar A. Poe, it is impossible to affirm that he considered him 'his model' and that the 'Philosophy of Composition' had had the consequences which you mention."[34] One of the ambiguities here centers on the word "model." Michel Duchesneau has ingeniously, but also cautiously, suggested that Ravel's testimony about how he composed the Sonata for Violin and Piano lines up with Poe's method: "When I began the Sonata for piano and violin [*sic*] . . . I had already determined its quite singular form, the instrumental writing [or textures], and even the character of the themes in each of the three parts before 'inspiration' whispered any one of the themes to me."[35] Thus Duchesneau proposes that we might read Ravel's successive enumeration of "singular form," "instrumental writing" [*écriture des instruments*], and "character of the themes" as analogous to Poe's methodical determination of "extent" (i.e., duration = "singular form"), "effect" (i.e., pleasurable elevation of the soul through beauty = "instrumental writing") and "tone" (i.e., affective register; melancholy as "the most legitimate of all the poetical tones" = "character of the themes"). Only later in his essay does Poe describe his invention of the semantic content of the poem (the lamenting lover as protagonist, the appearance of the raven); accordingly Duchesneau suggests an analogy between the creation of poetic meaning and Ravel's final stage of composing the themes themselves, the moment when "inspiration" whispered them to him.

Although without doubt the location of thematic invention after the mapping of form and decisions about textures bears Poe's strong form-before-content stamp, circumspection seems well placed here. For whereas Ravel unambiguously describes how he went about composing a *particular* piece (referring, for example, to its "singular" form and the character of the instrumental writing specific to the work), Poe does not clearly demarcate reflections on the overall nature of poetic composition from the specific creative acts associated with "The Raven." The poet's thoughts on extent, effect, and tone are general in nature. The solutions to the categories of extent and effect apply to a great many poems indeed (brevity to produce "unity of effect" in the first case, beauty to produce "elevation of the soul" in the second). Poe then describes "melancholy" as the ideal poetical tone, while implicitly leaving room for other affects. It is only at this point that he determines the structural principle to be employed in "The Raven": a refrain (once again a relatively generalized phenomenon) and the limitation of the refrain to a single word (now a much more individualized trait of this poem). In short, Ravel's description seems to have little in common with Poe's modulation from general principles for poetic composition (extent, effect, and tone) to the specific features of "The Raven." If anything, the "forme assez singulière" of the Sonata for Violin and Piano (Ravel's putative first step in the succession "singular form," "instrumental writing," "character of the themes," and then the themes themselves) would seem to correspond to Poe's broaching of actual meaning in "The Raven" with the choice of just a single word ("Nevermore") as refrain. Ravel's "instrumental writing" seems quite different from the poet's more abstract ideas about how effects should create Beauty. And, whereas Poe emphasizes the goal of unity of "tone" in poems, Ravel's "character of the themes" (posited by Duchesneau as analogous to Poe's determination of "tone") leaves the door wide open to contrasting affects in a single work (despite the unity that might prevail on the level of motivic derivation).

Such comparisons are perhaps most instructive about the perennial difficulties involved in analogies between music and language. "The Philosophy of Composition" seems relevant to Ravel not for the specific methodology it outlines but rather for the attitudes to which it gives witness, an orientation that is also consonant with Valéry's critical outlook. Like the poet, the composer remains completely lucid in the act of creation. Ravel is said to have once told the violinist André Asselin: "Inspiration—what do you mean—no—I really don't know what you mean. . . . What is most difficult for a composer, you see, is choice, yes, choice."[36] Poe predicates his treatise implicitly on writing as the rational selection of materials and procedures from among a host of variables. He makes it clear that originality, which he values highly, stems not from "impulse or intuition" but, rather, must be "elaborately sought" and "demands in its attainment less of invention than negation." This became a central tenet in Valéry's assessment of Mallarmé's art: "Serious work in literature operates according to rejection."[37] The more rigid the parameters, the greater the negation. And the greater number of pieces on the cutting-room floor, the greater the effort—and the greater the art. Ravel's thinking would seem to be nourished by this literary spirit, which in its turn harmonizes with Valéry's second point about classicism relating to order and discipline. Poe writes of having devised the original versification of "The Raven" by combining different metrical schemes that, taken individually, had all been used before; novelty lay in bringing them together, interlocking the "wheels and pinions" in new and interesting ways. Ravel's cultivation of extremely chromatic chords with strong bass fifth motion, or (from a higher vantage point) a classical orientation grounded in "the golden thread of tonality," seems tributary to Poe's quest for originality forged out of a judicious selection from well-tried syntactical elements. Seen from the perspective of the aesthetics of the dandy, which Michael J. Puri has recently urged upon critics as an approach broadly applicable to Ravel's oeuvre,[38] the construction of originality out of sanctioned, perhaps even pedestrian, materials accords with Baudelaire's observation that the dandy cultivates "an ardent desire to make himself original within an exterior frame of propriety."[39] When Ravel observes that "What is most difficult for a composer, you see, is choice, yes choice," we might locate that very challenge in a Poe-influenced strategic negotiation between originality and convention, a challenge Ravel associated, as we have seen, with "a return to classic standards."

Léon-Paul Fargue

Ravel never appears to have cited the poet Léon-Paul Fargue (1876–1947) as an influence. Links between their creative worlds that one might attach somehow to a classicizing impulse are considerably more attenuated than those inspired in Ravel by Poe's rational methodology. Yet remarking on the lifelong friendship between the poet and musician in his obituary for Fargue, the critic Émile Vuillermoz, who knew them both from a young age, observed: "Because of the spiritual influence [*l'influence spirituelle*] that he had on Maurice Ravel in particular, he has a place in the history of today's music."[40] Like many other writers, including Fargue himself,[41] Vuillermoz situates the beginnings of this camaraderie in the circle of the Apaches and attests to Fargue's impact on the group as a whole: "None of us could resist what one might call his deadpan lyricism [*lyrisme pince-sans-rire*]. Even in his most lively fits of enthusiasm he knew how to cultivate a kind of secret irony that put everything in its place."[42] The subject of Vuillermoz's characterization here might easily be mistaken for Ravel himself, well known for his dry humor and *pudeur*. Witness the artist Valentine Hugo's recollection of a nocturnal promenade in the company of the two men after a *soirée* at the Godebski salon in 1914:

> That night it was Mallarmé, that *Orphée intime* as Fargue called him, who sparked a vertiginous battle of poetic wits. Ravel . . . quoted verses, entire poems, and suddenly, at the height of emotion, increased by our own, he withdrew with a sharp, self-deprecatory joke, pricking himself with a comic needle in order to hide his emotion.[43]

Hugo notes how on that very night she came to understand the reciprocal affection between Fargue and Ravel: "Their mutual understanding was perfect, they completed each other, they adapted themselves to one another."[44] And further: "One of them heard the inaudible, the other saw the invisible"—a striking metaphor for an aesthetic convergence. Flash forward another fourteen years to 1927 or thereabouts, and the recollections of the writer André Beucler of his friendship with Fargue. In Beucler's extensive account of meeting his mentor in the company of Ravel, the composer and Fargue are still together wandering the streets of Paris at the cusp of daybreak as the *boulangers* of the city begin to ply their trade.[45] A strain of Satie's waltz song "Je te veux" caught in the air leads them to ruminations on popular song in general—the very essence of the urban soundscape, they agree, and an escape valve from the boredom of the office or shop. Fargue imagines a ballet called *Les violons de Paris* with a score pieced together from popular songs. A research trip to sheet music and record dealers in working-class *quartiers* follows. Ravel admires the craft of the popular artists of the day—Yvonne George, Maurice Chevalier, Mistinguett. Later, as they stroll along the Canal Saint-Martin in moonlight, the quiet hum of the working-class city enchants them: a counterpoint of radios, bicycles, café sounds. A simple, amicable solo female voice floats above this vast urban "concerto." "We all became silent, and then Ravel said 'There you have it, *Les violons de Paris*.'"[46] Popular song, and music more generally, waft through Fargue's urban poetry, reminiscent of *L'enfant et les sortilèges*. The Dragonfly's waltz, "Où es-tu? Je te cherche" in the garden scene of *L'enfant* partakes of the same lyrical register (and stock rhythmic gestures) as Satie's "Je te veux," the trigger for Ravel's and Fargue's ruminations upon *Les violons de Paris* in Beucler's account. These vignettes point up the many affinities between Fargue and

Ravel: their aversion to self-importance and snobbism; their love of Mallarmé and nocturnal peregrinations; their attraction to the poetry of the urban environment; their sympathetic appreciation of the working class; and their openness to popular culture.

The city of Paris itself, with its hidden alleys, mournful chimneys, quiet squares, lovers' shadows, and the silent witness of the Seine, nourished Fargue's creative world. Trains, locomotives, steam, and stations combine in a string of railway metaphors that Fargue spun out through much of his poetry. "Aux grandes orgues / De quelque gare / Gronde la vague / Des vieux départs," Fargue writes in "Rêves," the only one of his poems that Ravel set. The poem ends with a recursive summary of its own fleeting images—"Des choses brèves / Qui meurent sages"—a tribute to the taste for concision shared by both men.

In his prose poem "Aux longs traits du fer et des pierres," Fargue paints the masses that gather around live animals in a market with characteristically lugubrious hues: "Au fond d'une ruelle, la foule se voûte sur des cages sales où battent comme un cœur et s'éteignent des bêtes étranges et grelottantes. Plus tard les rampes de gaz de la rue aux bouges sourcilleront au vent du soir."[47] Baudelaire's *Le spleen de Paris* was an obvious influence, but Fargue's industrial urban *tristesse* and his startling shifts between grit and moonlight reinscribe nature onto the city, manufacture a dream world out of iron and stone—and thereby mark a distinctive voice. Whereas Fargue's tone in his landmark collection *Poèmes* (fully published in 1918; earliest *cahier* in 1907) may not be easy to locate in Ravel's music, the composer's responsiveness to factories and machines as a source for musical inspiration shares a kinship with Fargue's lyrical celebrations of the urban milieu. One recalls Ravel's enthusiastic description to Maurice Delage in 1905 of "the marvelous symphony of driving belts, whistles and formidable hammer strokes" heard during a visit to a foundry.[48] Almost thirty years later, he wrote an article for a British periodical about locating music in factories.[49] In one section, entitled "The Beauty in Industry," Ravel describes the silencing of the machines at the end of the working day, the dull roar of departing workers, and how "where a few hours before was noise and toil is stillness and desolation"[50]—an image redolent of Fargue's work, if less lyrically developed. Passages in *L'heure espagnole* and "Le grillon" sound as refractions of the disposition to hear mechanical sound as music. The end of the latter even transposes (avant L'heure) Ravel's evocation of quiet in the wake of mechanical sounds.

Aside from the *mélodie* "Rêves," perhaps the closest meshing of the creative worlds of Ravel and Fargue occurred around the piano suite *Miroirs*. The suite and Fargue's *Poèmes* were both dedicated to fellow members of Les Apaches. Ravel's dedications to members of the Apaches—to Fargue himself ("Noctuelles"), Ricardo Viñes ("Oiseaux tristes"), Paul Sordes ("Une barque sur l'océan"), Michel Dimitri Calvocoressi ("Alborada del gracioso"), and Maurice Delage ("La vallée des cloches")—have long been recognized as evidence of his attachment to this artistic circle. Philippe Rodriguez has recently discovered that Fargue also planned to dedicate the prose poems in his collection to members of the group.[51] Of twenty-eight dedicatees, sixteen were affiliated with the Apaches between 1902 and 1914. These tributes disappeared before the definitive publication of 1918, but do nonetheless mark common ground with *Miroirs:* Viñes, Sordes, Calvocoressi, and Delage all received their own dedications from Fargue. The poem that Fargue intended for Ravel, "Les festins qui sonnaient aux terrasses du soir," seems uncannily premonitory of the garden world in *L'enfant et les sortilèges* and of the child's world of *Ma mère l'oye,* particularly the "Jardin féerique."[52] Tiny insects of the night respond to a mantle clock, a "ville naine" where the fireflies "font leur ronde aux sons de sa boîte à musique." In this almost surrealist fairy-tale world, the oaks tower over the road where important personages will pass—Viviane and Myrdhinn, Faust and Marguerite, and Verlaine's "deux spectres du parc solitaire" (from his cruelly ironic poem "Colloque sentimental"). Mushrooms chatter in quiet groups. A nasicorn beetle in a winsome suit guides Turandot, the Chinese princess doll, down a dark path. And finally:

> Orphée prélude, et les yeux des bêtes attentives, dans l'ombre, entre les fûts des arbres, brillent sans lumière, comme des vins rares. Et je suis devant lui, lourd de ma peine, sous la futaie qui me rend invisible, au bord de la lisère mystérieuse—comme un homme que son âme empêche de dormir.

For many years, Delage provided the meeting place for the Apaches at his Auteuil property "separated by gardens, hidden in greenery."[53] With autobiographical panache, Fargue the noctambulist ("un homme que son âme empêche de dormir") stands in the shadows listening to Orphée's improvisations, doubtless the music-making of none other than Ravel himself.

Evocative echoes sound from Ravel's side, as well, in *Miroirs.* The title "Noctuelles" found an obvious dedicatee in Fargue the insomniac. Perhaps fluttering moths did indeed inhabit the magic garden in Auteuil. And maybe the doleful middle section of the piece stands for the poet "que son âme empêche de dormir."[54] Early editions of *Miroirs* contained an epigraph from Fargue's prose poem "La petite gare aux ombres courtes": "Les noctuelles des hangars partent d'un vol gauche, cravater d'autres poutres / Un oiseau chante, sur un ton de question," a clever way to introduce "Oiseaux tristes," the second piece in the collection.[55] Some of the other titles in *Miroirs* may echo Fargue's work. "Dans la rue qui monte au soleil" is a dreamy walking tour of the city, "depuis le canal d'or où l'ecluse trempe solidement dans l'émail chaud" (the Canal Saint-Martin?), past the "beaux regards et les bras nus de Carmen et de Juliette" and the "piano [qui] pense avec lenteur" to the "rue qui a un nom d'oiseau triste."[56] Despite the largely urban context, Fargue returns repeatedly to images of ships, rivers, and the sea. The speaker's father is "sage comme la barque amarrée dans le port."[57] In another poem, train headlights seem equivalent to the lanterns of boats while music rises all about the speaker in the city: "Des beaux accords plans se recouvrent. La mer qui remonte. Un rayon de Chopin m'arrive."[58] Ravel's title "Une barque sur l'océan" melds with Fargue's imagery. Although all of this is inconclusive as far as Ravel's creative intent goes, at the very least it cannot be assumed that the titles in *Miroirs* are attributable entirely to natural phenomena: Fargue's *Poèmes* unfold a host of musical metaphors for urban things, and Ravel's piano suite might be construed as an extension of this creative impulse. Following in this vein, one might add that Ravel once told Robert Casadesus that Parisian noon church bells provided the initial spark for "La vallée des cloches."[59]

Fargue's art bespeaks eclecticism generated by the urban context, the rubbing together of high and low culture and the cultivation of paradoxical juxtapositions. His poetry makes breathtaking leaps from hard reality to fairy-tale enchantment. Things are not always quite what they seem—in the city or in nature. On Ravel's side, witness the swan in *Histoires naturelles,* who causes the naïve listener to modulate sharply between fantasy and apprehension of material fact. The cycle then plunges into the dream world with "Le martin-pêcheur," whose final wispy G$\sharp$ in turn gets undermined by a semitone clash with G$\natural$ to set the raucous "La pintade" on its way.

In his writings on aesthetics, Fargue argued that there was no *a priori* hierarchy among the materials at the disposition of the creative spirit, a point of view consonant with Ravel's practice.[60] The working-class Canal Saint-Martin became as rich a fount of inspiration as any canal in Venice, and the guinea-hen (*la pintade*), that proletarian laborer of the barnyard, is as worthy of musical tribute as the magnificent kingfisher (*le martin-pêcheur*). For Ravel this creative disposition nourished the sense one has in his few aesthetic pronouncements about composition as *ars combinatoria*. The more variegated the resources, the greater the challenge of choice—and the more surprising the potential juxtapositions.

Clearly, Fargue gave greater importance than Ravel to the "mouvements du cœur et de l'âme" as generating factors in his art, and spoke little of a methodical, self-conscious constructivist orientation. Yet in a set of aphorisms published the year of Ravel's death, he declared that "les mauvais poètes sont des poètes inspirés."[61] Fargue's poetry flits adeptly from image to image as it avoids prolonged immersion in lyricism. Listen to his admonition: "Coupe les cheveux à ton lyrisme. Coupe lui-même un peu les ailes. Laisse voir tes yeux entre tes doigts. Scalpe l'emphase. Une grande phrase est un cri de mondaine. Un mot, rien qu'un petit mot bien placé, je t'en supplie."[62] Elsewhere, in the spirit of Mallarmé, Fargue enjoys the sheer materiality of the "word": "Au commencement fut le verbe. Les idées sont les parasites du verbe."[63] This could have been uttered by Valéry, accompanied by greater (Poe-influenced) self-consciousness about the act of writing, but with no less of a musical sense that words flow into the poet with a long history of connotations and a capacity to create unpredictable sparks when conjoined with other words in a well-structured arrangement. *Ars combinatoria* once again. To attribute classical or neoclassical qualities to Fargue's oeuvre would be wrong-headed, but taken individually and rearticulated in a different creative alchemy, say in certain works of Ravel, his terms of reference could adapt to that environment.

The same might be said of Fargue's obvious attachment to working-class Paris, and—more to the point—a traditional (and perhaps outdated) elevated regard for the artisan. The poet's father was a potter with a little workshop in the tenth *arrondissement*.[64] Fargue's empathy for working-class Parisians sprang from deep roots, and rhymes with Ravel's own apparent empathy, at least as exhibited by his leftist political orientation. The theoretical by-product is Fargue's essay "Artisans d'art," in which he argues that the dichotomy between artist and artisan was a false construction of seventeenth-century academic institutions.[65] No one could aspire to be a great artist without craft, wrote Fargue, though an artisan could not be a truly complete practitioner of a trade without imagination.

Calvocoressi once noted, "We should never forget that as a musician [Ravel] was first and last an artisan," whence his interest in varied sources that allowed him "to exercise his craft in fresh directions."[66] The composer himself downplayed natural genius in favor of a more artisanal orientation by claiming that any Conservatoire student could write works of equal value to his own with a sufficient amount of discipline and hard work.[67] Fargue observed that Ravel was "fou de perfection" (fixated on perfection) leaving to posterity only finished objects, like jewels, Chinese ivories, and lacquerware. "This great artist," he continued, "was served by a matchless artisan."[68] Reminding his readers that Ravel was a singularly French artist, Fargue noted within the same breath that he "produced objects in the spirit of eighteenth-century masters."[69] In light of his argument in "Artisans d'art," perhaps never was the distinction between the two so illusory. Perfection and emulation of great masters of the past: Fargue's description of Ravel's craft recalls two of Valéry's ways of understanding the classical. Yet all of this seems entwined in a marriage of souls cultivated on urban perambulations. In "Artisans d'art" Fargue tells of the tortuous alleys around Sainte-Geneviève-du-Mont where he heard the sound of hammers on stone or wood, smelled old leather and freshly cut wood: "le charme obscur, le charme profound du travail de Paris."[70] And in the mind's eye one sees him draw up to an artisan's window with Ravel to admire the handiwork—perhaps after recalling a verse or two of Mallarmé.

Tristan Klingsor

Like Fargue, the poet Tristan Klingsor (pseudonym of Arthur Justin Léon Leclère, 1874–1966) frequented the Apaches from the earliest days and would later reminisce about his socializing with Ravel in that milieu.[71] Their camaraderie did not outlive the circle itself, and just how close they ever were certainly remains open to further questioning (Ravel did *not* dedicate one of the *Miroirs* to him). Yet their contact bore fruit immediately for Ravel; he set three poems from the poet's anthology *Schéhérazade* within months after it had been published in 1903. Moreover, Klingsor claimed that Ravel's setting emulated his style of recitation in the rhythms of the vocal lines.[72] That a poet with a Wagnerian pseudonym produced verse on "oriental" themes certainly gives pause for reflection. Klingsor's own explanation of his moniker complicates the cultural mélange even further: "Tristan" not because of Wagner, but because his own first name encouraged him to look to Arthuriana, and "Klingsor" because of his enchantment with a little book of German ballads that he found along the *quais*.[73] Some of the *Schéhérazade* poems suggest an even larger cultural mosaic, as for example when he writes: "Tous les djinns d'Orient sont cachés, dit-on, / Ô Rimsky-Korsakoff, dans les instruments / Que tu fais jouer au signe de ton baton."[74] From one *Schéhérazade* to another. To Russian music, the Orient, Wagner, and Arthuriana, we might add Klingsor's predilection for pre-Raphaelite art in his youth, especially the figure of the *dame triste* surrounded by a lugubrious but mystical aura, as in the paintings of Edward Burne-Jones.[75] His taste extended to the assimilation of pre-Raphaelite style by well-known English illustrators of children's books such as Walter Crane and Kate Greenaway and, indeed, to a cultivation of children's verse himself, for which he remains best known today in France.[76] In Klingsor's anthology *L'escarpolette* (1899), fairy-tale characters Tom Thumb, Mother Goose, Cinderella, and Red Riding Hood mingle with figures from the commedia dell'arte tradition. Klingsor was a painter and composer, too, and in 1906 published a collection of songs on Mother Goose themes. Still in a fantastical vein, but now more appropriate for older readers, in *Squelettes fleuris* (Flowering Skeletons, 1897), elves and dwarfs frolic around the theme of love and death. Klingsor acknowledged the influence of Aloysius Bertrand's *Gaspard de la nuit* on this collection and on his youthful fascination with the Middle Ages in general, an enthusiasm that inspired him to copy out Bertrand's entire anthology by hand. For Baudelaire, writing in his dedicatory letter to Arsène Houssaye in *Le spleen de Paris* over thirty years before, *Gaspard de la nuit* was "a book known to you, to me, and to some of our friends," and therefore (he immodestly continued), "Doesn't it fully deserve to be called famous?"[77] Baudelaire championed *Gaspard de la nuit* as a set of prose poems that prefigured his own by an author who, like Poe, dealt in the macabre and was misunderstood. Bertrand remained a cultish object of reverence among those who admired Baudelaire and Mallarmé at the fin-de-siècle, as Klingsor certainly did.

Even a cursory overview of the themes of Klingsor's early poetry suggests a confluence of mutual interests and influences with Ravel, in range and actual subjects—witness Mother Goose and *Gaspard de la nuit*.[78] In his commemorative writing about Ravel, Klingsor wrote approvingly that the composer "adored puerile fantasy worlds."[79] Recall Fargue's confection of nasicorn beetles and Chinese princess dolls. Ravel's own poetry for his *Trois Chansons* would have been at home in the child's world of *L'escarpolette*, for the sheer quality of the verse and the fairy-tale subjects.

The poet Francis Carco wrote of Klingsor's attachment to "tiresome serenaders, rascal lovers, and Bohemian dandies." "All the legends that he recounts," Carco continued, "resonate with laughter and tears."[80] In wearing "irony like a mask" (Carco's expression) Klingsor fit in with a group of poets who published briefly under the banner *Groupe fantaisiste* and became recognized as precursors to the surrealists (Apollinaire was among them). Once again, the parallels to Ravel fairly leap from the page: the grotesque serenaders, the dandy, the would-be-rascal Don Inigo in *L'heure espagnole*. Klingsor would continue to work from an eclectic palette for the remainder of his long career. Writing late in life to Lester Pronger, the author of the only book-length scholarly study of him, the poet revealed that "beneath the diversity in my various works, which is more apparent than real, is always the same man under different masks."[81] For Pronger, Klingsor was a masked romantic, continually conflicted by the friction between his impassioned temperament and his rationalist and self-critical spirit. Much ink has been spilled in similar assessments of Ravel's character, including by Klingsor himself who noted that "He seemed mysterious because he was too discreet to reveal his profound ardor. A humorous edge helped him better to mask himself."[82] Or in Jankélévitch's words: "Ravel is the friend of *trompe-l'œil*, pretenders, merry-go-rounds, and booby traps. Ravel is masked; and that is why the carnival for him does not signify, as with Schumann, an orgy or a confusing witches' Sabbath, but pseudonyms, the oblique incognito, the *fête galante*."[83] This line of criticism has encouraged some to detect a substratum of genuine emotion in his work and to identify decoys that deflect the listener from this inner world. This need not be the only hermeneutic strategy. Elsewhere I have made the case—one more closely aligned to the artisanal spirit *tout court*—that Ravel operated with little anxiety as an artist in a non-self-revelatory eighteenth-century sense.[84] But, at the very least, on the level of reception at which Ravel *appeared* to wear masks, the distinction between private and public harmonizes with Klingsor's self-assessment.

In one of his essays on Ravel, Klingsor drew attention to the *Schéhérazade* poem "Art Poétique" as particularly instructive about his own aesthetic position during the Apaches days. The speaker—presumably Klingsor himself since he writes of his "barbe épaisse"—warns the reader to think of the poet not as a turbaned Oriental caught up in an opium-induced dream, but rather as one who cultivates a sensitive reaction to his surroundings, as, say, when sitting on a bench to watch passers-by:

Il regarde les costumes charmants
Des femmes aux voiles légers . . .
Il regarde les grimaces et les masques,
Les visages creusés de mille rides
Des vizirs, des marchands et des cadis,
Et c'est cela qu'il se contente de copier
D'un trait fin et rapide
Sur le papier.[85]

Observation over inspiration: doubtless at this stage of his career Klingsor would have agreed with Fargue's later remark, "Les mauvais poètes sont des poètes inspirés." But insofar as the oriental subject matter goes, here is the rub: Klingsor did not visit the Middle East before *Schéhérazade*. He once confessed his embarrassment at being unable to locate the cities mentioned in the collection on a map.[86] His *art poétique* stemmed not from observation of the Oriental milieu per se, but from looking around Paris and transposing the people and places to an eastern setting, arming passers-by with curved scimitars, coiffing them with pointed hats, transforming steeples into minarets. In the poem "Orient de Fantaisie" the speaker admits right away "Je n'ai pas fait tous les voyages de Sindbad" and asserts that his own powers of transformation allowed him nonetheless to fashion "un Orient adorable / D'une poésie exquise et choisie"[87] (An adorable Orient / Of poetry exquisite and select). Pronger calls this "la poétisation du réel." It is an approach that ultimately makes no pretense at authenticity. In the vein of Poe, Klingsor allows a backstage glimpse in some poems, where he admits that clever and imaginative transpositions take the place of genuine engagement with a distant milieu. Rimsky-Korsakov's mediation, already mentioned, also had its role to play in *Schéhérazade*. Such frank confessions rub shoulders with the unrequited desire of other poems, as in those set by Ravel in his own cycle *Shéhérazade*, where the attraction to faraway places expressed in "Asie" becomes rearticulated as sexual desire in "La flûte enchantée" and "L'indifférent."

Juxtaposition of yearning with admissions of artifice destabilizes the reader's perspective. Klingsor's project is not unrelated in this respect to Baudelaire's poem "À une dame créole," from which Ravel extracted the first line ("Au pays parfumé que le soleil caresse") as an epigraph to the "Habanera" from the *Sites auriculaires*. Baudelaire's speaker begins by recalling the exotic female in her native habitat, but concludes by imagining her in France "au vrai pays de gloire, / Sur les bords de la Seine" where she would certainly provide inspiration for "mille sonnets dans le cœur des poètes." Another armchair gateway to the exotic, now with the "real" conveniently (and colonially) transplanted to home soil. The "pays parfumé que le soleil caresse," Baudelaire seems to suggest, can merely be a contrived world triggered by the "importation" of exotic culture. He writes of a tropical milieu at the beginning of his poem, then of France, but

Ravel composes a Spanish habanera—or rather a piece where shards of habanera topics mingle in unexpected ways. One thing stands for another: where is the truth? "The lie, taken as the ability to create illusion, is the only way mankind is superior to animals; and, when it has an artistic dimension, the only way that the artist is superior to other men," Ravel once noted.[88]

This disposition also provides a path into Ravel's classicism, with the obvious replacement of geographic by temporal distance. Indeed, Klingsor created an eighteenth-century setting for his own poetic tribute to Ravel called "Jeux d'eau" in the anthology *Humoresques:*

> Les jeux d'eau dans le parc et la ribambelle
> Des fous,
> Le cœur troublé des belles
> Et le cœur ironique et tendre qui bat sous
> Le gilet de velours de Maurice Ravel,
> L'inquiète qui rougit sous l'ombrelle
> Et le gredin qui se met à genoux
> Devant elle,
> La guitare fausse que joue
> Un doigt rebelle,
> La vasque, le vieil arbre, la cascatelle
> Et l'arc fin de lune dans le soir d'août,
> Tout cela dans mon souvenir infidèle
> En accord très doux
> Se mêle . . . [89]

Memory is unfaithful and imprecise writes the poet; music—Ravel's music—captures ineffable filaments of the past. But which past? Ravel with his "cœur ironique et tendre" joins characters in an eighteenth-century *fête galante* with a parade of fools, a hard-to-get ingénue, and an out-of-tune guitar. Klingsor's verse recalls Verlaine's "Sur l'herbe," a string of fragments of a conversation among libertine characters caught in the wind. "Hé! Bonsoir, la Lune!" says the last of them. In Ravel's setting of "Sur l'herbe" as a minuet, the very soft piano cascade with flatward harmonic motion might have worked just as well for Klingsor's "l'arc fin de lune dans le soir d'août." Klingsor's speaker waxes nostalgic—that sentiment seems genuine enough—but how seriously to take the object of memory? Ravel functions at once as a player in the scene and one who provides perspective from outside, indeed from a much later time, suggesting that the reader take the point of view of the "cœur ironique et tendre" on the *fête galante.*

Such multivalence seems analogous to the ironic modulations between the here and now of Paris and distant geographical spaces in *Schéhérazade.* The poem called "Le menuet" from *Humoresques* tells of a "menuet délicieux de Mozart" that suggests to the speaker a park painted by Watteau where lovers engage in "useless dialogue" (*inutiles propos*) and where their laughter mingles with the fountain's melody.[90] The minuet "mélancolique et charmant et fantasque un peu" becomes drawn out in a stream of roses, roses that tumble from the hands of Mademoiselle. But—suddenly—we see not a mademoiselle of the eighteenth-century, but Laure, whose father Monsieur Durand listens to her obligingly while beating time on his belly. In the final stanza, as the tempo increases, Madame Durand slips an oblique glance to an ardent suitor.

> Et cette fois le menuet se brise
> Comme un jet d'eau sous la brise
> Au fond d'un parc.

Fête galante or duped contemporary cuckold?—the present becomes a mirror for eighteenth-century libertinage. In "La gavotte" the speaker apostrophizes Gluck and thanks him for evoking the world of wigs and pannier dresses.[91] On the floor above, the bourgeois slumbers in his Louis XVI bedroom as the speaker enjoins "his neighbour" to replay the piece:

> Car se soir j'imagine
> Que vous voici marquise
> Et m'accordant enfin votre joli corps:
> Le bourgeois obèse du dessus dort.

The speaker escapes middle-class drudgery by recreating the licentious and aristocratic *fête galante* to Gluck's music. In "Bonnard" an elegant eighteenth-century dance accompanies quotidian urban reality:

> Madame joue un air ancien,
> Un air tendre et cajoleur
> De gavotte;
> Monsieur descend faire pisser le chien.[92]

Her posture at the piano seductively reveals the nape of her neck. While Monsieur is away, the suitor lets his hands roam over her. But the key suddenly grinds in the lock, the suitor sinks back in his chair, and Madame takes up the gavotte "adorable et tendre" once again.

Klingsor's take on the eighteenth century and eighteenth-century music is playful, irreverent, and full of witty rejoinders between the past and present—all without recourse to pastiche or self-conscious claims to an avant-garde stance. The ludic atmosphere subsumes any sense of authentic commitment to past styles. Ravel's *Menuet antique*, written over twenty years before the publication of the *Humoresques* (though Klingsor wrote many of the poems earlier) shares this spirit. The musical mixture is further complicated because, as has been pointed out often enough, his piece also resembles Emmanuel

Chabrier's *Menuet pompeux* in the concluding cadences of the outer sections and texture of the trio. But although Chabrier's piece as a whole cleaves to the traditional ternary design with contrasting trio, his fiery and virtuosic outer sections belie the atmosphere or affect typically associated with the minuet. With boisterous guitar-strumming effects and massive chords, the music assumes the guise of an *anti*minuet, completely infusing the genre with Chabrier's impetuous temperament and style. Ravel restores more of the gestural language associated with the minuet to his outer sections. The immediate intertextual link, then, serves to remind us of just how much more of a minuet Ravel's piece is, of how he allows the past to speak with its own voice. Just like Klingsor with his Watteau-like images, one might say.

But is it productive to speak of a greater authenticity? Not quite, for Ravel's stronger allusions to the past serve another purpose: an ironic gloss on the model more trenchant than Chabrier's (and hence the full force of the intertextual reminder of the earlier piece) precisely because they are closer to an eighteenth-century ambience. Ravel's minuet begins with a pungent dissonance of the leading tone against tonic. A diatonic circle of fifths driven by suspensions follows in the third measure, so conventional a baroque progression as to suggest deprecatory pastiche. The ensuing cadence, analogous to Chabrier's, flattens the seventh to produce a modal sound. A more dreamy-sounding alternation between ninth chords and seventh chords follows in the second half of the outer section (e.g., mm. 13–14, 19–20). A long dominant pedal point prepares the return classically enough, but Ravel writes modern parallel chords above it. The return itself plays up the hint of the subdominant implied in the first theme with a manifestly overdone run of loud left-hand octaves that aim for B minor instead of the tonic F-sharp. An even more playful return occurs at the reprise of the lyrical theme in the ternary trio where the pungent minuet theme unexpectedly elbows its way into the predominantly elegiac atmosphere. Just as Klingsor plays with proximity and distance, present and past, the aristocratic *fête galante* in a twentieth-century urban milieu, so Ravel also enjoys tongue-in-cheek ironic juxtapositions, but not without a hint of nostalgia too—that "accord très doux" in Klingsor's poem about the composer. Both destabilize the position of the listener, who responds to both the irony and the sincerity in the music.

In Ravel's case this destabilizing effect was compounded by the title page of the first edition, which depicts Pan, naturalistically clothed in animal skin, beneath a title made to look like an archaic inscription. The rusticity that Pan conventionally represents is starkly juxtaposed with the stylized foliage of the surrounding border: a representation of nature as artifice. Such an odd association of an aristocratic minuet and salon decoration with the god of nature foretells the minuet-musette combination in *Le tombeau de Couperin*. Marguerite Long recalled the title page in her memoirs and spoke of it as a "hoax" that Ravel knew would confuse generations of future commentators.[93] Perhaps

that semitone clash at the beginning of the *Menuet antique* does have something of Pan's primitive *joie de vivre*. Nevertheless, Pan seems just as out of place
here as the bourgeois narrator of Klingsor's "La gavotte" might be in Watteau's
garden. *Antique/rustique*, high/low, jest/nostalgia, old/new: here Ravel's classicism creates a moving target in a witty *jeu d'esprit*.

Henri de Régnier

Ravel does not appear to have kept company with Henri de Régnier (1864–
1936), as he did with Fargue and Klingsor. Régnier was a decade older than
Ravel and his friends, and already quite well known when the Apaches formed—
indeed almost an establishment figure by virtue of the success of his novel *La
double maîtresse* in 1900. Accounts of Apaches gatherings do not mention Régnier's presence, and Ravel's name surfaces only twice in Régnier's copious diaries.
The first time was in 1913, where the description is merely a thumbnail sketch
of a man he barely knew: "Evening, supper at the Lebaudy house and Ravel's
music. He's a small man, thin and nervous, but looks intelligent."[94]

Often seen in Mallarmé's circle, Régnier had been heralded in the 1890s
as a young standard-bearer for symbolism: Fargue himself recalled much
later "the effect of a new poet, of a new passport into *féerie*," on his own creative world when he was in his teens.[95] Régnier married Marie de Heredia,
the second daughter of the Parnassian poet José Maria de Heredia, and his
poetic style moved away from symbolism to resemble that of his father-in-law.
The pre-Revolutionary eighteenth century became his ambience of choice, a
"beguiling and despotic presence" funneled through nostalgia and the dream
world.[96] This predilection was not uncommon among fin-de-siècle symbolists, but Régnier distinguished himself by the intensity of his absorption with
the Louis XV period. The music critic (turned politician) Robert Jardillier
once grouped Régnier with Verlaine as key figures who turned the page from
representations of a facile and carefree eighteenth century to one where evo-
cations of frivolity became tinged with soft melancholy and a "charme nostal-
gique."[97] Historical distance is a great leveler, suggests Régnier's alter ego in
one of his best-known novels, *Le passé vivant:* whereas if he had actually lived
in the period he would have swept up crumbs from beneath the nobleman's
table, the dream world allowed him to mingle with the likes of Madame de
Pompadour as an equal. But dilapidated remnants of the past—the silence of
abandoned parks and pavilions—also produced a sense of a lost paradise in
the mind of the isolated dreamer.[98]

Ravel's connection to Régnier was expressed in his setting of the poem "Les
grands vents venus d'outremer," a latter-day manifestation of spleen that will
not concern us here, and the epigraphs to two piano works that will. The first is
the inscription to *Jeux d'eau:* "Dieu fluvial riant de l'eau qui le chatouille" taken

from the poem "Fête d'eau" in the anthology *La cité des eaux* published in 1902. According to Arbie Orenstein, Henri de Régnier inscribed the quotation in his own hand on Ravel's autograph, but on both the working draft at the Bibliothèque Nationale and the clean copy in the Lehman collection of the Pierpont Morgan Library the writing clearly looks like Ravel's own.[99] The main ambiguity would seem to concern the date, because the working draft is marked November 11, 1901—that is, before the publication of the anthology. Ravel may have added Régnier's line after having completed the draft or had access to the poem before its publication through some other channel; it is possible that he met or heard Régnier sometime in 1901. We do know that Ravel insisted on the inclusion of Régnier's verse in the program for Viñes's premiere of *Jeux d'eau* in April 1902, as if it were important for the audience's understanding of the piece.[100] But we do *not* know (nor is this necessarily important) the extent to which the verse, the poem, or indeed the entire collection provided some sort of initial inspiration to Ravel. From the hermeneutic perspective the problem is much the same as with Ravel's citation of Baudelaire's "À une dame créole" for the Habanera in *Sites auriculaires:* a single line may have been chosen for its evocative power without intended allusion to the literary work as a whole. This has been the implicit perspective of writers and critics so far, but exploring the intertextual path illuminates Ravel's and Régnier's heretofore undervalued affinity. The "Fête d'eau" of the title refers to the fountains in the park of the château de Versailles, and the entire sonnet reads:

Le dauphin, le triton et l'obèse grenouille
Diamantant d'écume et d'or Latone nue,
Divinité marine au dos de la tortue,
Dieu fluvial riant de l'eau qui le chatouille;

La vasque qui retombe ou la gerbe qui mouille,
La nappe qui décroît, se gonfle ou diminue,
Et la poussière humide irisant la statue
Dont s'emperle la mousse ou s'avive la rouille;

Toute la fête d'eau, de cristal et de joie
Qui s'entrecroise, rit, s'eparpille et poudroie,
Dans le parc enchanté s'est tue avec le soir;

Et, parmi le silence on voit jaillir, auprès
Du tranquille basin redevenu miroir,
La fontaine de l'If et le jet du cyprès.[101]

Régnier describes a classical sculptural group of figures in the so-called Latona fountain in the gardens of Versailles: Latona (a Latinization of the Greek goddess Leto) stands in the center with her young children surrounded by various dolphins, tortoises, and unspecified river-god gargoyles. When the water is on, Latona glistens with mist and gold droplets. The speaker welcomes the aquatic laughter of the gods in their celebration of crystal and joy. The hinge of the sonnet becomes the deep silence that follows at dusk, as the waters flatten into a mirror that reflects the cypress and yew, mute surrogates for the fountains. In the preceding poem, "Latone," Régnier develops a similar mood of hushed wonder, writing "Le Silence qui songe et l'Écho qui recule / Bercent la douceur d'être en ce beau crépuscule."[102] Such melancholic reflection pervades the collection. The waters of the title refer mainly to stagnant pools that eloquently encapsulate a poetic condition produced by the stark contrast between the vibrant play of imagination about past grandeur and the abandonment of monuments. After the poet announces in the first poem of the collection, "Salut à Versailles," that "ce qu'il cherche en vous, ô jardins de silence . . . Ce qu'il veut, c'est le calme et c'est la solitude,"[103] the fountain's rare sound acts as a foil to his sought-after tranquility.

Ravel's *Jeux d'eau* is manifestly about the real sound of the Latona fountain, complete with mimetic effects that trace upward surges of water and vertiginous cascades. Henriette Faure noted that he chided her when she played it too solemnly: "Your *Jeux d'eau* are sad. It is almost as you haven't read Henri de Régnier's subtitle 'Dieu fluvial riant de l'eau qui le chatouille.'"[104] So, she played it again, a little faster and with tighter rhythms. Ravel responded, "This time it was fine, but now, when all is said and done, you can allow yourself to dream a little at the end." Marguerite Long wrote of the final appoggiatura, the famous last E-major-seventh chord, as prolonging "the dream beyond the last notes."[105] Despite the joyous ambience of the piece as a whole, one would not need this primary testimony to make a case for its dissipation into a more dreamy condition during the hushed final measures, the relaxed stepwise descent in the bass from A to tonic E, and the final evaporation on an unstable chord that seems to ask the listener to "complete" the sound in her mind's ear. Similar dreamlike suspension points dot Ravel's oeuvre, from his earlier setting of Mallarmé's "Sainte" to the minuet of *Le tombeau de Couperin*.[106] To bridge sound and silence in this way validates the latter as engendering an aesthetic experience on its own terms, an invitation to reach beyond the articulating frame of sounding music. Régnier's fountains structure his experience in the first part of "Fête d'eau," but the truly moving moment occurs in silence as the trees become the unheard echo of Latona's waters. Perhaps the cypress and yew along the ponds and basins of Versailles also lie in the *au-delà* after Ravel's final measures.

The classicism of *Jeux d'eau*, if classicism there is, lies in imagery and hints of a more extended reverie about a lost world. The other Régnier inscription in Ravel's oeuvre attaches to a piece that actually evokes another era, *Valses nobles et sentimentales*, named with reference to Schubert's waltzes. Ravel himself set the date as 1820 in the scenario for his own subsequent ballet based on this music, *Adélaïde ou le langage des fleurs*.[107] The epigraph "le plaisir délicieux et toujours nouveau d'une occupation inutile" comes from Régnier's *avertissement* to the reader in his short novel *Les rencontres de M. de Bréot* (1904). The book belongs to a subgenre that has been called the "roman costumé," in which Régnier emulates the general manner of seventeenth- and eighteenth-century writers without creating a pastiche of any one in particular. For literary critic André Guyaux, Régnier was a "styliste de l'anachronie" who was able to establish an identity as a pseudo-eighteenth-century writer by deploying a kind of "true-false style."[108] One contemporaneous reviewer of *Les rencontres de M. Bréot* spoke of "an elegant and a little bit burlesque variation, almost a pastiche, of libertine authors of the eighteenth century."[109] The novel begins by describing a performance in an open-air garden theatre, a rococo *fête galante* peopled by marquises and duchesses, where Madame de Blionne arouses the erotic instincts of Monsieur de Bréot as he watches her dance. At the end of the novel, she satiates his desire—while, not too subtly, "la fontaine, dans un sursaut de sa force, darda un jet éblouissant."[110] In between, Monsieur de Bréot meets a variety of other characters who tell him about their carnal experiences, naturally arousing in him thoughts of his own lust. Each story is more improbable and sensationalistic than the last, told in virtuosic conversation replete with shallow ruminations about the human condition and laced with witty and salacious imagery. The characters exist as pasteboard figures devoid of psychological development, several of them faintly ridiculous in the manner suggested by Klingsor's poem *Jeux d'eau*. Régnier warns his reader in the *avertissement* that they "do not place great stock in the idea that any part of us can survive beyond our material existence."[111] Like Ninon de Lenclos, Régnier says, they pity those who need religion to guide their actions because this attests to either of dullness or corruption. Monsieur de Bréot himself confesses to an interlocutor named Monsieur Floreau de Bercaillé that he has adopted a hedonistic lifestyle precisely because he has no faith in a Christian afterlife. As it happens, he is a musician:

> J'aime le plaisir et j'en ai goûté quelques-uns. L'un de ceux que je préfère est de chanter sur le luth. Je sais en accompagner agréablement une voix qui n'est pas vilaine. Je trouve une volupté singulière à joindre mon corps à un corps de femme. C'est à ces occupations que j'ai passé les années de ma vie jusqu'à l'âge de vingt-cinq ans où je suis aujourd'hui.[112]

Playing the lute and playing the libertine have been Monsieur de Bréot's main "occupations," "occupations inutiles," really, to adhere to the wording of the *avertissement*. Small wonder that a warning for polite company also motivates Régnier's prefatory note. Perhaps the best way to avoid an extended apologia, writes Régnier, is not to publish at all. He might have done this—and now we come to the complete version of Ravel's epigraph—but he feels that *Les Rencontres de M. de Bréot* is a book that well demonstrates that he has never aimed for anything but the "plaisir délicieux et toujours nouveau d'une occupation

inutile." In short, the *avertissement* implicitly sets up a mirror between superficial eighteenth-century gallant society consumed more by appearance than
metaphysical substance, and the fin-de-siècle writer who celebrates the sheer
surface joy of craft for its own sake. Sex, music, writing: all are shown to have
little use beyond pleasure.

From all that we know of Ravel's tastes, it is not difficult to imagine that
Les recontres de M. Bréot appealed to him enormously. Régnier's "true-false style"
reminds one of anecdotes concerning Ravel's own pleasure in showing phony
oriental bibelots to visitors to his house at Montfort-l'Amaury. Responding to
their enthusiasm, he would exclaim "But it's fake!" like a "triumphant child,"
in the words of Jourdan-Morhange.[113] The sheer circumlocutory brilliance of
Régnier's characters, their narcissistic absorption with articulating their point
of view in as florid and stylistically elegant a way as possible, recalls the dandified aspect of Ravel's comportment (though not the composer's actual spoken
demeanor, which was terse), and the enjoyment of style for its own sake. As a
literary work the novel is thoroughly anti-romantic, except perhaps in its fas-
tidious detail that suggests the keen eye of the realist writer (which Régnier, of
course, generally was not), repeated touches of the melancholia of fading sun-
light, and ironic twists (at the end, for example, another character comes upon
M. de Bréot's special wig fitted with tiny gold satyr horns and imagines them
as the cuckold's horns of M. de Blionne). Broadly speaking, the gathering of
irony, realism, and melancholy within an anti-romantic envelope makes for a
viable critical approach to many of Ravel's works as well.

That larger envelope would include the large-scale ground plan of the
Valses nobles et sentimentales. Ravel wrote a succession of seven discrete waltzes
in rounded binary form, which raises the critical question—one asked count-
less times of Haydn and Mozart minuets—of how he achieved aesthetically
appealing variety in handling the conventional formal sutures, for example the
cadence at the first double bar or the preparation of the return. A hint of *fête
galante* even surfaces in the work's incarnation as *Adélaïde.* Marguerite Long
used the term disapprovingly in her critique of the ballet.[114] Although the setting of 1820 is many decades after that of the novel and all wrong for a *real* pre-
Revolutionary *fête galante,* the exaggerated action of the suitor Lorédan would
not have been out of place in Régnier's novel: at the end he pulls out a pistol
at the feet of his beloved just before she falls into his arms. And despite the
Schubertian precursors, the setting is Paris.

In addition to all of this, the epigraph "le plaisir délicieux et toujours nouveau d'une occupation inutile" may be readily assimilated with a classicizing
point of view. It speaks to an idealized artisanal value of artistic creation for
the sheer pleasure of creating well. Skill and craft provide not only sufficient
justification for artistic endeavors and value judgments but a constantly replen-
ished resource. Pleasure becomes experienced in a new way each time, a kind
of unquenchable hedonism that Régnier equated with sexual desire. In this

additional way, then, the epigraph harmonizes with the sensuous end of the ballet scenario. The "occupation inutile" also breathes the spirit of *l'art pour l'art*. Whereas in a sociological sense this reflects the fin-de-siècle more than any pre-Revolutionary condition of the artist, taken in Ravel's immediate context it communicates fierce independence from moral imperatives. The foil for such a blatant unfurling of the aestheticist banner was the position of Vincent d'Indy and his followers, and their belief in the didactic mission of the artist. Roland-Manuel, it will be remembered, would use words like "religion" and "cult" to characterize the practices of Ravel's nemesis in his *Revue musicale* essays. Earlier, not long after the premiere of the *Valses nobles et sentimentales,* he called d'Indy's historicist orientation "haughty and solemn neo-classicism," the product of "willful and intellectual discipline."[115] For from the Ravelian perspective, the famous dissonant opening chords of the *Valses nobles et sentimentales* affirm the "golden thread of tonality" (Roland-Manuel's words once again) not for the sake of world order, but as a supreme test of craft that seeks to tax the tonic to the maximum without threatening it.[116] Like Régnier, Ravel enjoins his listener not to seek edification or enlightenment, but the same degree of pleasure as the artist who takes joy in his finished work.

The *Valses nobles et sentimentales* conclude with a very slow, soft waltz during which fragments from the preceding waltzes waft in and out, and the music finally fades away "en se perdant." In short, another suspension point conclusion. Here Ravel, consciously or not, obliquely associated a leitmotif of Régnier's aesthetic with a "roman costumé" where it is scarcely to be found. In collections such as *La cité des eaux* Régnier plays upon strong reminders of the past in monuments, the act of recuperating lost voices—and the ensuing melancholy at being unable to penetrate the veil of silence. Ravel's final waltz even operates recursively with its own material in this way: not only do motifs from earlier movements circulate and disappear, but in an extended coda over a tonic pedal, the first phrase of the last waltz itself gets taken up again at its opening transposition level, only to become abandoned just like all else in the *perdendosi* concluding measures. Everything slips away—the crafty dissonant affirmations of tonality, the slickly varied formal reprises. One might fancifully imagine Régnier at the château de Versailles or in the park, straining to see and hear *ancien régime* society in full panoply—encouraged by the completeness and multitude of the monuments—and catching glimpses and aural filaments in his reverie, only suddenly to become aware of the silence, then to be overwhelmed by it—the classical experienced as melancholic loss.

Notes

1. Alexis Roland-Manuel, "Maurice Ravel," *La Revue Musicale* 2 (1921): 20. All translations by the author, unless indicated.

2. Edgar Allan Poe, *Poems and Essays on Poetry,* ed. C. H. Sisson (Manchester: Fyfield, 1995), 138–50.

3. Roland-Manuel, "Maurice Ravel ou l'esthétique de l'imposture," *La Revue Musicale* (April 1925): 16–21. For Baudelaire's preamble see "La Genèse d'un poème," *Œuvres complètes,* vol. 2, Pléiade edition (Paris: Gallimard, 1976), 343–44.

4. Roland-Manuel, "Maurice Ravel," 10.

5. The incident occurred in 1906. François Lesure reviews some of the main points of contact between the two musicians in "Ravel et Debussy," in *Cahiers Maurice Ravel* 5 (1990–92), 27–33. On *Jeux d'eau* specifically, in his 1928 Rice Institute lecture, Ravel offered an understated defense of its innovatory character by noting that others had insisted that the score influenced Debussy's *Jardin sous la pluie.* Regardless of whether this is true or not, Ravel affirms that from an early age he established his own creative space.

6. Roland-Manuel, "Maurice Ravel ou l'esthétique de l'imposture," 21.

7. Ibid.

8. I borrow this term from Scott Peeples, "Poe's 'Constructiveness' and 'The Fall of the House of Usher,'" in *The Cambridge Companion to Edgar Allan Poe,* ed. Kevin Hayes (Cambridge: Cambridge University Press, 2002), 178–90.

9. Roland-Manuel's (unfootnoted) Valéry citation may be found in context in Paul Valéry, "L'Âme et la danse," in *Œuvres,* vol. 2, Bibliothèque de la Pléiade (Paris: Gallimard, 1960), 154.

10. Roland-Manuel, "Maurice Ravel," 20.

11. Roland-Manuel, "Maurice Ravel ou l'esthétique de l'imposture," 17.

12. Ibid., 18.

13. T. S. Eliot, "Tradition and Individual Talent," in *Selected Essays,* new ed. (New York: Harcourt Brace, 1967), 6–7.

14. Roland-Manuel, "Maurice Ravel ou l'esthétique de l'imposture," 19.

15. 1. Classé—modèle—alors Shakespeare et Dante sont classiques 2. Idée d'ordre—discipline—règles formelles, conventions 3. Une certaine simplicité—Économie de moyens 4. Achèvement—perfection du détail—*ad unguem* poli—fini. Paul Valéry, *Cahiers* 2, ed. Judith Robinson-Valéry (Paris: Gallimard, 1988), 1184.

Valéry also notes, however, that his typology is only a "vague" definition, and that "classique" is a notoriously fluid concept subject to slight redefinition every time it is used in serious criticism. For a discussion of this passage, mainly as it related to Valéry's admiration of Racine, see Maarten van Buuren, "Paul Valéry et le classicisme," in *Histoire, Jeu, Science dans l'aire de la literature,* ed. Sjef Houppermans, Paul J. Smith, and Madeleine van Strien-Chardonneau (Amsterdam-Atlanta: Rodopi, 2000), 25–36.

16. Scott Messing, *Neoclassicism in Music: From the Genesis of the Concept through the Schoenberg/Stravinsky Polemic* (Ann Arbor: UMI Research Press, 1988), 76.

17. For a valuable survey of different meanings attached to the word "classicism" see Ortrud Kuhn-Schliess, *Klassizistische Tendenzen im Klavierwerk von Maurice Ravel* (Regensburg: Gustav Bosse Verlag, 1992), 9–37. This dissertation is the fullest discussion of Ravel and the classical available in print. Much of it is given over to a close and sensitive analysis of the works with classical generic titles.

18. Arbie Orenstein, "Ravel's Creative Process," *Musical Quarterly* 53 (1967): 481.

19. Kuhn-Schliess, *Klassizistische Tendenzen,* 13. For more on classicism and French nationalism see Anya Suschitzky, "French Music and Its Others," *Musical Quarterly* 86 (2002): 398–448; Jane Fulcher, *The Composer as Intellectual: Music and Ideology in France 1914–1940* (Oxford: Oxford University Press, 2005), 88–198.

20. Nina Gubisch, "Le journal inédit de Ricardo Viñes," *Revue Internationale de la Musique Française* 2 (1980): 183.

21. James Lawler, "Daemons of the Intellect: The Symbolists and Poe," *Critical Inquiry* 14 (1987): 99.

22. See Stéphane Mallarmé, *Le tombeau d'Edgar Poe, Œuvres complètes,* vol. 1, ed. Bertrand Marchal, Bibliothèque de la Pléiade (Paris: Gallimard, 1998), 38.

23. On this point see also T. S. Eliot's famous essay "From Poe to Valéry," in *To Criticize the Critic and Other Writings* (London: Faber and Faber, 1965), 27–42.

24. Charles Baudelaire, "Études sur Poe," in *Œuvres complètes,* vol. 2, ed. Claude Pichois, Bibliothèque de la Pléiade (Paris: Gallimard, 1975–76), 305.

25. Deborah Mawer, "Balanchine's *La Valse:* Meanings and Implications for Ravel Studies," *Opera Quarterly* 22, no. 1 (2006): 106–10.

26. See Steven Huebner, "*L'heure espagnole:* La Grivoiserie moderne de Ravel," in *Aspects de l'opéra français de Meyerbeer à Honegger,* ed. Jean-Christophe Branger and Vincent Giroud (Lyon: Symétrie, 2009), 193–213.

27. Maurice Ravel, *A Ravel Reader,* ed. Arbie Orenstein (New York: Columbia University Press, 1990), 433.

28. Ibid., 450.

29. Ibid., 454.

30. Ravel, *Ravel Reader,* 45–46.

31. Paul Valéry, "Je disais quelquefois à Stéphane Mallarmé," in *Œuvres,* vol. 1, ed. Jean Hytier (Paris: Gallimard, 1957 [Pléiade edition]), 646.

32. Ravel, "Mes souvenirs d'enfant paresseux," *Musical* 4 (1987): 13.

33. Joseph Szigeti, *With Strings Attached: Reminiscences and Reflections* (New York: Knopf, 1947), 139–40.

34. May Garrettson Evans, *Music and Edgar Allan Poe—A Bibliographical Study* (New York: Greenwood, 1968), 6.

35. Maurice Ravel, *Lettres, écrits, entretiens,* ed. Arbie Orenstein (Paris: Flammarion, 1989), 326. See Michel Duchesneau, "Maurice Ravel et Edgar Allan Poe: Une Théorie poétique appliquée," *Ostinato rigore* 24 (2005): 16. My remarks on Poe largely supplement Duchesneau's study.

36. Ravel, *Lettres, écrits, entretiens,* 585.

37. Paul Valéry, "Lettre sur Mallarmé," in *Œuvres,* vol. 1 (Paris: Gallimard, 1957 [Pléiade edition]), 641.

38. Michael J. Puri, "Dandy, Interrupted: Sublimation, Repression, and Self-Portraiture in Maurice Ravel's *Daphnis et Chloé* (1909–1912)," *Journal of the American Musicological Society* 60 (2007): 317–72.

39. Charles Baudelaire, "Le peintre de la vie moderne," in *Œuvres complètes* 2, 710.

40. First printed in *Spectateur,* December 9, 1947, reproduced as Émile Vuillermoz, "Un grand musicien," in *Ludions: Bulletin de la Société des Lecteurs de Léon-Paul Fargue* 8 (2002–3): 273.

41. Léon-Paul Fargue, *Maurice Ravel* (Paris: Domat, 1949), 52.

42. Vuillermoz, "Un grand musicien," 273–74.

43. Valentine Hugo, "Trois Souvenirs sur Ravel," in *La Littérature française et la musique (1900 à nos jours),* ed. Raymond Schwab (Paris: Richard-Masse, 1952), 141.

44. Ibid., 140.

45. The account is excerpted in Roger Nichols ed., *Ravel Remembered* (New York: Norton, 1987), 150–56. For a fuller version, containing additional material on the composer, see André Beucler, *Vingt ans avec Léon-Paul Fargue* (Geneva: Éditions du milieu du monde, 1952), 44–63.

46. Beucler, *Vingt ans avec Léon-Paul Fargue,* 63.

47. Léon-Paul Fargue, *Poèmes suivi de Pour la musique,* rev. ed. (Paris: Gallimard, 1944; first published 1918), 96–97.

48. Ravel to Maurice Delage, July 5, 1905, in *Lettres, écrits, entretiens*, 74.

49. Maurice Ravel, "Finding Tunes in Factories" (*New Britain* 9 [August 1933]) is reprinted in Orenstein, *Ravel Reader*, 399–400.

50. Ibid., 400.

51. Philippe Rodriguez, "Les Apaches de Léon-Paul Fargue. À propos des pièces annexes à l'exemplaire des *Poèmes (Premier Cahier)* conservé à la bibliothèque littéraire Jacques Doucet," *Ludions* 8 (2002–3): 161–73.

52. Fargue, *Poèmes*, 118–22.

53. Fargue, *Maurice Ravel*, 53.

54. Michael Puri has also suggested that the fluttering moths represent the "late-night conviviality" of the Apaches group; see "Dandy, Interrupted," 360.

55. This has already been noted by Michel Faure, "Léon-Paul Fargue, amateur et ins-pirateur de musique," *Ludions* 8 (2002–3): 58.

56. Émile Vuillermoz, another Apache, for his part located the inspiration of *Oiseaux tristes* in the Fontainebleau forest; see "L'Œuvre de Maurice Ravel," in *Maurice Ravel par quelques-uns de ses familiers* (Paris: Éditions du Tambourinaire, 1939), 34. Ravel himself wrote of evoking "des oiseaux perdus dans la torpeur d'une forêt très sombre aux heures les plus chaudes de l'été." See "Esquisse autobiographique," in *Lettres, écrits, entretiens*, 45.

57. In Fargue, "Depuis, il y a toujours," *Poèmes*, 15.

58. Ibid., 36.

59. Marcel Marnat, *Maurice Ravel* (Paris: Fayard, 1986), 184.

60. Raoul Pelmont, "Léon-Paul Fargue et la poésie," *French Review* 31 (1958): 476.

61. Léon-Paul Fargue, *Sous la lampe* (Paris: Gallimard, 1937), 22.

62. Ibid., 22.

63. Ibid., 46.

64. For biographical roots of Fargue's aesthetics see Warren Ramsey, "'Words of Light' and 'Somber Leaves': The Poetry of Léon-Paul Fargue," *Yale French Studies* 9 (1952): 112–22.

65. Léon-Paul Fargue, "Artisans d'art," in *Lanterne magique* (Marseilles: Robert Laffont, 1944), 128–36.

66. M. D. Calvocoressi, "When Ravel Composed to Order," *Music and Letters* 22 (1941): 59.

67. Émile Vuillermoz, *Histoire de la musique* (Paris: Fayard, 1949), 355.

68. Fargue, *Maurice Ravel*, 58.

69. Ibid., 59.

70. Fargue, *Lanterne magique*, 134.

71. See Tristan Klingsor, "Ravel et l'art de son temps," *La Revue Musicale* (April 1, 1925), 9–15; "Maurice Ravel et le vers libre," *La Revue Musicale:* Hommage à Maurice Ravel (1938); "L'Époque Ravel," *Maurice Ravel par quelques-uns de ses familiers* (Paris: Éditions du Tambourinaire, 1939), 125–39.

72. Klingsor, "L'Époque Ravel," 132.

73. Pierre Menanteau, *Tristan Klingsor* (Paris: Editions Seghers, 1965), 20.

74. For the complete poem, see Ibid., 110.

75. Lester J. Pronger, *La Poésie de Tristan Klingsor (1890–1960)* (Paris: M. J. Minard, 1965), 25.

76. Ibid., 87.

77. Charles Baudelaire, "Le spleen de Paris," in *Œuvres complètes* 1, 275.

78. Ravel became acquainted with *Gaspard de la nuit* as early as November 1895 when Viñes lent him a copy; see Nina Gubisch, "Le Journal inédit de Ricardo Viñes," *Revue Internationale de musique française* 1 (June 1980): 188.

79. Klingsor, "L'Époque Ravel," 133.
80. Cited by Pronger, *La poésie de Tristan Klingsor,* 126.
81. Ibid., 10.
82. Klingsor, "L'Époque Ravel," 125.
83. Vladimir Jankélévitch, *Ravel,* ed. Jean-Michel Nectoux (Paris: Éditions du Seuil, 1995), 140.
84. For an extended discussion see Steven Huebner, "Maurice Ravel: Private Life, Public Works," in *Musical Biography: Towards New Paradigms,* ed. Jolanta T. Pekacz (Aldershot: Ashgate, 2006), 69–87.
85. Menanteau, *Tristan Klingsor,* 110–11.
86. Pronger, *La poésie de Tristan Klingsor,* 100.
87. Ibid., 101.
88. Ravel, "Mes souvenirs d'enfant paresseux," 13.
89. Tristan Klingsor, *Humoresques* (Amiens: Librairie Edgar Malfère, 1921), Project Gutenberg ebook, 29.
90. Ibid., 10.
91. Ibid., 8.
92. Ibid., 14.
93. Marguerite Long, *Au piano avec Maurice Ravel* (Paris: Julliard, 1971), 118.
94. Henri de Régnier, *Les cahiers inédits 1887–1936,* ed. David J. Niederauer and François Broche (Paris: Pygmalion, 2002), 682.
95. Cited by François Broche "Présentation de Henri de Régnier," in Henri de Régnier, *Les Cahiers inédits 1887–1936* (Paris: Pygmalion/Gérard Watelet, 2002), 26.
96. Mario Maurin, *Henri de Régnier: Le labyrinthe et le double* (Montréal: Les Presses de l'université de Montréal, 1972), 149.
97. Robert Jardillier, "L'Évocation du XVIIIe siècle dans la musique d'hier et d'aujourd'hui," *La Revue Musicale* (July 1, 1923): 216.
98. Frédéric Martinez, "Une 'Belle Époque' en dentelles ou à quoi rêvent les académiciens: La perception du dix-huitième siècle en 1900 dans *La leçon d'amour dans un parc* de René Boylesve et *La double maîtresse* de Henri de Régnier," *Revue d'histoire littéraire de la France* 106 (2006): 651.
99. For a facsimile of the first page of the working draft, see Gerald Larner, *Maurice Ravel* (London: Phaidon, 1996), 70. Larner claims that "Ravel actually asked the poet to inscribe that line in his own hand on the manuscript."
100. Ravel to Eugène Demets, March 3, 1902, in *Lettres, écrits, entretiens,* 67.
101. Henri de Régnier, *Œuvres,* vol. 1, *Les médailles d'argile / La cité des eaux* (Geneva, Slatkine Reprints, 1978), 267.
102. Ibid., 266.
103. Ibid., 251–52.
104. Henriette Faure, *Mon maître Maurice Ravel* (Paris: Les Éditions ATP, 1978), 95.
105. Long, *Au piano avec Maurice Ravel,* 124.
106. The poem "Sainte" plays upon the unheard music that the wooden saint plucks with the delicate tip of her finger on the "harpe par l'Ange / Formée avec son vol du soir," and Ravel matches this with a ritualistic block-chord ostinato that Jankélévitch aptly called *musique blanche* (*La musique et les heures* [Paris: Editions du Seuil, 1988], 10). Ravel returns to the original transposition level for Mallarmé's final naming of the statue as a "musicienne du silence," this time slowing it down and, more important, truncating its final iteration so that the listener must complete the pattern somewhere in the silence "beyond" the end of the piece. Other suspension-point endings include his setting of Mallarmé's "Placet futile," where the final four pitches outline a major-seventh chord in

which the unresolved seventh bears the weight of the speaker's unrequited desire. Here the music maintains a delicious, and characteristically Ravelian, ambiguity between major and relative minor, a feature of *Jeux d'eau* as a whole that lingers in attenuated form at its conclusion. In the minuet from *Le tombeau de Couperin,* Ravel specifies a broad *rallentando* at the end to the marking *très lent* and a final pianissimo haze of trills where the unresolved leading-tone appoggiatura participates in full tonic-ninth harmony.

107. For an authoritative discussion of the genesis of the piano piece and ballet see Deborah Mawer, *The Ballets of Maurice Ravel: Creation and Interpretation* (Aldershot: Ashgate, 2006), 125–48.

108. André Guyaux, preface to Henri de Régnier, *Romans costumés* (Paris: Mercure de France, 1992), iii.

109. Review by Jean de Gourmont, cited by François Broche, "Présentation de Henri de Régnier," 38.

110. Henri de Régnier, *Les rencontres de M. de Bréot* in *Romans costumés* (Paris: Mercure de France, 2002), 503.

111. Ibid., 319.

112. Ibid., 353.

113. Hélène Jourdan-Morhange, *Ravel et nous* (Geneva: Éditions du milieu du monde, 1945), 26.

114. Long, *Au piano avec Maurice Ravel,* 50.

115. Roland-Manuel, *Maurice Ravel et son œuvre* (Paris: A. Durand et fils, 1914), 32.

116. See Alfred Casella, "L'Harmonie," *La Revue Musicale* (1925): 36, and for a more detailed discussion of the passage, Peter Kaminsky, "Composers' Words, Theorists' Analyses, Ravel's Music (Sometimes the Twain Shall Meet)," *College Music Symposium* 43 (2003): 161–77.

Chapter Two

Re-presenting Ravel

Artificiality and the Aesthetic of Imposture

Barbara L. Kelly

Maurice Ravel as artist and man has always intrigued the critics
because he slides from their grasp, eludes the intellectual analyst as he
does the writer of romantic biographies.

Alexis Roland-Manuel, *Maurice Ravel*

Roland-Manuel's words capture something of the elusiveness of Ravel's legacy. This chapter assesses individuals and groups close to Ravel who had an
important role in shaping his aesthetic and the public understanding of his
music. The central figure in this process was Roland-Manuel—Ravel's student,
disciple, spokesman, and friend.[1] Roland-Manuel is frequently cited as his
first biographer, but his role in influencing and writing Ravel's legacy has not
been scrutinized. Roland-Manuel's efforts to relaunch the composer in pre-
and postwar France amounted to an important, if subtle, repackaging of Ravel
in the context of shifting postwar aesthetics. This study traces the emergence
of a discourse of artificiality and the "aesthetics of imposture"; while Roland-
Manuel identified a separation between the composer and his work, he also
made links between musical qualities and personal characteristics. Besides
Roland-Manuel, Calvocoressi, a member of Les Apaches, was the first to write
about artificiality in Ravel's music and personality, but he was also among the
first to identify the dangers of defining Ravel too narrowly. Comparing Roland-
Manuel's constructed image of Ravel with the composer's own writings on the
purpose, process, and outcome of composition reveals Ravel's nuanced perspective on a composer's relation to his work, a position that neither excludes
the creator nor regards the artwork as a reflection of the composer's character. Finally, a consideration of Ravel's posthumous reputation from 1938 to the
present day reveals the extent to which his earliest advocates impacted current
understandings of the composer in scholarship, film, and the novel.

Ravel the French Classicist and the New French Music

In the critical literature to date, Roland-Manuel is quoted as Ravel's principal biographer. Although Haine has recently identified him as a latecomer to Ravel's close artistic circle, Les Apaches, Roland-Manuel was Ravel's student and still on the margins of the group when he began writing his biography of Ravel in 1913.[2] Even though their families became closer during the war,[3] the teacher-student aspect of their relationship remained significant; many of Roland-Manuel's quotable statements, which have become associated so closely with Ravel himself, seem to reflect the certainty of the pupil remembering his teacher's clear words of advice. Yet Roland-Manuel's impact in shaping Ravel's legacy should not be underestimated; it reveals the very influential role of criticism and biography on perceptions of composers and their relationship to their art.

Roland-Manuel published the first biography of Ravel in 1914, in which he discusses Ravel's major works up until the *Trois Poèmes de Stéphane Mallarmé*.[4] He outlines innovative aspects of Ravel's musical personality, including his distinctive piano writing, his unequalled orchestration, and his interest in imagined worlds, particularly Spanish subjects, ancient Greece, and childhood. Regarding musical form, he emphasizes Ravel's classicism as a reaction to romanticism. While Roland-Manuel situates *Miroirs* firmly within symbolist and impressionist aesthetics, he reflects Ravel's changing musical priorities beyond those associated with symbolism.[5] First, he addresses the issue of harmony versus counterpoint. While Debussy's music is "exclusivement harmonique," Ravel's takes a path between harmony and counterpoint: "Without being horizontal, it often derives the rarest effects from a sort of harmonic counterpoint."[6] In so doing, he distances Ravel from his rival Debussy in the battle of the *Debussystes* versus the *d'Indystes,* while not committing him to the contrapuntal tendencies of the *scholistes.*[7] In the postwar period, Roland-Manuel would be able to be much more open about Ravel's interest in counterpoint, given the general renewed interest in counterpoint and melody. Second, Roland-Manuel also attributes the quality of *simplicité* to almost all of Ravel's works, including *Daphnis et Chloé,* and describes his quest for *simplicité* in *Ma mère l'oye* "as a protest against ridiculous romantic gravity."[8] Finally, he hints at Ravel's musical personality, highlighting his "délicate pudeur" (delicate reserve) in "Le gibet," and the "ironie musicale" and "la malice de l'observateur" in *Histoires naturelles.*[9] Only once does Roland-Manuel refer to Ravel as an artisan, preferring instead to emphasize the ability of his music to touch and move its audience.[10] More pressing in 1914 was the need to connect Ravel to enduring French traditions; having repeatedly ascribed "French" qualities of precision to Ravel, the young critic claims that "Maurice Ravel miraculously renews the broken thread of our purest tradition . . . of Couperin and Rameau."[11]

Roland-Manuel wrote a number of articles and books on Ravel between 1921 and 1938, some under his own name and others on behalf of the composer. The first of these was an article laconically titled "Maurice Ravel," which also appeared in *La Revue Musicale* in April 1921.[12] The timing of this article is significant in that Ravel's relevance had been questioned in a number of prominent postwar publications, most famously in Satie's malicious comment, "Ravel refuses the Legion of Honor but all his music accepts it."[13] The group, Les Six, had been launched for over a year and was attracting attention with its reportedly outrageous statements about Debussy, Ravel, and Impressionism.[14] Roland-Manuel's article also responds to Paul Landormy's well-known reflection on current musical aesthetics in France, "Le Déclin de l'impressionnisme," which appeared in the February issue of *La Revue Musicale*.[15] Here Landormy argued that Ravel's music pointed to a way out of Impressionism, but that, nevertheless, he cannot be regarded as the leader of postwar French music. In Landormy's view,

> He lacks assurance, vigor, application, the courage to say things, crudely, if necessary, which characterizes the newcomers. M. Ravel is distinguished by elegance, affectionate gentleness and even affectation, a taste that will go out of fashion. . . . It is because he is a product of his time. It was important at least to underline the manner in which he foreshadowed a new era.[16]

Roland-Manuel's article amounts to a relaunching of Ravel in the context of the postwar musical scene; he wants to prove that Ravel need not be considered out of fashion. He situates Ravel as a successor of Chabrier and Fauré, describing the former as "the precursor of the new French school,"[17] and in so doing, echoes the contemporary interest in Chabrier by the young French composers.[18] Perhaps surprisingly, he also acknowledges Satie's importance. He begins by reminding readers that Cocteau's "discovery" of Satie is not new; Ravel himself discovered Satie as a young composer in the 1890s, and subsequent works including the experimental "Surgi de la croupe et du bond" of 1914 reveal his influence. In Roland-Manuel's view, Satie's rejection of his own past can explain the "contradictory and sometimes cruel whim, which the musician of *Socrate* brings to everything,"[19] most notably in his public rejection of Ravel himself. By contrast, Roland-Manuel diminishes the importance of Debussy. He argues against the view that Ravel is an impressionist or a *Debussyste,* and pits the "sensualité et sensibilité" of Debussy against the "intelligence et sensualité" of Ravel.[20] While Debussy's uniqueness allowed him to escape the "harmful pitfalls of romanticism,"[21] he consigns the aesthetic of *Debussysme* firmly to the past. At the same time, he seeks to link pre- and postwar aesthetics in a determined public attempt to counteract the perceived rupture between pre- and postwar musical concerns, placing Ravel at the center.[22]

Roland-Manuel cites a number of distinctive traits in Ravel which were regaining popularity in the postwar period, in particular, his penchant for traditional "classical forms," and his distinctive melody, which was "toute différente" to *debussyste* melody, at once "supple but extremely clear."[23] While many younger composers sought, at least in their public discourse, a return to classical forms and qualities, the postwar period in France is noted for its preference for clear melodic outlines and phrasing, in contrast to the subtleties of so-called impressionist melodic writing. This preoccupation with melody—and its link to counterpoint—was shared by Ravel, Darius Milhaud, Arthur Honegger, and Florent Schmitt, and was due to a considerable extent to their tutelage under André Gédalge, who taught all of them counterpoint at the Conservatoire. Gédalge provides a crucial link between the composers who studied counterpoint with him at this time and key aesthetic and musical priorities of the period.[24]

Roland-Manuel touches on two other characteristics of postwar music and attempts to relate them to Ravel's technique: "polytonie" (polytonality) and "l'art dépouillé" (the stripped-down style). Skeptical of the flurry of interest in polytonality and its perceived link with Les Six, he wants to show that Ravel's *Valses nobles et sentimentales* can be analyzed in terms of one controlling tonality despite the appearance of multiple superimposed keys.[25] He presents Ravel as a composer who retains classical forms and adheres to the fundamental rules of tonality, as distinct from those (such as Milhaud) who claimed that their experiments in extending tonality were new. Roland-Manuel was eager, though, to embrace "le style dépouillé" in Ravel's music, detecting it in his works as early as the *Histoires naturelles*. While in 1914 he noted the "comique," the "malice de l'observateur," and the "raffinement musicaux" of the song cycle, by 1921 his focus has changed: "In *Histoires* the line is reinforced, the harmony has become more incisive, even more personal and neater. The style, clarified, stripped of the superfluous, succeeds in expressing itself with exactitude and perfect clarity."[26] He makes similar claims for the "marvelous concision" of the Trio, presenting it as an example of avant-garde tendencies: "At a time when theories of 'the stripped-down style' take hold of the avant-garde's journalistic columns, it is important to note that it is Ravel who has given us the most eloquent illustrations of this aesthetic to date."[27]

Roland-Manuel confirms that his motivation in promoting Ravel as the figure to represent both continuity and innovation in the postwar period was his desire to counteract the perception of Satie as the spiritual leader of French postwar music. His criticism of Satie is strong: "Our music must be wary of mixing up 'denuded art' with 'artistic corpses.'"[28] Roland-Manuel thereby announced his participation in the aesthetic battle in which he and the other young French composers were engaged concerning the direction and leadership of French music in the post–World War I period. Along with others, notably Louis Durey, Roland-Manuel saw "the perilous danger of naked simplicity" as championed by Satie and those intent on promoting him, including Cocteau, Auric, Poulenc, and Milhaud.[29] His purpose in writing this article immediately after Landormy's "Le Déclin de l'impressionnisme" was to argue that Ravel was the best model for young generation to follow: "Until now, Ravel seems to have been only overtaken by Ravel himself."[30] Central to the young critic's thinking was that Ravel was responding to new cultural and social conditions; moreover, he provided much-needed continuity between pre- and postwar contexts at a time of political and artistic instability.

Ravel and Artificiality: Man and Music

Roland-Manuel's 1925 article, "Maurice Ravel ou l'esthétique de l'imposture," which was written for a special Ravel issue of *La Revue Musicale,* had a different purpose and focus; it provided the opportunity for the author to develop a discourse of artificiality around Ravel, the man and his music. He was not the first to describe Ravel's art as artificial. Calvocoressi, the music critic and polyglot, had written as early as 1913 that "the artificiality of M. Ravel's art . . . is beyond question. One might say, indeed, that artificiality is natural to M. Ravel."[31] He later put these words into Ravel's mouth in the oft-cited comment: "But has no-one realized that I might be artificial by nature?"[32] In both statements, Ravel's nature enters into a discussion of his art. While Roland-Manuel had touched on some of these qualities in Ravel's music in his 1914 biography and his 1921 essay, by 1925 he was now less concerned with style and more preoccupied with the nature of the artist/artisan and artistic creation. He applies Baudelaire's commentary on Edgar Allan Poe's "The Philosophy of Composition" to Ravel, arguing that Ravel, like Poe, eschews "chance" in favor of "analysis and calculation."[33] In this and other references to Baudelaire, Roland-Manuel emphasizes the anti-romantic, classical qualities of Ravel, demystifying his role as an inspired artist: "Art doesn't intrude on him as it imposed on the romantic composers. It is not, in his eyes, the supreme truth, but the most brilliant lie; an amazing imposture."[34] Roland-Manuel pushes this notion of Ravel as a trickster, a conjurer, whose music may move the listener to tears, but who lacks emotional involvement with his art. His imposture is all the more impressive because "ce magicien" hides all trace of his tracks, even from those closest to him.[35] Roland-Manuel uses language associated with magic and sorcery to describe Ravel's art, in striking contrast to critics such as Louis Laloy and Émile Vuillermoz, who use language emphasizing nature and originality to describe the art of Debussy.[36]

In place of the "originality" of Ravel's arch rival, Debussy, Roland-Manuel claims that "[all] of Ravel's works were first of all pastiches."[37] While Ravel may have hidden his tracks about how he realized a composition, he was ironically more open about his use of models when preparing to compose. Roland-Manuel compares him to a copyist, for whom "the assimilation mechanism" remains hidden.[38] The young critic's choice of language is significant; in describing the process of moving from imitation to composition as a mechanism, he not only chooses a term that has continued to be associated with Ravel, but also demystifies and appears to diminish his master's creative ability.[39]

The young critic was clear in his aim of setting Ravel up as an anti-romantic figure who eschewed the confessional expression of the artist; he was also keen to identify him in opposition to Debussy, insisting that Ravel has never "solicited" or "submitted" to Debussy's influence. But this line of argument was not new in Roland-Manuel's criticism. Given the emphasis of "The Aesthetics of Imposture," it also made sense for him to align Ravel with other figures such as Baudelaire, Poe and Paul Valéry who shared views on the relationship of the artisan to the artwork, the ability of art to communicate, and the pursuit of technical perfection. He goes further; rather than relegating this aesthetic to a bygone fin-de-siècle sensibility, he counteracts the view that Ravel was no longer central to postwar debates by claiming that Ravel's aesthetic was distinctive in deliberately working against a modernism that was "dominated by the passion for originality."[40] In so doing, he places Ravel's music and approach to composition alongside other contemporary figures who were similarly rethinking and reacting to aspects of modernism, most notably Valéry, T. S. Eliot, and Stravinsky. In particular, by linking past to present in a reciprocal relationship that redefines both, he adopts an attitude not dissimilar to that of Stravinsky and T. S. Eliot, who not only regarded tradition as something acquired through effort and study, but also believed that past and present were linked in a fluid relationship, not simply determined by chronology.[41]

Most compelling is Roland-Manuel's subsequent statement that originality emerges in combining familiar things in new combinations:

> It is in his attachment to the most clearly defined objects that he perceives new connections between things. The more familiar they are, the more significant will the discovery be. The really original work of art will retain this association with the familiar.[42]

These lines are strikingly close to T. S. Eliot's idea of creating "new wholes" by bringing together disassociated material. In his essay "The Metaphysical Poets" (1921), Eliot argued that the poet's mind was always receptive to making new combinations and could combine the reading of Spinoza with the smell of cooking. Similarly, Stravinsky's musical practice, most striking in his neoclassical works, but traceable throughout his creative life, was to superimpose unrelated musical materials in new and original ways, often involving past and present, as in *Oedipus Rex, Le Baiser de la fée,* and *The Rake's Progress,* to mention only a few. While it is not clear to what extent Roland-Manuel, or Ravel, knew T. S. Eliot's work, it becomes apparent that he was thinking of Stravinsky when he situated Ravel in opposition to "the sectarians of Romantic subjectivism" and alongside the "artisans for whom style is art itself, and notably alongside Stravinsky."[43]

Roland-Manuel's article reveals an important shift in his attentions; whereas the 1921 publication was a defense in response to the perceived threat of Satie and Les Six, by 1925 several of the now scattered group had softened their attitudes toward Ravel and were beginning to seek recognition and greater acceptance by the public and the musical establishment. In addition, Roland-Manuel's 1925 intervention reveals the full impact of Stravinsky's new aesthetic in France. The Russian's neoclassicism had surprised and preoccupied the French since the "failure" of *Mavra* in 1922 and the subsequent success of the Octet (1923). Moreover, Stravinsky's writings outlining his neoclassicism were just appearing in print.[44] But Ravel and Stravinsky, although close in 1913, had grown apart, especially after *Mavra*, which Ravel found hard to appreciate because of its deliberate rejection of Rimsky-Korsakov in favor of Tchaikovsky.[45] Roland-Manuel defines Ravel's position in relation to Stravinsky, identifying their shared pleasure in mixing up "le *beau* et l'*utile*."[46] It is noteworthy that he quotes Paul Valéry's recent writings when identifying the two composers' shared preoccupation with the technical demands of achieving a particular effect, when the issue of craft dominates and controls all other parameters.[47]

Yet Roland-Manuel also specifies the differences in their approach to composition. Whereas Stravinsky employs "volumes, weights, or densities" to achieve a particular musical effect, Ravel, by way of contrast, only employs the raw musical materials as a means to an end; musical meaning extends beyond the physicality of the notes themselves.[48] Just as Roland-Manuel was partly motivated to write his 1921 article in reponse to Landormy's "Le Déclin de l'impressionnisme," he engaged with Ansermet's article "Introduction à l'œuvre d'Igor Stravinsky," (which had appeared the previous month) with Landormy's verdict on Ravel still on his mind. Ansermet identified two questions posed by a work of art: the "what" (subjective) and "how" (objective). In Stravinsky's case, according to Roland-Manuel, the "musical fact," the "how," supersedes every other interest, coincidence, or extra-musical element.[49]

Roland-Manuel distinguishes between Ravel and Stravinsky by appealing to French (Rameauian) traditions to justify Ravel's interest in both the "what" and the "how." He outlines a middle way between Stravinsky's formalist position and the German Romantic view that music is a way to express emotion: Ravel's music does not seek to "imitate" but to "evoke." His choice of evocation immediately connects Ravel's aesthetic to Symbolism and to Debussy, who used this term frequently to describe his quest for musical originality.[50] Roland-Manuel goes further in stating that unlike Stravinsky who proceeds by metaphor, Ravel proceeds by ambiguity: "antitheses, allusions, value transmutations [and] reversals of equilibrium."[51] He takes the familiar example of *L'heure espagnole* as an instance of Ravel's reversal of normal expectations, where people are heartless puppets with mechanical thoughts and clocks are imbued with human feelings, and argues that this reversal of expectation also occurs on a formal and timbral level; listeners are tricked through "equivocation and ambiguity."[52] In his view, Ravel also differs from Stravinsky in the essential aspect of trickery, of "imposture," which is central to his article. In summing up the relationship between the composer's technique and the evocative and dream-inspired world often associated with Symbolism, he returns to Valéry's Socrate: "A dream, a dream, but a dream that is fully penetrated by symmetry, all kinds of order, routine, and sequences!"[53] Yet both Roland-Manuel and Valéry seem unable to explain what takes place when disparate elements of the real, the imagined, and the intelligible unite to form an original work of art.[54]

Significantly, Roland-Manuel cites Valéry numerous times in this exposé of Ravel's aesthetic position, strongly suggesting that he had read his latest work, *Eupalinos* (1921), after Valéry's twenty-year silence, and that he recognized the many connections between Ravel and the French poet. They both had frequented Cipa and Ida Godebski's salon in the period preceding World War I, and, according to Haine, reading Valéry was one of the group Les Apaches' particular enthusiasms.[55] Moreover, they openly acknowledged the importance of Edgar Allan Poe, particularly "The Raven" and the essay "The Philosophy of Composition," with its emphasis on the construction of the work of art. They also shared an identification with classicism in its postwar context. T. S. Eliot was also fascinated by Valéry, and wrote a lecture entitled "From Poe to Valéry" in 1948, and supplying the introduction to the English edition of Valéry's *The Art of Poetry* in 1958.[56] Eliot's image of Valéry as the scientist-poet in his laboratory, fascinated with the problems of method and process, has resonances for Roland-Manuel's construction of Ravel.[57]

In sum, Roland-Manuel's "Maurice Ravel ou l'esthétique de l'imposture" is significant on a number of counts. First, there is no mention of Satie and Les Six; that perceived threat had dissipated. Second, the article fashions a place for Ravel adjacent to but distinct from Stravinsky, rooted in French traditions, and indebted to the thinking of his immediate predecessors such as Poe and Baudelaire as well as contemporaries, notably Valéry. His overriding claim is that both Stravinsky and Ravel make important contributions to the aesthetics and practice of contemporary music, particularly in reacting against the quest for constant innovation.

The article is also significant in that it links Ravel's personality to discussions of his aesthetic. Superficially the following assertion could suggest that his personal life is irrelevant to an understanding of this music:

> It is not necessary to know Ravel personally or to have delved deeply into his thoughts to be convinced that the methods of this musician, his technique, and his art in its entirety suggest deliberate research and mistrust of inspiration.[58]

However, a second reading of this passage suggests that Ravel's personality is self-evident from a study of his art.[59] While Roland-Manuel is keen to distance Ravel from artists who reveal their innermost soul through their work (which he links to German Romantic sensibility), he teases the reader to speculate on the nature of the man who plays tricks with a listener's emotions: "If this music pleases you, moves you, makes you cry, know that it is made by a man who did not go on his knees 'before or afterwards' [and] who did not cry while writing it."[60] Here he suggests a disjuncture between the man and the emotional power of the composer's art; unlike detractors, particularly Pierre Lalo, who argued that Ravel's music lacked emotional depth, Roland-Manuel seems to suggest that there was something lacking in the composer's emotional make-up, causing him to obscure his subjectivity to the extent he apparently did. Roland-Manuel portrays Ravel as an isolated, aloof artisan who remains distant from his art and whose fabrications are fakes, reproductions rather than inspired originals. Certainly he acknowledges Ravel's originality and consummate skill; however, such an understanding of Ravel's musical essence has persisted and has guided assessments of his significance to date.[61]

Calvocoressi points out the dangers of defining Ravel's importance too narrowly in a short contribution to the 1938 Special issue of *La Revue Musicale*, entitled "Ravel: Un point d'histoire et un point d'exégèse." He blames Ravel's first apologists, especially Roland-Manuel, for having "contributed to spreading this conception of an exceptional, artificial and precious art, based on the 'aesthetic of imposture,' which has tended to mask the very normal, classical, and especially human character of Ravel."[62] Calvocoressi returns to this issue in his 1941 article "When Ravel Composed to Order," pointing his finger at Roland-Manuel's "Maurice Ravel ou l'esthétique de l'imposture" article.[63] Yet, ironically, it was Calvocoressi himself who first discussed Ravel's artificiality in an article on Ravel in the *Musical Times* in 1913 and later attributed Ravel's arguably most quoted phrase to the composer himself in 1933.[64] Calvocoressi's remarks have sparked seventy years of discussion about the nature of Ravel's artificiality and how it continues to influence our understanding of his music, as this volume attests.

Ravel on Composition

An important issue persists: Ravel himself remains elusive in the shaping of his own legacy. Ravel's public statements consist of one formal presentation, "Contemporary Music" (1928), which was written with the help of Roland-Manuel for the Rice Lecture in Houston; an "Autobiographical Sketch" (1928), which he dictated to Roland-Manuel; and a number of articles which include "Take Jazz Seriously" (1928), written for the *Musical Digest,* and "Memories of a Lazy Child" (1931). In addition, he wrote reviews from the 1910s on and gave many interviews in the 1920s and early 1930s. Thus the most complete statements on his musical tastes are focused on 1928, only a few years after Roland-Manuel's article on the aesthetic of imposture. Ravel's tendency was to stand back from the mêlée; he only rarely commented on the attacks he received in the press, most notably when he responded to Pierre Lalo's claim that he had imitated Debussy.[65] Indeed, he did not defend himself against the attacks from Satie and Les Six in the postwar period, instead acknowledging his indebtedness to Satie and praising Milhaud as one of the most gifted young composers. He also acknowledged the right of the younger composers to reject his music. His failure to speak out more forcefully in the 1920s partly accounts for the perception that he was not a suitable figurehead in this period; Roland-Manuel's efforts on Ravel's behalf were matched only by one other composer and critic, Louis Durey, albeit in the British press. In explaining his aesthetic position, Ravel again equivocated, declaring that "I have never felt the need to formulate, either for the benefit of others or for myself, the principles of my aesthetic."[66] Despite such denials and his apparent wish to leave the elucidation of his ideas about music to others, his writings, although not contradicting Roland-Manuel's statements, provide the reader with a more nuanced glimpse into his understanding of the process of creation of a work of art, which Roland-Manuel's and Calvocoressi's writings omit or are unable to tackle.

Within his creative process, the materials of composition for Ravel consisted of the particular style, technique, or form. He described these in "Contemporary Music" as the "more superficial elements of [the] music, that is to say, [the] external manifestations rather than [the] inner content." In his view, "popular forms," such as the blues and jazz, "are but the materials of construction."[67] Similarly, the atonality of Schoenberg and the polytonality of Milhaud constituted "but the garb concealing or adorning [the works'] emotional sensitiveness"; while these elements are the surface traits of a work, he continues "sensitiveness and emotion constitute the real content of a work of art."[68] While Roland-Manuel acknowledges that a work of art could move a listener to tears, Ravel's purpose, in contrast, is different in emphasizing the distance between the emotion inherent in the work and the author; Ravel appears to search for the more essential and elusive aspects of the work of art.

Ravel also shows nuance in discussing the aim of composition and the means of achieving the "real inner emotion of the music" or the "inner content." In a number of articles from this period, he emphasized the importance of craft and the aim of technical perfection, most notably in "Some Reflections on Music" (ca. 1928):

> My objective . . . is technical perfection. I can strive unceasingly to this end, since I am certain of never being able to attain it. The important thing is to get nearer to it all the time. Art, no doubt, has other effects, but the artist, in my opinion, should have no other aim.[69]

In "Contemporary Music" he outlines the task and priorities of the composer in working with a particular style. He describes the "severe effort toward perfection" in which "no detail has been left to chance."[70] Yet, this mania for perfection does not preclude the individual.

Ravel was clear that the composer's individuality imposed itself on the particular materials as the work was being shaped.[71] He alludes to this on a number of occasions, most famously when urging his students to copy existing works; deviation from the model will emerge from the work of an original composer.[72] While this phrase has been given an authoritative spin by Roland-Manuel, it reflects Ravel's thinking regarding the individual character, traits, and roots of the composer imposing themselves on a work of art.[73] Indeed, Ravel developed the idea of individual consciousness in his lecture "Contemporary Music." He describes the laws of counterpoint and harmony as "the obvious and superficial part of the work of art," while the more significant elements are the "roots of the artist's sensitiveness and personal reaction," which are twofold: national consciousness and individual consciousness.[74] These elements inform the evolving work of art and distinguish between the task of the artisan and the achievement of the artist. While a composer may search widely for musical materials, he should engage with them according to these two roots, which constitute his particular heritage. Crucial to his thinking in this and other writings is that Ravel finds a significant place for the artist.

Throughout the above statements, Ravel appears to conceive of composition on two levels: technical craftsmanship, which permits the creation of a perfect object, and the individual and national consciousness of the composer, which leads to the "real inner emotion" and "inner content" of a work. At the same time he felt that such processes defied "classification and analysis,"[75] which explains his reluctance to talk about his aesthetics or, with notable exceptions, to analyze his music.[76] By contrast, he was quite happy to write about the technical side of composing.[77] In his view, technical mastery can be studied and achieved through hard work, while originality can only be sensed and is unknowable. Roland-Manuel acknowledged that Ravel kept his traces as a composer hidden even from close disciples like himself. For the young composer-critic, this concealment tied into his idea of Ravel's imposture. While imposture, artificiality and distancing are important aspects of Ravel as composer and personality, his own writings, although often not entirely free of Roland-Manuel's fingerprints, present a more complex picture that fits less comfortably into the particular aesthetic position espoused by his young disciple in the mid 1920s.[78]

Assessing Ravel in 1938

Immediately after Ravel's death, many writers attempted to assess his importance for French music and beyond. At play in many of these critical assessments is a

struggle over who really knew and understood Ravel. The most substantial tribute appeared as a Special issue of *La Revue Musicale* in 1938. Constituting the
official and state sanctioned assessments of the composer, it included a tran-
script of the funeral oration by minister of national education and fine arts
Jean Zay and contributions by musical establishment figures (such as Henry
Bidou, André Suarès, Alfred Cortot, Robert Brussel and Robert Bernard), and
foreign composers (including Bartók, Casella, and Malipiero). This collective
tribute provides a fascinating insight into competing views about Ravel's significance. For a number of contributors, Ravel's character and music were
reflections of French national traits, in revealing the nation's strengths as
well as its limitations, as noted by Minister Zay.[79] There was also considerable
consensus that Ravel was a classical composer who strove for perfection.[80]
For some authors these traits distinguished him from Debussy, although
other contributors, notably those from abroad, regarded the two composers
as inseparable, complementary, and even interdependent.[81] In a number of
these assessments, Ravel's contribution is regarded as supplementary to the
more overwhelming impact of Debussy; rather than revolutionizing French
musical taste, "Ravel will have been the surest guarantee and the most effective witness of national aspirations in our time."[82] The view of Ravel's special but limited contribution is borne out by subsequent prominent French
composers, notably Jolivet, Messiaen and Boulez, who trace their lineage
to Debussy rather than to Ravel.[83] Dutilleux, by contrast, stands out for his
more unequivocal admiration of the composer.[84]

Returning to the Special issue of *La Revue Musicale,* Robert Bernard's editorial reveals tensions over Ravel's fame and the discomfort of certain groups
close to Ravel regarding his international renown. In Bernard's view, these
groups wish to preserve the reputation of Ravel as an elite and private individual and resist the tendency to regard him as a popular international figure.
Bernard pits the elite against "la foule" (an evocative term with threatening
revolutionary connotations), the "tendance aristocratique" against the "goût
vulgaire."[85] He identifies a related group who do not want Ravel's work to be
misunderstood and therefore wish to guard his legacy jealously; moreover, he
claims that several in this group have declined to be involved in this public
and collective tribute. Justifying the volume's scope and purpose, he asserts
that "Ravel's celebrity status is an independent fact beyond our control,"[86] and
therefore, Ravel's legacy is out of the hands of his inner circle of supporters
and friends.

While some of Ravel's closest associates are not included in this volume,
there are contributions from former Apaches such as Viñes, Vuillermoz, Inghelbrecht, Klingsor, and from performers including Marguerite Long, Madeleine Grey, and Hélène Jourdan-Morhange.[87] Roland-Manuel chooses to
remain more distant, taking the role of "scribe" for Ravel in his publication
of and commentary on Ravel's "Autobiographical Sketch," reserving his own

revised perspective for his 1938 biography. The former group prepared their own more personal and anecdotal tribute in *Maurice Ravel par quelques-uns de ses familiers* (1939), in which they remembered the Apache days before World War I and their role in supporting Ravel's talent through musical and intellectual exchange. Their contributions give a valuable insight into the role of Ravel's private artistic network before World War I.[88] In the context of the 1938 Special issue, Ravel's friends play a part in counteracting the view that his personality and music lack emotional engagement.[89] Nevertheless, they contribute to the notion of Ravel as a masked figure who revealed his true self only to the few. Marguerite Long writes:

> Reserved, sacred, and distant with unwelcome visitors, he was the surest, most delicate, and most faithful of friends. By his exterior appearance, his witticisms, and his love of paradoxes, he has often contributed to crediting the myth of 'spiritual indifference,' but, in spite of these appearances, this great prisoner of perfection hid a sensitive and passionate soul.[90]

For Hélène Jourdan-Morhange, portraits of Ravel as dandified, dry, and formal were simply false. In her view too, "the true Ravel" was known and understood only by his friends: "His friends and those close to him looked for him in his work, sometimes remembering him in a rhythm, an unpredictable harmony, the fleeting memory of a look, a tender expression, where their lost friend was wholly revealed to them."[91]

There is an important connection between the friends who wanted to guard him jealously and those who used their knowledge of the composer to establish Ravel as the subject of scholarship. In this respect, Roland-Manuel stands partly in both groups; while close to Ravel, and, according to Haine, a late member of Les Apaches, he remained more of a disciple and student than a peer.[92] While the composer's circle resisted the view of Ravel as distant and lacking in emotional engagement, they were complicit with the idea of masks, which Jankélévitch developed for the first time in his 1939 biography.[93] Furthermore, in their eagerness to protect Ravel, they also proffered the view of the composer as childlike and in need of protecting. This portrayal of Ravel as a child is prominent in the special issue, and constitutes a defining issue in Roland-Manuel's posthumous biography.[94] Similarly, Ravel's friends bolstered the links between Ravel the man and his music, as Hélène Jourdan-Morhange reveals in the quotation above. Roland-Manuel had introduced the idea of studying Ravel's life in relation to his music in 1925; by 1938 he had presented his portrayal of Ravel as a dandy which has had a significant impact on subsequent Ravel scholarship. While the composer's friends remained engaged principally on an emotional level, Roland-Manuel stood apart in seeking to establish an intellectual discourse that was rooted in his privileged knowledge of Ravel's character and music.

Vladimir Jankélévitch was one of the first to consider Roland-Manuel's take on Ravel a subject for critical interrogation. Significantly, he did so in his contribution to the special issue, "Ravel vu par Roland-Manuel," in which he noted the significant role Roland-Manuel had played in initiating "une conception artificialiste" of Ravel as the artisan constructor.[95] In commenting on Roland-Manuel's latest biography, he first acknowledges the impact of Edgar Allan Poe and Baudelairean dandyism on Ravel, and also cites the influence of Valéry, Apollinaire, and Matisse. He thus places Ravel not only in his prewar generation, but also in the context of emerging strands of modernism.[96] While lamenting the lack of analysis in the biography, he declares that from now on this "literary musician's name [Alexis Roland-Manuel] is inseparable from that of Ravel."[97]

Jankélévitch is not content simply to act as a reviewer; he makes another significant contribution to the volume, which prepares the way for his biography of 1939. Entitled "La Sérénade interrompue," it tackles the issue of Ravel's hidden sensuality, desire and passion, which are evident in his works but masked behind irony and the image of the dandy.[98] Examining Ravel's output, he offers the image of the "sérénade interrompue," giving examples of strangled developments, terse and shortened melodies, and curtailed crescendos.[99] Discussions of sublimation and the search for explanations in Ravel's character and life have continued to preoccupy scholars, such as Lawrence Kramer and most recently Michael Puri.[100] Jankélévitch's writing represents an important moment in Ravel scholarship; he undeniably builds on the work of Roland-Manuel and others, but differs from them in not having been a disciple or friend of the composer.

Similarly freed from the responsibilities of intimacy, subsequent scholarship has tended to confirm the consensus about Ravel that began to emerge in 1938. Ravel scholars have largely accepted Roland-Manuel's discourse of artificiality and have shared a fascination with Ravel's life, with much speculation about his character and sexuality.[101] Such a fascination with Ravel's character has also informed interpretations of his music. For example, Lawrence Kramer characterizes *Daphnis et Chloé* as a work of self-conscious fakery, of beauty aimed at sensuality, pleasure, consumption, and ultimately commerce.[102] Steven Huebner has made important contributions to Ravel scholarship, most notably in his article "Maurice Ravel: Private Life, Public Works," in which he tackles the problematic issue of how biographers have portrayed Ravel's music as an expression of the composer's personal emotions. Huebner's observation that Ravel tried to keep his life private and separate from his art has certainly not discouraged writers from searching for traces of the man in his creative output.[103] Indeed, the contrary is true. Ravel's masks fascinated Jankélévitch in 1939 and continue to intrigue as recent and forthcoming studies by Deborah Mawer, Michael Puri, and Peter Kaminsky prove.[104]

Beyond musicology, this view of Ravel has materialized in the film *Un Coeur en Hiver*, which not only uses Ravel's chamber music both diagetically and nondiagetically, but contains a Ravel-like main protagonist who lacks normal human emotional responses, but who can relate to music, and more specifically to the mechanics of making beautiful music and beautiful objects. Jean Echenoz's novel entitled *Ravel* (2006) emphasizes Ravel's dandyism and emotionally distance, even to those closest to him. In portraying Ravel's last ten years, Echenoz paints his subject as an aloof and fading figure who is increasingly used as a cultural product by the state, representing France on his big foreign tours. Such a portrayal recalls Robert Bernard's caution in his editorial for *La Revue Musicale* that Ravel's fame exceeds the control of the select few. Alluding to the music and the man he attempts to capture Ravel's national status: "Today, his music is infused with new meanings, as is his character, and above all, both aspects increase in national, or, if you prefer, cultural value."[105] This statement is important in confirming that as early as 1938 Ravel was significant and meaningful for distinct and potentially competing constituencies. On a private level he was remembered as a friend and mentor, while simultaneously becoming a public national symbol and international celebrity. Yet this essay has also demonstrated the critical role of a select few in shaping how Ravel could be understood at various stages of his life and compositional career. Equally important, these contemporary notions of Ravel's essential characteristics as man and artist continue to exert a strong and to some extent unacknowledged influence on current Ravel scholarship. Importantly, Ravel's Frenchness is never in doubt in assessments of his value. For many contributors to the special issue of *La Revue Musicale,* Ravel symbolized the French creative spirit in both its qualities and limitations. In claiming this composer as their own, there has perhaps been a tendency to limit the nature, not only of Ravel's creativity, but by extension, the scope and purpose of French musical achievement itself.

Notes

The epigraph for this chapter is drawn from Alexis Roland-Manuel, *Maurice Ravel* (Paris: Editions de la Nouvelle Revue critique, 1938), 254; trans. Cynthia Jolly (NY: Dover Publications, Inc., 1938), 136. With the exception of Orenstein's translations of Ravel, translations are my own unless otherwise noted.

1. Alexis Roland-Manuel Lévy (Roland-Manuel) studied with Roussel at the Schola Cantorum from 1911 and took lessons from Ravel at the same time. He was introduced to both composers by Erik Satie. Roland-Manuel was a minor composer in his own right, but better known and respected as an insightful and articulate commentator on French music of this period. He became a ghostwriter, not only for Ravel, but also for Stravinsky, with whom he wrote *Poetics of Music* (1942).

2. Roland-Manuel stands on the edge of the group Les Apaches. According to Malou Haine he was "le plus jeune des Apaches et l'une des dernières recrues." Malou Haine, "Cipa Godebski et les Apaches," *Revue Belge de Musicologie*, vol. 60 (2007): 255. Jann

Pasler, by contrast, does not include him in her list of members in "A Sociology of the Apaches: 'Sacred Battalion' for Pelléas," in *Berlioz and Debussy: Sources, Contexts and Legacies*, ed. Barbara L. Kelly and Kerry Murphy (Aldershot: Ashgate, 2007), 149–66.

3. Roland-Manuel's mother, Mme Dreyfus, became Ravel's *marraine de guerre* (his wartime godmother). Ravel dedicated the 'Menuet' from *Le Tombeau de Couperin* to Roland-Manuel's stepbrother, Jean Dreyfus. See Arbie Orenstein, ed., *A Ravel Reader* (New York: Columbia University Press, 1990), 155, 162.

4. Ravel's letter to Roland-Manuel of August 27, 1913, reveals that Émile Vuillermoz was to have supplied the musical analysis for the biography at the suggestion of the publisher Durand. This collaboration never materialized. See Orenstein, *A Ravel Reader*, 140.

5. Roland-Manuel, *Maurice Ravel et son œuvre* (Paris: Durand, 1914), 16.

6. "sans être horizontale, elle tire souvent d'une sorte de contrepoint harmonique les effets les plus rares," Ibid., 36.

7. See Brian Hart, "The Symphony and National Identity in Early Twentieth-Century France" in *French Music, Culture, and National Identity, 1870–1939*, ed. Barbara L. Kelly (Rochester, NY: University of Rochester Press, 2008), 137, 146. See also Jane Fulcher, *French Cultural Politics and Music* (New York: Oxford University Press, 1999), 27.

8. "une protestation contre la ridicule gravité romantique." Roland-Manuel, *Maurice Ravel*, 23. He remarks that "la forte simplicité" of *Daphnis et Chloé* "nous touche plus que tel hurlement romantique." According to Scott Messing, the term was associated with pre–World War I *nouveau classicisme* but would soon become firmly linked to Satie and to postwar musical aspirations. See Scott Messing, *Neoclassicism in Music: From the Genesis of the Concept through the Schoenberg/Stravinsky Polemic* (Ann Arbor: University of Michigan Press, 1988), 76–77.

9. Roland-Manuel, *Maurice Ravel*, 19–20.

10. He alludes to Ravel as an artisan in *L'heure espagnole*. Ibid., 25. Talking up the emotive qualities of Ravel's work was surely a response to critics such as Pierre Lalo, who criticized the composer for his disengagement and apparent coldness.

11. "Maurice Ravel renoue miraculeusement le fil perdu de notre plus pure tradition . . . de Couperin et Rameau." Roland-Manuel, *Maurice Ravel*, 39.

12. Roland-Manuel, "Maurice Ravel," *La Revue Musicale* 2, no. 6 (April 1, 1921): 1–21.

13. "Ravel refuse la Légion d'Honneur mais toute sa musique l'accepte." Erik Satie, *Le Coq*, May 1, 1920. See also Georges Auric, "Jeux," *Nouvelle Revue française* 16 (January 1, 1921): 101–3.

14. See Georges Auric, "Bonjour, Paris" and "Après la pluie le beau temps," *Le Coq*, April and June 1920. Auric stated: "To imitate Debussy today seems to me to be no more than the worst form of vulturism" ["imiter Debussy ne me paraît plus aujourd'hui que la pire forme de la nécrophagie"]. Auric, *Le Coq* 1 (April 1, 1920): 1. See also Barbara L. Kelly, *Tradition and Style in the Works of Darius Milhaud: 1912–1939* (Aldershot: Ashgate, 2003), 6–7.

15. Paul Landormy, "Le Déclin de l'impressionnisme," *La Revue Musicale* 2, no. 4 (February 1, 1921): 97–113.

16. Il lui manque la vigueur, le trait appuyé, l'audace de tout dire avec crudité, la brutalité, s'il le faut, que caractérisent les nouveaux venus. Maurice Ravel a pour la distinction, l'élégance, les douceurs caressantes et aussi pour la préciosité un goût qui va passer de mode. C'est en quoi il est de son temps. Il importait de souligner du moins de quelle façon il annonçait déjà des temps nouveaux. (Landormy, "Le Déclin de l'impressionnisme," 101). Landormy based this article on an earlier piece that appeared

in *La Victoire*, August 10, 1920. See Barbara L. Kelly, "Ravel after Debussy: Leadership, Influences and Style," in Kelly and Murphy, *Berlioz and Debussy*, 168.

17. "le véritable précurseur de la nouvelle école française." Roland-Manuel, "Maurice Ravel," 4.

18. For Milhaud on Chabrier see Barbara L. Kelly, *Tradition and Style*, 36–37; for Ravel's interest in Chabrier see "Memories," in Orenstein, *A Ravel Reader*, 394 and Barbara L. Kelly, "History and Homage" in *The Cambridge Companion to Ravel*, ed. Deborah Mawer (Cambridge: Cambridge University Press, 2000), 12–14. Ravel writes about the importance of Chabrier in several articles.

19. "fantaisie contradictoire et parfois cruelle que le musicien de *Socrate* apporte à toutes choses." Roland-Manuel, *Maurice Ravel*, 5.

20. Ibid., 7–8.

21. "écueils funestes du romantisme." Ibid., 8.

22. Roland-Manuel changed his mind about the rupture between pre- and postwar composers in his unpublished article "Les Six devant Ravel," unpublished typescript. BNF Mus, 4 Vm⁰, Pièce 369, c. 1925, 1.

23. "souple mais extrêmement nette." Roland-Manuel, *Maurice Ravel*, 9.

24. Manuel Rosenthal confirms the importance of André Gédalge for Ravel, Schmitt, Koechlin, Rabaud, Roger-Ducasse, and Enesco, and later for Ibert, Honegger, and Milhaud: "Tout le monde voulait passer par les mains de Gédalge." *Maurice Ravel, Souvenirs de Manuel Rosenthal*, ed. Marcel Marnat (Paris: Éditions Hazan, 1995), 56–57.

25. As François de Médicis and I have shown, debates concerning polytonality were rife in the French musical press from 1921, and Médicis has shown just how closely polytonality was perceived to be aligned with the aims of Les Six, thanks mainly to Henri Collet's efforts, and despite the fact that the technique is most consistently evident in Milhaud's works, rather than in the works of the group as a whole. See Kelly, *Tradition and Style*, 142–68. Indeed, Poulenc and Auric publicly rejected polytonality in 1922. See also François de Médicis, "Darius Milhaud and the Debate on Polytonality in the French Press of the 1920s," *Music and Letters* 86, no. 4 (2005): 573–91.

26. Roland-Manuel, *Maurice Ravel*, 19. "Dans les *Histoires Naturelles* la ligne s'affermit, l'harmonie se fait plus incisive, plus personnelle encore et plus nette. Le style, clarifié, se dépouille du superflu et parvient à s'exprimer avec une exactitude, une limpidité parfaites." Roland-Manuel, *Maurice Ravel*, 17.

27. "Au moment où les théories de 'l'art dépouillé' défraient la chronique 'd'avant-garde,' il n'est pas utile de marquer que c'est un Ravel qui nous a donné jusqu'ici la plus éloquente illustration de cette esthétique-là." Ibid., 17.

28. "notre musique . . . doit se garder . . . de confondre 'l'art dépouillé avec les dépouilles des arts.'" Ibid.

29. "le sentier périlleux de la simplicité nue." Ibid., 18–19. Durey's article appeared in the same month as Roland-Manuel's, and was clearly part of a campaign to counteract derogatory writings about Ravel in the press. See Louis Durey, "Maurice Ravel," *The Chesterian* 14 (April, 1921): 422–26. Roland-Manuel prepared the way in an article on Durey in the February issue, in which he emphasizes Ravel's interest in Durey. Roland-Manuel, "Louis Durey," *The Chesterian* 13 (February 1921): 392.

30. "Ravel semble jusqu'à présent n'avoir été dépassé que par Ravel." Roland-Manuel, "Maurice Ravel," 18–19.

31. Michel Dimitri Calvocoressi, "Maurice Ravel," *Musical Times* (December 1, 1913): 785.

32. "Mais est-ce qu'il ne vient jamais à l'idée de ces gens-là que je peux être 'artificiel' par nature?" Calvocoressi, *Musician's Gallery* (London: Faber, 1933), quoted in Roger Nichols, ed., *Ravel Remembered* (London: Faber, 1987), 180.

33. "d'analyse, de combinations et de calcul . . ." Roland-Manuel, "Maurice Ravel ou l'esthétique de l'imposture," 16–17. This chapter goes on to discuss the importance of E. A. Poe to Ravel's idea of structure and imitation. See E. A. Poe, "La Genèse d'un poème," in *Histoires grotesques et sérieuses*, trans. Charles Baudelaire (Paris: M. Lévy Frères, 1871). See also Barbara L. Kelly, "History and Homage," in Mawer, *The Cambridge Companion to Ravel*, 16–17; and Michel Duchesneau, "Maurice Ravel et Edgar Allan Poe: une théorie poétique appliqué," *Ostinato rigore* 24 (2005): 7–24.

34. "L'art ne s'impose pas lui de la façon dont il s'impose aux romantiques. Ce n'est pas à ses yeux la suprême vérité, mais un mensonge, le plus brillant; une merveilleuse imposture." Roland-Manuel, "Maurice Ravel ou l'esthétique de l'imposture," 17.

35. Ibid., 18.

36. See Claude Debussy, "Pourquoi j'ai écrit Pelléas," *Monsieur Croche et autres écrits* (Paris: Gallimard, 1987), 64–65; Debussy, "A la veille de Pelléas et Mélisande," interview with Louis Schneider, *La Revue Musicale, Revue d'histoire et de critique* 2, no. 4 (April 1902): 138–40; Barbara L. Kelly, "Debussy and the Making of a *musicien français: Pelléas*, the Press and World War I," in Kelly, *French Music, Culture, and National Identity*, 59–60, 73; and Carlo Caballero, *Fauré and French Musical Aesthetics* (Cambridge: Cambridge University Press, 2001), 32–34.

37. "Aucune œuvre de Ravel qui n'ait été premièrement un pastiche." Roland-Manuel, "Maurice Ravel ou l'esthétique de l'imposture," 18.

38. Ibid., 18–19.

39. Indeed, there are many similarities between his discourse and that used both to support and to undermine Schoenberg's *Pierrot lunaire* at its French première. See Paul Le Flem, *Comoedia*, January 23, 1922; Dezarnaux, *La Liberté*, December 19, 1922; Jean Marnold, *Le Mercure de France*, July 1, 1922; and Vuillermoz, *L'Excelsior*, May 1, 1922.

40. Ibid., 19.

41. See T. S. Eliot, *The Four Quartets* (London: Faber, 1943); see also Barbara L. Kelly, "Time Present, Past and Future in the Writings and Practice of Milhaud: Comparisons with Stravinsky and Eliot," *Irish Musical Studies* 5 (1996): 294–320, and Kelly, *Tradition and Style*, 169.

42. "C'est en s'attachant aux objets les plus clairement définis qu'il percevra des rapports nouveaux entre les choses. Plus ces choses nous seront familières, plus la découverte aura de prix. L'œuvre d'art réellement, sainement originale se dégagera de cette dissociation du connu." Roland-Manuel, "Maurice Ravel ou l'esthétique de l'imposture," 19.

43. "des sectateurs du subjectivisme romantique"; "artisans pour qui le style est l'art même, et nommément à Igor Stravinsky." Ibid., 19.

44. Igor Stravinsky, "Some ideas about my Octuor," *The Arts* (Brooklyn, NY) (January 1924): 4–6; reprinted in Eric Walter White, *Stravinsky: The Composer and His Works* (London: Faber and Faber, 1979), 574–77; Ernest Ansermet, "Introduction à l'œuvre d'Igor Stravinsky," *La Revue Pleyel* (March 15, 1925): 19–20. Stravinsky, like Ravel, often involved critics to help him in his writings on music, most notably Arthur Lourié during this period.

45. José Bruhr, "An Interview with Maurice Ravel," *Le Guide du Concert*, October 16, 1931, and André Révész, "The Great Musician Maurice Ravel Talks about his Art," *ABC de Madrid*, May 1, 1924, in Orenstein, *Ravel Reader*, 482, 433.

46. Roland-Manuel, "Maurice Ravel ou l'esthétique de l'imposture," 19. The emphasis is his.

47. Ibid., 19; he quotes from Paul Valéry's *Eupalinos ou l'architecte* (1921).

48. "des volumes, des poids ou des densités"; "Ravel à la différence de Stravinsky, ne les évalue jamais sans une arrière-pensée." Roland-Manuel, "Maurice Ravel ou l'esthétique de l'imposture," 19.

49. Ibid., 20. Furthermore, Roland-Manuel's article is dedicated to Ansermet.

50. See Barbara L. Kelly, "Debussy's Parisian Affiliations," in *The Cambridge Companion to Debussy*, ed. Simon Trezise (Cambridge: Cambridge University Press, 2003), 25–42.

51. "antithèses, allusions, transmutations de valeurs, renversements d'équilibre." Roland-Manuel, "Maurice Ravel ou l'esthétique de l'imposture," 20.

52. "l'équivoque et de l'ambiguïté." Ibid., 21.

53. "Rêve, rêve, mais rêve tout pénétré de symétries, tout ordre, tout actes et séquences!" Ibid.

54. "Le réel, l'irréel et l'intelligible se peuvent fonder et combiner selon la puissance des Muses?," Ibid.

55. See Malou Haine, "Cipa Godebski et les Apaches," *Revue Belge de musicologie*, 60 (2007): 231–32.

56. T. S. Eliot, Introduction to *The Art of Poetry*, by Valéry (London: Routledge and Kegan Paul, 1958), vii–xxiv.

57. Ibid., xix–xx, xxiii. Stravinsky too was interested in Valéry's work. In the 1930s he became close to Roland-Manuel, who ghost wrote his *Poetics of Music* (1942). However, in the preface to Stravinsky's *Poetics*, George Seferis recalls that Stravinsky claimed that Valéry checked the drafts of his essays. See Igor Stravinsky, *Poetics of Music* (Harvard: Harvard University Press, 1942/1970), viii–ix. This completes the connection between Roland-Manuel, Ravel, Stravinsky and Eliot. In 1925 it seems that it was the young critic who has brought them together because of important shared artistic values.

58. "Il n'est pas nécessaire de connaître personnellement Maurice Ravel, ni d'avoir pénétré fort avant dans l'intrinsèque de sa pensée pour se convaincre que les procédés de ce musicien, sa technique et son art tout entier impliquent une recherche volontaire et la défiance de l'inspiration." Roland-Manuel, "Maurice Ravel ou l'esthétique de l'imposture," *La Revue Musicale*, numéro spécial consacré à Maurice Ravel (April 1, 1925): 17.

59. Steven Huebner, "Maurice Ravel: Private Lives, Public Works," in *Musical Biography: Towards New Paradigms*, ed. Jolanta T. Pekacz (Aldershot: Ashgate, 2006), 70.

60. "Si cette musique vous plaît, vous émeut, vous arrache des larmes, sachez qu'elle est faite par un homme qui ne s'est pas mis à genoux 'auparavant et après' [et] qui n'a pas pleuré en l'écrivant." Roland-Manuel, "Maurice Ravel ou l'esthétique de l'imposture," 18.

61. This is despite more nuanced assessments of Ravel's character and music in his *Ravel et son œuvre dramatique* (1928), in particular, the mixture of emotion and involvement apparent in *L'enfant et les sortilèges*. See also Jean Roy's preface to a reissue of the 1938 edition: Roland-Manuel, *Ravel*, préface et postface de Jean Roy (Paris: Mémoire du livre, 2000). It has opened the way for psychological studies of Ravel and his work. See Richard Langham Smith, "Ravel's Operatic Spectacles," in Mawer, *The Cambridge Companion to Ravel*, 188–210; Steven Huebner, "Ravel's Child: Magic and Moral Development," in *Musical Childhoods and the Cultures of Youth*, ed. Susan Boynton, Roe-Min Kok and Amanda Minks (Wesleyan University Press, 2006), 69–88; and Peter Kaminsky, "The Child on the Couch; or, Toward a (Psycho)Analysis of Ravel's *L'enfant et les sortilèges*" (this volume).

62. "contribué à répandre cette conception d'un art exceptionnel, artificiel, précieux, base sur 'l'esthétique de l'imposture'—ce qui naturellement tendait à en masquer

le caractère très normal, très classique, et surtout très humain." Michel Dimitri Calvocoressi, "Ravel: un point d'histoire et un point d'exégèse," *La Revue Musicale* (1938):
226–28.

63. Michel Dimitri Calvocoressi, "When Ravel Composed to Order," *Music and Letters*
22, no. 1 (1941): 54.

64. Calvocoressi, "Maurice Ravel," *Musical Times* (December 1, 1913): 785. See also
footnote 32.

65. See Ravel's letter to Lalo, February 5 1906, in Orenstein, *A Ravel Reader*, 79–80.

66. Maurice Ravel, "Some Reflections on Music," in Orenstein, *A Ravel Reader*, 38.
Orenstein notes that according to Roland-Manuel, this short statement originally concluded the "Autobiographical Sketch."

67. Ravel, "Contemporary Music," in Orenstein, *A Ravel Reader*, 42, 46.

68. Ibid., 42.

69. Ravel, "Some Reflections on Music," in Orenstein, *A Ravel Reader*, 38.

70. Ravel, "Contemporary Music," in Orenstein, *A Ravel Reader*, 46–47.

71. Ibid., 46.

72. Roland-Manuel, *Maurice Ravel par quelques-uns de ses familiers* (Paris: 1939), translated in Roger Nichols, *Ravel Remembered* (London: Faber, 1987), 143. This is yet another
instance of Ravel's most repeated views actually being penned by others. It suggests that
Ravel the teacher adopted a very different tone with his students than he did in other
contexts.

73. Ravel, "Contemporary Music," in Orenstein, *A Ravel Reader*, 46–47.

74. Ibid., 41. There is an interesting problem in separating Ravel's words from
Roland-Manuel's: the young writer helped Ravel write this article, and it therefore
becomes difficult to distinguish where Ravel stops and Roland-Manuel takes over. It is
noteworthy, however, that the articles officially in Ravel's name place a stronger emphasis on the artist and individuality rather than on the artisan's approach to composition.

75. Ibid., 41.

76. A notable exception is Ravel's "self analysis" of the Trio to the seventh of the
Valses nobles et sentimentales for René Lenormand's *Etude sur l'harmonie moderne* (1914).
See Orenstein, ed., *A Ravel Reader*, 517–23.

77. His oft-mentioned secrecy when composing and contrasting openness when
orchestrating, confirm this view. Roland-Manuel, *A La Gloire de Ravel* (Paris: *Nouvelle
Revue Critique*, 1938), 249–50.

78. Parallels may be drawn between Roland-Manuel's impact on Ravel and Robert
Craft's control of Stravinsky in his later years, in particular, in the conversation books.

79. Jean Zay, "Discours de M. Jean Zay aux obsèques de Maurice Ravel," "Hommage à Maurice Ravel," *La Revue Musicale* (December 1938): 24–28. This issue was also
addressed by Alfred Cortot, "Dans le souvenir de Maurice Ravel," *La Revue Musicale*
(1938): 37; and Roger Allard, "Le Secret de Ravel," Ibid., 144.

80. See Robert Brussel's prominent article, "Ravel, classique français," in which he
confirms traits identified by Roland-Manuel, including the centrality of perfection,
objectivity, Ravel as the artist-artisan, and the link between his nature and his art. Ibid.,
30–32. See other discussions of Ravel as classical in this issue; for instance, Migot, 43,
Suarès, 51, Closson, 241, and Alfredo Casella, 249. Jane Fulcher associates classical values with the political left. In her view, those who argued that Ravel's music was able to
move the listener were writing for right-leaning journals. See Jane Fulcher, *The Composer as Intellectual* (Oxford: Oxford University Press, 2005), 254. The emphasis of this
present chapter is different in tracing the association of Ravel with classicism to 1920s

discussions of Ravel's aesthetic position. It also argues that it was those closest to him who were determined to show that Ravel's music was able to move the listener. For discussions of perfection as a central aim of Ravel see contributors to *La Revue Musicale*, 1938, including Romain Rolland (33), Mauclair (38), and Suarès (48).

81. Both Liess (233) and Migot (43) placed Ravel in second place to Debussy. Charles Van de Borren (238–39), Closson (240–41), Bartok (244) and Vuillermoz (56) regarded them as inseparable and reflecting a particular time and place. Casella (241) and Tommasini (252) emphasized their differences, while Honegger (67) wondered how they could once have been regarded as so similar.

82. "Ravel aura été, dans notre époque, le plus sûr garant, le plus efficace témoin des aspirations nationales." Alfred Cortot, "Dans le souvenir de Maurice Ravel," ibid., 37.

83. See for example, Claude Samuel, *Entretiens avec Olivier Messiaen* (Paris: Belfond, 1967), 122–23, 131, 207–9. That Messiaen valued certain works of Ravel, particularly *Gaspard de la nuit,* is clear from his recently published analyses; see Olivier Messiaen and Yvonne Loriod-Messiaen, *Ravel, analyses des œuvres pour piano de Maurice Ravel,* Paris, Durand, 2003. See also André Jolivet, "Le Réveil des muses," in *La Revue Musicale* 198 (February–March 1946): 39–41 and Lucie Kayas, *André Jolivet* (Paris, Fayard, 2005).

84. "Sur Maurice Ravel: L'ombre d'un géant," *Le Monde de la Musique,* September 1987.

85. Robert Bernard, "La Gloire de Ravel," *La Revue Musicale,* 1938, 8–9. For a discussion of the revolutionary context of "la foule" see Gabriel Tarde, "L'Opinion et la Foule" (Paris: Presses universitaire de France, 1989). See also Edward Berenson, "Unifying the French nation," in Kelly, *French Music, Culture, and National Identity,* 23, 35–36. A consensus emerges in the special issue that the popularity of Ravel's *Boléro* has contributed to the composer's vulgarization.

86. Bernard, "La célébrité de Ravel est un fait indépendant de toute volonté."*La Revue Musicale* (1938): 9.

87. Notably absent from the volume are Léon-Paul Fargue, Maurice Delage, Dominique Sordet, Jacques de Zogheb, and Colette.

88. See footnote 2.

89. As we have seen above, even Calvocoressi criticized Roland-Manuel's "esthétique de l'imposture" for 'masking the very normal, very classical and above all very human character' of Ravel. Calvocoressi, "Ravel: un point d'histoire et un point d'exégèse," 227.

90. "Réservé, secret, distant avec les importunes, il était le plus sûr, le plus délicat, le plus fidèle des amis. Par son aspect extérieur, par ses boutades, par son amour du paradoxe, il a contribué souvent à accréditer la légende d'une 'spirituelle froideur.' Mais, en dépit de ces apparences, ce grand prisonnier de la perfection cachait une âme sensible et passionnée." Marguerite Long, "Souvenir de Maurice Ravel," *La Revue Musicale* (1938): 173.

91. "Ses amis et ses proches le cherchent dans son œuvre, parfois retrouvent dans un rythme, une harmonie imprévisible, le souvenir fugitive d'un regard, d'une tendre expression où se révélait, tout entier leur ami disparu." Hélène Jourdan-Morhange, "Mon ami Ravel," *La Revue Musicale* (1938): 197.

92. See footnote 2.

93. Vladimir Jankélévitch, *Maurice Ravel* (Paris: Editions Rieder, 1939).

94. The following contributions link Ravel's interest in fairytales and childhood with his own childlike nature. See Vuillermoz "Maurice Ravel," 58–59, René Chalupt, "La Féerie et Maurice Ravel," 128–34, Goldbeck, "Les Fées et les marionnettes," 152–54, Hélène-Morhange, "Mon ami Ravel," 193.

95. Vladimir Jankélévitch, "Ravel vu par Roland-Manuel," *La Revue Musicale* (1938): 281.

96. Ibid., 281–82.

97. Ibid., 282.

98. Vladimir Jankélévitch, "La Sérénade Interrompue," *La Revue Musicale* (1938): 145–49.

99. Ibid., 150–51.

100. Laurence Kramer, "Consuming the Exotic: Ravel's *Daphnis and Chloé*," in *Classical Music and Postmodern Knowledge* (Berkeley: University of California Press, 1995), 201–25; Michael Puri, "Dandy, Interrupted: Sublimation, Repression, and Self-Portraiture in Maurice Ravel's *Daphnis et Chloé*," *Journal of the American Musicological Society* 60, no. 2 (2007).

101. See Benjamin Ivry, *Maurice Ravel: A Life* (New York: Welcome Rain Publishers, 2000), and Lloyd Whitesell, "Ravel's Way," in *Queer Episodes in Music and Modern Identity*, ed. Sophie Fuller and Lloyd Whitesell (Urbana and Chicago: University of Illinois Press, 2002), 70.

102. Kramer, "Consuming the Exotic," in *Classical Music and Postmodern Knowledge*, 201–25. In moving from the man to the music to support his view he is less convincing, in that the qualities (or absences) he detects in *Daphnis*, such as "techniques of reproduction, reiteration, similitude" and an absence of "organicist logic of real motivic organization" could equally be applied to most French experimental music of this period (particularly that of Debussy), which deliberately sought a break from Austro-Germanic teleological procedures, and arguably is more revealing about prevailing attitudes toward French music. Ibid., 216–17.

103. Steven Huebner, "Maurice Ravel: Private Lives, Public Works," in *Musical Biography: Towards New Paradigms*, ed. Jolanta T. Pekacz (Aldershot: Ashgate, 2006), 70.

104. See for instance, Deborah Mawer's introduction to *The Cambridge Companion to Ravel*, Michael Puri's "Dandy, Interrupted, and Self-Portraiture," and the title of this present volume *Unmasking Ravel: New Perspectives on the Music*.

105. "Aujourd'hui, sa musique se charge de significations nouvelles, comme son personnage, et avant toutes choses, l'un et l'autre prennent une valeur d'ordre national, ou, si l'on préfère, culturel." Robert Bernard, "La Gloire de Ravel," *La Revue Musicale* (1938): 9.

Chapter Three

Adorno's Ravel

Michael J. Puri

It is not surprising that philosopher, sociologist, cultural critic, and musicologist Theodor W. Adorno (1903–69), steeped in the Western European art of his era, should have written about Maurice Ravel and his music. What is surprising, is the insightfulness of this writing, given Adorno's well-known devotion to the Austro-German repertory, a tradition with markedly different aesthetic priorities. It is not difficult to imagine reasons for these valuable texts having been overlooked for so long. For Adornians, they would likely have seemed insignificant and ephemeral when set alongside his voluminous writings on Beethoven, Wagner, Mahler, Schoenberg, Berg, and others. For Ravelians, Adorno's cultural credentials would immediately disqualify his writings on the French composer from being taken as seriously as, for example, those of the philosopher Vladimir Jankélévitch, who wrote about not only Ravel, but also his compositional kinfolk, Debussy and Fauré.

Whatever the actual reasons for this neglect may have been, this essay seeks to bring it to an end by collating and assessing Adorno's commentary on Ravel, which is scattered across decades of published and unpublished texts. After surveying this commentary, I demonstrate ways to appropriate it for musical analysis before concluding with some methodological reflections.

Adorno's Ravel

Adorno's most extended discussion of Ravel is an essay first published in a 1930 issue of *Anbruch*, the Viennese journal that Adorno edited from 1928 to 1930. This essay was later incorporated into the collection *Moments musicaux* (1964) with only minor revisions;[1] the relative invariability of the text over thirty-four years suggests the consistency of Adorno's understanding of Ravel over the course of his career. In several ways, the "portrait" of Ravel painted by Adorno in the 1930 essay recalls Albrecht Dürer's melancholic,[2] a figure sunk

Excerpts from Maurice Ravel's *Valses nobles et sentimentales*, Waltz I, II, III and IV, © 1911 Redfield B.V. / Nordice B.V., are reproduced with the kind authorization of Les Editions Durand.

in thought while the things of this world crowd in upon him.[3] Like the melancholic, Adorno's Ravel has sovereign command over his cultural inheritance but is stricken by the knowledge that it has grown obsolete and can no longer support faith in its continued reality.[4] The potency of this music derives paradoxically from its sense of impotence before the passing of the past—which, however, only increases Ravel's commitment to inscribe the "disappearing figures of his historical moment" before they completely disappear.[5] The notion of this music as a "prosthetics of memory" binds the 1930 essay to an earlier, unpublished fragment on Ravel from around 1928,[6] in which Adorno sets the composer alongside Marcel Proust in his ability to "extract the fragrance" of the past and incorporate it into his art.[7]

The imaginative scenario that crowns the 1930 essay also helps strengthen the connection between Ravel and Proust. It describes five o'clock in the afternoon—a twilit, presumably autumnal moment emblematic of Ravel's music—when children of a privileged class make one last round outside before evening falls. Recalling the youthful games of Marcel, Gilberte, and their companions on the Champs-Elysées described in *Remembrance of Things Past*, this carefree romp is overshadowed in both Proust and Ravel by the same factors: the constraining space of play, the vigilant eyes of the governesses, and the nostalgic mind of the narrator, all of which are potential symbols and executors of history in Adorno's scenario. Both delighting retrospectively in the Western European classical musical tradition and mourning its imminent demise, Ravel's music is the sound of freedom and innocence under negation.

According to Adorno, much of Ravel's music can be explained by its membership in French musical impressionism. Characteristic features of impressionism listed in Adorno's "Nineteen Essays about New Music" (1942) include the use of a "floating sound" that depends on suspension and displacement rather than progression and development, the application of infinitesimal sonic "dabs" (*Tupfen*) that combine to produce an iridescent and highly differentiated soundscape, an emphasis upon harmony and homophony rather than melody and polyphony, and an embrace of tonal elements and small forms.[8] Generating works that appear to radiate freedom and innocence in their openness to tonality, overt cultivation of beauty, and improvisatory, quasi-spatial approach to form, impressionism nonetheless is undermined, in Adorno's eyes, by its bad conscience toward history. As he argues in *Philosophy of New Music*, impressionism's "suspension of musical time consciousness corresponds to the entire history of the bourgeoisie, which, no longer seeing anything in front of itself, denies the process of history itself and seeks its own utopia through the revocation of time in space."[9]

Disavowing history and its immanence within the artwork as temporal progression, impressionism can avoid descent into "crass infantilism" only by somehow "compos[ing] out" consciousness of its own mortality.[10] For Adorno, this is exactly what Ravel did, except perhaps in his earliest works, such as *Jeux d'eau.*[11] Adorno continues by claiming that Ravel was not uniformly successful in transcending the liabilities of impressionism, since the peculiar modality he developed in his music ultimately did little to overcome impressionism's static tendencies.[12] Nevertheless, Ravel acknowledges the obsolescence of the tonal tradition by framing his impressionism within an aesthetics of the accidental and unreal.[13] Among other things, it is his particular situation in history that makes such irony and insight possible; his position at the outermost periphery of impressionism allows him retrospectively to grasp its successes and failures.[14]

Impressionism is only one aspect of the larger French classical-music tradition of which Ravel is the "last true representative."[15] The concept of tradition that Adorno invokes in discussing Ravel deals with compositional technique generally as "the heritage of handicraft" and specifically as "instrumental *peinture.*"[16] The latter term refers to multiple phenomena at once: the influential role that French painting played in the development of late-nineteenth-century French music; the inclination of French music toward a painterly, rational-spatial arrangement of its elements; the perfection and transparency of sound produced by mastering this art of arrangement; the flexibility to transpose this music from one instrumental setting to another; and the ability of the artwork to survive and even accommodate the vicissitudes of history by virtue of its complex substantiality.[17] The latter attribute of *peinture* is an index of the artwork's "vitality," which is "lodged deep within, under layers concealed in earlier phases which manifest themselves only when others have withered and fallen away."[18] The "Forlane" from *Le tombeau de Couperin* beautifully illustrates *peinture* by absorbing this hermeneutic-historical principle into itself. That is, as an antiquated form "plucked bare" (*entblättert*) by its astringently modern harmonies, the vitality of the "Forlane" lies, for Adorno, precisely in its estrangement from and vulnerability within the present.[19]

The clarity with which Ravel understood his position within history and society helped him transcend it. A member of the petty bourgeoisie,[20] he nevertheless cultivated an aristocratic persona in his music that renounced fundamental ideals of bourgeois art, including unmediated expressivity, sincerity, creativity, originality, organicism, interiority, and depth, all hallmarks of the romantic, "form-giving personality."[21] By invalidating these ideals through his double persona as both aristocrat and *Wunderkind*—whose very existence demystified the bourgeois myths of artistic autonomy and experience[22]—Ravel was paradoxically able to access new truths and disclose new depths by embracing the essential falsity of art and valorizing the surface over the interior.[23]

These assertions have potentially profound consequences for the way that we incorporate Ravel into narratives of music history. Most commonly compared with his contemporaries Debussy and Stravinsky (Adorno makes the comparisons himself in his 1930 essay), Ravel might actually be more tellingly associated with Chopin and Richard Strauss. Indeed, Adorno's following description of Straussian modernism might apply just as well to the French composer:

The chatter about Strauss's superficiality is irresponsible; all the depth of his music lies in the fact that its world is itself all surface, that it floats freely on the surface of the world, instead of letting the remainder of an albeit fragmentary external reality slip away in the futile hunt for an interiority that is itself completely unreal.[24]

Adorno's 1928 essay on Ravel, in turn, suggests that an artist's esteem for exteriority might be motivated as much by class identification as by modernist worldviews. Rather than locate eros in the ecstasies and sufferings of the lover, as Wagner does in his music dramas, both Ravel and Chopin devote themselves to the image of the beloved and allow it, rather than narcissistic self-consideration, to guide their forays into musical erotics.[25] For Adorno, the turn inward and emphasis on the subject are quintessentially bourgeois, the turn outward and emphasis on the object aristocratic.

Abnegation of the self and devotion to the other bring to mind the medieval knight, who also figures centrally in Dürer's woodcuts. In fact, Adorno seems to have just such an entity in mind when describing Chopin's careful guidance of beautiful themes across the landscape of his music as an aristocratic act of "chivalry"—a chivalry, however, of a melancholic sort peculiar to Ravel, as well as to Chopin.[26] With thoughts on duty and melancholy we spiral back to our original point of departure while simultaneously arriving at the core of Adorno's understanding of Ravel: the interpretation of his music, particularly its childlike moments, as the "aristocratic sublimation of mourning."[27] In the immediate context of this utterance, "sublimation" refers to the transformation and externalization of a negative emotion felt deeply by the artist into a more positive affect represented in the artwork, as well as the gain in poise and beauty that such a transformation entails.[28] One example of this procedure for Adorno is the modulation of a world-weary melancholy into the innocence of childhood, as in *Ma mère l'oye*. In another example, melancholy makes its presence-as-absence felt even more acutely: the first movement of the Sonata for Violin and Piano (1923–27) sublimates a whole bucolic world into only a few symbolic elements—its air, its trembling.[29] Upon distilling a wealth of experience into an idealized, even sentimentalized image, sublimation shades into nostalgic memory.

Viewing the *Valses nobles et sentimentales* through an Adornian Lens

Adorno's writings on Ravel represent criticism uncluttered by analytical detail.[30] This aspect brings them closer to a general readership while simultaneously distancing them from a practice he despised: the reduction or reification of music to the elements of a theoretical system, as mentioned above. This is not to say that Adorno rejected analysis as such; on the contrary, he believed unequivocally that "all criticism which is of any value is founded in analysis," a claim well supported by the frequent and elegant mediation between the two modes in his monographs on composers, as well as in numerous essays and articles.[31] Unfortunately, the lack of any analytical examples in his writings on Ravel, apart from the occasional reference to musical materials (to the key of G major in *Le tombeau de Couperin* or to sonata form in *Jeux d'eau*, for example), makes it difficult for scholars to figure out how to build on these ideas or to appreciate them as more than idiosyncratic musings.[32]

At the risk of putting an overly positive expression on the face of this (in)famously negative dialectician, I propose that it is indeed possible to develop a constructive understanding of Ravel that is at once Adornian, analytical, and illuminating. Rather than simply attempt to reverse Adorno's creative process by reconstructing the analytical findings that might have led to and justified his critical conclusions in his two essays on Ravel and elsewhere, I combine his general dialectical method of reasoning with some of his specific claims about Ravel to formulate a new perspective on this music. My strategy, therefore, is to engage Adorno's ideas creatively in the spirit of a "critical approach to tradition,"[33] an enterprise that he advocated for its ability to disencumber a system of thought from any "mystical authority" that has accrued to it,[34] and embrace it in its *Aktualität* ("currency" or "relevance") rather than its supposedly original, univocal, and fixed meaning.[35]

The repertoire that I have chosen to analyze here, Ravel's *Valses nobles et sentimentales* (1911), might seem more susceptible to Adornian dismissal than recuperation. Indeed, Adorno's single reference to it in *Philosophy of New Music* is hardly celebratory. It occurs within a disparaging discussion of Stravinsky's *Le sacre du printemps*, which "takes its pleasure openly in a profligate splendor that would have been easily understood in the Paris of Ravel's *Valse noble et sentimental* [*sic*]."[36] At first glance, in this sentence Adorno appears to judge the *Valses* as merely a mirror of *fin-de-siècle* cultural decadence in all its "profligate splendor," an embodiment of prewar hedonism so "easily understood" by its bourgeois audience that it could hardly be imagined to harbor any critical potency. However much we want this passage to comply with this interpretation, it nevertheless refuses to do so: it is in no way clear that Adorno is claiming here the validity or sufficiency of this verdict. In fact, the all-too-easy understanding of the *Valses* as decadent excess might be another self-serving delusion of the bourgeoisie, which characteristically does not recognize its own critique, especially one so subtly construed in the midst of the unsubtle frenzy of cultural consumption during the *belle epoque*.

A section from the 1930 essay on Ravel supports these conjectures as germane to Adornian thought. Asserting Ravel's music to be the "portrait" of the bourgeoisie's more privileged stratum, Adorno wonders why, then, it does not prefer Ravel's music to the relatively meretricious products of Strauss and

Stravinsky. In mulling over the possible causes for this phenomenon, Adorno selects two: lacking either self-awareness or an "aesthetic power" (*ästhetische Kraft*), society may no longer recognize its own likeness, and thus remains deaf to the intimations of its mortality in this music; or, this stratum might experience a cognitive dissonance with the utopian vision of a free society conjured up by this music.[37] Considering this evidence of Adorno's own interpretive position, it would probably be foolish to conclude that he shares with the bourgeoisie its understanding of the *Valses* as simple "profligate splendor" without any deeper, critical dimension. Indeed, the epigraph from Henri de Régnier that Ravel cunningly chose for the *Valses* has the special capacity to support both uncritical and critical understandings at once. While the one might take at face value the direct applicability of "le plaisir délicieux et toujours nouveau d'une occupation inutile" to the *Valses*, the other might discern—and savor— the irony in Ravel's choice.[38]

To my knowledge, Adorno does not discuss the *Valses* anywhere else in his musical writings.[39] Left to our own, we will do well to formulate an Adornian interpretation of this piece by first considering its relation to tradition—the tradition of the nineteenth-century waltz. With the *Valses* Ravel places himself in a compositional lineage whose most important members include Schubert, Chopin, and the Strauss family. Though named in homage to Schubert and his sets of "noble" and "sentimental" waltzes, the *Valses nobles et sentimentales* is an uninterrupted suite of eight waltzes for solo piano that encompasses the breadth of the tradition, from the shorter Schubertian phrases of Waltz III and the Chopinesque chromatic textures of Waltz V to the Straussian grandeur of Waltz VII. As the following passage indicates, the influence of the Strauss waltz did not disqualify the *Valses* for Adorno's serious attention.

> The music of Johann Strauss is set off from the art music of the time through its "genre" ["light music"], but this separation is not total; his waltzes leave room for harmonic differentiation and, furthermore, they are formed thematically out of small, contrasting units never subject merely to empty repetition. It is the surprising connection of these fragments which gives the Strauss waltz its charm, its "pungency" [*Pikanterie*], relating it at the same time to the tradition of Viennese classicism, from which it is derived via Strauss senior, Lanner and Schubert.[40]

Every comment here about Strauss's waltzes applies equally well to the *Valses*, regardless of the degree to which they literally sound like Strauss. Particularly remarkable in this context is the exquisite craft displayed in the transitions between one waltz and the next. Take, for example, the passage linking Waltzes III and IV, which may have been the most significant transition for Ravel: it is the only inter-waltz transition in the manuscript for the orchestral version that he marked "Enchaînez" (link together).[41] At the beginning of Waltz IV Ravel shrewdly undermines continuity in multiple parameters—dynamics, meter (including the hemiolas on both sides of the double bar line) motive, rhythm, melodic pitch, tessitura, and texture—with a piquant shift in harmony. This compositional sleight-of-hand, shown below in example 3.1, neatly exemplifies the mastery of *métier* that Adorno associated with Ravel.

Example 3.1. Ravel, *Valses nobles et sentimentales*, transition between Waltz III and Waltz IV

In part, the reason that Ravel's transitions between waltzes are so effective is that they acknowledge and negotiate the demands of a specific impulse in the waltz tradition: the creation and interrelation of different musical characters (generally, one character per waltz in a suite). This aspect of traditional composition is very important for Adorno, since:

> The articulation of music in terms of characters is what makes possible their principle of individuation. They are the qualitative element, not dissoluble into musical generality. The tendency to rationalization, however, that places Western music in the general movement of Enlightenment, is one that moves in the direction of quantification, reducing the individual element to an indistinguishable, interchangeable part of the whole, into which it goes without remainder.[42]

Looming over the tradition of musical characterization, however, is the threat of its imminent demise, which Adorno determines to be its "inevitable condition at this stage in history."[43]

Ravel's design of the *Valses* reflects an understanding of musical character, the waltz, and their mutual fate quite similar to Adorno's. In Waltz VIII, which the composer entitled "Epilogue," all of the previous seven waltzes (except Waltz V) return haphazardly and in fragmentary form. As shadows of their former selves, they bear witness to the obsolescence of the nineteenth-century waltz; their centrifugal dissipation into nothingness is staved off only by their subsumption into Waltz VIII. Despite the smoothness with which the sustained, slow *pianissimo* of Waltz VIII assimilates the citations of the previous waltzes, a tension is nonetheless palpable, even electrifying: standing at the brink of oblivion, the waltzes hold fast to their individual characters, which remain as unmistakable in Waltz VIII as they were before it. Such twilit struggle between memory and oblivion is a dialectic as quintessential to Adorno as it is to Ravel.[44]

This site of dialectical tension is counterbalanced by another at the opposite end of the *Valses*. Combining the clear-cut rhythms of the waltz with strange, strident harmonies, the opening measures of Waltz I present the central "problem" of the suite as one of stylistic schizophrenia: its simultaneous pull toward the familiar and the esoteric. This dialectic comes to a head in the retransition of Waltz I, as shown in example 3.2.

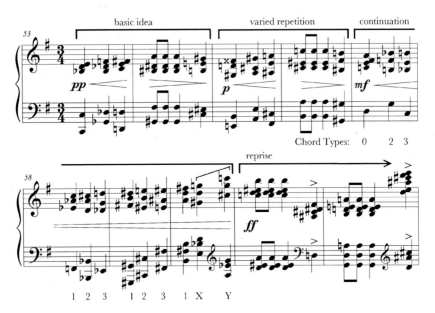

Example 3.2. Intensification of the retransition in Waltz I and two measures of its reprise (mm. 53–62)

After the opening of the B section, the waltz increasingly withdraws into a hermetic harmonic idiom—what we will call its "harmonic esotericism"— only to be restored to its initial vitality by a version of the initial gesture of the piece, one that now begins the retransition. However, before Waltz I is able to reshape this gesture to align more faithfully with the opening measures of the piece and thereby initiate the reprise, it undergoes an eight-bar intensification. Structured metrically and motivically as a Schoenbergian sentence, this phrase begins hesitantly, with the melody of the "basic idea" and its varied repetition ascending only three semitones each while their bass lines vacillate among various root progressions. Nonetheless, in the "continuation" the elements finally come into alignment: the melody rises consistently by semitone, the bass line latches onto a descending circle of fifths (one that will actually complete a full chromatic cycle at the downbeat of the reprise), the rhythm proceeds solely by quarter notes, the dynamics increase without intermediate fluctuations, and the harmony rotates through a cycle of three basic chord types, marked by Arabic numerals in example 3.2.

At the end of this orderly sequence a moment of chaos intrudes. As indicated by the bracket in example 3.2, in the second and third beats of measure 60 the melody suddenly breaks its chromatic ascent, moving up by the root interval of the circle-of-fifths sequence. Simultaneously, the harmony lands on chords X and Y (a transposition of X up a perfect fourth), two chords that not only challenge our present-day classificatory schemes, but would also have been difficult for the audience attending the 1911 premiere to comprehend aurally.[45] The rhetorical placement of this moment augments its hermeneutic force: right before the reprise sounds to confirm the waltz in its formal and tonal conventionality, the harmonic esotericism that has been building up during the retransition finally overflows the bounds of the sequence to expose the instability of the *Valses* as a stylistic experiment. In other words, content is inextricably bound up with form; the one receives its meaning from the other. For Adorno, attention to this dialectic was a crucial aspect of analysis, insofar as "that which is going on underneath [formal schemata] is not simply a second and quite different thing, but is in fact mediated by the formal schemata, and is partly, at any given moment, *postulated* by the formal schemata."[46]

It is equally Adornian to claim that harmony's challenge to form in Waltz I should be understood not as a rejection of tradition, but rather as an example of tradition's critical impetus, which stays true to itself by unsettling, or even exploding, its own self-assured continuity.[47] The strange and strident harmonies of the first four measures of Waltz I now seemingly accounted for by the retransition's esoteric sequence as its natural outgrowth, the beginning of the reprise can be heard paradoxically as the simultaneous celebration of both convention and its contravention. Initiating Waltz I as well as the entire set in unforgettable fashion, the dialectical image projected by these measures represents *in nuce* the status of the *Valses* as a whole.

Having determined the critical role that harmonic esotericism plays in the historical profile of this piece, we may now address the history of this esotericism itself—thereby suggesting, among other things, that it is not merely the result of ahistorical compositional caprice. Indeed, we may even be able to locate a potential source of the retransition's X and Y chords in a piece of incidental, esoteric music by Erik Satie, the first of the preludes for the Rosicrucian play *Le fils des étoiles* (1891; example 3.3).

Example 3.3. Satie, *Le fils des étoiles*, beginning of the *1er Prélude* (unmeasured)

If, reading registrally from bottom to top, we transposed the first and third notes of the U and W chords in example 3.3 down a semitone—which would also increase their dominant potential and harmonic dynamism, so to speak—they would be identical to chords X and Y in example 3.2. Now, there is no doubt that Ravel knew this piece and was thinking about it during his composition of the *Valses* in early 1911. A friend and admirer of Satie since his teens, Ravel not only chose to feature Satie's early piano music in one of the first concerts of his newly founded society, the Société Musicale Indépendante, but also performed it himself in a January 16, 1911 program which included three solo works by Satie: the second *Sarabande*, the third *Gymnopédie*, and the preludes to *Le fils des étoiles*.[48]

This concert may have brought Satie a recognition he had never before experienced, but it fulfilled other goals as well. First, it clarified the aesthetic identity of the fledgling SMI, which sought to promote works—like Satie's—of a less monumental design than those favored by its rivals, the Société Nationale and the Schola Cantorum. Second, it allowed Ravel to pay personal homage to a composer whose aesthetic priorities had shaped his own. Premiered two months later in the SMI concert of May 9, 1911, the *Valses* continue this homage to Satie, as even the audience sensed at the time. To stimulate listeners' participation at this concert of premieres, the organizers withheld the names of the composers, challenging the audience instead to guess them; after the dust had cleared and the votes were tallied, Satie came close to beating out Ravel for authorship of the *Valses*.

We can only speculate as to which elements of the *Valses* would have reminded the audience of Satie. The exuberant address of Waltz I could have recalled Satie's rambunctious *En habit de cheval,* a four-hand work also performed on the January concert, but no one besides Ravel himself could reasonably have discerned in real time the allusion in Waltz I to *Le fils des étoiles*—a shame, since the transplantation of these chords from an extremely static to an extremely dynamic context is such a delightful, Chabrier-like display of witty, irreverent parody. Waltz II, however, offers other possibilities for discerning the importance of Satie's esotericism both to the *Valses* and to our understanding of them from an Adornian perspective (ex. 3.4).

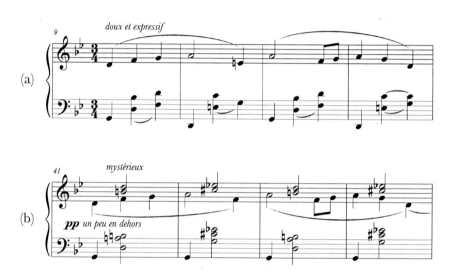

Example 3.4. Ravel, *Valses nobles et sentimentales,* primary lyrical theme of Waltz II (*a*, mm. 9–12) and its reprise (*b*, mm. 41–44)

Example 3.4a presents the primary lyrical theme from Waltz II, a *valse lente* audibly indebted to Satie's *Gymnopédies* for its sad modal sway and spare texture (and perhaps also to the *Gnossiennes* for its exotic ornamentation). In the reprise of this theme, shown in example 3.4b, Ravel intensifies the reference to Satie: the accompaniment reproduces the rhythm of the *Gymnopédies* with greater fidelity, while the expressive indication "mystérieux" calls attention to the passage's esotericism, an effect occasioned by the combination of strange harmonic oscillations, *pianissimo* dynamics, concealment of the melody in an inner voice, and ritualistic tolling on the second beat.

The intensification of esotericism over the course of Waltz II bespeaks a gradual heightening of reflexivity in the piece—not only of its debt to Satie, but also its historical obsolescence as a waltz suite. The three themes of Waltz II, through which it cycles twice to produce its binary form, may be interpreted as representing different phases in the psychological process by which the compositional persona works through these mortal thoughts. Example 3.5 provides an overview of these themes by excerpting the first two measures of each from their debuts.

Example 3.5. Opening measures of the three themes of Waltz II: "Grief" (*a*, mm. 1–2), "Melancholy" (*b*, mm. 9–10), and "Consolation" (*c*, mm. 25–26)

Part of a transition from Waltz I, Theme 1 (ex. 3.5a) thematically transforms the opening two measures of the latter and, as such, overtly shifts the tone of the *Valses* from high-spirited celebration to an intense grief that is expressed with each augmented triad. In Theme 2 (ex. 3.5b), the anguish expressed in Theme 1 is temporarily modulated into a doleful melody before erupting once more. Instead of a second statement of Theme 2 after the reappearance of Theme 1, we hear a more light-hearted Theme 3 (ex. 3.5c), which nevertheless devolves into a Theme 2-like cadence at the end of its phrase. The transitions among the multiple phases of this psychological experience—passing through grief, melancholy, grief again, brief consolation, and melancholy once more— are so carefully shaped that the musical flow is virtually unbroken.[49]

A seamless vessel, Waltz II catches tears like drops of rain. The tears belong to Adorno's Ravel, a Proustian figure beset by nostalgia for the past and the melancholy of its loss. As a musicologist, it is tempting to try to divvy up the individual numbers of the *Valses nobles et sentimentales* according to their apparent "nobility" or "sentimentality." From an Adornian viewpoint, however, the adjectives "noble" and "sentimental" simultaneously describe the suite as a whole. It is sentimental in a quasi-Schillerian sense, insofar as it is acutely conscious of the historical distance that separates it from the once-living tradition of the nineteenth-century waltz. And it is noble to the extent that it exemplifies Ravel's "aristocratic sublimation of mourning."

Adornian Analysis

Almost three decades after Rose Rosengard Subotnik published her groundbreaking essays on Adorno—during which time numerous Adorno-related books and articles have appeared, conferences have been convened, papers presented, and panels formed—it is still somewhat controversial in American music academia to invoke this philosopher and his ideas. More precisely, it is still wholly unresolved whether Adorno represents more of a benefit or a liability for American musicology.[50] Even for those who feel sympathetic toward Adorno's views, it is hard not to be unsettled by anti-Adornian sentiment. Richard Taruskin's exhortation that we no longer allow Adorno to "do our thinking for us" seeks to rouse our sense of autonomy and pride (and guilt) not only as independent-minded Americans but also as free-thinking heirs of the Enlightenment.[51] (Recall Kant's definition of Enlightenment as the transcendence of *Unmündigkeit*, a state of immaturity in which we literally cannot speak or, for that matter, think for ourselves.) However compelling Taruskin's phrase might be, it is nonetheless problematic in several respects. It implies that Adornian thought can simply and unthinkingly be parroted back as a sort of dogma, when it is, in fact, not only difficult and elusive enough to forbid such regurgitation, but also as vigorously self-critical as it is potentially doctrinaire. In addition, it wrongly depreciates an aspect of intersubjectivity that is as fundamental and beneficial to academia as it is to any other sector of the public sphere: allowing the thought of others to inflect the way we think is not equivalent to having someone else do our thinking for us.

While the preceding analysis is by no means an apology for Adorno, it nevertheless demonstrates how Adornian thought can help to generate insight—directly and indirectly—into repertory that does not fall within his usual purview of Austro-German music. Here, Adorno's perceptions of Ravel's critical devotion to tradition, his melancholy over its transience, and the aristocratic sublimation of this melancholy into his music have illuminated some structural aspects of the *Valses*. There are many promising issues that still await treatment: Ravel's relation to French musical impressionism; his relation to Wagner (a topic almost completely absent from Ravel studies, though not justifiably so); his personal handling of motivic design; his internationalism as a modernist; the alignment of his music with aesthetics of primitivism, organicism, and contingency; and so on.

Ideas imported indirectly here from Adornian thought and applied to Ravel include the differentiated use of musical motive and character in the compositional tradition of the waltz, and a general notion of dialectics which imputes a tense dynamism to the relation of form to content, conventionality to esotericism, and memory to oblivion—somewhat contrary to Adorno's later, more rigid understanding of French musical aesthetics as anti-developmental, which compelled him in the 1964 version of the Ravel essay to eliminate the few remaining references to dialectics in the original 1930 version. Adorno's self-censorship notwithstanding, a broader and more thorough consideration of dialectics in Ravel's music, whether involving these particular oppositions or others, may form another path of productive inquiry for future scholarship.[52]

Adorno laid out his understanding of music analysis as a whole most clearly and extensively in "On Musical Analysis," a lecture from the final year of his life. As elsewhere in his work, one of the most stimulating aspects of this text is the way he gradually and dialectically unfolds the notion of analysis over the course of the lecture. For our present purposes, though, it is helpful to condense this discussion into its most salient methodological points. For Adorno, analysis is a necessary means to a good and practical end: it enables performers to get to know the score intimately, forces them to confront important matters of interpretation, and thus helps generate a more satisfying performance; in similar fashion it allows the composer-as-analyst to actively participate in an ongoing musical tradition as both recipient and contributor. Just as important for Adorno, however, is the ability of analysis to ramify a piece of music into both a conceptual "force field" (*Kraftfeld*) and a scene of cognition whose immanent "truth content" (*Wahrheitsgehalt*) is released by the analytical act.

The dialectical procedure involved in such analytical practice gives rise to a performativity that assimilates analytical discourse to its object through a type of mimesis. In other words, analysts, for Adorno, should seek not merely to provide a heuristic basis for the meaningful performance of music, but also to transmute musical performance into linguistic performance. When Kofi Agawu says that music analysis today, in order to benefit fully from Adorno's legacy, must be willing to "stage ongoing enactments and reenactments of the musical work (or parts thereof) not only in actuality but, more potently, in imagination and in a manner consistent with music's performative essence," he appears to be responding to this impulse in Adornian thought, which wishes to open music analysis to the possibility of a discursive multivalence it is always in danger of foreclosing.[53] Defining analysis elsewhere in his lecture so broadly and humanely as "the achievement of imagination through faith," Adorno invites us to seriously consider the kinship of analysis, criticism, and poetics, all of which could reasonably fall under this definition.[54] Thus, in the continuing effort to carve out a future for Adornian thought in music analysis, it is just as important to invoke his specific concepts and methodologies as it is to strive for this possibility of discursive richness. The point here is not to let Adorno do our thinking for us, of course, but rather to take him as a model for more adventurous and perhaps even more rewarding modes of analysis.

Notes

I would like to thank Carlo Caballero, Berthold Hoeckner, Robert Hullot-Kentor, Brian Hyer, Martin Jay, and Richard Leppert for their helpful and thought-provoking comments on earlier drafts of this essay.

1. The original version is Theodor W. Adorno, "Ravel," *Musikblätter des Anbruch* 12 (April/May 1930): 151–54; the revised version is Adorno, "Ravel," *Gesammelte Schriften*, 20 vols. (Frankfurt am Main, DE: Suhrkamp, 1970–86), 17:60–65. All references to excerpts from the *Gesammelte Schriften* will henceforth be abbreviated as "essay title," *GS* volume number: page number(s).

2. Adorno describes this essay as a "portrait of Ravel" (*Porträt Ravels*) in the preface to *Moments musicaux*. "Vorrede," *GS*, 17:10.

3. A contemporary study of Albrecht Dürer's *Melencolia I* that is still important today is Erwin Panofsky and Fritz Saxl, *Dürers 'Melencolia I': Eine Quellen- und Typengeschichtliche Untersuchung*, in *Studien der Bibliothek Warburg*, vol. 2, ed. Fritz Saxl (Leipzig and Berlin: B. G. Tuebner, 1923). Incidentally, Adorno would surely have known about this study in 1930, having just read (and been deeply affected by) Walter Benjamin's *Ursprung des deutschen Trauerspiels* [*The Origin of German Tragic Drama*] (1928), trans. John Osborne (London and New York: Verso, 1977), which cites Panofsky and Saxl's book in several places. The constellation of melancholy, knowledge, history, and nature in Adorno's profile of Ravel, I would argue, betrays the influence of Benjamin and, more specifically, his *Trauerspiel* book.

4. The religious subcurrent of this diagnosis of cultural decline emerges more clearly in "Music and Technique," first published in 1958, where Adorno summarizes French musical aesthetics at the *fin de siècle* in quasi-biblical language as the "creaturely melancholy [*kreatürliche Trauer*] of sensuous happiness." Adorno, "Music and Technique," in *Sound Figures*, trans. Rodney Livingstone (Stanford, CA: Stanford University Press, 1999), 198.

5. "Er notiert sicher die entschwindenden Figuren seines geschichtlichen Moments." Adorno, "Ravel," *GS*, 17:61. Adorno describes Ravel here as if he were a Baudelairean "painter of modern life," a sketch artist who has the special talent, according to the poet,

of capturing "the transient, fleeting beauty of contemporary life." See Charles Baude-laire, "Le peintre de la vie moderne," in *Journaux intimes,* in *Œuvres complètes,* ed. Y.-G Le Dantec and Claude Pinchois (Paris: Gallimard, 1961), 1152–92; cited here from 1192.

6. The notion of a prosthetics of memory has recently gained currency, largely due to the publication of Alison Landsberg's *Prosthetic Memory: The Transformation of American Remembrance in the Age of Mass Culture* (New York: Columbia University Press, 2004), which discusses the ability and consequences of the media of American mass culture to sustain and produce collective memory. The idea itself is quite old, however, dating at least back to Plato's *Phaedrus,* in which he criticizes prosthetic memory—in the form of writing and other *aides-mémoire* (including the whole rhetorical tradition of an "art of memory")—for contributing to the neglect of natural memory. For a brief but focused discussion of the latter, see Frances Yates, *The Art of Memory* (London: Routledge and Kegan Paul, 1966), 37–39.

7. " . . . [den] Duft zu extrahieren." Adorno, "Ravel," *GS,* 18:274. Proust loomed large on Adorno's intellectual horizon throughout his life; sustained discussions of Proust by Adorno appear in "Short Commentaries on Proust," in *Notes to Literature, Volume One,* ed. Rolf Tiede-mann, trans. Shierry Weber Nicholsen (New York: Columbia University Press, 1991), 174–84; "Words from Abroad" (ibid., 185–99); "Theses Upon Art and Religion Today" in *Notes to Literature, Volume Two,* ed. Rolf Tiedemann, trans. Shierry Weber Nicholsen (New York: Columbia University Press, 1992), 292–98; and "On Proust" (ibid., 312–17).

8. Adorno, "Neunzehn Beiträge über neue Musik," *GS,* 18:57–87, supplemented by material from Adorno, "Musikalischer Impressionismus," *GS,* 18:79–80.

9. Adorno, *Philosophy of New Music,* trans. and ed. Robert Hullot-Kentor (Minneapo-lis, MN, and London, UK: University of Minnesota Press, 2006), 140.

10. "The convergence of music and painting also opens up the possibility of crass infantilism, at least in music: it is able to stave off this element only to the extent that it reflects it within itself, as an expression of decay, and composes it out, so to speak." Adorno, "On Some Relationships between Music and Painting," trans. Susan H. Gil-lespie, *Musical Quarterly* 79, no. 1 (Spring 1995): 68.

11. The distinction that Adorno perceived between Debussyan and Ravelian impres-sionism seems to have become sharper over time. Upon revising the *Anbruch* article for its publication in *Moments musicaux,* Adorno altered the original statement, "[Ravel's] Impressionism was once unmediated like Debussy's" ("Einmal war sein Impressionismus unmittelbar wie der Debussys") to "[Ravel's] Impressionism was never unmediated like Debussy's" ("Niemals war sein Impressionismus unmittelbar wie der Debussys"). For the former, see "Ravel," *Anbruch,* 152; for the latter, see "Ravel," *GS,* 17:62.

12. "The early piece Jeux d'eau is one of the least dynamic and least characterized by development of any of the works produced by [French musical Impressionism], in spite of its arrangement as a sonata. Since then, however, Ravel has sought a strengthening of the awareness of harmonic progression. This explains the particular role of modality in his music, utterly distinct from its function in Brahms. The church modes provide a surrogate for the tonal degrees. These, however, lose their dynamic quality through the abrogation of the cadence. The archaism of organum and fauxbourdon effects helps produce a kind of continuation by degrees while maintaining the feeling of a static jux-taposition." Adorno, *Philosophy of New Music,* 139.

13. Adorno diluted slightly the pessimism inherent in Ravel's historical wisdom from the earlier to the later version of the essay, originally describing his knowledge as "hope-less" (*ausweglos*) rather than "complete" (*rückhaltlos*). Compare "Ravel," *Anbruch,* 150, with "Ravel," *GS,* 17:63.

14. As expressed quite neatly in this concert review of *L'heure espagnole* from August 1932: "Ravel . . . holds to tradition, still on this side of the break: however, he surveys it like no one else, and his irony is its afterglow" (Ravel . . . hält sich in der Tradition, diesseits des Bruches noch: aber er überschaut die traditionale Region wie kein zweiter, und seine Ironie ist ihre Abendröte). Adorno, "Frankfurter Opern- und Konzertkritiken," *GS*, 19:231.

15. Adorno, "Der letzte gültige Repräsentant" (ibid., 56). Adorno's sympathy for Ravel's nationalist traditionalism undoubtedly springs from similar impulses of his own. The German context for what has been called (somewhat disparagingly, albeit accurately) Adorno's "cultural mandarinism" has been laid out in two classic texts: Fritz Stern, *The Politics of Cultural Despair: A Study in the Rise of the Germanic Ideology* (Berkeley: University of California Press, 1961), in particular, see the "Introduction," xi–xxx, and the "Conclusion: From Idealism to Nihilism," 267–98; and Fritz Ringer, *The Decline of the German Mandarins: The German Academic Community, 1890–1933* (Cambridge, MA: Harvard University Press, 1969).

16. Adorno, "On Tradition," *Telos* 94 (Winter 1993–94; orig. German 1966), 75.

17. Passages useful for an understanding of "instrumental *peinture*" in French music appear in Adorno, "Zum Verhältnis," *GS*, 18:142–43; "Motifs" in *Quasi una fantasia*, trans. Rodney Livingstone (New York: Verso, 1992; original German 1963), 20; and "Zemlinsky" (ibid., 128).

18. Adorno, "On Tradition," 80.

19. Adorno, "Ravel," *GS*, 17:63.

20. "Not a few musicians came from the petty bourgeoisie without developing its social character: the generous Ravel, the intransigent Schoenberg" (Nicht wenige Musiker stammten aus dem Kleinbürgertum und entwickelten jenen Sozialcharakter nicht: der generöse Ravel, der intransigente Schönberg). Adorno, "Ad vocem Hindemith," *GS*, 17:244.

21. "The Romantic conception of the immediate expression of subjectivity, unhampered by thing-like objectivities, was a product of the musical experience of the generation around 1800. Twinned with this are the experience of transcendence, of floating, of sound not rigidly fixed to any individual support, and, ultimately, the irrationalist ideal itself, which the Romantic movement set up in opposition to the rationalism of eighteenth-century enlightenment." Adorno, "Classicism, Romanticism, New Music," in *Sound Figures*, 114. Adorno provides insight into his understanding of the notion of "personality" in his "Gloss on Personality" (1966) in *Critical Models: Interventions and Catchwords*, trans. Henry W. Pickford (New York: Columbia University Press, 1998), 161–65. A helpful overview of the central features of bourgeois society and music in Adorno's thought can be found in Max Paddison, "The Historical Dialectic of Musical Material," chap. 6 in *Adorno's Aesthetics of Music* (New York: Cambridge University Press, 1993), 218–62.

22. The entry on the *Wunderkind* in Adorno's "Musical Aphorisms" is particularly helpful for fleshing out references to this phenomenon in the 1930 *Anbruch* essay. The following sentence from the former summarizes the bourgeois critique embodied in the *Wunderkind*: "Each one that is born destroys the musical and not merely musical order in its consciousness of dignity, autonomy, and freedom" (Jedes, das da geboren wird, verstört die musikalische und nicht bloss musikalische Ordnung in ihrem Bewusstsein von Würde, Autonomie und Freiheit"). "Musikalische Aphorismen," *GS*, 18:43.

23. On the point of the falsity of Ravel's music, compare the following from pages 136 and 137, respectively, of *Philosophy of New Music*: "Above all, Ravel's aesthetic of the sophisticated toy, the impossible stunt, the tour de force, acknowledges the verdict of

the Baudelaire of the *Paradis artificiels,* who no longer wrote 'nature poetry.' No music that participates in technological enlightenment can now escape this verdict. . . . Once the artificial element of music, the 'making,' becomes conscious of itself and acknowledges itself, it loses the sting of the lie of being a pure, primordial, and absolute sound of the soul. This is the gain in truth reaped through the expulsion of the subject" (137). Regarding the valorization of the surface over the interior, it is intriguing to consider the degree to which the following passage by Adorno from 1932 might apply to or even *imply* Ravel, especially in light of his 1930 *Anbruch* essay: "It might be possible for the most advanced compositional production of the present—solely under the pressure of the immanent development of its problems—to invalidate basic bourgeois categories such as the creative personality and expression of the soul of this personality, the world of private feelings and its transfigured inwardness, setting in their place highly rational and transparent principles of construction. Even this music, however, would remain dependent upon bourgeois production processes and could not, consequently, be viewed as 'classless' or the actual music of the future, but rather as music which fulfills its dialectic cognitive function most exactly." Adorno, "On the Social Situation of Music," trans. Wes Blomster, in *Essays on Music,* ed. Richard Leppert (Berkeley: University of California Press, 2002), 394.

24. "Unverantwortlich ist das Gerede von der Straussischen Oberflächlichkeit; die ganze Tiefe seiner Musik ruht darin, dass ihre Welt selbst ganze Oberfläche ist, dass sie auf der Oberfläche der Welt lose schwebt, anstatt in vergeblicher Jagd nach dem selbst ganz unwirklichen Innen den Rest einer wenngleich fragmentarischen Wirklichkeit des Äusseren aus Händen zu lassen." Adorno, "Richard Strauss: Zum 60. Geburtstage," *GS,* 18:256.

25. Just to make the provenance of these ideas absolutely clear, this sentence summarizes a few passages from Adorno's "Ravel" (c. 1928).

26. In a passage about Chopin, Adorno proposes that "the aristocratic nature of his music may reside less in the psychological tone than in the gesture of knightly melancholy [*schwermütigen Ritterlichkeit*] with which subjectivity renounces the attempt to impose its dynamism and carry it through." "Motifs," *Quasi una fantasia,* 17. For Adorno, the lack of dynamism is common to both Chopin and Ravel, whose music refuses any dialectical development.

27. "Die aristokratische Sublimierung von Trauer." Adorno, "Ravel," *GS,* 17:62.

28. In "Dandy, Interrupted: Sublimation, Repression, and Self-Portraiture in Maurice Ravel's *Daphnis et Chloé* (1909–12)," *Journal of the American Musicological Society* 60, no. 2 (Summer 2007): 317–72, I discuss sublimation in Ravel's music extensively, taking *Daphnis et Chloé* as a prime example in which sublimation appears as both "the psychic means by which raw sexual desire is modulated to produce seemly and even beautiful gestures of courtship" and "the musical process by which noise is transformed into serenade" (321). Max Paddison outlines the basic features and functions of sublimation for Adorno in *Adorno's Aesthetics of Music,* 128–34.

29. "Die Landschaft ist geschwunden; ihre Luft, ihr feines Zittern, allein übrig, macht die Musik aus." Adorno, "Ravel," *GS,* 17:64.

30. The distinction between criticism and analysis has been a site of active contestation in music academia ever since Joseph Kerman's initial polemics in "How we got into analysis, and how to get out," *Critical Inquiry* 7, no. 2 (Winter 1980): 311–31. Representative contributions to these debates, which became particularly heated during the emergence of New Musicology in the 1990s, include an exchange between Scott Burnham and Lawrence Kramer in the Summer 1992 issue of *19th-Century Music* 16, no. 1, 70–79; several essays by Marion A. Guck (e.g., "Rehabilitating the Incorrigible," in *Theory, Analysis, and Meaning in Music,* ed. Anthony Pople (Cambridge: Cambridge University Press,

1994), 57–73, and "Analytical Fictions," *Music Theory Spectrum* 16, no. 2 (Fall 1994): 217–30); and various chapters in *Rethinking Music,* eds. Nicholas Cook and Mark Everist (Oxford and New York: Oxford University Press, 1999), especially the editorial preface (v–xii) and Scott Burnham's "How Music Matters: Poetic Content Revisited" (193–216).

31. Adorno, "On Musical Analysis," 168.

32. A helpful consideration of Adorno's analytical practice is Ludwig Holtmeier, "Analyzing Adorno—Adorno Analyzing," in *Adorno im Widerstreit: Zur Präsenz seines Denkens,* eds. Wolfram Ette, Günter Figal, Richard Klein, and Günter Peters (Munich: Karl Aber, 2004), 184–98.

33. Adorno, "On Tradition," 78.

34. Ibid., 80.

35. The French-derived "Aktualität" is one of Adorno's trademark terms, foregrounded in such musical essays as "Mahlers Aktualität" (1960; *GS,* 18:241–43) and "Wagners Aktualität" (1965; *GS,* 16:543–64); the latter is now available in English as "Wagner's Relevance for Today," trans. Susan Gillespie, in *Adorno, Essays on Music,* ed. Richard Leppert (Berkeley: University of California Press, 2002), 584–602. Max Pensky defines Adorno's use of "Aktualität" to mean simultaneously "relevance for the present and its concerns," "up-to-date," and "still in fashion." Pensky specifies the "dialectical ambiguity" of this term as follows: "on the one hand, it expresses the quintessence of the modern ephemeral. . . . On the other hand, actuality denotes a kind of practical affinity between an element of an intellectual legacy and a self-reflective contemporary situation; an affinity that resists or ignores what is intellectually fashionable and instead wants to capture an aspect of a culture's authentic expression of what it needs." Pensky, "Editor's Introduction: Adorno's Actuality," in *The Actuality of Adorno: Critical Essays on Adorno and the Postmodern,* ed. Max Pensky (Albany: SUNY Press, 1997), 1.

36. Adorno, *Philosophy of New Music,* 113.

37. Adorno, "Ravel," *GS,* 17:60–61.

38. My thanks to Peter Kaminsky for noticing this connection and sharing it with me.

39. I leave aside here the indirect, passing reference to the *Valses nobles et sentimentales* in the following sentence: "Durch die Scheinregionen von noblesse und sentiment, durch die hochmütige Kinderlandschaft führt die Tournée seiner Musik ins Altertümliche" ("The tour of his music leads through the virtual regions of *noblesse* and *sentiment* and the high-spirited landscape of children into the antique" [my emphasis].) Adorno, "Ravel," *GS,* 17:63.

40. Adorno, "On the Social Situation," 428.

41. This manuscript score is stored in Box 300 of the Carlton Lake Collection at the Harry Ransom Humanities Center at the University of Texas-Austin; the direction "Enchaînez," which was not included in the Durand scores for either the piano or orchestral versions of the *Valses nobles,* appears in the margins of page 22. I thank the HRC for providing me access to this score.

42. Adorno, "Criteria of New Music," *Sound Figures,* trans. Rodney Livingstone (Stanford: Stanford University Press, 1999), 182.

43. Ibid., 186.

44. Another way to conceptualize Waltz VIII from an Adornian standpoint is as a piece of musical surrealism. The disintegration of the waltz suite in VIII demonstrates, like surrealism, the alienation of the past from the present, thereby "permitting social flaws to manifest themselves by means of a flawed invoice which defines itself as illusory with no attempt at camouflage through attempts at an aesthetic totality." Adorno, "On the Social Situation of Music," 396. Max Paddison discusses this passage on page 104 of *Adorno's Aesthetics of Music.*

45. It is wholly plausible, of course, to recognize chords X and Y as altered dominant sevenths that are related to other chords in the preceding sequence. Except for the dominant sevenths doubled in the left hand and lowered fifths, their structure is virtually identical to that of chord 2. Our ability to rationalize the structure of these chords as tonal and relate them to the preceding harmonic progression does not, however, negate my larger point that they are aurally provocative to an almost excessive extent, and thereby place the subsequent reprise—normatively, a moment that simultaneously creates and celebrates the rational and stabilizing influence of form upon musical flow— under considerable dialectical strain.

46. Adorno, "On Musical Analysis," trans. Max Paddison, in *Essays on Music,* ed. Richard Leppert (Berkeley: University of California Press, 2002), 164–65. The italics are Adorno's. Paddison treats this topic briefly in *Adorno's Aesthetics of Music,* 155–6.

47. Eva Geulen offers a detailed investigation of Adorno's dialectical notion of tradition in "Theodor Adorno on Tradition," in *The Actuality of Adorno,* ed. M. Pensky, 183–93. A classic text on tradition—one that, admittedly, does not refer directly to Adorno—is Edward Shils, *Tradition* (Chicago: The University of Chicago Press, 1981).

48. Ravel also appears to have orchestrated these Preludes around this time, but this orchestration has unfortunately not yet come to light. See Arbie Orenstein, *Ravel: Man and Musician* (New York: Dover, 1991); a slightly altered republication of the same title (New York: Columbia University Press, 1968), 243.

49. My impetus to invest Waltz II with deep subjectivity and emotional sincerity comes, at least in part, from Ravel's libretto for *Adélaïde ou le langage des fleurs,* the 1912 ballet version of the *Valses.* In this libretto, Waltz II accompanies the scene in which the hero Lorédan is introduced in all his youthful passion and inner torment.

50. I say "American musicology," rather than "Anglo-American" or "English-language musicology," because it seems to me that, judging from the work of Daniel Chua, Max Paddison, Michael Spitzer, Alastair Williams, and others, the musicological reception of Adorno in the UK has been broader and deeper than in the United States.

51. Taruskin made this statement in his review of *The Cambridge History of Nineteenth-Century Music* and *The Cambridge History of Twentieth-Century Music* in *19th-Century Music* 29, no. 2 (Fall 2005): 185–207.

52. One of the few gestures—and perhaps the earliest—in this direction is Randolph Eichert, "Kontrapunkte: Ravel gegen den Strich gehört," in *Hommage à Ravel 1987,* 193–95. Dialectical thought also informs my interpretive approach in "Dandy, Interrupted"; see, in particular, the subchapter "A Dialectics of the Dandy" (351–52), where I show how moments of sublime composure in Daphnis's Dance subtly refer to other moments in which this composure is shattered, and vice versa.

53. Kofi Agawu, "What Adorno Makes Possible for Music Analysis," *19th-Century Music* 29, no. 1 (Summer, 2005): 55. The article in this Adorno-centered issue of *19th-Century Music* that treats his analytical writing most fully as literary performance is Beate Perrey, "Exposed: Adorno and Schubert in 1928," 15–24.

54. Adorno, "On Musical Analysis," 169. Adorno's immediate definition of "imagination" (via Walter Benjamin) as "the capacity for interpolation into the smallest details" unfortunately does little to clarify this definition of analysis. More helpful are the accounts of "exact imagination" (or "fantasy") in Susan Buck-Morss, *The Origin of Negative Dialectics: Theodor W. Adorno, Walter Benjamin, and the Frankfurt Institute* (New York: The Free Press, 1977), 85–88, and Shierry Weber Nicholsen, *Exact Imagination, Late Work* (Cambridge, MA and London: The MIT Press, 1997), 1–13.

Part Two

Analytical Case Studies

Chapter Four

Ravel's Approach to Formal Process

Comparisons and Contexts

Peter Kaminsky

Precious little has been written about Ravel's approach to form. Even in works purporting to catalogue all the salient aspects of Ravel's musical language, the discussion of form is conspicuously absent. For example, in Vladimir Janké-lévitch's well-known study of Ravel, the headings under his second section, "Skill," comprise chapters entitled "Challenge," "Artifice," "Instrumental Virtuosity," "Rhythms," "Harmony," "Modes," and "Counterpoint."[1] One possible reason is the widespread assumption that for Ravel, form means little more than the choice of a conventional vehicle with which to convey his innovations in harmony, orchestration, and sonority. As Charles Rosen notes, "[Ravel's] musical forms are generally impeccable, if uninteresting, and almost in all cases adequate to convey the fantastic originality of his concern with sound."[2] A second reason is simply the difficulty of writing about form without taking a purely textbook approach: i.e., creating a taxonomy of formal hierarchy.

This is unfortunate, because form clearly is of vital importance to Ravel in his compositional thinking. In his own writings, he tends not to discuss form in his or other composers' works unless he regards it as deficient. (We shall see this below in his attitude toward Debussy.) His commentary, however, does provide some clue for what is evident over the course of his oeuvre: for virtually every work that he wrote, the *formal process*—which includes the formal hierarchy as well as the diachronic progress of its unfolding, in conjunction with tonal, harmonic, rhythmic, and thematic/motivic elements—is essentially *sui generis*. But such custom-made design creates another problem: how can one explore formal process in a coherent fashion if every piece is its own formal universe? Yet to focus exclusively on common factors simply offers reduction to the least common denominator.

My point of departure is twofold. First, while Jankélévitch does not explicitly talk about formal issues, he does put his finger on a central component of Ravel's aesthetic attitude. Drawing on Alexis Roland-Manuel's "aesthetics of imposture," Jankélévitch refers to an "aesthetics of challenge" which he describes as follows:

> Every composition by Ravel represents in this sense a certain problem to be solved, a game in which the player voluntarily makes the rules of the game more complicated; although nobody makes him do so he places restrictions on himself and learns, as Nietzsche would have said, "to dance in chains."[3]

From a form standpoint, one could interpret this as Rosen does: that Ravel relies on conventional tonal baroque and classical form in order to provide the necessary chains for his unique contributions in harmony, orchestration, and so forth. But I propose an alternative view: that the problem Ravel chooses to solve in a given work extends to and indeed is central to the *formal process* itself. Hence I shall extend the notion of aesthetics of challenge to the domain of form.

Second, I will employ the homely teaching principle of *comparison*—specifically, comparison of works with strong commonalities, in consideration with appropriate historical, stylistic, and/or structural contexts—to approach the issue of formal process for Ravel. I have chosen three pairs of works, not with the intention of illustrating some overriding theoretical principle (e.g., Ravel's use of augmented eleventh chords), but simply because they are exceptionally clear candidates for comparative analysis: (1) *Pavane pour une infante défunte* and "Pavane de la belle au bois dormant"; (2) Debussy's *Hommage à Haydn* and Ravel's *Menuet sur le nom d'Haydn;* and (3) Aloysius Bertrand's poem "Le gibet" and Ravel's piano work "Le gibet." Others could have been chosen: e.g., the muleteer Ramiro's two solo scenes from Ravel's opera *L'heure espagnole;* Debussy's "Nuages" (the first of the *Nocturnes* for orchestra) and Ravel's "Prélude à la nuit," the first movement of *Rapsodie espagnole;* the "Forlane" from the fourth of François Couperin's *Concerts Royaux* and the "Forlane" from Ravel's *Tombeau de Couperin,* and so on. The objective is not to be exhaustive, but rather to elicit the structural factors behind Ravel's approach to formal process.

Pavane pour une infante défunte and "Pavane de la belle au bois dormant"

Our first comparison addresses Ravel's two pavanes, the *Pavane pour une infante défunte* (1899) for solo piano and the opening movement from *Ma mère l'oye* (1910) for piano four hands, entitled "Pavane de la belle au bois dormant."

Looking back on his early works, the self-critical Ravel faulted the first pavane for its form and derivativeness: "It [the "Pavane"] is so much a matter of ancient history that it is time the composer handed it over to the critics. I no longer see its virtues from this distance. But, alas, its faults I can perceive only too well: the influence of Chabrier is much too glaring, and the structure [*la forme*] rather poor."[4] His student and disciple Roland-Manuel concurred: "It is a stern verdict, but not an unjust one."[5] Tracing its provenance from the baroque dance to the nineteenth-century pavanes of Saint-Saëns and Chabrier, Kuhn-Schliess notes the largely unmediated classical influence on all parameters of Ravel's piece—its form as a five-part rondo; its rhythm; its motivic development, which confers organic unity; its melodic range; its compositional means (e.g., repetition, sequence, pedal point, contrary motion, etc.); its texture; and its tonality, rooted at all times in G major (notwithstanding the conventional turn to G minor in the second episode and the extensive use of dominant ninth chords).[6] This is not to say the piece is devoid of interest. One could cite the rather exhaustive and almost mechanical development of the melody of the opening two measures, leading to its variant in measures 3–4 and subsequent sequence; its fragmentation, engendering the tonally ambiguous half cadence (mm. 6–7); the varied inversion of measure 1 leading off the new phrase beginning in measure 9; its anticipation of the quotation from Chabrier's *Gwendoline* in three octaves (mm. 10–11); and the little rising line (B–D–E–F♯) in measure 11 as a lead-in between phrases that provides the impetus for the central episode in G minor beginning in measure 40. While this sort of close melodic development is elegant and indeed characteristic of Ravel's more mature writing as well, it does not quite rescue the work from the composer's and his student's judgment.

At first glance, Ravel's approach to formal and tonal structure in "Pavane de la belle au bois dormant" appears little different from that adopted for the earlier pavane; indeed, the classical treatment of the parameters outlined above applies equally to both works. Set in A minor, the "Pavane de la belle au bois dormant" is composed of five four-measure phrases (a, b, c, a', b') and is cast as a ternary form with a clear and relatively conventional tonal and melodic organization. Only through closer examination of the harmony and tonal progression, the form, and their interactions can we observe how this work signals a later stage in Ravel's compositional development.

The formal and harmonic process may be modeled through a simple Riemann-inspired scheme of harmonic functions, shown in example 4.1a. Reading from left to right, the staff shows three principal and two derived harmonic functions: T (tonic), Tr (tonic-relative), S (subdominant), D (dominant), and D/S (dominant of the subdominant); these functions may be expressed as major or minor. Following the double bar are two possible functional superimpositions, where $\frac{T}{S}$ represents a D minor ninth chord, and $\frac{S}{D}$ an E minor eleventh chord.[7]

Example 4.1b presents a modified Schenkerian analysis of the movement. On the top the formal divisions are overlaid; on the bottom, below the roman-numeral analysis, is the progression of Riemannian functions. The opening phrase leads conventionally from tonic to dominant, supporting a stepwise treble descent from $\hat{5}$ to $\hat{2}$ that culminates in a half cadence. Measures 5–8 prolong the dominant, and lead to a modal v–i cadence. Harmonically, the dominant is actually $\frac{S}{D}$, as the tenor and treble voices together strongly imply a D-minor *Klang* over bass E. Measures 9–12 turn to the relative key of C major, prolonged until measure 11. Here the bass descends by step to V^7/D minor, whose succeeding resolution to D minor briefly implies both C major (as ii) and A minor (as iv). Significantly, at measure 13 the resolution coincides with the return of the opening melody, whose recontextualization is no less stunning for being achieved so simply: the opening tonal function T is replaced at the reprise by $\frac{T}{S}$.[8] This substitution creates a radical disjunction for listeners: the opening melody, initially heard as tonally stable and harmonized consonantly by the tonic, is reprised at pitch but harmonized dissonantly by the subdominant; in particular, the *Kopfton* E_5 is now perceived as an appoggiatura resolving to D. Analytically, this perceived disjunction arises through the lack of alignment between the formal structure—the small ternary form of 8 + 4 + 8 bars—and the tonal progression of 8 + 12 bars.

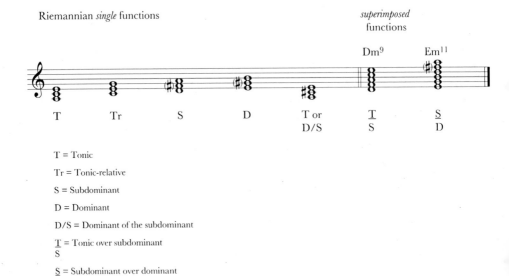

Example 4.1a. Riemannian functions in Ravel's "Pavane de la belle au bois dormant"

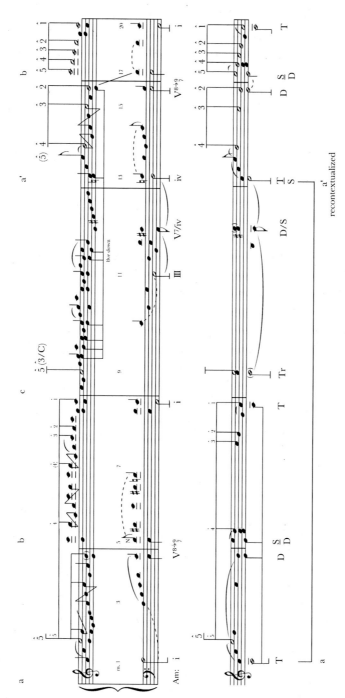

Example 4.1b. Form and voice leading in "Pavane de la belle au bois dormant"

On the one hand, the "Pavane de la belle au bois dormant," like the earlier Pavane, utilizes completely conventional elements: a melodic unfolding modeled by a Schenkerian 5-line within a three-part classical form. The mature Ravel's compositional wizardry emerges, however, through a transparent technical device—the superimposition of harmonic functions—resulting in the stark noncongruence between the formal articulation and the tonal structure. In this way, Ravel, working with formal and tonal norms, subverts their normativeness by rewiring their connections, thereby creating a unique structural process.

Debussy's *Hommage à Haydn* and Ravel's *Menuet sur le nom d'Haydn*

As is well known, the two works in question are part of a set of six commissioned from Debussy, Ravel, and other prominent French composers on the *soggetto cavato* B–A–D–D–G (based on the letters H–A–Y–D–N) as part of the centennial commemoration of Haydn's death.[9] Previous work comparing these two movements has noted the stylistic consequences of Ravel's and Debussy's choice of dance as a vehicle for the *soggetto*. Debussy chooses to open and conclude his homage with a distinctly un-Haydnesque and anticlassical slow waltz (whose possible model is Chopin's Waltz in A minor, op. 34 no. 1), framing a *de facto* set of variations on the *soggetto*. In stark contrast, Ravel chooses a minuet, which not only evokes the elevated tone and style of cultured nobility, but more importantly represents the exemplary and propaedeutic model for classical composition in its balanced phrasing, clarity of form, and economical thematic development.[10] My analysis will focus on the different compositional possibilities for the *soggetto cavato* seized by Debussy and Ravel, and their ramifications in relation to the formal process for the respective movements.

For Debussy's *Hommage à Haydn*, the unfolding of the opening waltz section (mm. 1–22)—its harmonic progression, introduction of the *soggetto*, phrasing, and cadence organization—sets the stage for the remainder of the piece and for its stylistic and structural content. It opens with a sinuous stepwise melody in the bass based on a consistent dotted-rhythm figure stated in sequence. This is accompanied by right-hand off-beat chords, and the composite rhythm defines the waltz gesture. The opening section comprises three phrases of irregular lengths (mm. 1–4, 5–14, and 15–22), the last of which overlaps with the variation section. Interestingly, each phrase begins on the same G half-diminished seventh chord in first inversion. While one should not automatically assume that every half-diminished seventh chord found in Debussy's oeuvre is a reference to Wagner's *Tristan und Isolde* prelude, here the progression and voice leading for the respective phrases suggest precisely that. Example 4.2a shows the first two phrases of the introduction and a simplified voice-leading reduction of their respective progressions, in comparison to the first phrase of *Tristan*. Phrase 1 resolves to G♭7, the voice leading strongly reminiscent of that in *Tristan*. Phrase 2 begins the same but substitutes the enharmonically equivalent E♮ for F♭. This in turn motivates the introduction of the motto "H–A–Y–D–N" in the treble voice, culminating in a full cadence (ii^7–V^7–I) and thereby establishing G major as tonic. Phrase 3 (not shown in the example) substitutes C♯ (enharmonic to D♭) for C♮ in resolving the half-diminished seventh, leading to V^7/V, which supports the restatement of the motto. Immediately following, the expected harmonic resolution to the dominant instead gives way to another half-diminished seventh, coinciding with a change in tempo and the beginning of the variations.

Given the disparate nature of the elements that make up the opening of Debussy's *Hommage*—the romantic-period slow waltz, the Tristan chord and voice leading, and the statement of the motto—and his minimal effort at blending them into a seamless whole, the piece takes shape as a play of dichotomous elements: a *bricolage*, if you will. Beginning at measure 23, Debussy's choice of variations allows for maximal compositional freedom. Retaining the motto at its original pitch level throughout, the main body of the piece is set in a wild array of rhythmic and harmonic contexts, including hemiola (mm. 23–30), chromatic mediant motion (mm. 33–34), floating parallel triads through the acoustic scale (mm. 47–53), linear chromaticism (mm. 58–86 and octatonicism (mm. 94–104). "Closure" takes place as the implied octatonic retransition truncates the motto to four notes ("H–A–Y/D–N"), giving way to an elaborated plagal cadence (C$_6$ to G$_6$), with the return of the opening waltz and its Tristan chord interpolated as a chromatic passing chord (ex. 4.2b).

In turning to Ravel's *Menuet sur le nom d'Haydn*, it is worth considering, if only briefly, his ambivalent attitude toward Debussy as a composer. Specifically, while he lauds Debussy as the greatest genius of French music and praises without reservation individual works such as *Pelléas et Mélisande* and especially *Prélude à l'après-midi d'un faune*, at the same time he faults him (albeit rather cryptically) for his lack of formal precision. From an interview in *The Morning Post* dated July 10, 1922, the unidentified reporter notes "[Ravel asserted that] Debussy had shown a *négligence de la forme*. . . . M. Ravel said that he followed Debussy in the ideal of economy of material, but he was at odds with him in his respect for forms."[11] Clearly Debussy's *Hommage* as *bricolage* would have been completely unsatisfactory to Ravel on formal grounds.

Ulrich Mahlert, addressing the opening phrase of Ravel's *Menuet*, suggests a structural context. His analysis divides the phrase, a 1 + 1 + 2 bar sentence structure, in two parts, the first implying the relative key of E minor and the second closing with a full cadence in the tonic. The minuet rhythm and classical phrase structure support the *soggetto cavato;* the outer-voice counterpoint, in particular the 9–7 voice exchange and B minor seventh chord as (temporary) dominant, provide the "*fin-de-siècle* sentiment." He concludes:

H A Y D N

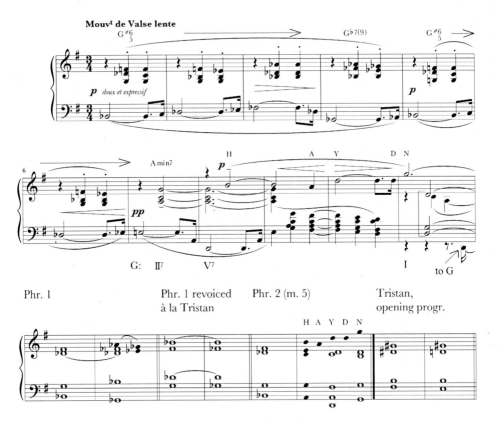

Example 4.2a. Opening, Debussy's *Hommage à Haydn*

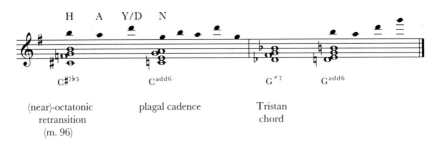

Example 4.2b. "Closure," Debussy's *Hommage*

In these four measures it already is evident how Ravel as an early twentieth-century composer solves the problem of a "Hommage à Haydn": he directs on the 'auditory stage' [*Hörbühne*] a masked dance in which archaic, classical, and modern elements pervade in a refined manner and act together in a complex game of exchanges.[12]

While Mahlert's view is persuasive, it also is relatively obvious in its identification of Ravel's characteristic mix of archaic, classical, and modern style elements as a "masked dance." Crucially, it begs the question of the nature of their interaction, and especially of how Ravel exploits the *soggetto cavato* in defining that interaction. My analysis will show that the archaic and modernist elements serve a thoroughly classical tonal and formal structure as opposed to Mahlert's notion of complex changing game—which in fact comes closer to describing Debussy's *Hommage* rather than Ravel's.

First, unlike Debussy's radical rhythmic variations, Ravel's composition employs only two rhythmic settings of the motto, both in equal quarter notes: the first, beginning on the upbeat, presents the "prime form," while the second, which begins on the downbeat, signals the motto's transformations. Also unlike Debussy, Ravel allows for canonical pitch transformations of the motto; however, except in one instance, Ravel keeps H (B♮) invariant.

Formally, measures 1–8 represent a conventional period modulating to the dominant, with both the antecedent and consequent phrases suggesting 1 + 1 + 2–measure sentence structures; the antecedent phrase not only introduces the motto but also implies its retrograde, thereby anticipating its subsequent transformation (ex. 4.3).[13] The overall form is cast as an outwardly conventional ternary: section A comprises the eight-measure modulating period and its written-out repetition; the developmental section B (mm. 17–42) culminates in a retransition (m. 38) that overlaps with the reprise of A at measure 43, which transposes and extends the consequent phrase to conclude in tonic.

It is only with section B and the reprise that Ravel's compositional strategy fully emerges. Example 4.4 provides an analytical reduction showing the motto and its (mostly) canonical transformations; their respective tonal, harmonic and pitch-collection contexts in relation to the bass progression; and the correlation of pitch organization with formal progression.[14] The middle section divides into three parts labeled B1, B2, and B3, defined respectively by the (overlapped) stepwise descent of the bass by third (G–E); by fourth (E–B); and by the prolongation of B, which simultaneously signals the onset of the reprise, whose third descent (B–A–G) completes the long-range octave descent. Unusually, the development begins not only with the motto at P_0 but with the inversion of its leap from ascending fourth to descending fifth. As a result, the motto migrates from the middle to the bass register and represents a near-cadence in tonic. (We shall see how the same disposition occurs at the end to provide structural closure.) Following R_0 and the cadential movement in VI, section B2 introduces RI_0,

Example 4.3. Opening, Ravel's *Menuet sur le nom d'Haydn*

which changes the perfect to an augmented fourth and, more importantly,
introduces C♯ as the first chromatic pitch in the motto's transformation. With
the transference of C♯ to the bass at measure 27, the passage enters into more
remote tonal regions. In the upper voice, the alternation of R_1, R_0, and R_1
against the sustained bass C♯ implies Mixolydian and Locrian contexts. At
measure 33, with the statement of the motto at R_5, the music veers into octatonic pitch space for the next six measures. (Note that Ravel attains the octatonic by repeating the treble figure from m. 29—G–A–F♯–E—at pitch, simply
changing the bass note and transposing the motto accordingly.)

In sum, the ongoing canonical transformations of the motto engen-
der a progressively more dissonant harmonic and pitch-collectional context, culminating with the sustained octatonic region. At the same time,
the underlying tonal progression for measures 17–39 is both completely
classical and characteristically Ravelian, consisting of II–V–I motion in G, E
minor (VI), and B minor (III). What follows is perhaps the most dissonant
portion of the piece, as the stepwise diatonic sequence in the treble scrapes
against the rising chromatic tritones in the middle register, all over the bass
pedal point on B.[15] Once again, however, the chromatic superimposition
belies a thoroughly classical succession. Thus at measure 38 beat 3, Ravel's
accent on the dissonant sonority D♯–A–A♯ (middle staff) hints at its status

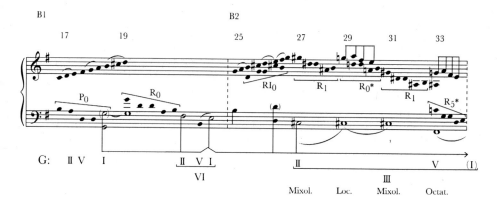

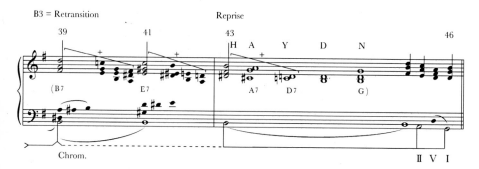

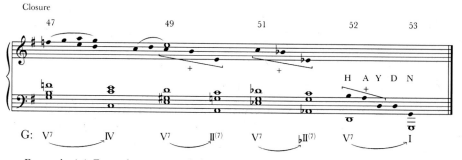

Example 4.4. Formal process and closure, Ravel's *Menuet*

as an appoggiatura chord; the resolution of A♯ to B in the next measure reveals it to be a B[7] chord, which initiates the motion by descending fifths through E[7]–A[7]–D[7]–G. Equally elegant is the treble succession: the brackets (designated with a + sign) show three iterations of a downward intervallic sequence, beginning on D, C, and finally B, the B reinitiating "H–A–Y–D–N" and the onset of the reprise.

At first glance, Ravel's reprise is the most conventional portion of the movement, a modifying of the opening period to conclude in tonic. This view, however, underestimates Ravel's aesthetics of challenge. Ravel's challenge appears to be to derive *all* the melodic material, as well as the means of progression and closure, from the *soggetto cavato.*

The lower staff of example 4.4 continues from the end of the upper and shows the concluding phrase in reduction. Tonally, the progression is again quintessentially classical, tonicizing in succession the subdominant, supertonic, and Neapolitan on the way to the final cadence. It is the melody that warrants closer attention. While measures 47–48 simply transpose measures 5–6, the material at 49 (marked *Retenu*) appears to have no direct antecedent, other than the obvious rhythmic precedent in measure 3. However, under the treble pedal point the melodic figure C–B–C–E–G is a more elaborated version of C–B–E, which in turn is a transposition of the "H–A–Y" of the motto. Looking back to the retransition at 38–42, the "H–A–Y" figure was stated three times in sequence, leading to a complete statement of the motto and the reprise. In the final phrase, the same figure is once again stated thrice: on C–B–E (supported by II); C–B♭–E♭ (by ♭II); and finally taken down a half step, leading once more to the complete motto which, having migrated to the middle and bass register (cf. mm. 17–18), supplies the final cadence. Thus the three principal formal junctures of the *Menuet*—the onset of the B section at measure 17, the retransition at measure 38, and the final cadence—all reuse the same basic material in a similar manner while articulating completely different formal contexts. (Such functional interchangeability of course is not exactly unknown in the classical period.)

In conclusion, we may consider Charles Rosen's view of the two homages:

> Ravel writes a minuet which does not appear to be based on the Haydn notes at all, but into which these notes are worked, starting from the first measure. . . . The final impression of the listener is one of richly shifting harmonies hidden under a simple exterior. This total impression comes mainly from the inner part-writing which contains the motto theme, but *the motto is not essential to the work* [my emphasis]; its conception provides only a way in which it may be inserted.
>
> Quite the contrary is true of the Debussy *Hommage à Haydn:* here the motto is not only essential, but it may be said to be the germinating element.[16]

From the standpoint of the overall structure and compositional strategy, the foregoing analysis has shown the opposite to be the case: for Debussy the motto has provided melodic material but little more; for Ravel, the motto, its intervallic succession, and its correlation to all levels of form from cell to section controls the *Menuet* in its entirety.

Bertrand's Poem "Le gibet" and Ravel's Composition "Le gibet"

Louis "Aloysius" Bertrand (1807–41) is remembered today solely for his slender volume of prose poetry entitled *Gaspard de la nuit: Fantaisies à la manière de Rembrandt et de Callot*. Almost exactly contemporary with Edgar Allan Poe, Bertrand's compact verse shares much with the American in its exploration of the subconscious, occult, diabolical, and fantastic.[17]

Within Ravel's *oeuvre*, "Le gibet" stands out as the piece that most clearly embodies Poe in its expression of obsession and terror. By way of introduction I shall briefly sketch the confluence of Bertrand, Poe, and Baudelaire prior to analyzing Ravel's "setting" of "Le gibet." While Baudelaire was an early admirer of Bertrand's *Gaspard*, he is better known for championing the work of Poe, especially his translation of Poe's most famous poem "The Raven" and the attendant explanatory essay "The Philosophy of Composition." Largely through Baudelaire's efforts, Poe became a central figure in both literature and music in France throughout the second half of the nineteenth century.[18] For Ravel, Poe and in particular "The Philosophy of Composition" exerted enormous influence.

> As for technique, my teacher was certainly Edgar Allan Poe. The finest treatise on composition, in my opinion, and the one which in any case had the greatest influence upon me was his *Philosophy of Composition*. No matter how much Mallarmé claimed that it was nothing but a hoax, I am convinced that Poe indeed wrote his poem *The Raven* in the way that he indicated.[19]

In his essay Poe, self-consciously eschewing any stereotypical notions of poetic inspiration, describes in precise analytical discourse the step-by-step process of writing "The Raven," even down to the phonological factors dictating the choice of the Raven's refrain "Nevermore." Clearly Poe's desiderata—the contemplation of Beauty, means of creation of effect, exaltation of sheer craft, abhorrence of chance and incomprehensibility, and so forth—found a most sympathetic fellow artist in Ravel.

For "Le gibet," it appears that Poe's aesthetic opened up for Ravel the possibility of completely expressing in musical terms the horrifying affect of the poem through the exercise of sheer technical craft. And, while Ravel did not actually set any of Poe's works to music, Bertrand's poem affords similar opportunities for expression. The text of "Le gibet" as it appears immediately preceding Ravel's score is given below, followed by a translation.

> Que vois-je remuer autour de ce Gibet?
> FAUST

> Ah! ce que j'entends, serait-ce la bise nocturne qui glapit,
> ou le pendu qui pousse un soupir sur la fourche patibulaire?

Serait-ce quelque grillon qui chante tapi dans la
mousse et le lierre sterile dont par pitié se chausse le
bois?
Serait-ce quelque mouche en chasse sonnant du cor
autour de ces oreilles sourdes à la fanfare des hallali?
Serait-ce quelque escarbot qui cueille en son vol
inégal un cheveu sanglant à son crâne chauve?
Ou bien serait-ce quelque araignée qui brode une demi-
aune de mousseline pour cravate à ce col étranglé?
C'est la cloche qui tinte aux murs d'une ville, sous
L'horizon, et la carcasse d'un pendu que rougit le soleil
couchant.

[What is it I see stirring around that gibbet?
FAUST

Ah! What do I hear? Is it the night wind howling, or
the hanged man sighing on the gibbet?
Might it be a cricket singing, hidden in the moss and
the sterile ivy with which the wood covers itself out of pity?
Might it be a fly hunting and sounding its horn around
those ears that are deaf to the slaughterer's triumph?
Might it be a cockchafer plucking, in its halting
flight, a bloody hair from its bald pate?
Or might it be a spider, weaving a length of muslin as
a scarf for that strangled neck?
It is the bell that sounds from the walls of a town
beyond the horizon, and the corpse of a hanged man that
glows red in the setting sun.][20]

In composing his celebrated piano triptych *Gaspard de la nuit,* Ravel selected
three from Bertrand's collection of some sixty-six prose poems: "Ondine," "Le
gibet," and "Scarbo." Each poem in the collection follows the same format: it
is headed by an epigraph that provides the point of departure for the poem,
which proceeds in short unrhymed and generally unmetered verses. The epigraphs are drawn from sources ranging from the Bible to literary reviews to
contemporary poets to myths and legends.

Of all the poems in *Gaspard de la nuit,* only "Le gibet" and one other poem,
"The Hour of the Sabbath" (L'heure du sabbat), have epigraphs consisting of
a single question; for "Le gibet," "Que vois-je remuer autour de ce gibet?"
FAUST ("What is it I see stirring around that gibbet?")[21] This would appear
to set the stage for the objective of the poem: to answer the question. But
then the sense abruptly shifts, as the poem proper begins "Ah! What do I
hear?" The sensate shift suggests that the act of seeing, of immediately verify-
ing what is swinging from the gallows, is being repressed. This hint of repression then is made explicit in the course of the first verse by none other than

the word "or": "Might it be the night wind howling, *or* the hanged man sigh-ing on the gibbet?" We know—and the poem's protagonist knows, at least subconsciously—that the answer can only be the latter. But each of the suc-ceeding verses save for the last represses this knowledge, suggesting in the sec-ond verse that the stirring might be a cricket's call. The questioning thereafter continues with progressively more grisly descriptions of various aspects of the still unidentified corpse (deaf ears, bloody hair, strangled neck). Syntactically, following the lead of the first verse, verses two through five begin with the con-ditional interrogative "Serait-ce?"—"Might it be?" In the final verse, the return to the present indicative "C'est"—"It is"—signals the break in the pattern of repression. Formally, it circles back not only to the question of verse one, but also to the question of the epigraph, and hence to the initial site of repression: the protagonist *hears* the bell tolling and *sees* the hanged man rotting.[22]

In an earlier essay on Ravel's vocal works, I demonstrate that he seeks to enact in musical terms essential syntactic aspects of his chosen texts; most often this entails idiosyncratic structural procedures involving harmony, tonal context, form, and voice leading.[23] For "Le gibet," Ravel follows a similar strategy in bas-ing the musical setting on fundamental elements of the poem by Bertrand: its formal circularity issuing from the question-answer framework; its undercurrent of repression leading to ultimate revelation; its tone of foreboding; and its pro-gressive intensification. Figure 4.1 below is a schematic outline of the central structural analogues between the poem and music. The subsequent analysis will show that Ravel's musical realization of these poetic elements constitutes a tonal-formal narrative deeply congruent with the unfolding of Bertrand's text.

Central to the tonal narrative as it unfolds are three interrelated elements introduced in the opening seven bars: the ostinato B♭ and its structural con-text; the battle for tonal supremacy between E♭ and B♭; and the status of the chromatic F♭ and its resolution.[24] Attempts at definition and/or resolution are continually offered but then repressed, the musical process aligning itself with the poem. In the end, structural resolution is isomorphic with the answer to the protagonist's "What do I hear?" further illuminating the initial sensate shift.

Example 4.5 shows how the opening of the piece sets in motion the tonal narrative. The piece begins by introducing its most famous feature, the repeated ostinato pedal point on B♭ (mostly doubled at the octave) that sounds without respite for the entire movement. While one is tempted to assign it a literal pro-grammatic meaning—the bell or the swinging of the hanged man—in a dia-chronic sense we do not know the meaning of the ostinato until the last verse of the poem, and, by extension, until the end of the piece. Less obvious is that the ostinato is cast as a four-beat isorhythm, indicated by the brackets. While some-what disguised by its displacement with respect to the bar line and the subse-quent departures from the exact rhythmic pattern (the first occurs at m. 14), the presence of isorhythm conveys a sense of the mechanical, the impersonal, and the inexorable even before the listener knows what the ostinato "means."

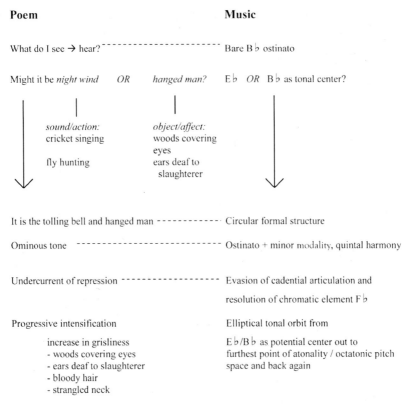

Poem   **Music**

What do I see → hear?   - - - - - - - - - - - - - - -   Bare B♭ ostinato

Might it be *night wind*   OR   *hanged man?*   E♭   OR   B♭ as tonal center?

sound/action:
cricket singing

fly hunting

object/affect:
woods covering
eyes
ears deaf to
slaughterer

It is the tolling bell and hanged man - - - - - - - - - - - Circular formal structure

Ominous tone   - Ostinato + minor modality, quintal harmony

Undercurrent of repression - - - - - - - - - - - - - - - Evasion of cadential articulation and

resolution of chromatic element F♭

Progressive intensification   Elliptical tonal orbit from

increase in grisliness   E♭/B♭ as potential center out to
- woods covering eyes   furthest point of atonality / octatonic pitch
- ears deaf to slaughterer   space and back again
- bloody hair
- strangled neck

Figure 4.1. Poetic and musical correspondences in "Le gibet"

Harmonically, the isorhythmic B♭ plays on the duality of pedal points, which conventionally imply either tonic or dominant. With the entrance of the left-hand quintal Theme 1 and in particular the bass note E♭2, it appears that E♭ represents tonic, while the ostinato B♭ provides reinforcement as the upper fifth. Its tonicity is weakened, however, by the presence of F as both a dissonant appoggiatura and as the (doubled) upper fifth of B♭, which suggests B♭ as an alternate tonic; indeed, the quintal chord E♭–B♭–F also implies both E♭ and B♭ as tonic. At measure 6, Theme 2 begins with a clear statement of B♭ minor harmony, the ostinato temporarily serving as bass. However, the melodic emphasis on F♭ (doubled by its displacement of F♮ in the inner voice), weakens B♭ as a tonic; and, while F♭ gives way to F♮ with the quintal return in measure 8 (and to the inner-voice E♭ in m. 12, not shown in the example), F♭ remains essentially unresolved. Even so, a path to eventual resolution is subtly suggested. In measures 6–7, the vertical lines in the treble outline the figure D♭–F♭–E♭–D♭ within the context of B♭ minor: omit the alto F♭ (or nudge it up to F♮) and the three pitch elements in the drama reach agreement. I

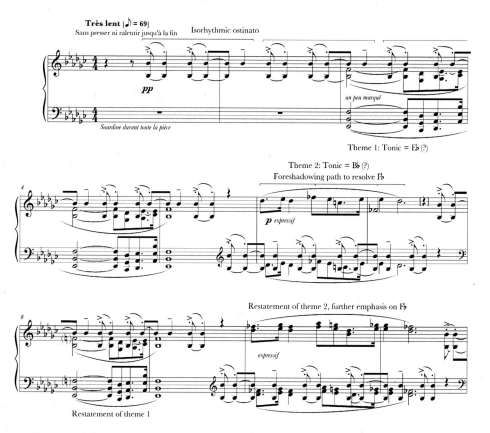

Example 4.5. Opening tonal narrative in Ravel's "Le gibet"

suggest that the understated repression of F♭'s resolution subsequently gives way to its climactic emergence.

In the absence of conventional cadences, thematic articulation plays a significant formal role. The piece unfolds five recurring themes within a structure that doubles back on itself: the piece ends up where it started, but concludes in a radically different structural and interpretive context.[25] Example 4.6 displays the five themes. The organum-like quintal Theme 1 begins and ends on E♭–B♭–F. In Theme 2, marked "*expressif*," the metric and contour emphasis on the chromatic F♭ signals its increasing importance throughout the movement. Theme 3, a transformation of Theme 1, preserves its rhythm and contour while altering its harmonies from fifths trichords to triads (with octave doubling), which migrate from bass to treble. Theme 4, a series of chords stated in contrary motion between left and right hands over a bass pedal, prolongs a single harmony (here, F♭9 over A♭) before leading to a chromatic descent in major thirds. Theme 5 initiates the second half of the movement; in contrast to

Theme 1 (m. 3, LH)

Theme 2 (mm. 6-7, RH)

Theme 3 (m. 12, RH)

Theme 4 (mm. 20-21, LH and RH)

Example 4.6. Main themes, "Le gibet"

Theme 5 (mm. 28-30, RH)

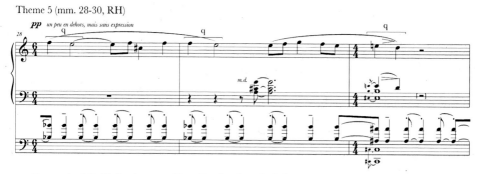

Example 4.6. Main themes, "Le gibet"—*(concluded)*

the marking on the earlier single-note melody of Theme 2, this is marked *sans expression* and features a two-note descending step motive (labeled q).

Formally, "Le gibet" unfolds the tonal narrative in six stages. Example 4.7a provides a schematic diagram of the form, and example 4.7b provides a harmonic reduction aligned with the formal designations. Both the schematic and the reduction are laid out so as to make explicit the circular nature of the form: the arrows indicate the relationships between the stages and the themes. Each stage in example 4.7a is designated according to its function within the tonal narrative; formal divisions generally are motivated by the entrance of the respective themes. S1, *tonal ambiguity,* alternates the two statements of Themes 1 and 2. S2, *attempted tonal clarification,* transforms Theme 1 into Theme 3. In this process, first B♭ and then E♭ is cast as a dominant seventh chord supporting an incipient cadential progression and stepwise melodic descent of scale degree 4–3–2; in both instances resolution is evaded. Harmonically, the second evasion at measure 20 is crucial in leading to S3, *failure of clarification.* In Theme 4, the combination of the bass motion E♭–A♭—implying V–i in A♭ minor—with the upper voices rooted on F♭ (VI) results in what Rameau in his *Traité de l'harmonie* designates a "deceptive cadence."[26] F♭, the note responsible for the cadential deception, is associated with the willful self-deception of the poem's protagonist; and by extension, as long as F♭ remains unresolved within a definite tonal context, the act of repression continues. Although the deceptive cadence keeps the passage at least in potentially tonal territory, at measure 23 the motion of the bass from A♭ down to G destroys any semblance of tonality. Specifically, the sonority G–D–G♯–B–E is a subset of the octatonic collection (G–G♯), which is completed by the arrival at the end of the phrase on C♯[7] with augmented ninth.[27] Example 4.7c shows that only one pitch class change—G♭ to G♮—is involved in turning the pitch space from tonal, as reflected by the dominant ninth sonority, to nontonal and octatonic. As noted recently by Elliott Antokoletz and other scholars, symmetrical collections in late-nineteenth- and early-twentieth-century music, in particular the octatonic

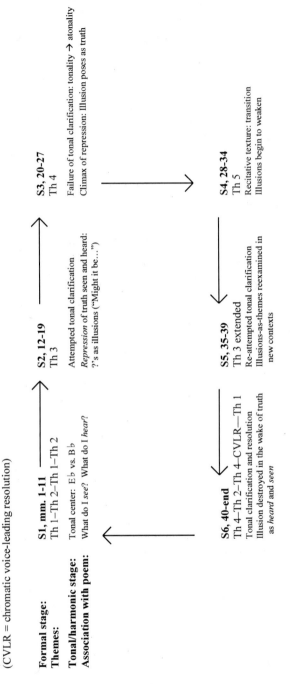

(S = *stage* in the musical process)
(Th = Theme)
(CVLR = chromatic voice-leading resolution)

Formal stage:
Themes:
Tonal/harmonic stage:
Association with poem:

S1, mm. 1-11
Th 1–Th 2–Th 1–Th 2
Tonal center: E♭ vs. B♭
What do I *see*? What do I *hear*?

S2, 12-19
Th 3
Attempted tonal clarification
Repression of truth seen and heard:
?'s as illusions ("Might it be…")

S3, 20-27
Th 4
Failure of tonal clarification: tonality → atonality
Climax of repression: Illusion poses as truth

S4, 28-34
Th 5
Recitative texture: transition
Illusions begin to weaken

S5, 35-39
Th 3 extended
Re-attempted tonal clarification
Illusions-as-themes reexamined in
new contexts

S6, 40-end
Th 4–Th 2–Th 4–CVLR—Th 1
Tonal clarification and resolution
Illusion destroyed in the wake of truth
as *heard* and *seen*

Example 4.7a. Formal overview, "Le gibet"

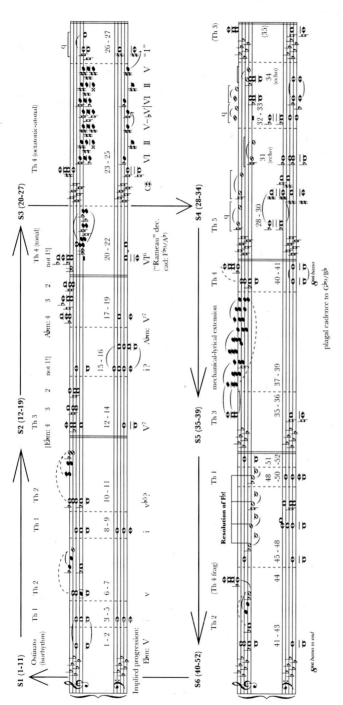

Example 4.7b. Harmonic reduction and circular form, "Le gibet"

Registral voice leading
(3 "registral" common tones)

Pitch-class voice leading
(4 pitch-class common tones)

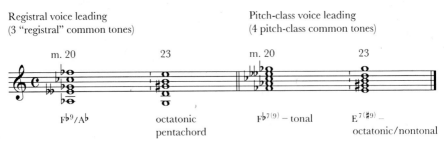

(First chords of the two statements of Theme 4, "très lié")

Example 4.7c. Tonal vs. octatonic implications in "Le gibet"

and whole-tone collections, are often employed to represent the supernatu-ral and fantastic, while asymmetrical tonal and modal collections are used to represent the human and normal.[28] By casting the octatonic domain as the destination of Part I of "Le gibet," Ravel takes the poem's repression to its extreme, i.e., to the furthest point from resolving the tonal narrative. Even the semblance of V–I motion at measures 25–26 (bass G♯ to C♯) is a cruel parody of a cadence not delivered earlier.

Stages 4, 5, and 6, which constitute the second half of the movement, mirror their counterparts S3, S2, and S1, respectively, from the first half (see ex. 4.7b). While S4 (mm. 28–34) begins by stating a new theme, its pitch content and bass motion by minor third (C♯–B♭–G) extend the preceding octatonicism concluding S3 (C♯–D–E–F–G–A♭–B♭–B, with A as the only nonoctatonic pitch class). Measure 35 initiates S5 and signals a renewed attempt at tonal clarifica-tion. The return of Theme 3 prolongs a single chord—C half-diminished sev-enth—and, diatonically, implies several plausible cadential outcomes: as vii°7, an authentic cadence in D♭ major; or as ii°7, the supertonic in B♭ minor as agent of a plagal cadence. Unlike the earlier continuation of Theme 3 that Ravel brings to a semblance of harmonic (though not melodic) resolution (cf. mm. 14–15), the three-bar Debussyesque extension ratchets up the suspense by further prolonging the C half-diminished seventh harmony (see the dotted-line connection mm. 35–39). (Closer inspection reveals that this apparently lyrical interlude shares with the ongoing ostinato B♭ the quality of mechanical and thus horrifying repetition, here consisting of three iterations of the same dynamic and contour sequence.)

At measure 40, the bass motion from C to B♭ confirms the plagal interpreta-tion;[29] moreover, the continuation of octave B♭ in its lowest register as a bass pedal for the remainder of the piece essentially resolves one of the principal tonal elements—the centricity of E♭ versus B♭—in favor of the latter. How-ever, with the return of Theme 4 (mm. 43ff.), the Rameauian sonority from measure 20 is transposed up a whole step placing the G♭ dominant ninth over

Bb. As a result, Fb now represents the chordal seventh and hence reiterates its need for resolution. Thereafter, the permutation of the original order of themes, Theme 4 → Theme 2 (at its original pitch level) → Theme 4 fragment, prolongs Fb and magnifies its structural prominence.

With measures 44–48, the question "What do I hear?" is finally answered, coinciding with the structural resolution of the three central tonal elements. The most dramatic of these is Fb, now sounded in stark isolation against the three-octave Bb ostinato, which descends chromatically in sequence culminating with the thrice-repeated Db–Bb.[30] By resolving definitively to Db, the complete minor triad on Bb is explicitly sounded for the first and only time in the piece. At the same time, in measures 46–end the opening isorhythm returns in its original metrical placement, now reinforced by the sustained bass notes corresponding precisely to each iteration of the talea. Consequently, when Theme 1 returns for its final statement in measures 47–49, the tonal force of Eb, so prevalent in its introduction at measure 3, is now totally eviscerated by the overwhelming presence of Bb. Even granting Ravel's prodigious powers of musical representation, "Le gibet" stands out among his programmatic works in the uniqueness of its tonal and formal scheme and its virtual isomorphic relation to Bertrand's poem.

It is hard to imagine the shape taken by "Le gibet" without the influence of Poe's "Philosophy of Composition." About the nature of refrain, repetition, and suggestion, Poe writes:

As commonly used, the refrain, or burden, not only is limited to lyric verse, but depends for its impression upon the force of monotone, both in sound and thought. The pleasure is deduced solely from the sense of identity—of repetition. I resolved to diversify, and so heighten, the effect, by adhering, in general, to the monotone of sound, while I continually varied that of thought: that is to say, I determined to produce continuously novel effects, by the variation of the application of the refrain, the refrain itself remaining, for the most part, unvaried.

But in subjects so handled, however skillfully [sic], or with however vivid an array of incident, there is always a certain hardness or nakedness, which repels the artistical eye. Two things are invariably required: first, some amount of complexity, or more properly, adaptation; and, secondly, some amount of suggestiveness, some undercurrent, however indefinite, of meaning. It is this latter, in especial, which imparts to a work of art so much of that richness . . . which we are too fond of confounding with the ideal.[31]

While Ravel's ostinato Bb is assuredly not a refrain, Poe's elucidation of monotonous repetition engendering novel effects readily describes its artful succession of structural allegiances. Equally apt is his stress on hidden complexity and the undercurrent of meaning to transform mere craftsmanship into artistry. Musically, Ravel goes way beyond the sheer novelty of the ostinato, counterpointing the chromatic and dynamic element F♭ against the static B♭ as they converge in expressing the poem's suggested repression and its final obliteration. Ravel's assertion of Poe as his most important compositional mentor is not as facetious as first appears.

To conclude, let us take up the question posed at the outset: what constitutes Ravel's approach to formal process, as viewed through the foregoing analyses? Do any consistent principles emerge? My response draws on the striking consistency of metaphors employed by many commentators in describing Ravel's music. Debussy describes Ravel as "exceptionally gifted, but what irritates me is his posture as a 'trickster,' or better yet, as an enchanting fakir, who can make flowers spring up around a chair."[32] Jankélévitch brings up the paradox of Ravel's *poverty* of materials and *opulence* of result, saying, "Some aspects of this poverty, through energy and tour de force, become more opulent than opulence [including melodic, harmonic, and polyphonic poverty]."[33] And of course there is Roland-Manuel's aesthetics of imposture. These statements all speak to a fundamental dichotomy central to the character of Ravel's music. Applied to the nature of his formal process, this dichotomy becomes manifested as *minimal* compositional materials serving in *maximal* formal/structural contexts. This elementary maxim underpins the reharmonization of the simple opening theme in "Sleeping Beauty," the redeployment of material at the formal junctures of the elegant *Menuet,* and the syntactic circularity as question leading to psychologically devastating answer in "Gibet."

Notes

1. Vladimir Jankélévitch, *Ravel,* trans. Margaret Crosland (New York: Grove Press, 1959). More recently, Jean-Claude Teboul's study entitled *The Musical Language in the Piano Works of Ravel* comprises chapters on melody, harmony, counterpoint, rhythm and tonality, but not form.

2. Charles Rosen, "Where Ravel Ends and Debussy Begins," *Cahiers Debussy, nouvelle série* 3 (1979): 32. Arbie Orenstein, *Ravel: Man and Musician* (New York: Columbia University Press, 1975), 135 and *passim* and, in a more nuanced manner, Martha M. Hyde, "Neoclassic and Anachronistic Impulses in Twentieth-Century Music," *Music Theory Spectrum* 18, no. 2 (fall 1996): 206, both take similar positions.

3. Jankélévitch, *Ravel,* 68–69. See also Roland-Manuel, "Maurice Ravel ou l'esthétique de l'imposture," *La Revue Musicale* 6, no. 6 (April 1925): 16–21.

4. Alexis Roland-Manuel, *Maurice Ravel,* trans. Cynthia Jolly (London: Dennis Dobson, 1947), 28–29; original source February 1912, *Bulletin de la S.I.M.* The texture and layout resemble Chabrier's "Idylle" from the *Pièces pittoresques,* and Ravel also quotes the cadence from Chabrier's opera *Gwendoline.* See also Ortrud Kuhn-Schliess, *Klassizistische Tendenzen im Klavierwerk von Maurice Ravel* (Regensburg: Gustav Bosse, 1992), 108–11; and Roy Howat, "Ravel and the Piano," in *The Cambridge Companion to Ravel,* ed. Deborah Mawer (Cambridge: Cambridge University Press, 2000), 72–73.

5. Roland-Manuel, *Maurice Ravel,* 29.

6. Ortrud Kuhn-Schliess, *Klassizistische Tendenzen*, 115–16.

7. In Daniel Harrison, *Harmonic Function in Chromatic Music: A Renewed Dualist Theory and an Account of its Precedents* (Chicago: University of Chicago Press, 1994), 64 and passim, he shows an incipient version of superimposed functions in his "functional mixture." Of course jazz theory frequently constructs extended harmonies as the superimposition of two or more chords.

8. My use of the term "recontextualization" is consistent with that of Dora Hanninen, "A Theory of Recontextualization in Music: Analyzing Phenomenal Transformations of Repetition," *Music Theory Spectrum* 25, no. 1 (spring 2003): 59–98.

9. The other composers were Paul Dukas, Reynaldo Hahn, Vincent d'Indy and Charles Marie Widor; they were commissioned by the editor of the *Revue musicale de la S.I.M.* (Société internationale musique). See Ulrich Mahlert, "Gebannte Improvisation und Maskentanz: Die 'Haydn'-Stücke von Claude Debussy und Maurice Ravel," *Musik und Bildung* 19, no. 12 (Dec. 1987): 912.

10. Ibid., 913–16.

11. Arbie Orenstein, ed., *A Ravel Reader* (New York: Columbia University Press, 1990), 421–22.

12. Ulrich Mahlert, "Gebannte Improvisation und Maskentanz," 915. "In diesem Viertakter bereits wird greifbar, wie Ravel als Komponist des frühen 20. Jahrhunderts das Problem einer 'Hommage à Haydn' löst: Er inszeniert auf der 'Hörbühne' einen Maskentanz, in dem Archaisches, Klassisches und Modernes sich auf raffinierte Weise durchdringen und in einem komplexen Wechselspiel miteinander agieren." (The translation is my own.)

13. Ortrud Kuhn-Schliess, *Klassizistische Tendenzen*, 99, notes the implied retrograde.

14. Designating transformations of the motto follows normal serial practice: thus "H–A–Y–D–N" = P0, "N–D–Y–A–H" = R0, etc.

15. Indeed, Kuhn-Schliess, *Klassizistische Tendenzen*, 104–5, refers to mm. 39–41 as *bitonal*, albeit in the formal context of a retransition to the reprise. It is assuredly not bitonal, even in the loosest sense of the term.

16. Charles Rosen, "Where Ravel Ends and Debussy Begins," 35.

17. See John T. Wright, trans., *Louis "Aloysius" Bertrand's Gaspard de la nuit: fantasies in the manner of Rembrandt and Callot* (Lanham, MD: University Press of America, 1994): vii and passim.

18. See Jean Alexander, ed., *Affidavits of Genius: Edgar Allan Poe and the French Critics, 1847–1924* (Port Washington, NY: Kennikat Press, 1971), preface, ii; and Baudelaire (in Alexander), 97–98 and 122–25. From this volume, see Stephen Huebner, "Ravel's Poetics: Literary Currents, Classical Takes," chap. 1; and Barbara Kelly, "Re-Presenting Ravel: Artificiality and the Aesthetic of Imposture," chap. 2.

19. Orenstein, *A Ravel Reader*, 394, from an interview dated July 12, 1931.

20. The English translation is by Roger Nichols (1991), editor of the Peters Edition of *Gaspard de la nuit* (London and New York: Edition Peters, 1991).

21. Interestingly, "The Hour of the Sabbath" has the identical form of "Le gibet" comprising six short verses, the final one beginning "C'est ici le gibet!"—Here are the gallows

22. In its obsessive refrain and macabre subject matter, Bertrand's poem bears a strong resemblance to poems by Edgar Allan Poe (see "The Telltale Heart," "The Raven," etc.), a point undoubtedly not lost on Ravel, who by his own admission considered Poe his most important influence in aesthetics as well as the art of composition. See Gerald Larner, *Maurice Ravel* (London: Phaidon, 1996), 33.

23. See Peter Kaminsky, "Of Children, Princesses, Dreams and Isomorphisms: Text-Music Transformation in Ravel's Vocal Works," *Music Analysis* 19, no. 1 (2000): passim.

24. Roy Howat, "Ravel and the Piano," in Mawer, *The Cambridge Companion to Ravel,* 83, also cites the centrality of these elements.

25. Norma Doris Pohl, "*Gaspard de la nuit* by Maurice Ravel: A Theoretical and Performance Analysis" (PhD diss., Washington University, 1978), 45, notes accurately that thematic content flows from two cells. Her highly reductive perspective, however, does not adequately account for the recurrence of themes in different tonal and formal contexts, especially in relation to the unfolding of the poem.

26. See Jean-Philippe Rameau, *Treatise on Harmony,* trans. by Philip Gossett (New York: Dover, 1971), 71–73, on deceptive cadences.

27. I am designating the octatonic collection according to its first two pitch classes; the complete scale would be G–G♯–A♯–B–C♯–D–E–F.

28. The association between octatonic and symmetrical collections in general and the supernatural is discussed by Elliott Antokoletz, *Musical Symbolism in the Operas of Debussy and Bartók: Trauma, Gender, and the Unfolding of the Unconscious* (Oxford: Oxford University Press, 2004), 56–57, and by Richard Taruskin, "Chernomor to Kashchei: Harmonic Sorcery; or, Stravinsky's 'Angle,'" *Journal of the American Musicological Society* 38, no. 1 (Spring 1985): 103.

29. The final cadence of Ravel's "Ondine" features the same motion (in C♯ major); see mm. 88–89.

30. Howat, "Ravel and the Piano," 84, cites the centrality of F♭ within the tonal argument but does not discuss its resolution.

31. Edgar Allan Poe, *The Raven: with The Philosophy of Composition* (Boston: Northeastern University Press, 1986), 26–27 and 35.

32. Orenstein, *A Ravel Reader,* 87, from a letter from Debussy to musicologist and critic Louis Laloy.

33. Jankélévitch, *Ravel,* 69–70.

Chapter Five

Repetition as Musical Motion in Ravel's Piano Writing

Daphne Leong and David Korevaar

Ravel use des formes classiques, comme le jongleur des balles, des plumes, des éventails, des mille objets qui volent entre ses doigts.

[Ravel uses classical forms as the juggler uses balls, feathers, fans, the thousand objects that fly between his fingers.]

André Suarès

In Ravel's writing for the piano, the tactile dimension influences and sometimes determines aspects of musical structure. We consider physical motions—the gestures of the performer—as a dimension of musical structure in Ravel's piano-centered writing, and demonstrate how the conjunction of physical and musical features produces distinctive units, which, repeated and varied, create characteristic qualities of musical motion.[1]

Consider the opening of *Jeux d'eau* (ex. 5.1), with its ascending right-hand arpeggiation <D♯–G♯–D♯–F♯> requiring the fingering <1, 2, 4, 5>—a figure that is inspired in part by the way the hand lies on the keyboard.[2] This figure, set in motion by the rolling of the hand over the black keys, is immediately extended by retrograde (the return down the opening arpeggio), and then by a neighboring figure in halved note values (down a step in thirty-second notes, retaining the G♯ as the second-finger pivot). The initial four-note figure and its transformations combine to form ever-larger units, eventually creating, in this example, half-measure, then (by literal repetition) one-measure units, the third measure roughly sequencing the first up a fourth.

Example 5.1. *Jeux d'eau*, mm. 1–3

While certain aspects of the figure remain fixed in the first half measure (the contour and fingering of the four-note arpeggio), others change (the neighboring pitches and rhythmic diminution of the thirty-second-note arpeggio, the I–IV harmonic oscillation of the left-hand accompaniment). This varied repetition, animated by the choreographic arc of the pianist's hands and by the harmonic rhythm ♩., ♪, produces musical motion. The quality of the motion is not determined by the passage's basic pitch-rhythmic-physical structure: played without pedal and with light clear articulation, the excerpt sounds like a wind-up music box,[3] but played according to Ravel's indications (slurs, *1 corde,* and the pedaling implied by these markings and the piece's title),[4] it expresses subtle and fluid motion. It is the "dance of the performer"—the necessary rhythmic swing, the pedal clarifying the harmonic rhythm—that turns mechanical activity into dynamic waves, the music a metaphor for a fountain, itself a mechanical creation emulating nature.

This example presents syntactic *units* defined musically and physically, in terms of pitch-rhythmic structure and performed gesture. Our concern is to examine how the structure, repetition, and variation of such units create distinctive qualities of motion in Ravel's writing for the piano. We will show (1) how the characteristics and treatment of the units tend toward "mechanical" or "dance-like" types of motion; and (2) how the combination of these two types of motion characterizes particular pieces, wherein the composer, in tandem with the performer, creates, animates, and choreographs musical motion.

To do so we will draw upon Lawrence Zbikowski's recent work on categorization and conceptual blending. A category is a cognitive construct that groups similar items into a class. We will work with Zbikowski's "Type I" categories, in which membership in a category is graded according to conformance to a standard of "typicality" derived from existing members of the category.[5] For our units, this standard is based on some set of musico-physical characteristics in the domains of pitch, rhythm, and/or physical gesture.[6] For this type of category, boundaries are fuzzy, and category definition can shift over time depending on context, function of the category, and related factors.[7]

Our units range in size from the single note to the musical figure, motive, theme, and beyond. Essential to all of our units is the characteristic of being discrete and aurally recognizable. The units form hierarchies in which each level relates by inclusion to the next;[8] the primary level in our discussion will be that of the musico-physical *figure,* a unit larger than that of the single note that contains no meaningful intermediate units (for example, the first four notes in the right hand of *Jeux d'eau*). This level corresponds roughly to the "basic level" of category theory, that level which optimizes cognitive efficiency and informativeness.[9]

To evaluate how the features and treatment of units resemble either mechanical or dance-like motion, we call upon the notion of *conceptual blending,* which Zbikowski defines as "a dynamic process of meaning construction" in which "structure from two correlated input spaces is projected into a third, blended space."[10] We present five basic interrelated conceptual blends, on three different levels, from general to specific: (1) musical motion, (2) mechanical motion and dance-like motion, and (3) object and dance.

Musical motion is a generic conceptual blend of physical motion and musical structure. In the physical domain, motion occurs when an entity changes location over time, resulting from some expenditure of energy. In the musical arena, motion occurs when some parameter is held constant while others change, resulting from the action of some agent. For instance, in the *Jeux d'eau* passage, the initial one-measure unit moves upward by a fourth to the third measure: melodic contour, rhythmic structure, harmonic relations, and physical gesture remain largely the same, but change their pitch "location" to a fourth higher; the literal agent is the performing pianist.

The type of musical motion depends on the traits and treatment of the unit in question. For our discussion of Ravel's works, we present two specific types of musical motion—mechanical motion and dance-like motion—dependent respectively on two particular types of units—musical object and dance.

Mechanical motion involves units that resemble physical objects. Physical objects are discrete entities with relatively fixed boundaries; they can be viewed from multiple perspectives but are themselves inanimate. *Musical objects* are relatively discrete pitch-rhythmic entities with clearly defined temporal boundaries and proportions; multiple musical "perspectives" can be gained by slight alterations or additions to the basic pitch-rhythmic core. The inanimate nature of musical objects is generally represented by static harmonic and melodic structure.[11]

Mechanical motion in Ravel's music tends to resemble small-scale mechanical motion in the physical world, exemplified by the miniature toys and mechanisms of which the composer was so fond.[12] Such motion is characterized by regular repetition on a small physical scale, and translates musically into repetition accompanied by fast activity (usually at the subpulse level) and often, submetric regularity. Since mechanical motion involves musical objects, it tends to preserve the essential pitch-rhythmic features of these objects, and to repeat them as whole units, frequently creating hypermetric regularity. The opening passage of *Jeux d'eau* thus resembles mechanical motion, as we have already noted, in imitation of nature.

Dance-like motion involves units that reflect dance's blend of music and physical motions; thus a *musical dance unit* borrows from both the musical and the physical domains. It may incorporate the rhythmic-melodic-harmonic patterns and metric regularity (and often hypermetric irregularity) of particular dance musics (for example, waltz, habanera, forlane) and may translate physical dance motions into analogous motions of the pianist's limbs, into melodic contours, or into harmonic progressions.[13] Dance plays a central role in Ravel's oeuvre; as Deborah Mawer writes, "[in Ravel's music] dance is ubiquitous and its connection to physical movement, as choreography, inherent."[14]

In the works we analyze, dance-like motion resembles physical and natural motions in that, while core units are present, they are linked in a much more fluid and flexible manner than the objects of mechanical motion. Thus, repetition of dance units may be more elastic, stretching or shrinking temporal dimensions, significantly altering pitch relationships, changing affect, and so on.

In short, mechanical motion animates musical objects, while dance-like motion choreographs musical dance units. Though the sense of motion in both results from the varied repetition of units, the resulting hierarchies are of distinctive types. The structure of pieces governed by mechanical motion resembles a bottom-up assembly of components; components on each level are contained within those on the next level. That of pieces characterized by dance-like motion seems motivated by a top-down force.[15]

Yet as illustrated by the *Jeux d'eau* example, the two types of motion rarely occur independently in Ravel's music. While one or the other usually predominates, mechanical motion is usually tinged with dance-like motion, and vice versa; the particular blend of the mechanical and dance-like produces many different qualities of motion, from the clockwork of the last movement of the Piano Concerto in G Major to the spinning of the mysterious dwarf in "Scarbo."

Because of this blend of motion types, as well as Ravel's love of intricate detail and elegant craftsmanship, we will argue that for Ravel, the small levels—those of the figure and its neighboring levels—are always of prime importance in the generation of musical motion. Thus in this chapter we will take a bottom-up hierarchical approach, examining first repeated notes, then repeated figures, motives, and themes, and repeated layers. We will discuss (1) the repeated notes of the Toccata from *Le tombeau de Couperin* and the alternating-hands figures of the finale of the G-Major Piano Concerto; (2) the figures and motives of "Noctuelles" and "Une barque sur l'océan" from *Miroirs;* and (3) the layering of figures and themes in the second movement of the G-Major Piano Concerto. We will then explore Ravel's use of all of these types of units in a complete movement, "Scarbo" from *Gaspard de la nuit.*

Mechanical Motion

Repeated notes make a logical starting point for this discussion of Ravelian units. They occur throughout Ravel's oeuvre and take multiple forms. Heard slowly, as in "Oiseaux tristes" or "Le gibet," they are evocative of melancholy or horror; at high speed, as in the Toccata from *Le tombeau,* they are intrinsically virtuosic and physical (usually requiring a rapid change of fingers on the piano).[16] As building blocks for musical development, repeated notes are initially the most mechanical of units, although, as we shall see, they have the potential to dance as well.

The Toccata from *Le tombeau de Couperin* ranks among the most technically difficult piano works ever written (ex. 5.2). Ravel here extends the initial musical object—four sixteenth-note Es, the first played with the left hand, the next three with the right—into a marvelous mechanism. As can be seen in the example, the initial pitch-rhythmic core undergoes slight alterations and additions; in measures 3–4, for example, upper and lower neighbors (F♯ and D) enter, the alternating-hand distribution changes from 1 + 3 to 2 + 2 sixteenths, and the registral space expands from E to the surrounding octave via clockwork-like eighth-note Bs in alternating octaves. It is as if the original object had been rotated to exhibit more facets. Another "rotation" occurs in measures 5–8, featuring a new rhythm (quarter-eighth-eighth) and an augmentation of the neighbor-tone idea (D–E).

Example 5.2. Toccata, mm. 1–10

The piece's perpetual sixteenth-note motion in quarter-note pulses strongly suggests the mechanical, as does the constant presence of the opening object implied by this perpetual motion. The original repeated-note object also reappears in its most basic form to delineate the sonata-form structure of the piece (for example, the F♯s beginning in m. 42 as a transition to the second theme, and the five measures of Bs beginning at m. 81 as a transition to the development).[17]

Yet the physical feel of this passage introduces another element: while playing the initial repeated notes requires a kind of rotation of the hand in one place, the motion in measures 3–4 is dance-like, with the hands exchanging symmetrical gestures with each other. The new rhythm in measures 5–8 further animates the dance of the hands. The physical techniques of the repeated notes, alternating hands, and implied three-hand writing evident in these opening measures are intrinsic to the nature of the piece; the effect of the piece in performance depends on the player's ability to continue executing these intensely physical figures for its duration.

In the G-Major Piano Concerto, Ravel set out to create the effect of virtuoso display through technical tricks; his original goal, sadly unrealized because of his declining health, was to compose a work that he would be able to play himself.[18] The soloist's opening of the last movement (ex. 5.3) displays a musico-physical figure whose treatment exemplifies many of the characteristics of mechanical motion. Articulated by an alternating-hand technique, the initial figure of four sixteenths is executed with each hand in a single position; the left-hand fingering is 5–2, 3–1, and the right-hand fingering is 1–4, 2–5. The shape of the piano keyboard facilitates the choreography of the overlapping hands, with the C♯ on the third sixteenth and the F♯ on the fourth. The melodic content is created out of the middle notes, as is clear from Ravel's beaming, while the alternating hands imply a clearly articulated execution as a by-product of the technique.[19]

Example 5.3. G-major Piano Concerto, III, mm. 5–8

As in the Toccata, the basic figure is ubiquitous, and gives rise to fast regular rhythmic activity. The entire movement is built around this mechanical-technical trope. Thus, for example, the E♭-clarinet and piccolo licks at rehearsal 1 and 2 prefigure the piano's version of that material at the point of recapitulation, rehearsal 20.[20] The pianist, in playing this material, splits it once again between the two hands. The second theme (rehearsal 7 in the exposition) is also first given by the orchestra; it is only the piano entrance at rehearsal 9 that shows the alternating-hands origin of this idea. Furthermore, the effect of alternating hands is to make two hands sound as one—a reversal of the act of imposture in Ravel's own contemporaneous Piano Concerto for the Left Hand, where one hand masquerades as two.[21]

The Dance of Nature:
Evoking the Organic through the Mechanical

The line between mechanical and dance-like motion is hard to limn precisely. As we have seen, the essentially mechanistic opening of *Jeux d'eau* gives rise to wave-like motion; the dance of the hands in the Toccata and the finale of the G-Major Concerto animate initially mechanical musical units. In his more descriptive piano works, including especially *Miroirs* and *Gaspard de la nuit*, Ravel evokes the natural world by juxtaposing and subtly blending both kinds of motion.

The initial impulse in "Noctuelles" from *Miroirs* (ex. 5.4) is, once again, essentially mechanical in its use of the pianist's hands. However, the consequence of this mechanical motion is an organic-seeming physical metaphor for the flight of the creatures of the title.[22] The opening two sixteenth notes exploit the natural division between the thumb and the rest of the hand, with the thumb on a white note and the second and another finger on black notes; the resulting motion seems analogous to the fluttering of wings—be they of moths, owlets, or bats. This opening figure is repeated a total of five times at various pitch levels in the first measure. The physically inspired alternation of white and black notes creates a chromatic mixture in the right hand that is effectively contrasted by the whole-tone content of the left. Measures 4 and 5 present a new and more diatonic (A major) pitch manifestation of the same choreography, with further developments interpolated throughout measures 63–84. It is easy for a pianist to imagine this right-hand figuration divided between the hands (as at the beginning of Liszt's *Totentanz*). Ravel entertains that very idea by way of a coda in "Noctuelles" (ex. 5.5), raising the possibility that the opening figure is a kind of imposture, substituting the fluttering dance of the right hand for a passage more technically suited to left and right hands in alternation.[23]

Example 5.4. "Noctuelles," right hand, m. 1

The opening measures of "Une barque sur l'océan" from *Miroirs* present a repeating idea split between the hands, whose complex choreography helps evoke the title subject (ex. 5.6). Ravel's initial materials are limited to the minor-third pairs {F♯, A} and {C♯, E}. The left-hand pattern is thoroughly pianistic, involving a rolling motion over <F♯, C♯, E, A>, an extension of that motion up a second octave, and a return to the lower part of the pattern,

Example 5.5. "Noctuelles," mm. 126–28

rolling over it twice. The physical action of playing this arpeggio creates a large-scale rhythmic articulation of <♩, ♪, ♪,> literally executed by the left-hand fifth finger on the lowest pitch. There is a swing and dance to the motion, animating material that is harmonically static and that repeats itself exactly in every measure.

Example 5.6. "Une barque sur l'océan," m. 1

The hands deal with the initial note pairs in mirror motion to one another. Where the left-hand pattern has {F♯, A} outside of {C♯, E} first ascending and then descending, the right hand sets descending <E, C♯> followed by ascending <C♯, E> an octave below around a descending <A, F♯> with a passing G♯ between. The rhythm of the right hand, directly and clearly expressed, reverses the traditional habanera pattern <triplet, duplet> into <duplet, triplet>, with the middlemost note tied across between the beats.[24] Thus animated and combined, the left-hand arpeggio and the right-hand dance rhythm blend mechanical motion (associated with static harmony and repeated figuration) and dance-like motion (through flexible rhythm and the habanera trope), evoking musical waves.[25]

Layering

Repeated figures lead naturally (in the case of Ravel's music especially) to contrapuntal layering—the combination of different musical strands. By the end of his creative life—the time of the two concertos—Ravel had extended layering to a level of dissonance and rhythmic sophistication that shows not only his own expanding craft but also the liberating influences of Stravinsky, Schoenberg, and jazz (by way of Gershwin).[26] Ravel's complimentary review of

Stravinsky's *Le rossignol,* a work based on the story of a mechanical nightingale, is suggestive. He writes, "I am referring to this absolute contrapuntal liberty, this audacious independence of themes, rhythms, and harmonies, whose combination, thanks to one of the rarest of musical sensibilities, offers us such a fascinating ensemble."[27] Here Ravel celebrates his friend's ability to combine threads of apparently mechanical motion (represented by the nightingale of the title) into a simulacrum of the organic—a more sophisticated version of the process described above in *Jeux d'eau.*

The slow movement of the G-Major Piano Concerto presents the accumulation of layers derived originally from dance-like units, resulting in mechanical motion of surprising complexity. Beginning with two primary layers—a waltz bass and a sarabande-like melody—Ravel successively increases complexity through acceleration, modal clashes, metric dissonance and rhythmic transformations, and cumulative layering. Example 5.7 shows the two primary layers. The moderate waltz bass in $\frac{3}{8}$ meter, introduced by the pianist's left hand, persists throughout the movement, generally in the background. The adagio sarabande-like melody in $\frac{3}{4}$ meter in the pianist's right hand creates a pervasive hemiola effect against the left.

Example 5.7. Opening of G-major Piano Concerto, II

The first increase in complexity comes at rehearsal 2 (ex. 5.8), with modal clashes between melody and accompaniment, and metric and rhythmic development in melody and bass. The pianist's right hand has an oscillating triadic figure followed by a descending scalar pattern, initially just two notes, then expanded to four notes, articulating C♯ natural minor against the left hand's C♯ melodic minor. In contrast to the opening, the melody here features a three-sixteenth-note anacrusis; its main surface pulses have sped up from the sarabande's quarter and eighth notes to eighth and sixteenth notes. The waltz bass introduces a new emphasis on the third quarter note of the measure, undercutting the pervasive $\frac{6}{8}$ ($\frac{3}{8} + \frac{3}{8}$) pattern. From rehearsal 2 to rehearsal 4, the entire passage unfolds an aab form, in which the four-measure phrase shown in example 5.8 is first sequenced down from C♯ minor to B minor, then followed by a culminating third four-measure phrase in D major. This closing phrase temporarily releases tension, with a return to the texture, rhythm, and melodic smoothness of the opening of the movement, and a consonant harmonic progression leading to a perfect authentic cadence.

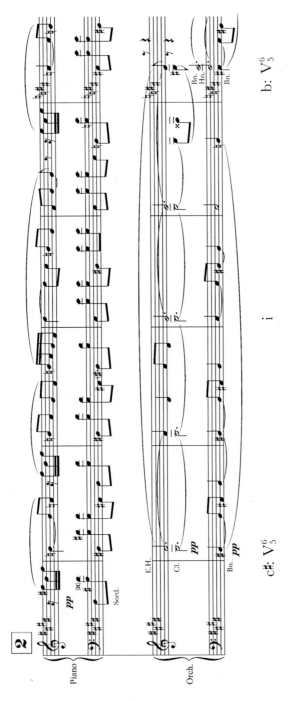

Example 5.8. G-major Piano Concerto, II, rehearsal 2

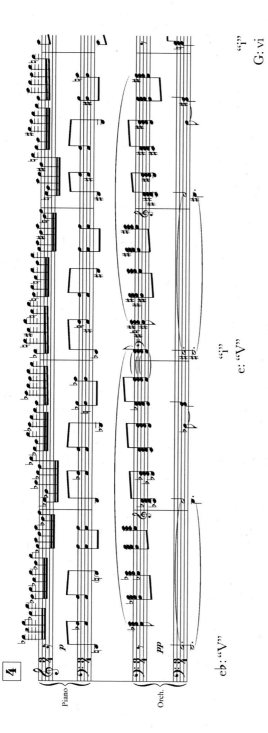

Example 5.9. G-major Piano Concerto, II, rehearsal 4

Immediately following this cadence (ex. 5.9), complexity continues to increase, as the right-hand figure of rehearsal 2 speeds up to new surface pulses of triplet eighth and triplet sixteenth notes (still over the waltz bass). Meanwhile the orchestra adds a new layer of ascending scales in parallel triads in E♭ major, in opposition to the E♭ minor mixed modes of the piano. There are only three layers operating here—the left-hand waltz pattern and orchestral bass, the right-hand melodic figuration, and the ascending triads—but Ravel dynamically opposes them, with the ascending triads of the orchestra grinding against the descending broken arpeggios and scale patterns of the piano's right hand.

The sense of compression created by the right hand's acceleration is heightened by formal compression: the 4 + 4 + 4 measure structure of the immediately preceding aab passage is shortened to 2 + 2 + 4 measures, with overlaps occurring at phrase boundaries. The three phrases now move from E♭ minor in the first phrase, sequenced to E minor in the second, concluding with G major in the third. (The dominant-tonic progression within each of the first two original four-measure phrases now occurs just at the downbeat overlap between the shortened two-measure phrases, the tonic ending the preceding phrase becoming the dominant for the following phrase.) The melodic structure now begins *after* the beat, rather than before it, and this afterbeat grouping facilitates the phrase overlaps. (While the final phrase is four measures, its afterbeat melodic structure forces Ravel to condense the first two measures of the corresponding four-measure phrase of rehearsal 3.)

At rehearsal 5 the opposition of descending scales in eighth-note triplets in the piano with the inexorably ascending eighth-note scales in the orchestra culminates in the climax of the movement (labeled below the score in example 5.10). Just before the climax, the piano's right-hand figuration again speeds up its surface pulses, doubling them to triplet sixteenths and triplet thirty-second notes. The climax—underlined by the entrance of the entire orchestra—reaches a level of dissonance startling in this unassuming movement. Here the bass line splits into two layers, suspending the lower G while simultaneously also moving it up to G♯. The opposition of G and G♯ stands in for the superimposition of E minor (the harmony that precedes the bass line's split) and the soon-to-come key of E major (represented here by G-sharp minor triads), an effect that continues the modal mixture begun at rehearsal 2.

Each step in the process leading to the climax increases tension through accumulating rhythmic, harmonic, and melodic complexity, as well as through the addition of new layers of material. Each of the movement's primary layers—the ubiquitous waltz bass (sometimes taking on $\frac{3}{4}$ meter characteristics, rather than $\frac{3}{8}$), the sarabande-like melody in $\frac{3}{4}$, the right-hand arpeggiation and scale passages articulating accelerating pulse levels,[28] the orchestra's parallel triads and ascending scales—retains its distinctive identity even through metric or modal shifts. Furthermore, each tends to occupy its own harmonic plane,

Example 5.10. G-major Piano Concerto, II, 6 mm. before rehearsal 6

and even, within sections, its own metric plane. Within these layers, constant repetition of figures generates regularity on multiple metric levels. Thus, though beginning with the dance-like figures of waltz and sarabande, the movement transforms them into a kind of infernal musical mechanism.

Immediately after the climax, the pianist's right hand returns to its surface triplet eighth- and sixteenth-note pulses (1 measure before rehearsal 6), and then, at rehearsal 6, reaccelerates to sixteenth- and thirty-second-note pulses. Despite the speed of this motion—a rate of activity superseded only by the two measures of the climax—the effect is one of an elegant dance, articulating a basic contour that repeats itself every two measures. At the same time, the English horn reintroduces the opening sarabande-like theme, and the return of this theme—together with the return of E major, consonant harmony, a *piano* dynamic, and more transparent texture—resolves the tension of the climax. Thus musical figures combine in the layering process of the movement, leading to apparent chaos; then, with a scraping of gears, they resolve into a quietly purring mechanism—like the mechanical nightingale of Stravinsky's opera.

Form as Motion

We now examine musical motion in a complete movement, "Scarbo" from *Gaspard de la nuit*.[29] We have already made the point that Ravel combines mechanical and dance-like types of motion in distinctive ways in different pieces. In the slow movement of the G-Major Piano Concerto, the layering of dance-derived units creates a primarily mechanical quality of motion. In "Scarbo's" depiction of a pirouetting dwarf, by contrast, musico-physical figures combine and transform into ever-larger units to express a largely dance-like quality of motion.

Our discussion of "Scarbo" begins with its text. Ravel chose three poems from Aloysius Bertrand's collection of sixty-six prose poems *Gaspard de la nuit: Fantaisies à la manière de Rembrandt et de Callot* as the basis for his musical *Gaspard de la nuit: Trois poèmes pour piano d'après Aloysius Bertrand*. In the original edition of Ravel's *Gaspard*, each movement is preceded by its poem,[30] and our translation of Bertrand's "Scarbo" and its epigraph is shown below.

SCARBO

> He looked under the bed, in the
> fireplace, in the chest;—no one. He
> could not understand how he had
> entered, or how he had escaped.
> HOFFMANN.—*Contes nocturnes.*

Oh! how many times have I heard and seen him, Scarbo, when at midnight the moon shines in the sky like a silver coin on an azure banner sown with golden bees!

How many times have I heard his laughter buzzing in the shadows of my alcove, and his nails rasping on the silk of my bed curtains!

How many times have I seen him descend to the floor, pirouette on one foot and roll around the room like the spindle fallen from a sorceress's distaff!

Did I believe him to have vanished? the dwarf would grow between the moon and me like the spire of a gothic cathedral, a little golden bell swinging from his pointed cap!

But soon his body would turn blue, translucent as the wax of a candle, his face would pale like the wax of a candle-end,—and suddenly he would go out.

The dwarf Scarbo is a fantastic and faintly malevolent being, unexpectedly appearing and disappearing, rapidly changing in size and color, constantly active and full of motion. His motion is described in both anthropomorphic and object-like terms: rasping nails, pirouetting on one foot, rolling spindle, expanding cathedral spire, swinging bell, flickering candle. The poem itself exhibits a kind of circularity, evidenced in the statement "how many times . . ." stated thrice. The dwarf's continually changing manifestations are colored, literally, by the silver, blue, and gold of the moon, midnight sky, and stars, the golden bell of the gothic cathedral, and the translucent blue of an expiring candle.

Without claiming literal correspondence between the sequential events in the poem and those of the music, we will show how Ravel's use of musico-physical figures expresses the aspects of the poem described above, and particularly how it creates musical motion of both dance-like and mechanical kinds, embodying the antics of the dwarf Scarbo. We begin with two central figures, show how they transform into four themes, and demonstrate how these themes unfold in three formal sections, all governed by the motivating force of Scarbo.

The movement grows from two basic figures labeled p and q in example 5.11. Implying a G-sharp-minor tonality, the two figures complement one another: both are based first on semitone neighbors, and second on the interval of the fifth and its inversion the fourth. Figure p, muted, deep in the bass, sounds a mysterious three-note motive in which F$\times$ acts as lower neighbor to G$\sharp$ which rises a fifth to D$\sharp$. Cut off by a rest, this D$\sharp$, dominant of G$\sharp$, is picked up an octave higher by q where it vibrates in the left hand, surrounded musically by its upper and lower semitone neighbors E and C$\times$ and physically by the fact that both of these neighbors are played by the splayed right-hand thumb. The doubling of the E up an octave at the top of the right-hand chord draws out its importance, and emphasizes the symmetry of the p and q figures: F$\times$ lower neighbor to G$\sharp$ answered by E upper neighbor to D$\sharp$, the ascending fifth to D$\sharp$ in measure 1 answered by the falling fourth to B in measure 5, all elaborating G$\sharp$ minor. The close and intertwined hand positions, the muted dynamics dwindling to rests, and the soft accents beginning both p and q—on the downbeat in the first case and on the second beat in the second—contribute to the suspense of these opening measures.

Appropriate to the mysterious appearances of the dwarf, the pairing of figures p and q appears three times in this introductory section, first as shown in example 5.11, then again with q's right-hand chords an octave lower, and finally in an accelerating traversal of the keyboard from bottom to top, an alternating-hand crescendo of the p figure and p and q sonorities.[31] This dramatic growth in dynamic, register, and tempo brings us to the movement's primary tempo, *Vif,* and its first complete theme. Theme i (for introduction), shown in example 5.12, expands figures p and q. Its opening measures stretch p's contour to embrace an octave from D$\sharp$ to D$\sharp$ before falling through C$\sharp$ to B to regain p's original intervallic span. This gesture is then completed by melodic motion

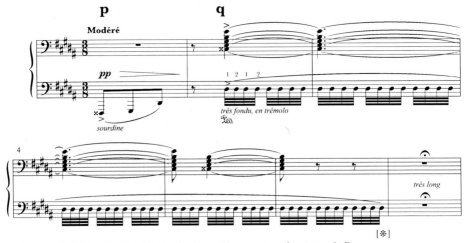

Example 5.11. "Scarbo," Introduction, Figures p and q, mm. 1–7

Example 5.12. "Scarbo," Introduction, Theme i, mm. 32–45

through two step-related fourths <G♯, D♯> and <E, A>. Measures 37–44 extend figure q by restating its melodic falling fourth and its repeated-note accompaniment, now expanded from single notes to arpeggiated chords.

The transformation of figure p into the opening of Theme i creates waves of pitch motion in both hands, and implied hemiolas in the right hand. These and other features are strongly suggestive of waltz topics used by Ravel in other pieces (compare the theme to the oboe solo at rehearsal 18 in *La valse*). Note the metric regularity articulated by the left-hand pitch contours, the cutting across these bounds by the right-hand hemiolas, the hypermetric irregularity, and the sense of swirling motion created by these rhythmic features, the waves of pitch motion, and the physical gestures required to realize these waves.

Example 5.13. "Scarbo," Exposition, Theme 1a, mm. 51–57

The particular quality of motion engendered by the theme also results from its harmonic basis. The arrival of D♯ major harmony (dominant of G♯) in measure 32 resolves the suspense of the cadential $^6_4$ implicit in all of the preceding material, and provides the impetus for Theme i's waltz-like motion by recontextualizing the elements of p incorporated here. Theme i exchanges p's metric placement of consonance and dissonance: the downbeat is now consonant, allowing for the grounding of the waltz-like motion, and the *second beat* is now the neighbor note, here a complete neighbor surrounded by (octave-displaced) D♯. Significantly, this use of the pitch classes D♯ and E translates q's *harmonic* clash into a *melodic* line.

From measure 32 to measure 50, the type of motion gradually changes to a more mechanical one, as the left-hand arpeggiation decreases in range and duration from two measures (m. 32) to one measure (m. 37), quarter notes (m. 41), and finally eighth notes (m. 45). The static harmony, the small size of the repeated figures, and (from m. 37) the basic hypermetric regularity contribute to this mechanical quality.[32] The entire passage takes place over a <D♯, C♯, B> bass descent (arriving at B in m. 51), related to the <D♯, C♯, B> descent in the head motive of Theme i (m. 33), as well as to the <D♯, B> articulated by the final melodic notes of figures p and q respectively.

Just as the dwarf Scarbo is ever-elusive, so too his musical portrayal shifts between two tonics, G♯ minor and its relative major B. The arrival at B in measure 51 (ex. 5.13) announces the beginning of the exposition proper and the movement's true tonic. The repeating bass figure with its tonic pedal B continues the mechanical motion, while also recasting an identifying pitch feature of the opening. The oscillating {F, G} neighbors an absent F♯ (dominant of B),[33] just as in figure q, {D, E} ({C×, E}) surrounded D♯ (dominant of G♯); the correspondence between these two-note pairs {F, G} and {D, E} becomes explicit in measures 55–56.

The main figure of Theme 1a enters in measure 52, and it incorporates the repeated D♯s and neighbor-note elements of the opening, influenced by the shape taken by these features in Theme i. The <D♯, D♯, D♯, C♯, D♯> figure condenses and inverts the upper-neighbor figure of Theme i, retaining its downbeat location, and then answers this figure (as did Theme i) with a pair of stepwise-related melodic fourths. The perpetual-motion sixteenth notes, repetition of small figures in both hands, small range and close hand position,

Example 5.14. "Scarbo," Exposition, Theme 1b, mm. 94–98

Example 5.15. "Scarbo," Exposition, Theme 2, mm. 121–24

un peu marqué and *staccato* markings, and harmonic stasis all contribute to the mechanical quality of the motion. At the same time, certain physical and musical attributes also suggest the dance (a reference that will be realized more strongly in Theme 1b). That is, Theme 1a's separation into primary melodic material all on the *black* keys and accompanimental material all on the *white* keys lends the theme a physical bounce;[34] registral crossovers (mm. 55–56) require the left hand to leap over the right; the hairpin dynamic, pitch wave, and associated physical motion in measure 54 create a miniature surge—all aspects that suggest an undercurrent of dance.

As shown in example 5.14, Theme 1b, Theme 1a's alter ego, returns to D♯ (dominant of G♯ minor), and expands Theme 1a's primary figure directionally, intervallically, and temporally. The neighbor motion now extends both up and down (having appeared each way in preceding Themes i and 1a), spans a third with passing motion rather than a second, and covers two measures rather than one. (The neighbor-note origin of this right-hand theme is clarified by the upper voice of the accompanying left hand.) More significantly for the theme's character, it accentuates beat two rather than beat one, suggesting the flamenco (a flavor that becomes much more prominent when this theme reappears in the development at m. 256).[35] "Wedge" staccato markings and tight overlapping hand positions provide a physical sense of the theme's energy.

As can be seen from the foregoing, figures p and q and Themes i, 1a, and 1b evidence a cumulative development; all three themes grow from p and q, each successive theme taking on and transforming traits of the preceding themes.

We detail just one additional way in which this successive shape-shifting happens. The movement's repeated-note figure contains change in the form of the pianist's finger changes on alternating notes. From p and q through to Theme 1b, Ravel merely steps up the change: repeated pitches (figure q), semitone neighbor (Theme i), whole-tone neighbor (Theme 1a), and minor-third upper and lower "neighbors" (Theme 1b)—all centered on D♯.

Theme 2, the first theme in which D♯ does not play a primary role, also differs from Themes i, 1a, and 1b in its succinctness. As shown in example 5.15, its primary figure comprises only two chords. This figure appropriates the {B, F, G} of Theme 1a's accompanying ostinato (see ex. 5.13) and turns it into its outer voices: B, E♯, and Fˣ, with the melodic E♯ and Fˣ occurring on the second and third sixteenths of the measure, just as they did in measure 51. The first chord's inner voices slide down a semitone to those of the second chord, although the physical semitone motion, generally from white to black key, steps *upwards* in finger height, and this white-to-black key step-up mirrors the semitone rise of figure p. As with figure q, Theme 2's sustained chord is animated by repeated notes (here in broken octaves), featuring the same pitch, E, that was so prominent in q. The diaphanous fabric of these Es and the complete octatonic collection (articulated by the combination of Theme 2's second chord, the repeated Es, and the bass B of the first chord) create an uncanny air, abetted by the markings *sourdine* and *très fondu*, further evidence of the theme's connection to p and q. (As Theme 2 unfolds, it also incorporates the complete neighbor-note element found in Themes i, 1a, and 1b; see mm. 131–33.)

Thus "Scarbo's" opening figures p and q successively take on four incarnations in the work's four themes i, 1a, 1b, and 2. Ravel's choreography of these figures and themes in turn creates a thematic cycle, that of the sonata-form movement's introduction and exposition, shown in example 5.16a.[36] In the following we will show how this thematic cycle itself recurs, transformed, in the development and in the recapitulation,[37] and thus how varied repetition on the expanding levels of figure, theme, formal section, and movement as a whole express the dwarf's continual motion and changing shapes. (In example 5.16a themes in parentheses are interjections or fragments; themes in italics are augmentations; theme i acts as a boundary marker.[38])

Example 5.17 diagrams the development. The themes are listed across the top of the example. Just below this, the line labeled "model/copy" shows that each theme expresses a version of the classical development technique "model-copy(-fragments)," where the "model" (m) is the first statement of material, the "copy" or "copies" (c) its sequential restatement or restatements, and the "fragments" (c'), where present, shortened versions of sequential restatements.[39] An extension (x) uses preceding motivic material.

As diagrammed in example 5.17a, Theme 1a states a model with F♯-major harmony, then its copy with C♯-major harmony, in a pattern of ascending fifths that brings us to the G♯-major harmony of Theme 1b. Theme 1b unfolds in

(a) Thematic Layout

Section:	Introduction		Exposition					Development				
Measure:	1	32	51	94	110	121		214	256	314	366	386
Theme:	p,q	i	1a	1b	i	2		1a	1b (1a, 2)	i/1b (2) (1a)	2 (1)	i

Theme 1 area

Section:	Recapitulation Introduction		Recapitulation proper		Conclusion		
Measure:	395		430	477	580	592	616
Theme:	p,q		1a	2	i (2)	1a (2)	p/q

(b) Formal Reinterpretation in the Recapitulation

Section:	Introduction		Exposition			
Measure:	1	32	51	94	110	121
Theme:	p,q	i	1a	1b	i	2

Theme 1 area

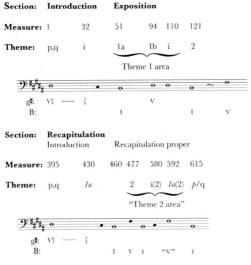

Section:	Recapitulation Introduction		Recapitulation proper				
Measure:	395	430	460	477	580	592	615
Theme:	p,q	1a	2	i(2)	1a(2)	p/q	

"Theme 2 area"

Example 5.16. "Scarbo," Form (parentheses indicate interjections or fragments, italics indicate augmentation)

two parts, set off by interjections of Themes 1a and 2. In the first part (mm. 256–76) the theme is stated twice over G♯-major harmony, then once over F♯ as the dominant of B minor. Fragments of Themes 1a and 2 then occur in B minor. In the second part (mm. 277–313) Theme 1b occurs first twice over G-major harmony, with B in the bass, then twice over E-major harmony, with G♯ in the bass. A shortened version of these statements then occurs over an A♯ dominant $\frac{4}{2}$ (notated in the score as B♭ $\frac{4}{2}$), continuing the preceding G♯

Example 5.17. "Scarbo," Development, Thematic and Harmonic Structure (themes in parentheses are interjections or fragments, themes in italics are augmentations; m = model, c = copy, c' = shortened copy, x = extension)

bass. Hence the entire Theme 1b area (mm. 256–313) prolongs the bass G♯, acting as neighbor to the larger-scale F♯.[40]

Theme i brings back the bass F♯, initially underlying a D♯ minor harmony that resolves the preceding A♯$^4_2$ (B♭$^4_2$). The Theme i/1b area (mm. 314ff.) proceeds in an overlapping sequence of falling (enharmonic) major thirds: the model expresses the harmonies <D♯ minor, F♯ major, B minor>, the copy <B minor, D major, G minor>, and the shortened copy <G minor, A♯ (B♭) major . . . > leading eventually to the D♯-major harmony of the reca- pitulation. The entire sequence can be reduced, as shown in the example, to a series of ascending fourths <F♯–b, D–g, A♯/a♯–D♯> sequenced at the descending interval of the major third. The last ascending fourth, that from A♯ to D♯, is expanded over time (although, as indicated by its c′ designa- tion above the staff, its thematic reference to the model is *shortened*, consist- ing only of broken-up statements of the model's antecedent phrase). Its A♯ dominant-seventh harmony at measure 343 (notated as B♭ dominant seventh with F in the bass) is extended by a passage elaborating a D half-diminished- seventh harmony (mm. 345ff.), which leads temporarily to V of C major (m. 362), and to the C major of the Theme 2 area (m. 366). This brief Theme 2 area, occurring just before the arrival of ii^7 of G♯ minor ushering in the recapitulation, represents the culmination of the development. The diagram shows the structural growth leading to this climactic point: beginning with the first Theme 1b area in measure 256, successive sections increasingly elab- orate the model-copy framework, expanding from <m, c′> to <m, c, c′> to <m, c, c′, x>. When the climactic Theme 2 arrives, it, along with the follow- ing augmented statement of Theme i, concludes the development, moving stepwise from D through C down to attain the awaited bass A♯ (notated as B♭), supporting ii^7 of G♯. The <D, C, B♭> descent echoes the <D♯, C♯, B> descent prominent in the exposition. The entire development, as shown in example 5.17b, moves from V of B major to ii^7 of G♯ minor, to lead to the cadential $^6_4$ of G♯ minor that begins the recapitulation.

To demonstrate how Ravel choreographs themes and the pianist's physi- cal motions via the model-copy-fragment process, we now look more closely at the Theme i/1b section (mm. 314ff.), shown in example 5.18 (cf. ex. 5.17). Model (m), copy (c), shortened copy (c′), and extension (x) are labeled to the left of the example. The model and copies, as labeled between the staves, consist of antecedent-consequent phrases of Theme i, answered by interjec- tions of Theme 1b (and once also of Theme 2 and of Theme 1a). Previously we identified Theme i as waltz-like in its motion; here it takes on even greater kinetic energy than in the exposition, beginning on beat 2 and expressing an even clearer hemiola structure. Theme 1b, identified with the flamenco, yet retaining some of the mechanical aspects of its twin Theme 1a, contrasts in the quality of its motion with Theme i.

Example 5.18. "Scarbo," Development, Themes i and 1b juxtaposed, mm. 314–52
(m = model, c = copy, c' = shortened copy, x = extension)

The two themes swirl around one another as each grows in complexity and drama. Theme i increases in stature from single notes (m. 314), to octave doublings (m. 320), to chordal doublings with arpeggios sweeping across the registral compass of the piano (m. 325), all the while rising in register. Theme 1b also grows: its interjections appear at measures 318, 335, 339, and 343; at measure 335 it appears for the first time as chords split between the two hands.

The pianist has a visceral sensation through this passage of the sweep of motion created by the increasing complexity and thematic dialogue. The legato motion of Theme i is undercut by the jagged interpolations of Theme 1b; the growth of both themes demands increasingly larger physical gestures, particularly with the swirling hand exchanges and registral expansion of measures 325ff. The two-hand rendition of Theme 1b at measure 335 adds to the theme's physical palette, for articulation of the repeated chords now requires a throwing of the hand onto the keys. At measure 345 the metamorphosis of the two themes in this passage—Theme i and Theme 1b—is complete: Theme 1b becomes a waltz-like sweep of octave hand positions resembling Theme i, its characteristic repeated pitches now forming pivot points for the accordion-like motion of the right hand. Its staccato articulation (notice the progression from m. 318 through mm. 335, 339, and 343), flamenco character, and mechanical facets have transformed into a legato waltz-like wave: compare measures 345–46 (Theme 1b) with 341–42 (Theme i), noting how the two hands have essentially changed roles.

Thus it is that Ravel's choreography turns one theme into another, expressing motion of ever-increasing dimensions. Comparing this choreographic section with the other model-copy sections of the development, we see similar processes of thematic transmutation and registral ascent at work. For instance, in the Theme 1b section of measures 256–76, Theme 1a interjections take on the second-beat placement of Theme 1b. Another example occurs just after the section in example 5.19. In measures 353–65, Theme 1b fragments, consolidated to closely resemble Theme 2's main figure, repeat and grow to build to the climactic arrival of Theme 2 at measure 366. This arrival, the apex of the development, has been preceded by registral ascents in each of the preceding thematic sections; the motion of the development as a whole therefore parallels the dwarf's immense expansion into the size of a cathedral spire. The growth, appropriate to the multiple manifestations of the dwarf, has occurred through transformed repetition on multiple levels: that of individual themes within passages, of passages within thematic sections (via the model-copy process), and of the entire thematic cycle (borrowed from the exposition).

Transformation of the opening thematic cycle occurs on an entirely different scale in the recapitulation. We begin by showing how the cycle reappears in the recapitulation, and then demonstrate how this apparent thematic parallel is itself reinterpreted. Our discussion references example 5.16 primarily,

Example 5.19. "Scarbo," Recapitulation, Theme 1a augmented, mm. 430–33

accompanied by musical illustrations in examples 5.19 and 5.20. As shown in example 5.16a, the recapitulation articulates the introduction-exposition thematic cycle in condensed form. The recapitulation brings back figures p and q, Theme 1a (representative of the first-theme area), and Theme 2, and follows this condensed thematic cycle with a rough expanded retrograde of the introduction (Theme i . . . figures p and q).

But, reflective of the dwarf Scarbo, Ravel continues to transform themes within this cycle. The recapitulation's Theme 1a—the sole Theme 1 representative in the main body of the recapitulation—is wholly altered, as shown in example 5.19. Augmented visually (notated in eighth notes in $\frac{3}{4}$ meter) and durationally (occurring in the slower tempo of the introduction's triple meter), and accompanied by D♯ harmony (dominant of G♯ minor), this dreamlike version of the theme suggests the flickering translucency of the dwarf near the end of Bertrand's poem ("but soon his body would turn blue, translucent as the wax of a candle").[41] From this slow beginning, the recapitulation only gradually regains the movement's primary tempo *Vif*—and the movement's true tonic B—achieving them just before the recapitulatory statement of Theme 2 (m. 477). Theme 2 is now over F♯ harmony (dominant of B), and it is developed, as in the exposition, over approximately a hundred measures.

Returning to example 5.16a, the concluding section re-presents the elements of the introduction in roughly reverse order. Theme i (m. 580), expanded registrally and temporally over C♯ harmony (recall the importance of C♯ harmony underpinning Theme i in the introduction as a conduit to B major), announces the beginning of this closing section. Just as the movement's introduction wound up to Theme i, this closing section winds down from Theme i, descending, decrescendo-ing, and decelerating in the pace of its activity. Snatches of Theme 2, with the interpolation of an expressive augmentation of Theme 1a, participate in this descent. The passage arrives at B major in measure 615 (ex. 5.20). Over the B pedal, figures p and q return, the

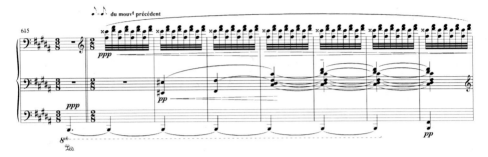

Example 5.20. "Scarbo," Conclusion, Figures p and q, mm. 615–22

repeated D♯ and the C× neighbor of q reappearing in the right-hand
tremolo, and the three-note motive of p occurring in the left-hand octaves.
This closing p statement answers the opening one (cf. example 5.11), for
whereas that initial statement outlined a G♯ minor tonic triad within a
dominant context, this closing statement frames a dominant chord within
a B-major tonic context. The tenuto {F♯, D♯} third that responds to p at
measure 620 stands in for q's chordal sonority that responded to p at the
opening of the work.

The recapitulation thus condenses the introduction-exposition thematic
cycle, and then concludes the work by roughly mirroring the elements of the
introduction. Example 5.16a showed thematic correspondences between the
movement's introduction-exposition and recapitulation by vertical alignment.
But Ravel has fooled us with a formal sleight-of-hand: the two large sections
follow essentially parallel harmonic plans, and example 5.16b realigns them
according to this harmonic structure.[42] Notice the resulting realignment of *thematic* material. The recapitulation omits the introduction's Theme i (m. 32)
and replaces it with its augmented Theme 1a (m. 430). This theme leads via
an accelerating crescendo to the primary tonic B (m. 460), the resumption of
the primary tempo *Vif* (m. 464), and not Theme 1a as in the exposition, but
Theme 2. Theme 2 unfolds in B major, leading to the movement's climax in
measure 563, where it reestablishes the tonic with a powerful V-I motion. The
lengthy Theme 2 is followed by two brief sections quoting first Theme i and
then Theme 1a in augmentation, all held together by interjections of Theme
2 material, forming a "Theme 2 area" corresponding to the tripartite Theme 1
area of the exposition (a longer Theme 1a section followed by shorter 1b and
i statements). The recapitulation achieves its final tonic at measure 615, just
preceding the recall of figures p and q, paralleling the exposition's expression
of its final tonic in its concluding Theme 2 section. After the expected Theme i
does not appear in the recapitulation's "introduction," it is as if the subsequent

thematic sections all shift one step earlier, each taking the harmonic and formal place of its predecessor.

Thus the apparent *thematic* parallels between introduction-exposition and recapitulation (ex. 5.16a) are reinterpreted by the *harmonic* parallels between the two large areas (ex. 5.16b)—a masterful reinterpretation of thematic design by harmonic structure. This functional restructuring explains in part the slow and dreamlike form of Theme 1a in the recapitulation (m. 430), for the theme is now introductory in function (though still resonating with its previous meanings). As a result, thematic and harmonic focus shifts to Theme 2, and the movement's true final cadence takes place across the seemingly "tacked-on" Themes i, 1a, and figures p and q.[43] Ravel's choreography does not stop with the transmutation of motivic figures into distinctive themes, nor with the synthesis of these themes into dance-like motion, but reaches even to the shape-shifting of the form itself, creating a musical movement worthy of the virtuosic dwarf Scarbo. The piece thus reflects the dwarf's ever-changing guises on multiple levels: the generation of a trove of different themes from figures p and q; the ways in which the themes seem to arise out of one another and turn into one another over the course of the movement; and the rotation and transformation of the basic thematic cycle through exposition, development, and recapitulation.

*   *   *

Musical motion is an illusion, a cognitive construct arising from the conceptual blend of physical motion and musical attributes. In Ravel this motion characteristically results from the varied repetition—animation and choreography—of musical objects and musical dance units, resulting in mechanical and dance-like motion respectively. The size of object and dance unit most strategic to this sleight of hand is the figure, the smallest meaningful unit larger than the single note.

We have argued that the pianist's physical gestures form an intrinsic part of these crucial figures and units, all the more so because of the centrality of piano writing—and of Ravel's own investment in virtuosic piano playing—to Ravel's oeuvre.[44] These gestures not only help to define and characterize units, but act in fact as the real "movers" in the animation and choreography of these units.[45]

As we have noted, mechanical and dance-like motion shade into one another in Ravel's works, and the combination often results in naturalistic depictions of water, creatures, or anthropomorphic beings. One can even posit a stylistic spectrum from mechanical (*Le tombeau de Couperin,* the G-Major Piano Concerto, the Piano Trio) to dance-like and organic (*Jeux d'eau, Miroirs,* the Left-Hand Concerto, *Gaspard de la nuit*), with the former lending itself more to the neoclassical, and the latter to the extramusical and pictorial.

In the end, the distinctive qualities of motion that result are characteristically Ravelian, centering on repetition of figures and units transformed
in many ways. In mechanical motion the transformations leave basic
pitch-rhythmic characteristics intact, while in dance-like motion, deeper
transformations of material result. We find Ravel the composer a juggler
indeed—able to keep thousands of perfectly choreographed objects flying
from his pianist's fingers for our pleasure.

Notes

The epigraph to this chapter is drawn from André Suarès, "Pour Ravel," *La Revue Musicale* 6, no. 6 (1925): 6. Unless otherwise specified, translations are by Korevaar and Leong.
  1. A pianistic physicality informs Ravel's writing as a whole. Arbie Orenstein, in *Ravel:
Man and Musician* (New York: Dover, 1991), 135, states, "The piano is the privileged instrument in Ravel's art, not only because he was a pianist and composed at the keyboard, but
because virtually all of the fresh trends in his style first appear in the piano music."
  2. Maurice Ravel, *Jeux d'eau*, Urtext edition by Roger Nichols (London: Peters, 1994).
Throughout this chapter, we use angle brackets < > to indicate ordered sets, and curly
brackets { } to show unordered sets.
  3. Henri Gil-Marchex, in "La technique de piano," *La Revue Musicale* 6, no. 6 (1925):
40, points out the harpsichord-like clarity implied by the technique of *Jeux d'eau*, men-
tioning Scarlatti in particular—perhaps a reaction to the repetition and sequencing of
keyboard-derived figurations that are common to both composers' styles.
  4. Although Ravel indicates only "1 corde" in the score, the performance tradition of
the time as evidenced by pianists who worked with Ravel demands generous use of the
damper pedal. See Roger Nichols's preface to his urtext edition of *Jeux d'eau* (London:
Peters, 1994), 6.
  5. Lawrence Zbikowski, *Conceptualizing Music: Cognitive Structure, Theory, and Analysis*
(Oxford: Oxford University Press, 2002), 36–40.
  6. Although our work intersects somewhat with that of Robert Hatten (*Interpreting
Musical Gestures, Topics, and Tropes: Mozart, Beethoven, Schubert* [Bloomington: Indiana
University Press, 2004]), our concern lies more with literal physical gestures and musical
units that may be construed as gestures, rather than with the semiotic or specific expressive meaning of such gestures.
  7. Compare to Ian Quinn's "Fuzzy Extensions to the Theory of Contour," *Music Theory Spectrum* 19, no. 2 (1997): 232–63, and his application of fuzzy set theory to contour
theory.
  8. We use the term "hierarchy" here in the straightforward sense in which it describes
taxonomies in category theory: Zbikowski, in *Conceptualizing Music*, 31, uses the categories "housecat, feline, mammal, and living organism," for instance, as examples of hierarchical levels related by inclusion.
  9. See Zbikowski, *Conceptualizing Music* 31–32 for a discussion of this level. Zbikowski
correlates "basic level" with "musical motive" (34).
  10. Ibid., 94.
  11. Deborah Mawer likens certain of Ravel's musical building blocks to "objects"—
"fixed" and "passive" entities which, though viewable from multiple angles, do not

themselves move or develop. See Deborah Mawer, "Musical Objects and Machines," in *The Cambridge Companion to Ravel*, ed. Deborah Mawer (Cambridge: Cambridge University Press, 2000), 48–49.

12. Hélène Jourdan-Morhange, in *Ravel et Nous* (Geneva: Éditions du Milieu du Monde, 1945), 27–28, describes the miniatures in Ravel's studio at Montfort-l'Amaury: mechanical toys, music boxes, a miniature sailboat that pitched on cardboard waves, a tiny nightingale that flapped its wings and sang.

13. Dance topics of course associate with a whole range of sociocultural meanings beyond those with which we are primarily concerned.

14. Deborah Mawer, "Ballet and the Apotheosis of the Dance," in Mawer, *The Cambridge Companion to Ravel*, 141.

15. This dichotomy roughly corresponds to Zbikowski's "atomistic" and "chain-of-being" hierarchies (Zbikowski, *Conceptualizing Music*, 287–321).

16. Serge Gut suggests a possible semantics of repeated notes, from horror (the slow repetitions of B♭ in "Le gibet") to grotesque laughter (the nearly unplayable sixteenth triplets of "Alborada del gracioso"). Gut also points out that the use of repeated notes (and, by extension, repeated figures) allows Ravel to animate certain musical parameters while allowing others to hover in place through repetition. See Gut, "Le phénomène répétitif chez Maurice Ravel. De l'obsession à l'annihilation incantatoire," *International Review of the Aesthetics and Sociology of Music* 21, no. 1 (1990): 37–38, 43. Gut's classification does not allow for the potential playfulness of repeated notes, an aspect that Ravel also exploits.

17. We might draw a parallel to the use of the drum for the scene changes in Stravinsky's *Petrouchka*.

18. Orenstein, *Ravel: Man and Musician*, 101–2.

19. The sheer pianism of this passage is convincingly demonstrated by how nearly impossible it is to execute by various instruments in the orchestra following rehearsal 14.

20. Maurice Ravel, *Concerto pour piano et orchestre* (Paris: Durand, 1932), 61–62, 86.

21. Daphne Leong and David Korevaar, "The Performer's Voice: Performance and Analysis in Ravel's *Concerto pour la main gauche*," *Music Theory Online* 11, no. 3 (2005), paragraphs 21–23, http://mto.societymusictheory.org/issues/mto.05.11.3/toc.11.3.html. On the performer, and particularly the keyboard player, as mechanism, see Carolyn Abbate "Outside Ravel's Tomb," *Journal of the American Musicological Society* 52, no. 3 (1999): 477–82.

22. The definition of "Noctuelles" is ambiguous; in the nineteenth century the word could refer to both nocturnal moths and small owls. Colette compared Léon-Paul Fargue, dedicatee of the work, to both a nocturnal bird and a bat (David Korevaar, "Ravel's Mirrors" [Doctoral document, The Juilliard School, 2000], 32).

23. Just as in alternating-hands chromatic-scale passages by various nineteenth-century composers, the equal partition of the octave into six and then three parts leads to strong whole-tone implications. In this final passage, the chromatic scale in the middle is harmonized by D♭, F, and A-major triads—a distinctly Lisztian progression.

24. This rhythm is reversed, creating a traditional habanera pattern, in the second theme beginning in measure 44. See Korevaar, "Ravel's Mirrors," 105.

25. See Korevaar, "Ravel's Mirrors," 104–6, for a more extended analysis of the symmetries inherent in this passage. The entrance of the horn calls between the hands in the middle register in mm. 4–10 further suggests the "barque" of the title, or at least a human presence on the ocean. These horn calls take pitches from the original ostinato

and reorder and slow them down, creating a new melodic line from already-present material. The rhythm of this new melody is related, by augmentation and retrograde, to the rhythm of the right-hand ostinato (Korevaar, "Ravel's Mirrors," 106, example IV-2b). Thus, Ravel delineates layers that are organically related, introducing the symbolic unity of ocean and boat through the blending of different types of musical motion.

26. Regarding Schoenberg's influence, Ravel wrote, "I am quite conscious of the fact that my *Chansons madécasses* are in no way Schoenbergian, but I do not know whether I ever should have been able to write them had Schoenberg never written" (quoted in Orenstein, *Ravel: Man and Musician*, 126). Regarding the influence of Gershwin and jazz, see Michael Russ, "Ravel and the Orchestra," in Mawer, *The Cambridge Companion to Ravel*, 132.

27. Maurice Ravel, "New Productions of the Russian Season: *The Nightingale*," trans. Arbie Orenstein, in *A Ravel Reader: Correspondence, Articles, Interviews*, ed. Arbie Orenstein (New York: Columbia University Press, 1990), 381. (Original: "Les Nouveaux Spectacles de la saison russe: *Le Rossignol*," *Comœdia illustré* 6, no. 17 (1914): 811–14.)

28. The acceleration in the right hand occurs within a larger process of transformation from melody into figuration, as the opening sarabande-like melody first becomes the arpeggiated and scalar melody of rehearsal 2, which itself becomes increasingly diminished until reaching the movement's climax.

29. Maurice Ravel, *Gaspard de la nuit*, Urtext edition by Roger Nichols (London: Peters, 1991).

30. Ravel's score, published in 1909, used the 1908 Mercure de France edition as the source for its reproduction of the three Bertrand poems (Maurice Ravel, *Gaspard de la nuit: 3 Poèmes d'après Aloysius Bertrand* [Paris: Durand, 1909], 2, 16, 22).

31. Ravel finds the piano's ambitus to be too small here: in m. 15 the keyboard's lower limit forces him to write <A, A♯, D♯> rather than <F×, G♯, D♯>. A similar limitation occurs at the recapitulation in m. 395.

32. The change from triplet subdivisions of the beat to duple ones may also contribute to the mechanical quality; the qualitative differences between triple and duple subdivisions may have affective connotations.

33. See Roy Howat, "Ravel and the Piano," in Mawer, *The Cambridge Companion to Ravel*, 85–87, for discussion of this semitonal neighbor figure.

34. A specific physiological trait of the composer, his spatulate thumb, has influenced his choice of pitches in the accompanying voices. The {F, G} and {D, E} white-note pairs, when written vertically (mm. 55–56), are played with the thumb covering both notes; the thumb also plays the pairs on the second, fourth, and sixth sixteenths of m. 57. This natural motion is encouraged by the thumb's relative comfort on the white keys while the other fingers are working the higher black keys.

35. Howat, in "Ravel and the Piano," 87, identifies Theme 1a and 1b material as flamenco-influenced.

36. The sonata-form designation for this movement is based more upon thematic than upon harmonic structure. The movement, in addition to slipping between two tonalities (G♯ minor and B major), exhibits many other harmonic aspects unusual for sonata form, from vocabulary (octatonic collections, for example) to large-scale structure. Although Howat, in "Ravel and the Piano," 85, also identifies the movement as a sonata form, his view of the form seems to be based largely on its ternary design. His view thus differs significantly from ours: his exposition begins with m. 1, and his recapitulation with m. 386; he identifies five separate themes.

37. See James Hepokoski and Warren Darcy, *Elements of Sonata Theory: Norms, Types, and Deformations in the Late-Eighteenth-Century Sonata* (Oxford: Oxford University Press, 2006), 16–20, 205–7, 611–14 for their presentation of "rotational form" in the Classical sonata.

38. Theme i ends the introduction, the exposition's first-theme area, and the development, and begins the conclusion.

39. See William Caplin, *Classical Form: A Theory of Formal Functions for the Instrumental Music of Haydn, Mozart, and Beethoven* (Oxford: Oxford University Press, 1998), 141–47 for his discussion of this development technique, which he calls "core technique," after Erwin Ratz.

40. The Theme 1b section in the development echoes the structure of the Theme 1b section in the exposition, while successively intensifying its features. In the exposition the theme occurs thrice, the third time fragmented; all three statements occur over the same harmony. In its first appearance in the development the theme also occurs thrice, the first two times over the same harmony and the third time harmonically shifted. In its second appearance in the development the thematic section expands through repetition: the theme occurs five times, in groups of 2 + 2 + 1, with each group now occurring on a different harmonic level. In all three appearances, in the exposition, development, and again in the development, the theme's statements gradually increase in textural and rhythmic complexity, as well as rising in register.

41. At m. 430, "♩ = ♪ du mouv^t précédent" relates to the tempo at m. 395; because of the durational augmentation at m. 418, acceleration is needed to smooth the connection between the motivically-equivalent bar at m. 429 and quarter note at m. 430. Ravel himself must have been confused by the notation here, for the autograph manuscript notes "♩ = ♪." at m. 430, which would equate the quarter-note at m. 430 with the bar at m. 429, but express an untenably slow tempo were no speeding up to occur between measures 395 and 430. Many recorded performances accelerate between m. 422 and m. 430. See critical commentary in Roger Nichols's urtext edition of *Gaspard de la nuit* (London: Peters, 1991), 46.

42. Roman numerals indicate basic tonal function only; Ravel often articulates these functions with nontraditional means. The exposition Theme 2, for example, begins with much octatonicism in the pitch-center context of B; the "V" in the recapitulation is entirely octatonic ($OCT_{0,1}$) over an F♯ bass.

43. Ravel's use of sonata form in "Scarbo" bears some striking resemblances to Haydn's sonata forms: Haydn's development sections frequently recycle exposition themes in order, and they sometimes do so while reinterpreting thematic *function* harmonically, as in the first movement of Sonata Hob. XVI/41 in B♭.

On transformed repetitions, see Dora Hanninen, "A Theory of Recontextualization in Music: Analyzing Phenomenal Transformations of Repetition," *Music Theory Spectrum* 25, no. 1 (2003): 59–98.

44. Ravel aspired to be a virtuoso pianist in his days in Charles de Bériot's class at the Conservatoire, and his interest in virtuoso keyboard music from the French clavécinistes through Liszt, Saint-Saëns, and the Russian school is well documented. For example, see Gerald Larner, *Maurice Ravel* (London: Phaidon Press, 1996), 161–62, here discussing the influences of Couperin, Liszt, and Saint-Saëns on *Le tombeau de Couperin*. See also Orenstein, *Ravel: Man and Musician*, 136 (Scarlatti, Couperin, Saint-Saëns, Chopin, Liszt); and Roland-Manuel, *Maurice Ravel*, ed. and trans. Cynthia Jolly (New York: Dover, 1972), 30 (Liszt and Scarlatti as influences on *Jeux d'eau*).

45. Similarly in *L'enfant et les sortilèges*, the flesh-and-blood child is the conduit through which the audience enters an enchanted world of dancing objects and talking animals. Speaking of the moment when the Child loses consciousness and the Animals suddenly fall speechless, then laboriously learn to speak, Abbate says, "Ravel is making a critical point about the 'enchanted' nature of all we have heard up to the instant the Child becomes unconscious. The Animals, the trees, the books, the teapot, the wallpaper: none of these things could speak, dance, or sing. They had *seemed* to, but their animation and voices are now understood as an illusion, engendered by [the child's] 'picturing gaze'. . ." (Abbate, "Outside Ravel's Tomb," 512–15).

Chapter Six

Playing with Models

Sonata Form in Ravel's String Quartet and Piano Trio

Sigrun B. Heinzelmann

If you have something to say, this something will never emerge more distinctly than in your unintended unfaithfulness to a model.

Introduction

Ravel's advice to his students quoted above points to the central role that models played in his composing.[1] A composer arguably with little overt "anxiety of influence," Ravel sought inspiration both in past conventions and in the innovations of his contemporaries. Ravel's appropriation of baroque and classical forms implies both homage and provocation: playing with models, Ravel entices his listeners to place his creations in the lineage of the composers whose heritage he evokes while at the same time distancing himself from them. Jankélévitch's assertion that "every composition by Ravel represents . . . a certain problem to be solved"[2] applies especially to works that are in sonata form: each presents a unique response to formal, harmonic, and motivic conventions of sonata-form "principles"—from early binary designs like those of Scarlatti to classical prototypes derived from Mozart to third-related key schemes à la Chopin.[3]

My aim in this essay is to show how Ravel adapts, manipulates, and even subverts sonata paradigms of the past.[4] To do so I will examine the respective first movements of the String Quartet and the Piano Trio. Separated by about a decade, the two movements represent very different solutions in Ravel's engagement with the form. The analyses also shed light on compositional developments in Ravel's prewar style that led toward condensation of form;

Excerpts from Maurice Ravel's String Quartet, © 1987, are used by permission of Dover Publications, Inc.

more sophisticated integration of motivic, harmonic, and formal substance; and increasingly complex interaction of diatonic and nondiatonic collections.

While formal models, which can be considered objects of the past, represent "musical objects" on a relatively large scale, pitch-class sets, scales, and specific harmonies form small musical objects in Ravel's music that help to shape and convey the formal structure.[5] In both the Quartet and the Trio, motives and their transformations not only highlight formal processes for the listener, but also contribute to the overall coherence of the four-movement sonata as a cycle. The sonata cycle itself has historical and aesthetic connotations that play a significant role in the Piano Trio; I will take up this issue at the close of this chapter.

The essay focuses primarily on Ravel's adaptation of sonata form, viewed principally through Hepokoski and Darcy's *Elements of Sonata Theory*.[6] The concepts and vocabulary developed by Hepokoski and Darcy offer both the flexibility to interpret unconventional features of Ravel's sonata forms and historical templates against which to contrast his designs. Within this formal context and methodology, the analyses combine a Schenkerian approach with motivic analysis, as well as consideration of the formal and rhetorical functions of nondiatonic collections.

String Quartet, I

> My String Quartet . . . reflects a preoccupation with musical structure, imperfectly realized, no doubt, but which appears much clearer than in my previous compositions.[7]

Composed in 1902–3, Ravel's String Quartet is among his earliest compositions in sonata form.[8] Ravel shapes the first movement's sonata form by creating tension not only between keys but also by juxtaposing diatonic and nondiatonic collections. The movement's tonal framework is characterized by the interplay of the F-major tonic and its submediant D minor. Into this F-major/D-minor framework Ravel integrates octatonic and whole-tone passages that each fulfill specific functions.[9] In the course of the analysis, I will focus on three main structural features (1) the sonata design and its creative dialogue with classical paradigms; (2) the F-major/D-minor ambiguity (suggested in the very opening phrase) and the functions of whole-tone and octatonic collections within this ambiguity; and (3) the role of motivic objects and their transformations in our perception of the movement's form.

Model and Form

Various authors mention Debussy's String Quartet as a model for Ravel's. There are obvious surface similarities that are easily perceived by the listener— namely, character, texture, and a cyclic design. As far as aspects of form are concerned, however, Ravel's first movement adheres to traditional principles of sonata form much more explicitly than Debussy's.[10]

Figure 6.1 shows the movement's formal subdivisions (the sections and segments are approximately proportional to the number of measures they occupy). For the sake of clarity, the terminology key for the example is shown below:

Sonata-Theory Terminology and its Abbreviations
Type 3 sonata form = "textbook" sonata form with exposition, development, recapitulation
P = P-zone, primary theme zone
TR = transition
S = S-zone, secondary theme zone (here represented as TM^3)
C = C-zone, closing zone
' = caesura
/ = structural cadence
TMB = trimodular block, dividing the space between P and C into three phases:
TM^1 = first module of TMB, a new theme following the first proposed medial caesura (MC^1)
TM^2 = second module of TMB, dissolving the new theme and, with energy-gaining TR rhetoric, leading to a second medial caesura (MC^2)
TM^3 = third module of TMB, establishing the "true" S-theme leading to the EEC
EEC = essential expositional closure
ESC = essential structural closure
V-lock = dominant lock in preparation of S

Thematic and Motivic Labels
p^1 = first P-theme
p^1 tra = transitional form of p^1
p^1 dom = dominant form of p^1
p^1 clos = closing form of p^1
p^1 end = ending form of p^1
p^1 clim = climax form of p^1
p^1 den = denouement form of p^1
p^2 = second P-theme
p^3 = third P-theme
s = S-theme
sf = fragment of s
wth = waiting-third motive

Other Abbreviations
lin. n.-d. coll. = linear nondiatonic collection
WT = whole-tone collection
OCT = octatonic collection

ROTATION 1

Exposition

mm. 1–83	P		TR	TMB									C			
zones	P		TR	TMB									C			
sections	A	B	A' → MC¹	TM¹		TM²		V-lock	MC²	TM³ (S)		EEC?	C			
rehearsal				A		B		C		D			E			
measure	1	9	17 21	24 28 31		35 39		44	50	55		62	69	74	77	80
thematic material	p¹	p²	p¹ wth	p³ p¹tra		p¹chr wth		p¹dom		s		s	s/p¹clos			p¹end
measure groups	4 4	8	4 3	4 3 4		4 6		10		8		6	5	3	3	4
n.-d. coll.			WT₁	OCT₀,₁	OCT₁,₂	OCT₀,₁ OCT₁,₂							WT₀ progression to d minor (elision w. development)			
key areas RN: F: d:	F/d I/vi III/i	g C ii V iv VI	F/d [G] I/vi V/V III/i V	C [F] E [a] mod. V I V/iii V/iii V/v		c# V/vi/vi vii°		A V/vi V		d vi i		d	B♭ A♭ G♯ E → WT₀ progression			
bass	F(scale)	G C	F(scale) G	Gped E ped E♯ G♯		C♯/E C♯		A				d				
lin.-d. coll.								37 OCT₀,₁								
dynamics	p	pp	pp p/f	pp pp/p mf p		ff p		pp JJ		mf p		pp	mf p mf/pp			

ROTATION 2

Development

mm. 84–128	P-based		S-based				P-based		
zones	P-based		S-based				P-based		
sections				trans.		trans.		climax + retrans.	
rehearsal	F		G				H		
measure	84	91	99	102	106	110	119	122	126
thematic material	p²	p²	wth	s/p²	s/p²	wth	p¹den	p¹tra	
measure groups	7.1 e 8 e		3	3.1		9	10		
	1.3 2.1 3.1 4	1.3 2.1 4	3	4.3 2.3 3		3	2.2 7.2		
n.-d. coll.				OCT₂,₃		OCT₂,₃	OCT₀,₁	WT₀	
key areas RN: F: d:	d/F [odd.6 i7]	f♭⁷/ab	F♭	d♯°⁷	d♯°⁷	f♯°⁷ /b5	F♯⁷ /b5 Gr⁺⁶/F♯⁺⁶ (=♭II)		
bass	→ D	F	F	D♯	D♯	D♯/F♯ ↑OCT₁,₃	F♯ F♯		
lin.-d. coll.	!						OCT₂,₃ !		
dynamics	pp/p pp	pp/p pp	mp p	mp p	p	p	PP JJ	JJ f mf/mp	

Figure 6.1. Ravel, String Quartet, I: Type 3 sonata form with TMB

ROTATION 3

	Recapitulation											
mm. 129–213												
zones	P		TR	TMB						C		codetta
sections	A	B	A' → MC¹	TM¹	TM²	V-lock	MC²	TM³ (S)	ESC?	C		
rehearsal	I	I		J	K	L		M				
measure	129	137	145	152 156 159	163 167	173	180	184	192	198	204	209
thematic material	p¹	p²	p¹	p³	p¹chr wth	p¹dom		s		s/p¹clos		s/p¹end
measure groups	4 4	8	4 3	4 3 4	4 6	11		8 6		3 3 3 2		5
n.-d. coll.	$OCT_{2,3}$		WT_1	$[OCT_{0,1}]$ $[OCT_{1,2}$ $[OCT_{0,1}]]$							WT_1 progression	
key areas / RN: **F:** **d:**	F/d I/vi III/i	F/Ab/B	F/d [G] I/vi V/V III/i V	C [F] Eb [Ab] mxd V I V/₃III		C V/i!		F#add6 I		F I		F I
bass	F(scale)	F/Ab/B C	F(scale) G	Cped. Ebped. E.G	Db/Ab Db	C	G/C	F Eb	G C F	C# B A G		F Eb FGF
lin. ne. coll.												
dynamics	p pp	pp p f	p	pp pp/p mf p	pp ff mf p	p mp p		pp		mf p p		pp

Figure 6.1. Ravel, String Quartet, I: Type 3 sonata form with TMB—*(concluded)*

The P-zone forms a small rounded—although tonally open—binary structure. It includes the main P-theme (p^1), a parallel period (antecedent mm. 1–4, modulating consequent mm. 5–8), and a contrasting p-based sentence (p^2). The partial return of p^1, which forms a dissolving reprise (mm. 17–20), comes to a first moment of repose, a three-measure caesura-gesture on V/V (mm. 21–23). Harmonically, one can interpret the V/V gesture in two ways: as an anomalous ending of the P-zone (in which case m. 24 is construed as the beginning of the transition), or, more likely, as a premature MC (in which case the previous p^1 theme lacks the energy gain normally associated with a transition). In either case, Ravel's design eschews the normative "defaults" (according to Hepokoski and Darcy). Melodically, the segment exemplifies Ravel's predilection for repeated thirds (such as the upper-voice F–A) within such preparatory passages. Alternating between two tones of the same harmony, these thirds provide a sense of biding time until the music is ready to move on. When Ravel uses them in this manner, I shall refer to them as "waiting thirds." (The waiting thirds originate from mm. 13–15, where the cello alternates the open fifths, G–D and B♭–F; they also underlie the p^1 theme in mm. 24–30 and play a central role in the first module of TM^2 in mm. 35–43.)

Beginning in measure 24, the rhetoric resembles an energy-gathering transitional section suggesting a "declined MC" (a premature caesura that fails to launch the secondary theme).[11] The music following the "proposed MC" normally declines it by remaining in tonic, either returning to the primary theme or introducing a new one. Here, the "new theme" (p^3) both derives from p^1 and elaborates the "waiting third" immediately preceding (vln. 1); moreover, its return to tonic is destabilized via $\frac{6}{4}$ inversion and especially by the octatonic undercurrents in the violin 2 and viola.

In turn, the declined MC here leads to a new thematic unit that becomes the first segment of a "trimodular block" (TMB), characterized by "two separate launches of new themes (pre-EEC themes) following those MCs."[12] Since p^3 (m. 24) is a closely related transformation of p^1 and "drifts back" to the original tonic (albeit in the guise of a $\frac{6}{4}$ chord) it cannot function as a true secondary theme. The ensuing TM^2 (mm. 35–50) has a TR-like texture and function: an ascending octatonic progression in the cello (which foreshadows a larger octatonic progression in the development) propels the music (mm. 37–38) toward the passage's melodic and dynamic goal (m. 39). Its denouement (mm. 39–43) prepares the arrival of a dominant lock (V/vi; mm. 44–50), which finally produces the second MC (MC^2) in measure 50 (with caesura fill in mm. 50–54), followed by a bona fide S-theme beginning measure 55.

Broadly, the notion of a TMB privileges the tonal scheme Ravel chooses for the MCs and the succession of themes, where a false (and declined) MC^1 produces a half cadence in the conventional "correct" key (V) that does not lead to a successful launch of an S-theme, and a true MC^2 yields a half cadence that does lead to the successful launch of the S-zone in measure 55, but now in the "wrong" key (vi). The TMB also highlights the gestural similarity of the two MCs.[13]

Beginning in measure 55, the S-zone in D minor is launched with a sentence-like eight-measure antecedent phrase leading to the half cadence at measure 62. Instead of leading to a consequent phrase of equal length providing the EEC, the phrase peters out after reiterating the basic idea (2 + 2 measures of plagal oscillation plus a static extension at mm. 67–68). Melodically, the pentatonic upper voice moves past the D_5 (m. 63) to circle around the S-theme's appoggiatura E an octave lower (mm. 65–68).[14] When E finally resolves to D in measure 69, the D-minor chord of mm. 67–68 is undermined by the subposition of B♭, which turns the consonant D-minor triad into a dissonant B♭-major seventh chord.[15] The effect calls to mind one of Hepokoski and Darcy's possibilities for failed expositions, "the last-minute elusiveness of the goal satisfaction at the end of the exposition—a PAC within easy reach that slips away like a phantom."[16]

The whole-tone bass motion of measures 69–84, shaping what should be the closing zone, muddies the formal function of this section. Does the double bar at measure 69 signal the beginning of the development? If so, the passage could represent Caplin's notion of "pre-core" function, a kind of "transitional introduction" to the development;[17] analogously, *pace Elements of Sonata Theory*, the presence of p^1 could signal a P-based beginning of a new rotation. Further, the dynamic shift from *pp* to *mf*, coupled with the likely easing of tempo at measures 67–68 and the *a tempo* at 69, invites performers to mark measure 69 as a formal point of departure. However, the failed EEC and the continuation of S-based fragments throughout measures 69–83 suggest that S-space within the exposition is still open; at the same time, in lieu of structural closure, the passage must fulfill some kind of concluding function. Supporting that interpretation are the repetitive neighbor motions of P- and S-theme fragments, the static pedal tones and parallel fifths, and especially the fact that—notwithstanding its nondiatonic provenance—the whole-tone progression connects the two D-minor harmonies at either end (mm. 67–68 and 84). Moreover, the corresponding passage in the recapitulation (mm. 198–213) serves to end the movement. Accordingly, figure 6.1 favors the parallel alignment of the two whole-tone progressions, showing them as belonging to the expositional and recapitulatory rotations, respectively. Consequently, the development may be construed as a tripartite space—one that is delineated by changes in texture, thematic material, and governing collections—thereby preserving a sense of thematic, sectional, and formal symmetry.

In the development proper, p^1 is conspicuous by its absence. A transformation of theme p^2 characterizes the development's first zone (mm. 84–101). The waiting thirds in measures 99ff. recall MC^1 and prepare the listener for the second zone, which features transformations of the S-theme (mm. 102–18). Reinterpreted enharmonically as D♯–F♯ from measure 102 on, the thirds propel the development toward the climax (m. 119). Here the development enters its first octatonic phase, almost entirely governed by collection $OCT_{2,3}$.[18] The collectional shift to $OCT_{0,1}$ at the movement's central climax in measure 119 signals the second octatonic phase and final zone (mm. 119–28) of the development, the p^1-based denouement which provides the retransition to the recapitulation; here a chain of p^1-fragments foreshadows the P-theme's impending return. Having been absent from most of the developmental space, p^1 provides a strong sense of return for the recapitulation in measure 129. (The collectional and harmonic aspects of this passage will be elaborated shortly.)

In essence, the recapitulation reiterates the exposition's zones and thematic units. Three notable "surprises" occur in relation to our formal-tonal expectations; these are displayed in example 6.1. Each surprise grows out of a key structural principle for the movement (and for Ravel's works in general): the deployment of minimal thematic or motivic material in maximal harmonic and collectional contexts. The first surprise (ex. 6.1a) occurs in the P-zone, when p^2—which for recapitulatory purposes could remain identical to its expositional form—sounds in an octatonic transformation, following the octatonic climax of the development shortly before (the subsequent p^1 nonetheless returns unchanged). As the upper voices prolong the diminished seventh chord A–C–E♭–G♭ above F in the cello, the resulting major-minor ninth chord on F briefly assumes a subdominant flavor (V/IV), but the F-major return of p^1 in measure 145 via the C-major dominant in measure 144 denies a true subdominant function to the octatonic passage. Again, Ravel seems to reference a classical sonata-form topos (the recapitulatory motion to the subdominant) while transforming its spirit for his own purposes: here, to recall the octatonic processes of the development.

The second surprise (ex. 6.1b) comes with the TMB's first (false) MC and the subsequent TM^1. The recapitulation's MC^1 (mm. 149–51) is identical to that of the exposition. Consequently, TM^1 also *begins* as in the exposition (mm. 152–54 are identical to mm. 24–26), but measure 155 changes the accompanying harmonies while keeping the first violin's melodic line identical. Just when we settle into this realization, both the melody and harmony undergo notable changes. Instead of supporting the p^3 theme as before, the bass shifts a half step lower to E♭. At the same time, the arpeggiation that resolves the appoggiatura, which previously outlined F major above an A-minor $^6_4$ chord (m. 29), now outlines F minor above an A♭-major $^6_4$ chord (m. 157); even with the semitone shift in the bass, the high note C_6 and succeeding "letter names" of the melody are preserved, albeit with altered accidentals. Compared to the ascending bass line in the exposition (D–D♯–E), the descending bass line here (F–E–E♭) effects a kind of dimming, a drop in energy that contrasts strongly with the brightening of sound and energy gain in the exposition. The resulting motion into the flat region resembles the motion to the subdominant familiar from classical recapitulations.

The third surprise occurs at MC^2 and the subsequent S-theme (ex. 6.1c). The preparation by MC^2 (mm. 180–83) for the return of S is ambiguous: as in the exposition, violins 1 and 2 seem to prepare for a D-minor S-theme; the viola and cello, on the other hand, articulate a dominant ninth chord on C (C–G–B♭–D) in preparation for a return to the F-major tonic. Both preparations

Example 6.1a. String Quartet, I: p^2 comparison

meet with success: Ravel reharmonizes the D-minor S-theme in F major, thus emphasizing the movement's F-major/D-minor ambiguity (and pitch-level economy) where conventional sonata form would be the least ambiguous, since S's purpose in the classical recapitulation is to restore (not obscure) the tonic key. The ESC—although "failed"—ultimately decides in favor of the F-major tonic as the reharmonization provides an approximation of a full cadence in F in measures 190–92. Parallel to the exposition's closing, the whole-tone progression reaches its goal, F, with the fifth whole step in measure 209, so that the remaining measures (209–13) serve as a codetta, with whole-step chordal neighbors ♭VII^7 and II$^{9/7}$ confirming the tonic arrival on F major.

Exposition

Example 6.1b. String Quartet, I: MC^1/TM^1 comparison

Exposition

Example 6.1c. String Quartet, I: MC²/S comparison

Tonality and the Interaction of Collections

Rather than basing the movement's tonal design on the tonic-dominant polarity associated with conventional major-mode sonata forms, Ravel explores the pairing of third-related keys that we usually associate with minor-mode sonata form. This shift in structural orientation entails unique strategic moves, resulting in the expanded role of the submediant relationship.[19] First, instead of treating the two related keys as opposing forces, Ravel exploits their shared collection as an element of tonal ambiguity from the first phrase of the movement. The underlying diatonic collection of the opening measures (mm. 1–4) seems to feature equally D minor and F major (D in violin 1, F in the ascending parallel tenths of cello and violin 2). That the F-major/D-minor juxtaposition becomes the central tonal issue of the sonata design is not a question of outright conflict but one of competitive coexistence: whatever tonic takes control of the bass also controls the harmonic motion—if not necessarily the details of the upper voices. For example, in measures 24–25, the bass progression implies a resolution from the dominant C to F in the cello. While the violin 1 also resolves its appoggiatura E to F during the downbeat of measure 25, the violin 2 pursues a progression that leads from the diminished seventh chord C♯–E–G–B♭ to D minor. Similarly, the S-theme, harmonized in D minor in the exposition, returns at the identical pitch level in the recapitulation, but now in the context of F major. This competitive coupling of relative keys (which we also find in the *Introduction and Allegro* and the outer movements of the *Sonatine*) is a predecessor to what I shall argue is the Piano Trio's full-fledged double-tonic complex.

Second, octatonic and whole-tone passages that fulfill specific formal functions within the F-major/D-minor rivalry replace some of the classical-period tonal conventions. As unordered collections, WT_0 and WT_1 serve as buffers between $OCT_{0,1}$ and the diatonic F-major/D-minor collections. As ordered stepwise progressions in the bass, they outline the trajectory of the movement's closing zones (WT_0 is associated with D, WT_1 with F). $OCT_{2,3}$, which includes the pitches of both the F-major and D-minor triads, forms the connective tissue between these keys and collection $OCT_{0,1}$ during the development. The task of $OCT_{0,1}$ is to destabilize F major in the exposition (thus enabling D minor), and to dramatize the movement's climax before WT_0 negotiates the return of F major. In addition, Ravel employs the chromatically-altered versions of the minor mode: he uses the melodic minor to leave the diatonic for the octatonic sphere, and the harmonic minor as dominant preparation to return from octatonic to diatonic sections. Each of these collections is linked to specific thematic ideas and formal segments, so that we associate thematic content, identity of collection, and formal function. To create smooth transitions between different collections, Ravel carefully crafts the succession of referential collections and maximizes common tones. Example 6.2 illustrates the principal relationships between the collections.

The interaction of all three types of collections—diatonic, whole-tone, and octatonic—culminates at the end of the development (see ex. 6.3). Moving toward its climax, the development is driven by a linear ascending progression of $OCT_{2,3}$. Although the collection contains the pitch classes F and D, Ravel centers the passage on the diminished seventh chord D♯–F♯–A–C (respelled as F♯–A–C–E♭ as the build-up nears its peak). At the moment of climax in measure 119 (in triple *fortissimo*), the sudden change to $OCT_{0,1}$ introduces a collection that includes neither D nor F. Only by alternating this collection with WT_0, with which it shares a four-note subset, is D reintroduced to the pitch repertoire. The shared four-note subset, F♯–A♯–C–E, functions as (enharmonically spelled) ♭II ♯9/♭7/4 chord, which substitutes for the dominant (a V^7 chord with simultaneously raised and lowered fifth, in 4/3 position). The presence of enharmonic relationships helps reinterpret the voice

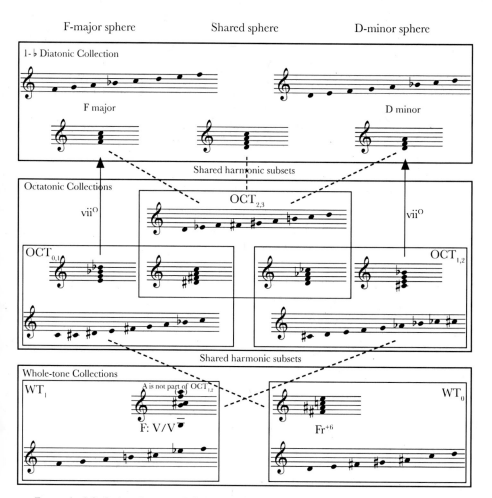

Example 6.2. String Quartet, I: Subset relations among referential collections

leading, gradually shifting the underlying harmonies' functions. At measure 119, the harmony appears to outline a V $\frac{9}{7}$ chord on F♯. In measures 122 and 124, the cello's C_2 appears structurally superior to the previously prolonged F♯2 and thus seems to announce the arrival on the dominant. When it yields again to the F♯$_2$ at the last moment (mm. 126 to 128), we witness, literally, a "tritone substitution." The four-note subset shared by $OCT_{0,1}$ and WT_0, C–E– F♯–A♯/B♭, can form both the French augmented sixth chord F♯–A♯–C–E and the V^7 chord C–E–B♭ (without fifth, G). At this moment of retransition, it is the dominant harmony that reaches back to earlier tonal practice. Oscillating between diatonic and chromatic dominant-preparations, the passage alternately invokes the possibilities of a diatonic (C–F) or chromatic (F♯–F) resolution.[20] Ultimately, the bass's F♯ resolves enharmonically to the tonic F (suggesting a Phrygian G♭–F motion); the upper voice's E_4 passes through F♯ and G♯ to regain the first theme's initial tone, A, in measure 129.[21] The limitation of the pitch-class repertoire to $OCT_{0,1}$ and WT_0 throughout measures 119–28 results in F being withheld. In fact, the last F we hear before the recapitulation is the chromatic passing tone in the viola in measure 114. The unusual progression of the French augmented sixth chord (spelled as ♯I, but resolving like a ♭II) thoroughly exploits subset properties; in addition, its enticing coloration makes the arrival of the tonic F a special event.

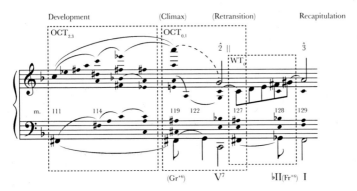

Example 6.3. String Quartet, I: Voice leading and collections at the retransition

Each of the referential collections thus forms an essential thread in the sonata form's pitch-class fabric and tonal design.[22] In signaling this succession of changing referential contexts, motivic transformations become the aural markers that help us track the various zones of the sonata form.

Musical Objects and Motivic Transformation

Motivic transformation might be compared to the notion of stagecraft, where changing lighting alters how we perceive the same characters or objects. By tracing the history of two musical objects, I will demonstrate such transformations in the String Quartet's first movement: a scale with turning figure that forms the counterpoint to the movement's main theme that I shall call the "counter-p" theme (cp), and theme p^2, the second component of the P-zone.[23]

The Counter-p Theme. What at first appears to be a simple accompanying scale in the cello's and second violin's opening measures turns out to be a significant thematic unit that supplies much of the motivic substance of the movement. To account for the theme's contrapuntal role, I designate it as the "counter-p theme," or cp. Like the other themes, cp undergoes a series of transformations related to its different formal functions. Example 6.4 shows four instances of

cp at important structural moments: cp's original diatonic form at the opening
of the exposition (cello), its octatonic transformation at the onset of TM^1 (violin 2), another octatonic transformation leading to the development's climax
(cello), and its whole-tone transformation at the retransition to the recapitulation (moving from violin 2 to violin 1).[24]

Example 6.4. String Quartet, I: Counter-p theme (cp)

In its original form, cp takes up four measures and divides into three consecutive tetrachords (designated tc^1–tc^3) and a turning figure (tn); since cp's
continuation often features a descending second (ds), measure 5 is included
as an extension. Latently present in the diatonic scale are the whole-tone and
the minor/octatonic tetrachords (see brackets above the staff) that through
sequential repetition in the subsequent transformations create the purely
octatonic or whole-tone transformations shown in the example. Again, the
collectional identity of each transformation is closely associated with the specific

role it fulfills in the formal process: the original diatonic form at a steady quarter-note pace denotes the relatively stable environment of expositional and recapitulatory openings; the octatonic forms serve the energy-gaining forward drive of TM^1 and the acceleration toward the development's climax; and the decelerating whole-tone transformation shapes the retransition to the recapitulation.

Transformations of Theme p^2. Although closely related to the primary theme p^1, this short theme creates a contrasting middle section within the primary theme zone. Its transformations throughout the movement reflect the changing collectional environments through which it passes (ex. 6.5). Originally outlining a D-minor triad in the exposition (mm. 9–10), p^2 outlines a diminished seventh chord on A at the corresponding moment in the recapitulation (mm. 137–38), where p^2 has been mapped onto the octatonic collection $OCT_{2,3}$.[25] Accompanied by an interval transformation of the motive's first interval from a fourth into a third, the underlying chord structure changes from a triad into a seventh chord. This octatonic form of p^2 is a result of a larger transformational trajectory from the exposition through the transformations of p^2 in the development. In measures 86–87, the same kind of interval transformation changes theme p^2 from its expositional triadic shape into a minor-seventh-chord outline (D–F–A–C), which contains as overlapping trichordal subsets the competing F-major/D-minor triads. The mapping of p^2 onto a rotation of A♭ melodic minor in measures 93–94 (with F as the lowest note of the collection) then transforms p^2 to outline a half-diminished minor seventh chord (F–A♭–C♭–E♭). Finally, the context of $OCT_{2,3}$ changes the half-diminished-seventh-chord form of p^2 into the recapitulation's fully-diminished-seventh-chord form G♭–E♭–C–A. The chain of p^2 heads that prepares for the return of p^1 after p^2's octatonic episode in the recapitulation features an elegant motivic parallelism (an enlargement of p^2) that bridges across the modular transformation from the octatonic to diatonic collections.[26]

By assigning the developmental task to p^2, Ravel draws our attention to the p^2 transformations, which create a perceptible path from exposition through development to recapitulation. This can work because the rhythmic motives of p^2 are different enough from those of p^1 that we hear p^2 as a contrasting theme—in spite of its intervallic relation to p^1. Therefore, since the p^1-based themes are absent throughout most of the development, when they come back in the recapitulation, we associate them more strongly with return. This process of withholding and returning an object is essentially different from the situation in which a primary theme is deconstructed during the development and restored to its original form at the beginning of the recapitulation. Ravel's "preoccupation with musical structure" in the String Quartet thus invokes another aspect of stagecraft: in addition to illuminating the transformation of the movement's characters—themes and motives—in the changing lights of referential collections, formal processes become highlighted by careful direction of the characters' presence on and off the stage.

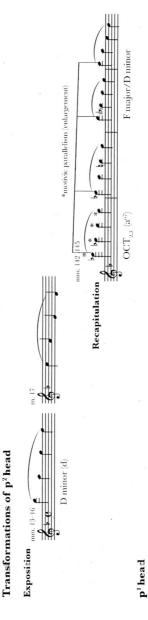

Example 6.5. String Quartet, I: Transformations of theme p^2

Piano Trio, I

In all the arts, the subject is of primary importance, for everything flows from it.[27]

Ravel's Piano Trio, completed in 1914, is the pinnacle of his prewar chamber music. In the first movement, Ravel achieves the utmost concentration of motivic, harmonic and formal design: a central object, the pitch-class set A–C–E–G, functions almost like a Schoenbergian "idea" in that it not only generates the motivic substance of the themes but also forms the harmonic framework for the movement's A-minor/C-major double-tonic complex (DTC). The DTC goes hand in hand with the double-rotational (binary) design of this sonata form and also has implications for the Trio's four-movement cycle as a whole.

Before addressing the motivic and structural organization, it is helpful to examine the primary theme's relationship to the Basque *zortziko*.[28] Previous authors have ascribed the "Basque flavor" of Ravel's Piano Trio to the *zortziko* (dance) rhythms in the first and fourth movements.[29] I suggest here that the first movement's primary theme is indebted to the *zortziko* as a *poetic* form. Basque poetry is sung and improvised to existing tunes with a mostly syllabic distribution of text.[30] To assist improvisation, the melodies are classified according to poetic meter. The *zortziko,* one of the more common meters in Basque poetry, has eight lines (*zortzi* means eight) and comes in two forms: the *zortziko handia* (large) alternates lines of ten and eight syllables, the *zortziko txikia* (small) lines of seven and six syllables.[31] In Ravel's Piano Trio, the first movement's primary theme follows the syllabic and verse structure of the *zortziko txikia:* the seven notes in each measure correspond to the seven syllables per line; and the eight measures of the repeated theme correspond to the eight lines of the poetic structure (ex. 6.6). The syllabic correspondence may explain why Ravel expanded the more typical $\frac{5}{8}$ *zortziko* meter to $\frac{8}{8}$ (3 + 2 + 3).[32] Instead of alternating measures with seven and six notes, which would have interrupted the melodic and rhythmic flow, Ravel invokes a "feminine" ending for all eight measures. While in the folk tunes the eight short lines are each different and form a single large unit, the division of the Trio's first eight measures into two thematic units of 4 + 4 incorporates the parallelism of classical phrase structure. Thus, we have reason to believe that just as the Malay pantoum inspired the second movement, a literary model also inspired the first movement (or at least its primary theme).[33]

The primary theme features other musical characteristics associated with Basque folk tunes: the meter is often composite or irregular, the melody moves mostly by seconds and thirds, leaps rarely exceed a fifth, the overall range is limited, the tunes are often modal, and the melodies proceed mostly at an *andante* pace. Ravel's tempo marking, *modéré,* thus associates his *zortziko* with the

Amodioa baida (19th-Century *zortziko txikia*)   **Ravel, Piano Trio, I**: P-theme

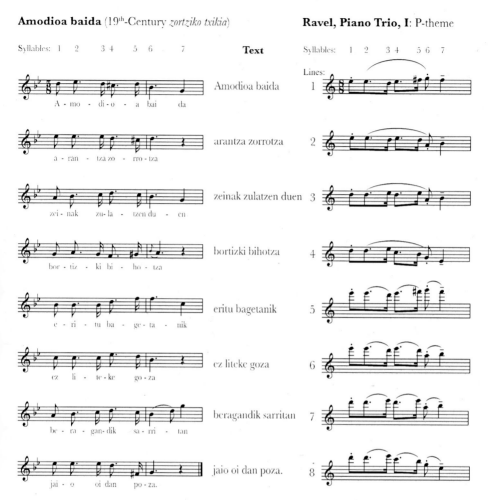

Example 6.6. Ravel, Piano Trio, I: Zortziko txikia structure of P-theme

sung tradition, rather than with the faster tempi of danced *zortziko*. The theme also shares specific melodic traits with certain nineteenth-century *zortziko txikia* tunes—for example, the Dorian mode found especially in the Lapurdi province (the region near Saint-Jean-de-Luz).

As the Basque topos invokes an idealized heritage, it invites hermeneutic interpretation—especially since the first movement's coda so obviously looks back to the opening measures.[34] Recalling the A-minor *zortziko* in C major— Ravel's marking *lointain* (from afar) conveys the distance in time and space— the transformed *zortziko* captures the movement's tonal and expressive crux in a moment of exquisite beauty (more on that later).[35]

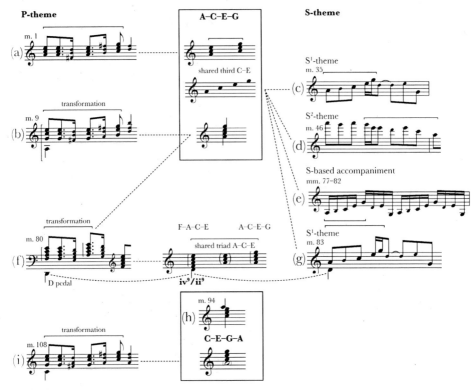

Example 6.7. Piano Trio, I: The pc object A–C–E–G

Motivic Substance and Tonal Process

Turning to the tonal-formal process, the pc object A–C–E–G permeates all levels of the movement. It not only shapes the motivic substance of the primary and secondary themes, but its minor-seventh-chord sonority appears at important formal junctures and is the source of the movement's A-minor/C-major double-tonic complex (DTC). Example 6.7 highlights the most salient relationships between motivic instances (melodic and harmonic) of the set, their roles in the overall design, and the overall tonal trajectory. While the combination of A-minor and C-major chords characterizes the primary theme in all its guises (see ex. 6.7a, b, f, h, and i), the melodic motion through an A-minor seventh-chord arpeggiation shapes the secondary theme and its derivations (ex. 6.7c, d, e, and g).

In the original primary theme (ex. 6.7a), the A-minor and C-major triads fall on the *zortziko*'s strong beats; the top voice's Dorian inflection further emphasizes the melodic motion to G. Ravel's subtle reharmonization of the theme's beginning in measure 9, with a C-major rather than an A-minor chord in the piano's right hand above the bass tone A1, features A–C–E–G as a single sonority (ex. 6.7b). The A-minor seventh chord initiates a descending circle-of-fifths motion from A through D (m. 11), G, and C (m. 13) to F (m. 14) to launch the P-based TR section.

The S-zone's first theme, S^1 (ex. 6.7c), outlines the A-minor minor seventh chord in melodic fashion, while the S-zone's second theme, S^2 (ex. 6.7d), traverses the A-minor pentatonic collection, a five-note superset of A–C–E–G. The transposition of the S-theme to D in measure 38, outlining D–F–A–C (not shown), foreshadows that harmony's role as structural subdominant (of A minor) or supertonic (of C major) in measure 80 (ex. 6.7f). More strikingly, the theme's varied continuation in measure 39 arpeggiating D–F–A–C–E, with E echoing the violin's 9–8 suspension, anticipates the large-scale suspension of measures 80–86.[36] S^1 becomes the basis for an S-based accompanying figure in the strings (ex. 6.7e),[37] while the piano plays a climactic variant of the P theme.[38]

At the moment of climax, the subposed D derails the triumphant return of the P theme (m. 77, last eighth note) to prepare for a minor-ninth chord whose upper three pitches contain the theme's original A-minor triad. In measure 80, the combined sets of the A–C–E–G accompaniment and the piano's D-minor ninth chord form a superset (ex. 6.7f), the eleventh chord D–F–A–C–E–G. Just as the double-tonic complex interprets the source set A–C–E–G as two triads, A minor and C major with the shared third C–E, Ravel parses the superset into a seventh chord A–C–E–G (strings) and a ninth chord D–F–A–C–E (piano), with the shared triad A–C–E. At this crucial juncture, the minor ninth chord on D functions as a kind of pivot chord: originally relating as a iv chord in A minor, its upper voice, suggesting a 9–8 suspension, hints at ii of C major.[39]

The return of S^1 at the original pitch level is still subposed by the supertonic D, which undermines the S-theme's A minor (ex. 6.7g). The upper voices hold on to the old tonic (A minor) while the bass moves inevitably toward the new (C major). The modulation to C major is confirmed at measure 85 with the characteristically Ravelian motion II–V to bass G, and the corresponding transposition of S^1 down a fifth (D–F–A–C). The final resolution to the C-major tonic remains in limbo until measures 93–94, providing the movement's essential structural closure (ESC) in C major (ex. 6.7h). With its added sixth A, the new tonic maintains the complete source set, now configured as C–E–G–A.

Beginning in measure 108, the P-theme returns in the coda, for the first time with the same melodic contour, texture, and dynamics as in the beginning. While the upper voice returns at pitch, the harmonization now reflects the new tonic C (ex. 6.7i). The C-major transformation casts the theme in a new and softer light: as if slightly blurred, it appears only a memory of its former self.

The double-tonic complex unfolds like a filtering-out process of components of the referential sonority A–C–E–G. First, A is filtered out in the bass but persists as an added sixth at the ESC (m. 94). Then, the closing zone (mm. 96–107) shifts three of the four pitches (all but C) down by a half step to a

ROTATION 1

59 m.	Exposition								$\hat5$ CF	S				/ C		
form	Exposition															
zones	P	TR							$\hat5$ CF	S				/ C		
segments	P	TR^1			Climax	Den.	TR^2	V_{lok}	link	S^1			S^2	EEC	P_C	
rch. no.		**1**			**2**		**3**			**4**			**5**		**6**	
m.	1–4	5–8	9–12	13–16	17–19	20–23	24–27	28–31	32–34	35–37	38–41	42–45	46–49	50–51	52–55	56–59
measure groups	4	4	4	4	3	4	4	4	3	3	4	4	4	2	4	4
bass	E	A	A–G	G–F	C#	C#♮B	B	E	E	A	D♭	A–G–F	E	A	A	A
RN	i	i	VI	VI	#iii	V/II	ii	V	V	i			V	i	i	i

ROTATION 2

58 m.	Development						Tonal Resolution					/ C				Coda		
form	Development						Tonal Resolution									Coda		
zones	P	TR					S					/ C				P		
segments	P_C	TR^1		Climax	Den.	link	S^1		S^1	S^2 ESC			P_C			P		
rch. no.	**7**	**8**		**9**			**10**			**11**			**12**			**13**		
m.	60–63	64–67	68–71	72–73	74–76	77–79	80–81	82–84	83–85	86–89	90–93	94–95	96–99	100–103	104–107	108–111	112–115	116–17
measure groups	4	4	4	2	3	3	2	3*	3*	4	4	2	4	4	4	4	4	2
bass	D#	C#	B♮…	B♭	A–D	D	D	D♭	G	G	C	C	C	C	C			
RN	i	D#	a:iv	a:ii	C:ii	ii	ii	v	V	II	I	I	I	I	I			

* Overlap of two three-measure groups = four actual measures

Figure 6.2. Piano Trio, I: Type 2 sonata form

Exposition

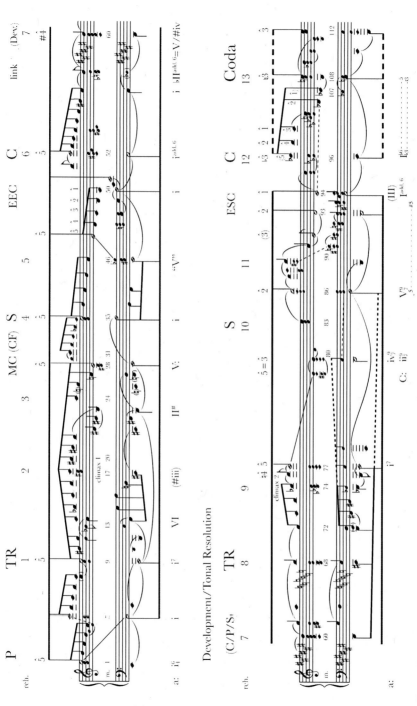

Development/Tonal Resolution

Example 6.8. Piano Trio, I: Middleground aligned with a Type 2 sonata form

neighboring common-tone augmented-sixth chord, further clouding the C-based sonority (for motivic consistency and voice leading, Ravel spells the chord's F♯ as a G♭). Finally, the coda filters out the harmonic turbidity of the flats and added sixth to sound a pure C major. In this vein, the final C major represents what is left of the double-tonic complex's seventh-chord sonority A–C–E–G after its root has been filtered out.

Formal and Structural Considerations

The C-major ending is a result of the unusual harmonic path the music takes through the highly condensed "Type 2" double-rotational sonata form (see fig. 6.2).[40] The exposition's secondary-theme zone does not sound in the relative major but instead remains in the tonic. The double-tonic complex arises because Ravel defers the motion to III, expected during the second half of the exposition, to the point of essential structural closure (ESC). Ravel's key scheme turns the classical harmonic paradigm upside down: the exposition's secondary theme sounds in the tonic key, whereas the movement's ESC and coda are in the relative major. This tonal scheme has implications for the structural voice leading. Compared to other sonata forms of Ravel's prewar period, the Trio's background structure appears furthest removed from Schenker's paradigm for a minor-mode sonata: it neither prolongs a single tonic nor shows the large-scale interruption of an *Ursatz* at the end of the development section and its subsequent completion at the end of the recapitulation.[41] To highlight Ravel's original treatment of tonal structure, my discussion of the graph focuses on "deviations" from the prototypical Schenkerian model of sonata form.

Example 6.8 presents a middle-ground graph of the movement aligned with the Type-2 sonata formal divisions. The *Kopfton* E is prolonged throughout the exposition since—unlike "standard" minor-mode sonata forms—the secondary-theme zone (S) continues to prolong the A-minor tonic.[42] Both primary and secondary themes feature two complete tonic fifth-descents. In both themes, the first descent is in the obligatory register (E_5 to A_4); the second descent is an octave higher in the P theme (E_6 to A_5) and an octave lower in the S theme.

The transition (TR) departs from normative expectations in its harmonic path toward the medial caesura (MC). TR begins in a fairly typical manner: melodic and harmonic alterations signal that the P theme is destabilizing, gathering momentum to launch the TR phase. TR first traverses a linear ascent from E_5 to E_6 (colored with F♯ and B♭, $\sharp\hat{6}$ and $\flat\hat{2}$ in A minor) culminating in the movement's first climax on C-sharp minor (reh. 2). From there, however, the denouement reverses the direction of the linear progression. The cadence on B major (V/V, m. 23), an octave below the obligatory register, turns out to be temporary: the second phase of TR returns to E_4 and a V:PAC medial caesura (m. 28).[43] As a consequence of the E-major MC, the S-zone opens in A minor.[44]

The Schenkerian graph makes S look deceptively strong in enshrining the tonic A minor. In the listener's actual experience, though, several factors weaken the sense of that tonicity. The imitative counterpoint of the S-theme itself at the pitch levels of A (m. 35), D (m. 38), and the descending-fifth stretto A–D–G–C (mm. 42–45) loosen A minor's hold on S. The A–D–G–C levels of imitation not only fit into A minor, but could function also, more strongly, as vi–ii–V–I in C major. The extended V $\frac{4}{2}$ in C, measures 44–45, and the lack of a leading-tone confirmation of A minor cast further doubt upon A minor's tonic status (hence the structural V in quotation marks in the graph at reh. 5). Part of the structural narrative here entails the exposition's S as playing with the possibilities of "A or C" with the nod barely going to A. This then sets up the return of S, which only needs a barely breathed sub-posed G to escort the tonal structure to C major.

The second rotation (beginning in m. 60) is notable for three aspects. The first concerns the degree to which Ravel blurs the boundary between developmental and recapitulatory aspects of the rotation. Measures 68–71 recall the opening theme while continuing the S-based accompaniment and maintaining the two-measure call-and-response pattern between the piano and the strings of measures 60–67. The parallelism of thematic sequence suggests that, as in the first rotation, this statement of P—in E minor over a C♯ pedal tone—launches TR. This is confirmed by the subsequent measures, 72–76, which match the approach to the climax of measures 15–19. Alluding to its precursor in the exposition, the thematic correspondence leads us to believe that we have unwittingly slipped into recapitulation territory. The passage's tonal instability, on the other hand, calls this judgment into question. In measure 68, E minor above the C♯$_2$ pedal (doubled with C♯$_1$) forms a passing half-diminished seventh chord which is part of a large-scale whole-tone trajectory in the bass that eventually leads (via the subposed D discussed in the next paragraph) to the structural dominant G in measure 86: initiated by D♯ in measure 60, the progression continues to B in measure 72, and moves toward the movement's second climax above the chromatic passing tone B♭ (mm. 74–76) to arrive at A in measure 77. This large-scale whole-tone trajectory achieves an interpenetration of developmental and recapitulatory aspects more deeply embedded in the overall structure than the S-based tonal resolution we expect for the second rotation of a Type 2 sonata form.

The second aspect is the process of reinterpretation of the *Kopfton* from $\hat{5}$ of A into $\hat{3}$ of C triggered by the "hostile" subposition of D, which thwarts P's triumphant return to A minor in measure 77. The transformation of E from the stable *Kopfton* of the fundamental line into a suspension that must—eventually—resolve to D initiates the final descent toward the ESC (mm. 93–94). The denouement, measures 78–79, parallels the exposition (mm. 21–22) but then merges with the approach to S. Unlike the exposition, the approach here does not articulate a caesura. On the contrary, the melodic descending-fifth line, formerly the caesura-fill E–D–C–B♭–A, continues into the S-space: while the cello begins the secondary theme in measure 83, the piano completes the descent from E to A in measures 83–85. Still undermined by the subposed D, the returning S-theme cannot accomplish its "normal" mission and provide tonal resolution. As if paralyzed by tonic inertia, it once again fails to move to III—now the new tonic. C major is accomplished *despite* the S-theme's insistence to return at pitch.[45]

The third aspect pertains to the provisional nature of structural closure for the movement. To assess if the ESC of this sonata movement marks the final tonal goal and completes the structural descent—albeit in a different key—and thus to answer our initial question about the DTC's tonal function, we must consider the prolongations and linear progressions of the closing zone and coda, both of which follow the ESC. The closing zone (mm. 96–107) imitates the exposition's 5-line that ultimately eluded the second rotation (development/tonal resolution). Although the descent here has the major quality (inflected with a Lydian ♯4) that we might have expected as a final transformation of the original 5-line, it arrives too "low." Not only do we hear the pitches B♭ and A♭—a half step below the B and A that would complete the A-minor fundamental line—we hear them an octave below the obligatory register. Ironically, this major-mode descent serves as a prolongation of ♭$\hat{3}$—the scale degree that we now interpret as a minor-mode inflection of the new tonic, C.[46]

Ravel restores scale-degree 3 to its natural major-mode state in the coda. (As in the movement's opening, the theme arpeggiates downward to E_4 instead of cadencing on C_5.) However, the last sonority of the movement leaves us with the sound of the third E_5 above C_5. Rather than confirming the $\hat{3}$–$\hat{2}$–$\hat{1}$ descent in C major, the coda prolongs E_5. This suggests that the *Kopfton* E has been recontextualized from A minor to C major but not truly displaced by a descent of the fundamental line. Perhaps it has yet to complete its journey to $\hat{1}$. Though tilting toward C major at the end of the movement, the double-tonic complex seems to create an equilibrium that allows the E to remain suspended as if in midair. At the very end of the movement, after the cello's C-major pizzicato, our ears are left with the sound of the third C–E, leaving open the possibility of a return to A minor at a moment's notice. Indeed, the second movement's opening A_2 immediately absorbs the third (back) into the A-minor sonority. From a prolongational perspective, the movement may be interpreted as incomplete—not only because the descent of the fundamental line is not entirely satisfactory, but also because the fundamental sonority has shifted its root from A to C, changing its manifestation from a seventh chord (A minor) to an added-sixth chord (C major).[47]

The Piano Trio's backward-looking C-major coda evokes the idea of memory, referring to a *past* reality; in its dreamlike quality, it might even signify a loss of that reality.[48] The classical paradigm's relative-major promise of relief from the minor-mode burden, on the other hand, looks to the *future,* the attainment of the parallel major. (Perhaps Mozart's "not yet" is Ravel's "not anymore.") The "Basque flavor" of the Trio's primary theme provides additional support for such an interpretation. Composing the Trio at Saint-Jean-de-Luz, Ravel might have conjured up idealized memories of childhood or, at the least, invoked his Basque heritage.[49]

The Four-Movement Cycle

From both the Schenkerian perspective and that and Hepokoski and Darcy, the lack of tonal closure at the movement level has consequences for the overall tonal plan of the Trio. First, we expect the Trio's sonata cycle to accomplish the harmonic closure not achieved by the first movement. Second, if Ravel follows classical paradigms, the Trio's sonata cycle eventually has to transform the "burden" of the minor-mode sonata by attaining the major mode in the tonic key. We have reason to believe that the major-minor dichotomy to some extent remained relevant during Ravel's lifetime. In his treatise on composition, d'Indy explains how in César Franck's Piano Quintet the keys of the outer movements, F minor and F major, form "poles of attraction, always in antagonism, until the victory of one over the other."[50] Paraphrasing d'Indy, Wheeldon describes the relationship between major and minor as follows: "The eventual triumph of the major tonic over the minor—or, metaphorically, of light over darkness—ends the antagonism between keys."[51] The correspondences between this model and Ravel's Piano Trio are the more striking as the first movement's failure to attain the major-mode tonic, or even to achieve tonic closure in the monotonal, Schenkerian sense, calls exactly for this kind of tonal plan to remedy both failures.

In the four-movement sonata cycle, Hepokoski and Darcy note that a 2 + 2 binary grouping of the "standard four-movement pattern" provides large-scale symmetry.[52] While the most common order of the movements is Allegro (tonic), slow movement (often nontonic), Minuet (tonic), and finale (tonic), Ravel's Trio features the alternative ("second-level default") ordering of Allegro, Minuet or Scherzo, slow movement, and finale, which is usually associated with the persistence of the tonic into the second movement. Ravel's key scheme matches this "heavily weighted tonic-balance in the work's first half":[53]

Modéré	Opening movement, sonata form	A-minor/C-major DTC
Pantoum	Scherzo/Minuet-type form with Trio	A minor
Passacaille	Slow movement, ternary form	C♯ Phrygian
Final	Fast final movement, sonata form	A major

Movement 1	Rotation 1		Rotation 2	
Section	P +TR	S+C	P +TR	S+C (+coda)
Key	a (E)	a	e above C#	C
Thematic Symmetry	P = p¹, p², p³, p⁴			P = p¹, p², p³, p⁴
Formal Symmetry	P-theme opens			P-theme closes

Four-Mvmt. Cycle	Pair 1		Pair 2	
Movement	I Modéré	II Pantoum	III Passacaille	IV Final
Key	a (C)	a	c# (Phrygian)	A
Thematic Symmetry	P = a, b¹, b², c			P = a, b¹, b², c
Formal Symmetry	Sonata Form	Large Ternary	Large Ternary	Sonata Form

Figure 6.3. Piano Trio: Movement-cycle parallelism

The double-tonic complex transfers the harmonic task—the attainment of the major tonic—of the first movement to the whole sonata cycle. As the DTC-based background structure of the complete first movement resembles that of a typical minor-mode exposition, harmonically, the first movement relates to the whole sonata *cycle* as an exposition would to a sonata *movement*.[54]

By comparing the key relationships within the first movement to those of the cycle, we find another parallelism that relates the binary symmetry of the Type 2 sonata form to that of the four-movement sonata cycle (fig. 6.3). In the first movement, the initial rotation cannot escape the tonic A minor. In the second rotation, the primary theme returns in E minor above a passing C♯. Although in a Schenkerian sense the E minor is not stable, formally this passage represents the first half of rotation 2 because here the modified P-theme returns; C major represents the second half of rotation 2. In the four-movement cycle, the first half remains in A minor. In this larger context, C major serves as the boundary between the two A-minor movements, just as in the first movement's exposition, the E-major medial caesura forms the boundary between the exposition's two halves. The Passacaille takes a first step toward attaining A major by centering its three-sharp diatonic collection on C♯, the major third of the overall tonic key. Similarly, we can interpret the primary theme's E-minor return in the first movement as centered on the C-major tonic's major third.

The shared collections are not the only indication that Ravel clearly designed the four movements as two pairs of related movements. Example 6.9 shows that movements I and II share the motivic parallelism of E–E–D (more specifically, motivic enlargement), while movements III and IV are closely

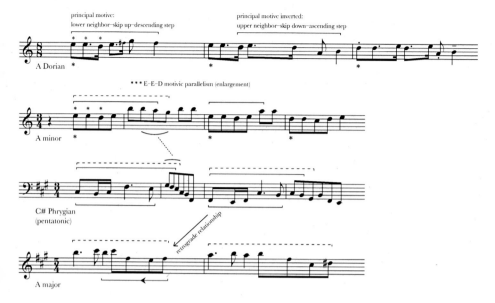

Example 6.9. Piano Trio: Inter-movement connections among P-themes

linked through their motivic substance, sharing pentatonic subsets in their main themes. Moreover, Ravel separates the last two movements only by a thin double bar, instructing the players to link them (*enchaînez*, literally, to chain, to thread). In addition to the overall tonal plan, the shared thematic substance among all four movements fulfills the second condition of d'Indy's *sonate cyclique*.[55] Example 6.10 summarizes some of the Piano Trio's most salient cyclic features, which include symmetry of form (sonata in the outer movements, ternary forms in the inner); shared collections between the two movement pairs (no sharps or flats in I and II, three sharps in III and IV); and symmetrical aspects of meter (asymmetric compound meter in the outer movements, triple meter in the inner).

Conclusion

According to Roland-Manuel, "The fundamental coherence and purity of conception of the Trio in A shows a quality of mastery quite different from the frenzied melancholy which with infinitely less sureness of touch animates the Quartet."[56] Viewing the analyses of the first movements of the String Quartet and the Piano Trio side by side affords two kinds of insights: where the two sonata movements share qualities or compositional techniques, we may detect trademarks of Ravel's style. Where they differ, we may (cautiously) deduce trends in

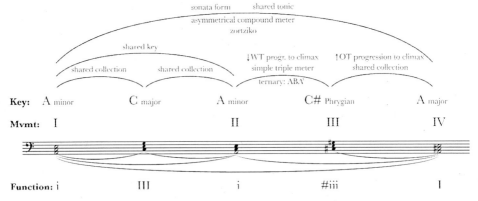

Example 6.10. Piano Trio: Cyclic aspects

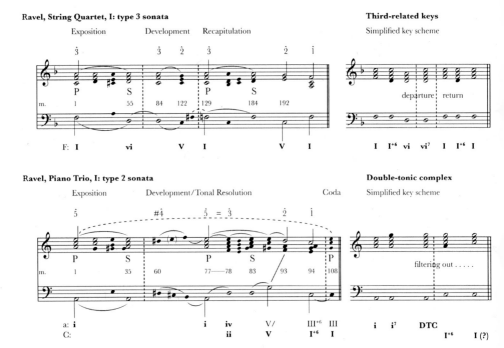

Example 6.11. Quartet and Trio: Key scheme and sonata-type interrelationships

Ravel's compositional craft. Both movements are part of a larger four-movement cycle with the general pairing Allegro-Scherzo and slow movement–fast finale. Although both works incorporate inter-movement relationships, the cyclic process of the Trio functions at deeper structural levels; the tonal plan is integral to the cycle and the motivic interrelationships are more essential.[57] In both opening movements, Ravel explores third-related keys of a single shared collection. F major and D minor function as competing keys in the String Quartet's first movement; A minor and C major form a double-tonic complex in the Trio's.

Example 6.11 demonstrates how each key scheme is inextricably linked with the respective movement's sonata type. The Quartet's type 3 sonata is based on the traditional concept of departure and return associated with tripartite forms, even if Ravel's design and the means by which it is achieved depart in many ways from tradition. The Trio's type 2 sonata is double-rotational because its tonal trajectory has no point of return (at least not within the movement); the original tonic has been filtered out. The two movements' simplified key schemes almost mirror each other in the way thirds are added above and below, and minor sevenths are turned into added sixths. However, the tonal trajectory of the Trio is much more adventurous and forward-looking (literally and figuratively). If we consider the path from the Quartet's bifocal tonality to the Trio's double-tonic complex as part of a larger trajectory, we might cast a line from here to Ravel's postwar explorations of the major-minor hybrid tonality of the *Sonata for Violin and Cello* and the (quasi-)polytonality in the Sonata for Violin and Piano.[58]

In both movements Ravel subverts the models he adopts; what differs is *how* he distances himself from them. The unconventional features of the Quartet's first movement ultimately do not keep us from tracking the type 3 sonata form, even if the juxtapositions of diatonic and nondiatonic material and the associated motivic transformation change *how* we track the form. In the Piano Trio, we still recognize a kind of sonata form, but one of the essential elements we associate with the form, that of tonic return—if not that of the primary, then at least of the secondary theme—has eluded us. Herein lies the element of subversion: Ravel entices us to hear and accept the movement as a (double-rotational) sonata form when at the same time he withholds the most central tenet of the sonata principle: the tonic return.

Ravel departs from his models when he alters the harmonic paradigms or the functions we associate with sonata form. In his harmonic praxis, third-relationships and nondiatonic collections serve to create ambiguities rather than outright conflict, a subtler kind of tension than direct confrontation. Ambiguities also obscure the formal functions of sections—as clearly delineated as they may appear at the music's surface. In evoking sonata paradigms while at the same time distancing themselves from them, Ravel's sonata forms play with their models and with our perception. In that, Ravel's advice to his students parallels our experience: where what we hear differs from what we already know, we perceive what is new.

Notes

The epigraph for this chapter is drawn from Maurice Ravel, as quoted by Roland-Manuel. See Roland-Manuel, *Ravel*, trans. Cynthia Jolly (New York: Dover, 1972), 134. The exact wording of the English translation here is found in Deborah Mawer, "Musical Objects and Machines," in *The Cambridge Companion to Ravel*, ed. Deborah Mawer (Cambridge: Cambridge University Press, 2000), 56.

1. For an extensive documentation on the historical and cultural background of Ravel's use of models, see Elisabeth Winnecke, *Ravel und die Modelle: Kulturhistorische Untersuchungen zum Gebrauch von Modellen und Beiträge zu einer Ästhetik Maurice Ravels*, Musik Kontext, vol. 1 (Frankfurt am Main: Peter Lang/Europäischer Verlag der Wissenschaften, 2001).

2. Vladimir Jankélévitch, *Ravel* (New York: Grove Press, 1959), 69.

3. In a 1932 interview Ravel links his love for Mozart to his own ideal of pure forms: "Mozart's great lesson for us today is that he is helping us to liberate ourselves from music, to listen only to ourselves and to our eternal heritage, to forget what immediately preceded us: this accounts for the present return to *pure forms*, this neoclassicism . . . which delights me, in a certain sense." See Nino Frank, "Maurice Ravel Between Two Trains," in Arbie Orenstein, *A Ravel Reader: Correspondence, Articles, Interviews* (New York: Columbia University Press, 1990), 497.

4. Works in or related to sonata form include the *Sonate posthume pour piano et violon* (1897); *Jeux d'eau* (1901); the *Quatuor à cordes* (String Quartet, 1902–3); the *Sonatine* (1903–5); the *Introduction et allegro* (1905); "Ondine" and "Scarbo" from *Gaspard de la nuit* (1908); the *Trio pour piano, violon et violoncelle* (Piano Trio, 1914); the *Sonate pour violon et violoncelle* (1920–22); the *Sonate pour violon et piano* (1923–27); the *Concerto pour la main gauche* (Concerto for the Left Hand, 1929–30); and the *Concerto en sol majeur* (Piano Concerto, 1929–31).

5. See Scott Messing, *Neoclassicism in Music: From the Genesis of the Concept through the Schoenberg/Stravinsky Polemic* (Ann Arbor: UMI Research Press, 1988), xvi; and Mawer, "Musical Objects and Machines," in Mawer, *The Cambridge Companion to Ravel*, 47–67.

6. See James Hepokoski and Warren Darcy, *Elements of Sonata Theory: Norms, Types, and Deformations in the Late-Eighteenth Century Sonata* (New York: Oxford University Press, 2006).

7. Maurice Ravel; see "An Autobiographical Sketch by Maurice Ravel," in Orenstein, *A Ravel Reader: Correspondence, Articles, Interviews*, 30.

8. The sonata forms that precede the Quartet are unpublished exercises from Ravel's studies at the Conservatoire and the posthumously published *Sonata posthume pour piano et violon*, composed in 1897 (Paris: Editions Salabert, 1975).

9. Thomas Kabisch was the first to point to the structural role of nondiatonic collections in the first movement of Ravel's String Quartet. See his "Oktatonik, Tonalität und Form in der Musik Maurice Ravels," *Musiktheorie* 5, no. 2 (1990): 117–36; see especially the subsection "'Une construction musicale plus nette'—Oktatonik, Tonalität und Sonatenform im Kopfsatz des Streichquartetts," 121–22.

10. Recent analyses of form in the first movement of Debussy's String Quartet include Richard S. Parks, *The Music of Debussy* (New Haven: Yale University Press, 1989), 217–20;

Teresa M. Davidian, "Debussy's Sonata Forms" (PhD diss., University of Chicago, 1988), 110–36; and Annie Ka-Po, "Continuity and Formal Organization in Debussy's *String Quartet*" (PhD diss., Yale University, 1992).

11. Hepokoski and Darcy, *Elements of Sonata Theory*, 45.

12. Hepokoski and Darcy describe three phases that each shape a module of the "trimodular block": (1) the first new theme after the MC (TM^1); (2) the first theme's dissolution and the preparation of the second MC (TM^2); and (3) the second new theme "starting its own, renewed journey toward the EEC" (TM^3). See *Elements of Sonata Theory*, 170.

13. An alternative interpretation is feasible: If p^3 is not heard as a new theme, the first caesura gesture (mm. 21–23) merely interrupts an extended transition (TR), whose second phase (mm. 35–50) leads to the actual MC (mm. 50–54) and S in measure 55. That both interpretations—trimodular block or resumed transition—seem plausible demonstrates how Ravel plays with classical conventions by creating ambiguity between thematic content and tonal expectation.

14. A "PAC that is immediately overridden, perhaps through thematic repetition," results in a "failed EEC" and thus a "failed exposition" (since it fails to produce the satisfactory cadence that is the single goal of the S-zone). *Elements of Sonata Theory*, 177.

15. Peter Kaminsky defines subposition in Ravel's music as "the placement of a root, interval, or chord below a previously stated sonority, generally either defining or altering its functional implication." See Peter Kaminsky, "Of Children, Princesses, Dreams and Isomorphisms," *Music Analysis* 19, no. 1 (2000): 35.

16. *Elements of Sonata Theory*, 178. Also relevant for Ravel is the authors' suggestion that, in the nineteenth or early twentieth century, a failed exposition or failed recapitulation "can imply a critique of the inadequacy of the older, Enlightenment solutions in more complex, modern times"—although Ravel's creative use of models might be rather an expression of ironic distance than a "critique of inadequacy." Ibid.

17. See William E. Caplin, *Classical Form: A Theory of Formal Functions for the Instrumental Music of Haydn, Mozart, and Beethoven* (New York: Oxford University Press, 1998), 147.

18. The subscripts of the $OCT_{2,3}$ indicate that this collection includes D and E♭. The single exception is the pitch C♯ in the second violin which belongs to this instrument's accompanying chromatic line (B–C–C♯–D).

19. Among the many scholars on nineteenth-century music who have written about expanded tonal relations in sonata form are James Webster, "Schubert's Sonata Form and Brahms's First Maturity," *19th-Century Music* 3, no. 1 (1979): 52–71; Charles Rosen, *Sonata Forms* (New York: W. W. Norton, 1980; rev. ed. 1988); Harald Krebs, "Third Relation and Dominant in Late 18th and Early 19th-Century Music" (PhD diss., Yale University, 1980); and Rey Longyear and Kate Covington, "Sources of Three-Key Expositions," *Journal of Musicology* 6, no. 4 (1988): 448–70.

20. For another discussion of this passage and the Quartet's nondiatonic collections, see Steven Baur, "Ravel's 'Russian' Period: Octatonicism in His Early Works, 1893–1908," *Journal of the American Musicological Society* 52, no. 3 (1999): 547–55.

21. The augmented sixth chord's resolution directly to the tonic is covered in chapter 27 of Tchaikovsky's harmony treatise: "[Chords of the augmented sixth] are nothing more than the inversions of certain chords resolving into the tonic triad, and having the 2nd degree of the scale chromatically lowered." Peter Ilyitch Tchaikovsky, *Guide to the Practical Study of Harmony*, trans. Emil Krall and James Liebling (Leipzig: P. Jurgenson, 1900; repr., Mineola: Dover, 2005; Russian original published 1871), 106.

22. Thomas Kabisch explains the structural role of octatonicism in Ravel's String Quartet as follows: "Whereas the role of octatonicism in the exposition serves to

create a transition between functionally clearly defined key areas, in the development the octatonicism becomes the intrinsic principle of organization." [Dient die Oktatonik in der Exposition dazu, einen Übergang zwischen funktional eindeutig bestimmten Augangs- und Zieltonarten zu schaffen, so wird sie in der Durchführung des Quartetts zum eigenständigen Organisationsprinzip.] See "Oktatonik, Tonalität und Form in der Musik Maurice Ravels," 123, my translation.

23. For a fuller consideration of the movement that traces the history of the opening p idea as well see Sigrun B. Heinzelmann, "Sonata Form in Ravel's Pre-war Chamber Music" (PhD diss., City University of New York, 2008), 136–61.

24. Further transformations of cp occur in measures 9–16, 45–48, 91–92, and 172–76.

25. The shifting harmonic contexts for these transformations, while beyond the scope of this analysis, represent an important facet of the passages in question. Thus, for example, following the bass line at measures 9–10, the harmonies are (approximately) G^9–$B\flat^7$–Dm^{add6}–$B\flat m^{M7}$; in contrast to this varied palette of chord types, the octatonic measures 137–38 have only the dominant seventh type—$F^7\flat^9$–$A\flat^7$–B^7–$A\flat^7$.

26. The concept of motivic enlargement is discussed in Brian Alegant and Donald McLean, "On the Nature of Enlargement," *Journal of Music Theory* 45, no. 1 (2001): 31–71.

27. Mawer, "Musical Objects and Machines," 49.

28. "The Trio, whose first theme has a Basque flavor, was composed entirely in 1914 at Saint-Jean-de-Luz." Maurice Ravel, "An Autobiographical Sketch by Maurice Ravel," in Orenstein, *Ravel Reader*, 32.

29. The first reference to the *zortziko* dance rhythm in Ravel's Piano Trio seems to appear in Hans Heinz Stuckenschmidt, *Maurice Ravel: Variationen über Person und Werk* (Frankfurt am Main: Suhrkamp, 1966), 191. See also the English translation *Maurice Ravel—Variations on His Life and Work*, trans. Samuel R. Rosenbaum (London: Calder and Boyars, 1969), 149. For a description of the *zortziko* as a musical dance, see Denis Laborde, "Basque Music," *Grove Music Online*, ed. L. Macy (accessed July 30, 2007), http://www.grovemusic.com. The typical *zortziko* rhythm is ♪♪.♪♪.♪.

30. Small exceptions are possible; e.g., in some *txikia* tunes, the six-syllable lines musically imitate the seven-syllable lines' "feminine" ending by adding a note to the last syllable.

31. A search for ninetheeth-century *zortziko txikia* tunes at the Basque website, http://www.bertsozale.com, dedicated to the tradition of the Basque folk poetry, yielded 545 matches. See Laborde, "Basque Music," *Grove Music Online*; Israel J. Katz, "*Bertsolaritza* and Its Musical Foundations: Some Observations," in *Voicing the Moment: Improvised Oral Poetry and Basque Tradition*, ed. Samuel G. Armistead and Joseba Zulaika (Reno: University of Nevada Press, 2005), 343–70; and Gorka Aulestia, *Improvisational Poetry from the Basque Country*, trans. Lisa Corcostegui and Linda White (Reno: University of Nevada Press, 1995), 22–24.

32. Stuckenschmidt mentions the Basque song "Errefusa," arranged by Charles Bordes, which shows the same metrical grouping. See Hans Heinz Stuckenschmidt, *Maurice Ravel*, 226–27; page 182 in the English translation. Since there are no significant similarities between the song and Ravel's tune, I contend that Ravel's meter was modeled on the metric characteristics of the folk poetry rather than a specific song.

33. For a discussion of the second movement, see Brian Newbould, "Ravel's Pantoum," *Musical Times*, 116 (1975): 228–31. It is likely that Ravel was familiar with the pantoum form through French poems by Hugo and Baudelaire.

34. We find internal and external references to past objects among the other movements as well: the second movement incorporates the verse structure of the pantoum, the third movement employs the baroque passacaille, and the fourth movement recalls the *zortziko* rhythm once more. As each movement's primary theme is derived from the same thematic substance, each also references the primary themes of the previous movements.

35. Biographical evidence links the Trio to Ravel's concern for his mother, as he worked on the Trio while contemplating to enlist for military service in the war. The strain of the situation is clearly evident in a letter to Maurice Delage from August 4, 1914: "If I left my poor mother, it would surely kill her. . . . Yes, I am working [on the Trio] with the sureness and lucidity of a madman. But as I work, something gnaws at me, and suddenly I find myself sobbing over my music!" See Arbie Orenstein, *Ravel: Man and Musician* (New York and London: Columbia University Press, 1975), 72.

36. See also examples 6.9 and 6.10.

37. The first to point to this motivic relationship was Jürgen Braun, in *Die Thematik in den Kammermusikwerken von Maurice Ravel*, Kölner Beiträge zur Musikforschung, vol. 33 (Regensburg: Gustav Bosse, 1966), 121.

38. The almost obsessive reiterations of the S-derived accompaniment figure in the strings at and after the movement's final climax (mm. 77–82) prepare for the reentry of S^1. Although this figure presents the original source set A–C–E–G, it is locally subordinate to the transposed, subdominant set D–F–A–C.

39. Editor's note: In the opening movement of *Ma mère l'oye*, "Pavane de la belle au bois dormant," Ravel does almost exactly the same thing—same chord, same keys—at the formal juncture between the middle section and the reprise; cf. chapter 4, example 4.1b.

40. A Type 2 sonata is a two-part or *bi-rotational* structure (its historical predecessor can be found in the piano sonatas of Scarlatti). The first rotation is usually a standard exposition, while the second rotation combines developmental and recapitulatory functions: with P-theme space occupied by the developmental function, it is most commonly the secondary theme (S) that fulfills the recapitulatory function (*tonal resolution*). See chapter 17 of *Elements of Sonata Theory*, 353–87.

41. See *Elements of Sonata Theory*, 344.

42. Chopin's early formal-tonal practice provides a precedent and possible model for Ravel's structural theme. For example, in his Piano Sonata op. 4 (I) the exposition's S-zone never leaves the C-minor tonic; and in the first movement of the E-minor Concerto op. 11, the exposition's S-zone sounds in the parallel key of E major. In the recapitulation, S returns in G major before the movement's conclusion finds its way back to E minor. The third relationship, i(I)–III, between the two S-zones is the same as that in the first movement of Ravel's Piano Trio. See Charles Rosen, *Sonata Forms*, rev. ed., 392; John Rink, "Tonal Architecture in the Early Music," *The Cambridge Companion to Chopin*, ed. Jim Samson (Cambridge: Cambridge University Press, 1992), 79–97; and Anatole Leikin, "The Sonatas," ibid., 160–87.

43. The harmonic path of returning to V of the tonic after pretending to aim for another key area is usually associated with TR's role in the recapitulation.

44. Hepokoski and Darcy offer a whimsical image for the role of the MC: "It may be thought of as metaphorically analogous to the moment of the opening of elevator doors onto a higher floor—making S-space possible or opening to the second part of the exposition." See *Elements of Sonata Theory*, 25. In this case, when the elevator doors open, we find ourselves still on the first floor!

45. Mark DeVoto's description of the second theme here as "harmonised first subtly, and then decisively, in C major," captures the spirit, if not quite the structural implications of the moment: as often in Ravel, a most subversive adaptation of a model seems to pass below the radar. See Mark DeVoto, "Harmony in the Chamber Music," in Mawer, *The Cambridge Companion to Ravel*, 105.

46. The C-zone's C major is colored with F♯ (which initially had provided the dorian inflection of A minor) and harmonizations whose A♭ and B♭ carry the vestiges of the C-zone's A-flat major harmony (Riemann's *Leittonwechselklang*/leading-tone-exchange chord of C minor).

47. Among others, Boyd Pomeroy has shown convincing background structures for third-related DTCs; see "Tales of Two Tonics: Directional Tonality in Debussy's Orchestral Music," *Music Theory Spectrum* 26, no. 1 (2005): 87–118. The particulars of this movement here, however, lead me to interpret the movement's tonal structure as somewhat "incomplete."

48. This contrast brings to mind the A-minor/C-major contrast in the first act of *Tristan und Isolde*. Based on research by Lorenz and Bailey, William Kinderman summarizes this tonal relationship in *Tristan* as "a pairing and alternation of A minor and C major to underscore the dichotomy between the real world of the lovers and the external world, the dreaded realm of 'Day.'" See William Kinderman, "Wagner's *Parsifal*: Musical Form and the Drama of Redemption," *Journal of Musicology* 4, no. 4 (1985–86): 432. Perhaps Ravel's tonal pairing is an ironic play that reverses Wagner's tonal relationship into one where C major is the key that represents the internal and intimate.

49. Since Ravel spent only the first three months of his life in Ciboure before his family moved to Paris, he would not have remembered the place. However, his frequent visits to the nearby Saint-Jean-de-Luz suggest that the place and his Basque heritage were important to him.

50. Vincent d'Indy, *Cours de composition musicale, IIe livre, Ire partie* (Paris: Durand, 1909), 389–90; Merle Montgomery, "Vincent d'Indy, *Cours de composition musicale*, English translation of the sixth edition (1912)" (PhD diss., University of Rochester, Eastman School of Music, 1948). Quoted in Marianne Wheeldon, "Debussy and *La Sonate cyclique*," *Journal of Musicology* 22, no. 4 (2005): 665.

51. Ibid., 666.

52. *Elements of Sonata Theory*, 337.

53. Hepokoski and Darcy imply a parallelism between the key schemes of a first-movement minor-mode sonata form and that of a minor-mode sonata cycle. In the sonata *movement*, the S-zone's motion to III during the exposition promises a release from the "burden" of the minor mode, but only the recapitulation's attainment of the major-mode tonic brings true liberation; in the sonata *cycle*, the major-mode finale redeems the opening minor-mode movement(s). *Elements of Sonata Theory*, 311.

54. This parallelism between movement and cycle does not equate the remaining movements with other sections of standard sonata form: the *pantoum* and *passacaille* do not function like developmental sections within the whole cycle, even if the *final* does fulfill the harmonic task we otherwise ascribe to the recapitulation.

55. See Wheeldon, "Debussy and *La Sonate cyclique*," 662–66.

56. Roland-Manuel, *Maurice Ravel*, 75.

57. That the Trio was conceived from an overarching idea might explain the curious remark of Ravel to Maurice Delage reported by Stuckenschmidt: "My *Trio* is finished. I only need the themes for it." Stuckenschmidt, *Maurice Ravel—Variations on his Life and Work*, 149; page 189 in the German original.

58. DeVoto uses Jan LaRue's term "bifocal tonality" to describe the type of diatonic tonal ambiguity between third-related tonics featured not only in the *Introduction and Allegro* but in other works. See DeVoto, "Harmony," 102–4; Jan LaRue, "Bifocal tonality: An explanation for ambiguous Baroque cadences," in *Essays on Music in Honor of Archibald Thompson Davison* (Cambridge: Harvard University Department of Music, 1957), 173–84; rept. in *Journal of Musicology* 18, no. 2 (2001): 283–94. See also Peter Kaminsky, "Ravel's Late Music and the Problem of 'Polytonality,'" *Music Theory Spectrum*, 26, no. 2 (2004): 237–64.

Chapter Seven

Spiral and Self-Destruction in Ravel's La valse

Volker Helbing

In *La valse* two aspects constitutive of Ravel's work converge in an ideal and characteristic manner: a tendency toward "distancing appropriation"—the ever-alienating incorporation of pre-found musical material into one's own musical language—and the formal conception of the "spiral," with its acceleration and intensification toward a final culmination. The work is to a large extent choreographically shaped with tendencies toward caricature, the fateful, and the (self-)destructive to a degree that is singular in Ravel's oeuvre. This study will explore the aspects of distancing appropriation, spiral, and self-destruction.

Spiral Forms

Repetition, circular motion, and dance shaped Ravel's music at least since the *Habanera* (1895). These tendencies became integral to an unmistakable musical physiognomy as soon as Ravel succeeded in (1) making them serve in larger linear contexts; (2) differentiating the circular figures and functionally adjoining them to one another; and (3) developing formal conceptions that accommodated the choreographic orientation of the music.[1] One of these formal conceptions, which I shall designate as the "spiral," first appears primarily in finales: in the third movement of the *Sonatine* (1905), "Feria" (*Rapsodie espagnole*, 1907), "Scarbo" (*Gaspard de la nuit*, 1908), the "Danse guerrière" and "Danse générale" from both suites from *Daphnis et Chloé* (1912), and the "Toccata" from *Le tombeau de Couperin* (1917).[2] All of these compositions combine a tendency toward periodicity with a prevailing escalating, teleological direction entailing all dimensions of the work. In other words, these works appear to move in progressively shorter and more intense oscillations encompassing more and more registral space toward a climax before the end of the piece (immediately before the coda), unless this final point of repose is itself over-shot. Most of the compositions divide either into two analogous parts, or they combine binary and ternary formal principles by modifying aspects of the tra-ditional formal development, recapitulation, and stretto in a single, coherent second part. The spiral construction is primarily manifest in the second (or, depending on the piece, the second and third) part. The first part is an "expo-sition" insofar as it anticipates this process, which will lead to the highest stage of intensification only in the second and third part.[3]

While most of these pieces are relatively short, within their narrow frame they unfold a remarkable pianistic or orchestral expansiveness.[4] If one also considers that the three orchestral movements resemble *La valse* in subject matter as a mass dance with a tendency toward the repetitive and orgiastic, that the "Feria"—even more so than *La valse*—works with quotations, and that the spiral construction in each of these movements arises through an emphasis on another compositional parameter, then it seems that these were preparatory exercises for a project that, although already conceptualized by 1906 before most of these spiral movements were composed, Ravel first found himself in a position to realize at the end of 1919.[5]

The Poetic-Choreographic Idea and Formal Conception

According to Ravel's autobiographical sketch, the subject matter of the work is "a sort of apotheosis of the Viennese waltz, mingled with, in my mind, the impression of a fantastic, fatal whirling."[6] Thus it represents, on the one hand, the "Grand Waltz" as "a sort of homage to the memory of the Great Strauss" as the work was originally conceived; and, on the other hand, the image of a fantastical and fatal vortex, a "dancing, whirling, almost hallucina-tory ecstasy, an increasingly passionate and exhausting whirlwind of dancers, who are overcome and exhilarated by nothing but 'the waltz.'"[7] The concep-tion of the waltz as a gradual intensification culminating in an orgiastic whirl is hardly Ravel's invention; indeed, from the opera and concert repertoires of the second half of the nineteenth century alone, there are at least three ball scenes which attempt to realize this exact conception. Not coinciden-tally, two of these set the same scene from the Faust myth—the waltz finale from Act II of Gounod's *Faust* (after Goethe, 1859) and Liszt's *Tanz in der Dorfschule* (after Lenau, 1860).[8] Yet it appears that the full realization of this concept first becomes possible at the beginning of the twentieth century, as the harmonic and metric foundations of tonality were irrevocably delimited as historically bound, thereby enabling composers to view such foundations "from the outside"; or more concretely, to musically work through the fatal whirling to its logical conclusion.

And herein the relationship of *La valse* to its musical "models" is defined: even if it may sound so at times (e.g., in the second waltz, Reh. 18–25, mm. 148–211), *La valse* is never "just" a waltz or a suite of waltzes but is a realization of a conception of "the waltz" as a musico-choreographic action for the stage, whose actors (the waltzes themselves) step back and forth, cut each other off and become entangled with one another through means of expansion, acceleration, montage (spatial and stylistic), distancing, and exaggeration.[9]

Formally, the first part of *La valse* is an exposition and the second part the actual spiral. The first part presents itself—in the above-mentioned theatrical sense—as an introduction and waltz suite, whose nine individual waltzes divide into three groups (see fig. 7.1a). While waltzes 1 and 2 remain in the primary key of D major, waltzes 3 to 6 move to the contrasting tonal region of B♭ major (and its subdominant and dominant), which then leads to a dominant prolongation in D. The return to the primary key, a close relationship with the first waltz, and the manner of its arrangement and emergence establish the seventh waltz as a quasi-recapitulation. Finally, structural commonalities join waltzes 7 through 9 into a group that simultaneously emphasizes various closing functions (see below) as well as anticipates developmental techniques that will be determinative for the second part of the piece.

Mm.	Reh.	Waltz	Tonal area(s)
1–66	1–8	Introduction	
I		**I**	
67–147	9–17	No. 1	D major
70–106	9–13^1	First Period	(modulation to A)
107–147	13^2–17	Second Period	
148–211	18–25	No. 2	D major (F♯ minor – D major – B minor) – E♭ major – D–major
II		**II**	
212–243	26–29	No. 3	B♭ major
244–275	30–34	No. 4	E♭ major
276–291	35	No. 5	F major?
292–331	36–40	No. 6	F major
308–331	38–40	Dominant pedal	
III		**III**	
332–371	41–45	No. 7	D major – F major – D major
372–405	46–50^1	No. 8	B♭ major – D♭ major
406–441	50^2–53	No. 9	A major – "C major"

Figure 7.1a. Ravel, *La valse*, Exposition (Part I)

Phase	Mm.	Reh.	Quoted Waltzes	Tonicized Key Areas	Refrain
I	442–458	54–56	(Nr. 1), 443–449 corresponds to Introduction 12–19	(G♭)	450–458
II	459–480	57–59	(Nr. 1), 459–480 corresponds to Introduction 40–57	**G♭ – A♭ – A**	473–480
III	481–501	60–62	No. 3	**A** (F♯, E)	493–501
IV	502–521	63–65	No. 6	**C** (D, E, F♯, min 3rd cycle)	–
V	522–557	66–72	No. 5 (and Refrain)	**E♭** (G♭, A♭, B♭, C, min 3rd cycle)	547–557
VI	558–579	73–75	No. 4	**C – A**	–

Boldface: Structurally prior key areas (see also key signatures in mm. 424 [no signature], 473 [A], 502 [C], 522 [E♭], 532 [G♭], 542 [A♭], 547 [C]: Only A♭ is not part of the minor third axis.)

Figure 7.1b. Ravel, *La valse*, Development (Part II, first section)

Phase	Mm.	Reh.	Quoted Waltzes	Key Areas	Choreographic Function
I	580–645	76–84	No. 7 586–601 and 610–625 corresond to 348–363	D major, D♭ major, E major	Beginning of the end: Reaching back and liquidation
II	646–664	85–87	No. 8 646–657 correspond to 372–382	F major	Gathering and explosion
	665–693	88–93	(No. 1, 8 etc.)		Centrifugal sequence I Fanning out toward the cadence
III (Coda)	694–722	94–97	No. 1, cadential progression and No. 2, mm. 712-713 correspond to 148-149	D major	Approach to the cadence: Gathering and explosion.
	723–738	98–99			Centrifugal sequence II (8+8)
	739–755	100–01	No. 1, Cadential progression	"D major"	Gathering (2+2) Reaching back (4x1+7x1) Termination (2)

Figure 7.1c. Ravel, *La valse*, Recapitulatory Stretta (Part II, second section)

184 ANALYTICAL CASE STUDIES

The second part (figs. 7.1b and 7.1c) follows this grouping insofar as (1) the "development"[10]—after a variant of the introduction—draws exclusively on material from the second group; (2) the entrance of the seventh waltz again achieves the initial key and is staged as "the beginning of the end"; and (3) the seventh and eight waltzes are the only ones that are quoted in more than a mere fragmentary manner. Only a small passage from the first group is finally taken up in the coda: the final cadence of the first and two introductory measures of the second waltz.

The following analysis concentrates on three formal turning points: the first waltz, in which the seed is sown from which all of the following waltzes will grow; waltzes 7 and 8 that introduce the end of the work; and the catastrophic end itself.

The First Waltz

The first waltz (reh. 9–17, mm. 67–147) sets in motion the choreographic process determinative for *La valse:* in a spirally-formed—that is, accelerating and intensifying—progression it moves from a region of harmonic and metric deception and vagueness (as is characteristic of the introduction) into a more circumscribed field of four-measure periodicity and major-minor tonality. The exact moment of this emergence and arrival at the beginning of the cadential progression in measure 139 is marked in the score by the scenic direction to suddenly illuminate the ballroom. While this "setting-in-motion" is form-defining at a local level of structure, it also establishes the contours of the frame for the entire piece. The cells from which it is composed function as models and continue to develop as the piece unfolds.

Example 7.1 provides an annotated reduction of the first waltz (mm. 70–147) showing its phrase structure. The waltz divides into two periods of 37 and 41 measures (mm. 70–106 and 107–47), ending in cadences in the dominant and tonic keys respectively. Both are expansions of a more fundamental thirty-two-measure framework. The expansion arises in the first case through the addition of two "empty measures" at the end of the first three eight-measure groups (mm. 78–79, 88–89, and 98–99) and in the second case through a cadential expansion (mm. 139–47). The irregularity thus comes about because the beginning and end of the second period fall in the "eighth measure" of an ideal eight-measure schema. The overall impression of this setting-in-motion is achieved by means of melodic ambitus and rhythm: the melodic range ascends from a narrow register around D_4 up to two octaves above this; and the rhythmic condensation proceeds from the smallest repeated rhythmic units (termed "cells" in the following), which correspond to ten-measure phrases in the consequent of the first period and repeated one-measure motives immediately before the end of the second.

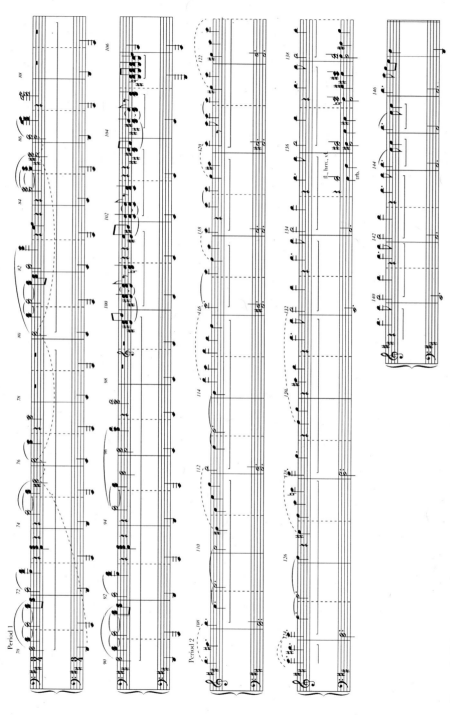

Example 7.1. *La Valse*, piano reduction of mm. 70–147

Both periods within the choreographic inner structure relate to one another in a correspondingly dynamic way: whereas the first begins with bipartite, ten-measure cells (see the horizontal beams in example 7.1), the second begins with simple, four-measure cells which then shorten into two-measure and eventually one-measure cells.[11] Whereas the figures of the first period emphasize melodic lowpoints and swing upward (the highpoints fall on unaccented beats), the circular motions of the second period find their climaxes in a series of accented recurrent high notes.

The impression of a rather slow beginning in the antecedent of the first period (mm. 70–89) is also reinforced by an expanded presentation of a standard harmonic-syntactic model, sometimes called *chiasmus*.[12] The origin of this expansion is a twofold broadening. On the one hand, given the latent six-voice texture of the motive, the chordal arpeggiations are too spacious for one to identify a single melodic layer as the primary one (as in *An der schönen blauen Donau*). On the other hand, the rhythm is an elastic augmentation of a simple triple meter: if one halves the note values of measures 70–77 (see the durational reduction in example 7.2a), then certain rhythmic and intervallic figures that are paradigmatic of the Viennese waltz (e.g., the "guitar bass"—example 7.2b—and the yodel figure in parallel thirds—example 7.2c) emerge, even if this particular hemiola configuration is largely without precedent.[13]

Two other elements in the opening period—while initially not accorded much weight because they only arise in hindsight as exaggerations of more or less idiomatic traits—become essential to the sound world and unfolding of the entire piece. These are (1) the tonic chord in an enriched form with added sixth (the return of V–I is likewise covered in the upper voice of the latent six-part melodic frame); and (2) the chromatic progression from scale degree 1̂ to 3̂ (D to F♯) (see the dotted slurs below the staff in example 7.1) at the deepest layer of the melodic frame.[14] The latter is integrated into several chromatic passing motions, or rather apparent passing tones which function primarily as neighbor tones to the following chords. These broad metric foundations sketch the essential aspects of the "formula" of *La valse*.

In the second half of the modulating consequent phrase (mm. 100–106) a sudden character shift takes place, as if a phrase from a trio has been dropped into the middle of the main scherzo. Without any mediating material, the melody

Example 7.2a. *La Valse*, durational reduction of mm. 70–77

Example 7.2b. Joh. Strauss, *Künsterleben* op. 316, no. 4, mm. 1–8

Example 7.2c. Joh. Strauss, *Künsterleben* op. 316, no. 4, mm. 17–24

abruptly condenses to a two-measure sequence, the harmonic rhythm to a two- and then one-measure pulse, the accompaniment pattern to a one-measure "guitar bass." The final cadence in the melody is achieved through a terse, idiomatic formula that—as the seventh measure of an ideal eight-measure scheme—for the first time is not elongated through two empty measures, but rather abbreviated through the stretched-out upbeat to the second period (m. 107). Regarding the cadential model, Strauss uses the formula

exclusively to express a "terse" closure in the sixteenth or thirty-second measure of a period (ex. 7.3a–c); in his waltzes the condensation and momentary metric displacement in the closing four-measure group usually interrupts a two-measure pulse and effectively brings about the final cadence.[15] By contrast, in this case the formula already ends in the thirty-first measure (if we don't count the six "empty" measures). That this idiomatic "lapse" went unnoticed by Ravel is surely out of the question; rather, the context indicates a purposeful thwarting of expectations.

The second period is expanded from 32 to 41 measures by means of an elongated upbeat (m. 107) and a twice-repeated cadential progression. Significantly, its periodic segmentation, articulated through a weak caesura at the end of the phrase (m. 122), is overridden by a spiraling structure encompassing both phrases.

This spiral formal conception is made manifest first through a condensing of the harmonic rhythm from four to one measures (see the harmonic changes

Example 7.3a. Joh. Strauss, *Wiener Blut* op. 354, no. 2, last 4 measures

Example 7.3b. Joh. Strauss, *Lagunen-Walzer* op. 411, no. 1b

Example 7.3c. Joh. Strauss, *An der schönen, blauen Donau* op. 314, no. 1b

in the left-hand system in measures 108–38, example 7.1), culminating in measures 135–38 where the chromatically ascending thirds of flutes, horns, and violins (representing a harmonic rhythm of one measure and shorter) are superimposed by the chromatic progression in quarter notes of the trombone. Second, there is an abbreviation of the melodic cells connecting the accentuated high notes (which, until m. 134, coincide with the points of harmonic change; see the horizontal beams in example 7.1). The four-measure cells in measures 108–11 and 112–15 are compressed in measures 116–19 to two-measure cells, then, after recommencing with four-measure cells (mm. 124–27 and 128–31), to two-measure units narrowing on the high notes; the last compression to one-measure cells takes place in measures 144–45.[16] Third, in both phrases (mm. 107–22 and 123–38) the upbeat figurations (see the dotted slurs above the staff in example 7.1) are progressively elongated until the upbeat to the third four-measure unit (the upbeats to mm. 116 and 132, respectively). In addition, the rhythmic constriction at the end of the first phrase (in mm. 116–23) is absorbed and carried forward by the upbeat to the second (mm.

121–23). Finally, the actual one-measure upbeat to the first cadential progression (m. 131) becomes elongated by an upbeat "to the second degree" (mm. 129–30), and in this manner contributes to the impulse of the proceeding upbeats in concentrated form. The result is an ever-increasing drive toward the cadence, and—insofar as this condensation occurs within the cadential progression—toward the end of the phrase.

Beginning in measure 107, the second period also may be viewed with respect to the tradition of the Viennese waltz. The antecedent is associated with a tonal model, for which the second period in the first waltz of the *Lagunen-Walzer* could have served as a precedent (see ex. 7.4). There, after a transitory tonicization, the chord on V resumes its function as a dominant, and is prolonged and linked back to the tonic. The dominant-tonic oscillation, serving as the prolongation, is spanned by a chromatic middle voice moving from the leading tone to scale degree $\hat{3}$ (see the dotted slurs in example 7.4). This eight-measure model is broadened to sixteen by Ravel and sequentially extended. An additional deviation is that the chromatic steps fall on accented (odd) measures in the grouping; moreover, the uppermost layer of the melodic skeleton, which in Strauss is parallel to the chromatic progression, becomes rhythmically displaced from the inner voice to form a succession of ascending high notes, which in turn becomes an independent, momentarily immobile layer. In comparison to the Strauss waltz, Ravel's is a broader conception in which the tonal model is indeed present but no longer determinative.

In the closing cadential phrase (mm. 131–47), two allusions to Strauss seem to be superimposed, one of which is determinative for the harmonic-syntactic form, the other (which is discussed at greater length below) in part for the sonic surface. The *Schatz-Walzer* (here excerpted from the second finale of *Der Zigeunerbaron,* example 7.5) provides a precedent for the harmonic-syntactic schema. The analogy extends beyond the eight-measure model and includes the phrase expansion through the use of an imperfect authentic cadence, the rhythmic contour (especially the upbeat hemiola), the position of scale degree $\hat{8}$ as a treble pedal, and the lingering of scale degree $\hat{6}$ in the $^6_4$ suspension. The further intensification of the second cadential progression—accomplished through a postponement of the cadence until the final bar of the eight-measure schema (m. 146)—may also be found in examples from Strauss's waltzes.[17]

Example 7.4. Joh. Strauss, *Lagunen-Walzer* op. 411, no. 1b

Example 7.5. Joh. Strauss, *Schatz-Walzer* op. 418, no. 1, conclusion

The cadence of the second period concludes what may be considered the "genesis" of spiral construction for *La valse*. This takes place as a crescendo and accelerando composed out in a number of dimensions: first, a broad three-step registral ascent over two octaves (from D_4 to D_6); second, an extensive instrumental crescendo; and third and above all, a rhythmic compression in several dimensions.

With respect to the harmonic rhythm, the leap between the first three phrases and the fourth phrase of the first period clearly anticipates a step in the condensation process that first comes to fruition in the course of the second period. (In this sense m. 105 may be understood as a "lapse in idiom," i.e., as the "false" anticipation of a cadential formula first possible only at the end of the second period.)

1st Period: (mm. 70–89)	Antecedent	**6 + 4** **6 + 4** **20**
Consequent (mm. 90–107)		6 + 4 2 + 2 + 1 + 1 + 2^{18} 18
2nd Period: (mm. 108–23)	Antecedent	**4 + 4** **2 + 2 + 2 + 2** 16
Consequent (mm. 124–47)		4 + 4 2 + 2 + **2** + **2**^{19} 2 + 2 + 3 + 1 24 (16 + 8)

The difference between the first and second periods becomes more apparent when we consider individual models of harmonic progression. First, if one takes the progression D^9–T^{add6} (with suspended scale degree $\hat{6}$) as a reference point, then the second ten-measure group of the first period (beginning m. 80) would correspond to the first eight-measure group of the second period (m. 108) and the second four-measure group of the cadential progression (mm.

136–39).[20] Second, if one considers the groupings spanning the chromatic progression (marked in bold in the above diagram), then the twenty-measure antecedent of the first period would correspond to the sixteen-measure antecedent of the second period and the second four-measure phrase (plus upbeat) of the cadential progression (mm. 135–39). Through the additional incorporation of a chromatic progression in quarter notes (first trombone), the process goes "prematurely" into a spin prior to its definitive occurrence at measure 638.

A similar tendency manifests itself in motivic dimensions. Between the immediately repeated circular and repetition figures, we hear a gradual unfolding from ten measures (first phrase of the first period) to four and two measures (units within the second period) to one measure immediately before the final cadence. Thus the cadential progression is based rhythmically on a diminution, contraction, and chordal repackaging of the opening motive (now shifted to begin on an upbeat), such that

The "Formula" and Its Historical Precedents

The first waltz presents a number of guidelines that prove essential for the entire cycle. These guidelines may be roughly categorized as (a) general, i.e., concerning the whole piece; or (b) specific to the first, fifth, and seventh waltzes, thus becoming a kind of recognizable "formula" of *La valse*. Examples 7.6a–f—mostly cadential progressions from the first part of the work—illustrate several of these guidelines:

1. A well-defined waltz character, with spatially and temporally expanded, "elastic" turning motions at the beginning; these become gradually narrowing, accelerating, and "heating up" motions after the start of the second period.
2. An unadorned, cadential-harmonic framework with an equally unadorned bass (but nonetheless appropriate for a waltz).
3. A preference for D–T progressions in which scale degree $\hat{6}$ characteristically functions as the ninth of a D^9 chord and as the added sixth of the tonic T^{add6}. (This tone often lies in the upper voice, see example 7.6a–c.)

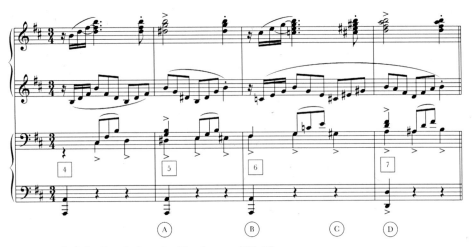

Example 7.6a. Ravel, *La valse*, No. 1, mm. 135–38

4. A middle-voice progression characterized on the one hand by multiple chromatic neighbor note displacements (usually ascending) and on the other by applied leading-tone alterations; and by chromatic progressions leading in multiple voices (ex. 7.6a–c) or in a single voice (ex. 7.6d–e) to cadential progressions or phrase endings.
5. A melody that, as essentially pendular in motion, presents a fixed upper pivot, while the lower turning point—as the latent middle voice—tends to ascend chromatically (ex. 7.6b–e).

While this general outline allows for a number of different realizations, that of the first cadential progression may be taken as paradigmatic, or "formulaic" for the harmonic style specific to *La valse*, insofar as it returns almost exactly in waltzes 5 and 7. The individuating features for this formula are:

1. A progression of D^9–T^{add6}, decorated by parallel chromatic major thirds and (at times) complete major triads in the middle voices.
2. A suspension preceding a resolution to the dominant ninth chord (marked in example 7.6 as A), in which the fifth is suppressed through a raised fourth (usually in a middle voice), and in which the third of the chord (scale degree $\hat{7}$) is omitted.
3. The minor $\frac{9}{7}$ chord (marked as B) as a suspension (7.6b) or passing chord (7.6c–e).
4. A dominant often featuring three "leading tones" (a raised fifth or $\sharp\hat{2}$, and seventh or $\sharp\hat{4}$ in addition to the normal leading tone $\hat{7}$, marked as C).
5. A tonic with added sixth as goal sonority (marked in example 7.6 as D).

Example 7.6b. Ravel, *La valse*, No. 5, mm. 275–78

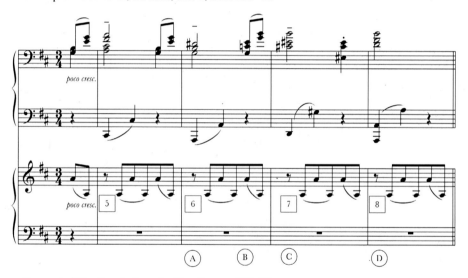

Example 7.6c. Ravel, *La valse*, No. 7, mm. 336–39

Another feature especially characteristic for the second and third waltzes is a rhythmization of the chromatic progression that condenses—somewhat like a hemiola—as it approaches the goal sonority (see ex. 7.6d–f).

On the one hand, the aesthetic intention of such a formula is to combine an unadorned harmonic-syntactic framework with a harmonic foreground whose complex results, while strictly controlled by tonal voice leading, sound at first as if they are wandering, functionally errant, or distorted; in extreme cases the

Example 7.6d. Ravel, *La valse*, No. 2, mm. 180–83

Example 7.6e. Ravel, *La valse*, No. 5, mm. 288–91

expected tonic remains undecided until the last moment of the cadence.[21] On the other hand, the formula contributes to the dynamic character in the broadest sense: a tendency toward the last chord of the cadence, characterized by chromatically ascending middle voices which, insofar as a diatonic framework is overridden by a "mechanical" chromatic pattern, drive past a strictly tonal goal, thereby becoming simultaneously affirmative and destructive. (It is no

Example 7.6f. Ravel, *La valse*, No. 3, mm. 212–17

coincidence that this should be signaled in the end by the chromatic progression of the trombone, which seemingly moves between layers of the formula.)

The formula itself is formative for the entire first part of *La valse*, while a variant introduced in waltz 2 is formative for waltzes 3, 4, and 6. Herein one may speak of a set of variations, to the extent that the formula and its variants are adapted as models for four-measure units, either at the beginning of phrases or at cadences.

From a broader perspective, the progression D^9–T^{add6} with suspended scale degree $\hat{6}$ and the chromatic middle voice appears to have been inseparable from the waltz for Ravel. A cursory glance at the *Valses nobles et sentimentales* (1911) confirms this: a passage from the second waltz is exemplary (ex. 7.7).

Example 7.7. Ravel, *Valses nobles et sentimentales*, No. 2, mm. 25–26

Here the probable (conscious or unconscious) source for this turn of phrase becomes transparent. In Strauss's *Kaiser-Walzer* (ex. 7.8), the chromatic progression in the middle voice rests on a prolongation of a dominant seventh chord, which moves in three steps from an incomplete neighbor tone over the "actual" chord to an altered dominant before reaching the tonic. Although the progression is certainly not obvious, its harmonic-metric hierarchies remain untouched—the incomplete neighbor on the downbeat resolves to the dominant chord on the second beat and the altered chord on the third beat functions as a passing chord and upbeat to the following tonic. Yet this unambiguousness is no longer present in Ravel's "formula," neither in *Valses nobles et sentimentales* nor in *La valse*. Through "mechanical" parallel triads the individual stages of the passing motion are concealed; but the diatonic framework—the dominant $\frac{9}{7}$ chord—is never heard in its entirety.

Passages such as those given in examples 7.9 and 7.10 may also be superimposed on the model in stages of the creative process. Yet unlike Ravel, Schumann and Tchaikovsky both clearly limit the chromatic progression to the prolongation of the D $\frac{9}{7}$ chord through the use of diatonic frame chords. In sum, it appears that the "formula" of *La valse* originated from a combination of clichés that Ravel associated with the waltz—clichés that could not claim universality as style attributes, but rather ones that had been impressed upon him in the form of several prominent individual works.

Example 7.8. Joh. Strauss, *Kaiser-Walzer* op. 437, No. 3

Example 7.9. R. Schumann, *Scenen aus Goethe's Faust*, No. 1, mm. 5–6.

Example 7.10. Tchaikovsky, *The Nutcracker* op. 71, no. 13 (Waltz of the Flowers)

The Construction of Closure and Reopening: Waltzes 7 and 8

The waltzes of the third group behave in a formally ambivalent manner. The return to the tonal areas D and B♭ major, as well as choreographic and harmonic characteristics of the first and third waltzes, impart to the seventh and eighth waltzes a quasi-recapitulatory function within the "exposition." That the ninth waltz begins in the key of the dominant appears to be a nod to the conventions of major-minor tonality. And each of the waltzes articulates another conventional end-oriented trajectory. But, as each of them simultaneously features another aspect of the "fatal whirling," they open up possibilities for development in Part II. This tendency is also manifest in the harmonic disposition: not only do each of the consequent phrases begin in the key of ♭III (in F in m. 348, D♭ in 388, and C in 424), but the tonally-open endings of waltzes 8 and 9 anticipate essential aspects of the harmonic unfolding of the development section; in particular, the ninth waltz introduces a minor-third axis on A that becomes structural for the harmonic outline of the development.

The Seventh Waltz

The seventh waltz is in several aspects a variant of the first. The model for the beginning of both phrases (mm. 332–39 and 348–55)—a chiasmus combining a latent two-voice polyphony and doubling in parallel thirds—corresponds to a condensed variant of the beginning of the first waltz (mm. 70–89). The idea of a gradual transference in register from the tenor to the descant is also taken over and even expanded to reach an octave higher. As at the end of the first waltz, an initial cadential progression (mm. 356–63) is followed by a more conclusive variant (mm. 364–71), wherein the retransition links the mediant key (F major) of the consequent to the beginning key of D major. The model for the cadential progression, in particular the initial one, follows the formula almost exactly, as did the initial cadence in the first waltz. Here it is not only exemplary for the cadential progressions, but for all concluding measures of melodic groupings.

The different ways in which this "formula" is deployed in relation to the ideal eight-measure framework shows the degree of distance and distortion that has been attained up to this point (see exx. 7.6a and 7.6c). In the cadential progression of the first waltz, which is displaced from the ideal eight-measure framework, a chromatic motion in three middle voices leads to a T^{add6} chord at the beginning of "measure 7" in the scheme (see the boxed numbers in the example). In the seventh waltz (ex. 7.6c) this progression is displaced forward by one measure, so that the penultimate sonority (marked as C), which had hitherto fallen on a weak sixth measure in the schema—thus being heard as an altered passing chord to the tonic—now appears as an accented chromatic lower appoggiatura to T^{add6} in the strong seventh measure. The chromatic appoggiatura (as well as the whole-tone suspensions in mm. 336 etc.) accompanies a turning melodic motion, whose momentum largely stems from the interaction between the accented, multiple dissonance and the unadorned harmonic cadential framework. Both the turning motion and the emphasis on the harmonically ornamental sonorities are characteristic for the position of the seventh waltz within the dramaturgy of the piece as a whole.

In particular, the broadening out of the chromatic progression is decisive for the "fatal" element of the seventh waltz. The durational reduction in example 7.11 shows this process. The "formula," appearing five times in a mostly rising succession (see the boxed passages), becomes the driving element in a nearly relentless circling and rhythmically insistent ascent. It lends subliminally forward and upward momentum even to the falling lines at the end of both phrases. The progression is driven onward in the odd four-measure groups, while the even groups contain a slight sense of recession. With the exception of the concluding phrases, this alternation is coupled with a continuous crescendo. These findings are consistent with our earlier observation regarding the first waltz. That is, in the "formula," a fundamentally "classical" phenomenon—the harmonic-rhythmic drive to the cadence—becomes subordinated in the long run to a more destructive principle: a forward and upward-rising process that precipitates "fatal" harmonic effects. Yet despite this subversive tendency, the unadorned tonal framework and the inevitability of the dominant-tonic progression of the waltz remain audible in this first entry of the seventh waltz.

The seventh waltz may also be related back to an earlier model: the middle section of the first waltz from C. M. Ziehrer's *Weaner Mad'ln* (ca. 1887, example 7.12). This most likely was available to Ravel and resembles his seventh waltz in the choice of the eight-measure chiasmus, the rhythm of the four opening measures, and the rhythmic and harmonic positioning of the inserted chromatic neighbor tones.[22] The insistence on the neighbor-tone figures—which in Strauss are essential for their ornamental function and rhythmic profile—here works together with a continuously iambic fundamental rhythm, creating an obtrusive and almost obsessive effect.[23] In the seventh waltz, and above all

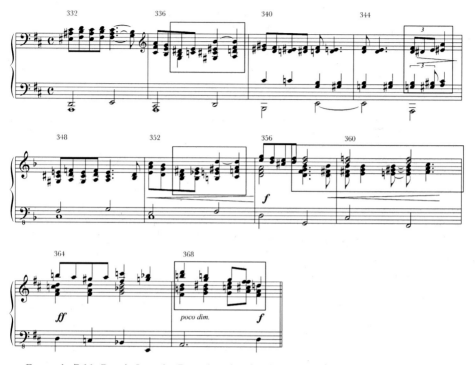

Example 7.11. Ravel, *La valse*, Durational reduction of No. 7

Example 7.12. C. M. Ziehrer, *Weaner Mad'ln* op. 388, No. 1b

its reworking in Part II of the work, it appears as though Ravel is preoccupied with foregrounding and exaggerating this obsessive tendency within the tradition of the genre itself.

The Eighth Waltz

In contrast, the eighth waltz conveys a strong sense of opposing qualities. It initially presents itself as a moment of relaxation, a lyric, dynamically recessive idea with a largely "falling" tendency. This gives way, however, to a sense of "letting go" (m. 373), "bouncing" (m. 374/1), and a rash, seemingly rhythmically uncoordinated rebounding shock (mm. 374/3–375/3). Moreover, this figure appears to be an elastic augmentation of, yet again, a two-measure model from Strauss (ex. 7.13). This choreography also corresponds to an arc of harmonic tension and relaxation based on a functionally dissonant chord with altered raised tones (m. 372), an accented neighbor-tone insertion (m. 374) and a diatonic resolution (mm. 374–75). In sum, it represents a cadential progression with applied chords or, yet again, a further variant of the "formula."

Example 7.13. Joh. Strauss, *Geschichten aus dem Wienerwald* op. 325, No. 2

While the antecedent (mm. 372–87) remains wholly within the four-measure mold, the surface melodic rhythm reveals a clear tendency toward abbreviation: the three successive melodic groups last 12, 10, and 8 quarters respectively, then expand in the fourth melodic group lasting 13 quarters. The incomplete cadential progression accompanying this reversal follows a rhetoric of exaggeration typical for Ravel: a moment of shock—the one-bar overlap between the third and fourth melodic group, accompanied by a complex suspension (m. 383)—marks the transition between chromatic alteration and elastic discontinuous linearity on the one hand, and a diatonic conclusion (an enriched tonic with added sixth) and broad legato on the other.

It is fitting for the dramaturgy of *La valse* that, in addition to anticipating the catastrophe of Part II at the end of Part I, the cadential progression of the consequent "no longer succeeds." A multilevel liquidation, beginning in measure 398, effects an elastic, seemingly continuous acceleration. Herein the driving tendencies of the work—rhythmic climax and chromatic progression—are condensed in a way that will prove exemplary for the catastrophe at the end of Part II.

The Stretta

Measures 580–755 combine aspects of a recapitulation with the choreographic image of a climactic staged finale. This section is recapitulatory insofar as (1) the tonic is reclaimed after the climax of the development, here over a dominant pedal; (2) a melodic shape first introduced in Part I as a "small recapitulation" (the seventh waltz) is taken up again; and (3) the sequential order of the waltzes largely follows that of Part I. From the beginning, however, the intensifying harmonic, dynamic, and metric distortion creates an ascending, accelerating, and increasingly compact turning motion that by measure 646 encompasses the entire registral space of the orchestra.

Each phase of the stretta is marked by the appearance of variants of earlier material: the seventh and eighth waltzes, and the cadential progressions of the first waltz (see earlier figure 7.1c). The choreographic functions of these phases and their components are elucidated below.

Phase I

The recapitulatory variant provided by the seventh waltz in essence marks a "beginning of the end" for *La valse*. Characteristic for this formal function (the turning point after the penultimate climax) are the sudden drop into the bass register and the rapid and constant pounding of the double basses and percussion, as well as a bubbling line of running eighth notes (a figure specific to *La valse*).[24] Taken together, these actions unmistakably signal the beginning of a relentless, rising, and escalating movement.

The consequent phrase material of the seventh waltz is first taken up again in measures 586–601 and then repeated at the interval of a diminished octave (!) in measures 610–25. Both phrases lead into a Schoenbergian liquidation, during which a mechanized variant of the chromatic progression spreads from the bass to the entire setting. This nullifies any possibility of periodic closure of the kind characteristic of the waltz's first appearance in Part I. In its place enters a relentlessly self-propelling ascent ultimately headed for oblivion. The formula itself is still audible in the cadencing measures and in this way even achieves a transitory tonal orientation. Yet the chromatic impulse of this ascent, in contradiction to the harmonic implications of the upper voice, broadens to exceed the limits of the tonally-controlled phrase.

Example 7.14 provides a durational reduction of the first phase of the stretta. Already in the opening D major thematic statement, the chromatic progression in the middle voice is spread across the original figure, bringing about a continuous and increasingly polyphonic chromatic ascent. The tonal framework (I–ii–V–I) remains as determinative as before. Yet as three chromatic voices are closely led in parallel motion, several gradually narrowing triadic mixtures follow in measures 586–601, including minor triads (with a suspended upper voice), major $^6_4$ chords, minor $^6_4$ chords, and major triads (see the second system). In addition, the bassoons form a chromatic layer, first in major, then in minor (parallel) thirds.

The possibility of tonal closure is progressively undone in the Db-major statement. Over the pedal point and seemingly free from the almost unchanged waltz melody, a spinning off, mechanization and amplification of the chromatic progression lead to harmonic redundancy, whose consequence is that the harmonic progression increasingly escapes tonal control. In measures 602–9 and 626–45, essential spiral components of the seventh waltz that otherwise were "restrained" by the periodic tonal waltz melody—turning motion, chromatic progression, and acceleration—now completely break through to the surface (see fig. 7.2). The turning of the upper voice shortens from a four-measure to a one-measure figure, while the bass, until now a pedal point, becomes caught up in the rhythm of the chromatic middle-voice lines and accelerates into quarter notes. Measures 642–45 achieve the highest stage of the spiraling acceleration.

As we have seen, however, the driving forces of this development, i.e., the turning motion and a distinct tendency for neighbor-note embellishment and chromatic ascent, are anticipated in the history of the genre. And, to the degree we are persuaded by Ravel's rhetoric, this catastrophe is not enforced by an external intervention, but the final consequence of a "fatal" historical tendency.

Phase II: Gathering and Centrifugal Sequence I

The "over-the-top" recapitulatory version of the eighth waltz (mm. 646–64) has three principal dramaturgical functions, which together create the effect of upheaval at the end of the piece and which may be described as a "gathering" process (see fig. 7.1c). That is, in its immediate connection to Phase I of the stretta, the eighth waltz functions simultaneously as its climax, as a moment of retardation, and as the "backswing" for Phase II. The result is that Phase II, with an expanded phrase structure, begins anew, but in such a way that when it is introduced (mm. 646–50), the metric impulse and the traversed registral space from the end of Phase I are completely taken over in the registrally expansive centrifugal figure.[25]

The figure divides into three segments: "impulse" (m. 646, beat 2), "sliding fall" (mm. 646/3–649/1) and a "double springing back" (mm. 649–50). It then is repeated twice in abbreviated and softened form before the actual liquidation begins (m. 658). The moment the impulse seems to abate (mm. 655–58) the figure is exploded and the interrupted accelerating and upward tendency is taken up again (mm. 657–64). Yet the specific part of this motion, whose splitting off and development initiates the renewed "pulling upward," is that of the "springing back" segment. In this manner the waltz becomes a quasi-sentential, open structure that serves as a model for the second phase of the stretta that it triggers (mm. 665–93). Choreographically speaking, measures 665–68 enter in the place of measures 646–54; similar to these previous measures, they encompass previously traversed registral space with a compact figure and offer a transitory stasis. Accordingly the unisono units (mm. 669–74,

Example 7.14. Ravel, *La valse*, Durational reduction of mm. 586–645

Measure numbers	586	602	610	(618)	626	634	638	642
Upper-voice groupings	8+8	4+4	8+8		4+4	2+2	3x4/3	4x1
Stages of acceleration of the ascending bass	I	IIIa			IIIb		IV	
Stages of acceleration of the ascending eighth-note groups – see arrows in ex. 7.14, middle staff	I		II III				IV	V

Stage I: pedal note/repetition of single eighth-note group.
Stage II: continuous progression by seconds.
Stage III: continuous chromatic progression. In the ascending bass, IIIa and IIIb each mark a beginning with B1.
Stage IV: final acceleration: change from dotted half notes to quarter notes in the bass, shortening of the eighth-note groups from 6 to 4 notes.
Stage V: Eighth-note figure (and turning figure in the upper voices) entangled in a "rotating standstill."

Figure 7.2. Ravel, *La valse*, Spiral acceleration in the Stretta, mm. 586–645

679–84) assume the same function as mm. 657–64, that is, a "pulling upward" or a long upbeat. Yet through a broadening out to extreme registers, the figures in these measures introduce simultaneously a "final escalation."[26]

The dramaturgy of this "trajectory to the climax" is clear: after the premature aborting of the cadential progression in measure 658, an ascending major-third sequence (mm. 665, 675, and 685) prepares a climax that clearly represents a breakthrough—insofar as it is linked with a tonal cadence. Yet such an effect is avoided through the harmonic, registral, and rhythmic disposition of the passage.

The skewed variants of the cadential measures of the first waltz (mm. 665–68, 675–78, 685–87 and mm. 131–38) function as stages of this intensification and simultaneously as a premature appearance of the expected breakthrough. In these measures, in a manner typical for Ravel's dramaturgy of crisis, descending perfect fifths (e.g., ii–V–I in the closing cadence of the first waltz) are replaced by diminished fifths and tritones.

As regards meter, within these cadential groups measures 2 and 4 (mm. 676 and 678) are relatively strong, while measures 1 and 3 gather the preceding unisono figure (mm. 669–74) into a collective upbeat. However, this moment is violently arrested by the explosion of the third cadential group in measures 688–93. The process is driven by a technical-formal topos that I call a "harmonic spiral"[27]—a texture comprising layers of chromatic chords moving in contrary motion. Beginning in measure 688, the upper voice progresses through a reaching-under progression (*Untergreifzug*) from the lower octave of the prematurely left $G\sharp_6$ leading toward D_6, which is clearly beneath this last high point, thus lying "in the shadows" of the entire passage. Both dynamically and harmonically the cadential progression does not fulfill the expectations it raises.

Phase III: Cadential Progression, Centrifugal Sequence II, and Conclusion

Our impression that a swift and violent turning motion encompassing the entire sonic space is not absorbed by a single cadential progression, but rather only momentarily arrested, is strengthened by the following series of alienating events that initially seem marginal, but subsequently encompass all essential parameters of the composition. These consist of (1) a thorough expansion of the chromatic progression by two measures (beginning in m. 696 instead of 698, which would be analogous to 135–38); 2) the insertion of further variants of the preparatory cadential progression from measures 702–9 in extreme metrical and dynamic dispositions; (3) a montage of a fragment of the second waltz (mm. 712–13) into the actual final cadence (mm. 710–18); and 4) a deferral and ultimate nullification of the final cadence (mm. 719–21).

The deceptive cadence turning toward B♭ minor (m. 723), whose entry triggers the final centrifugal sequence, becomes the starting point of a piling up of three- to five-note chords (mm. 723, 731, and 739; see example 7.15). The goal is an expanded return of the same augmented $\frac{4}{3}$ chord over B♭ (m. 739), whose repetition at the end of the first centrifugal sequence (m. 688) surprisingly failed to appear, and now takes over the function of an antepenultima.[28]

From a choreographic perspective this second centrifugal sequence is a compression of the first. The driving elements are variants of the two-measure motive which introduced the deceptive cadence (mm. 721, 729, and 737) and eighth-note runs (mm. 723–28 and 731–36). Similar to the "cadential" measures of the first centrifugal sequence, the "beating" units (mm. 721–22) take on a gathering function, in which they rapidly encompass a registral space opened up earlier. This movement occurs in a condensed succession of

* C#$_6$ as appgoggiatura to B#$_5$

Example 7.15. Ravel, *La valse*, Reduction of mm. 687–739

impulses and the continuation of a chromatic ascent interrupted by the cadential measures (mm. 688–93; see example 7.15). Similarly the "whirling" units (mm. 723–28 and 731–36) are taken from the strongest dynamic elements of the piece (cf. mm. 293–95, 503–5 and 642–45) and combined into a repeated three-measure cell, presented as a variant of analogous cells of the first centrifugal sequence (mm. 669–74 and 679–84). The combination of condensation and orchestral emphasis strongly conveys the impression of a ballroom literally enrapt in a fury of dance.

Brought about in this way, the antepenultima (m. 739) appears as a dominant (or rather the applied dominant of the dominant) with a suspended sixth and with a "raised eleventh" (as a neighbor to the fifth) in the bass. The "resolution" of the suspension to B♯ leads to an augmented chord, equally relatable to E and A♯ as fundamentals. (The tonal orientation is primarily indicated by the upper voices which in measures 743–53 suggest a plagal cadence in D.) This tonal ambivalence, or, more exactly, multivalence, is mirrored by the material of measures 740–53 in which, with the exception of the (suspended) C♯, a whole-tone scale is outlined:[29]

A♯   B♯   [C♯]   D   E   F♯   G♯

It speaks to the entirely unconventional teleology of *La valse* that a step toward the cadence is always a step deeper into the fatal whirling. Moreover, the broadening-out and hovering on a quasi-whole-tone sonic plane does not coincide with the *finalis* (as in most of Ravel's other spirally-formed pieces, which more often employ a simple major chord or the acoustic scale), but rather with the antepenultima. At measure 753, as a kind of alienated substitution for a $\frac{6}{4}$ suspension, an F♯ seven-with-lowered-thirteenth chord enters, immediately preceding the extremely terse concluding bass figure which only allows the dominant to enter upon reaching the penultimate note.

Rhythmically the final condensation entirely follows the principle of a spirally-formed climax. Proceeding from the ten-measure units of the first centrifugal sequence (mm. 665–74, 675–84, internally divided in 2 x 2 + 6) to the eight-measure units of the second (mm. 723–30, 731–38, internally divided in 2 x 3 + 2), the passage in measures 739–52 abbreviates the movement of the most salient structural pulse from a two-measure hypermeter to a one-measure hypermeter-as-tactus.[30]

Summary and Conclusion

An exceptional role is allotted to the seventh waltz (originally stated at mm. 332–71) within the recapitulatory stretta, as it anticipates and to a large degree determines the latter's path in a single "reaching back" motion. The waltz accomplishes this through (1) its threefold, progressively broadening and accelerating chromatic ascent from the bass register; (2) an arpeggiated ascent of the upper voice over four octaves; (3) a climaxing and finally self-accelerating turning motion, which doesn't break off until it has reached a turning frequency of one measure; and (4) an increasing harmonic distortion. A consistent dominant coloration through a dominant pedal (A, then A♭) as well as through a chromatic dominant prolongation over B, contributes its part in evoking an atmosphere of great, albeit unspecified, expectation.

In the second phase (mm. 646–93) the threefold escalation is initially arrested so that it can begin anew in two further staggered progressions and lead toward the cadential progression of the first waltz and the actual final cadence. However, the waltz quotations taken up here, while initially seeming intact like the seventh waltz, are unable to resist the pent-up and incessant forward-pushing impulse. This can be seen in the sonic and choreographic overkill (above all in the eighth waltz) as well as in an ongoing, only momentarily suppressed tendency toward detonation and liquidation that affects all dimensions of the composition. Both the first and the eighth waltzes become "involuntary" carriers of a relentless and uncontrollable impulse to which they are subordinated. Both centrifugal sequences produced from these detonations are "breakthroughs" insofar as they enable the musical material to express an augmented dynamic impulse. At the same time, these seemingly uncontrollable outbreaks show an affinity to the dance from which they originated: in both sequences, distorted fragments of waltz cadences become supporting pillars of a registrally expansive and sequential rhythmically-bound turning figure.

In both centrifugal sequences, distorted forms of what originally were cadential units function as transitory collections, insofar as they abruptly encompass a previously traversed registral space. Here as earlier, a seemingly triumphant return of previous (quasi-)cadential material takes place. Given the manner in which the cadential group of the first waltz is embedded into the context—nearly unchanged in its original parts, but with an incessant tendency toward explosion (in place of the traditional "expansion")—clearly the dynamic development in the passage is far beyond the possibility of an affirmative, "well-rounded" conclusion. Consequently the vanishing point of the development is not the final cadence, but rather the eight-measure whirling provisionally broken by it. This violent end is the last consequence of a musical attitude determinative for all the endings after Part I. (See the end of the eighth and ninth waltzes, the development and Phase I of the stretta; the last formal cadence that does not dissolve into whirling is that of the seventh waltz, mm. 364–71.)

Thus one may not speak of an apotheosis, as did Ravel, if one understands by it an affirmative or successful conclusion. All three attempts to arrive at a cadence—with the seventh and eighth waltzes as well as with the cadential group of the first waltz—fail, because the reused thematic material becomes overburdened in the process. In contrast to all of his other spiral-formed compositions, here Ravel abstains from an expansion of the final tonic in which pent-up impulses could release themselves. Instead the movement becomes bogged down in an antepenulitma that has little in common with previous tonal models.

For Ravel's *La valse,* the central musical, dramaturgical, and choreographic impulse—assimilating notions of turning, escalation, distortion, and ascent—is traceable in almost all its details back to topoi in the tradition of the genre. And, most importantly, its "fatal" tendency is immanent to the genre. Ultimately it is in this "fatal" sense that *La valse* may be understood as an "apotheosis of the waltz."

—Translated by Nicholas Betson

Notes

This chapter represents a condensed and revised version of Volker Helbing, *Choreografie und Distanz: Studien zur Ravel-Analyse* (Hildesheim: Olms, 2008), chap. 5 (283–351). Underlying that study is a comprehensive "musical physiognomy" of Ravel (Helbing *Choreografie und Distanz,* chaps. 1 and 2, pp. 1–174), the outlines of which can only be suggested in the space available here.

1. The presence of repetition, circular motion, and dance is especially palpable in the overture *Shéhérazade* of 1898, which, while later withdrawn from publication by Ravel, is thoroughly original in sound. As to Ravel's learning process in the construction of larger forms, see Thomas Kabisch, "Oktatonik, Tonalität und Form in der Musik Maurice Ravels," *Musiktheorie* 5 (1990): 120–24.

2. Like all metaphors, the use of "spiral" has its shortcomings. If one only considers the temporal aspect of the escalation (e.g., the abbreviation of the period lengths), then one might more properly speak of an "inverted" (inward-directed) spiral. A broadening process determines all other parameters (e.g., dynamics, ambitus, and instrumentation). Besides finales, the spiral process also affects the *Prélude* of *Le tombeau de Couperin* as well the developments (or more generally, middle sections) of *Jeux d'eau,* "Ondine," and "Les Entretiens de la belle et de la bête."

3. For an extensive presentation of the "choreographic direction" and "spiral form," see Helbing *Choreografie und Distanz,* 1–56.

4. Despite differences in interpretation, the average performance time for both piano finales is around 4 minutes, the finales from both *Daphnis et Chloé* suites around 4.5 minutes, and "Feria" around 6.5 minutes. Only "Scarbo," with its duration of over 9 minutes (and 628 measures), approaches the length of *La valse.*

5. The manuscript score of *La valse* is dated from December 1919 to March 1920. In a letter of April 13, 1920, Ravel reports having finished the score the previous evening. See Arbie Orenstein, ed., *A Ravel Reader: Correspondence, Articles, Interviews* (New York: Columbia University Press, 1990), 200–201. While it may appear obvious that the inception of *La valse* is related to his experience of the war and Europe's collapse, Ravel energetically opposed such interpretations. Moreover, the experience of World War I—which brought personal losses for Ravel—was overshadowed by the death of his mother in 1917.

6. Quoted from the *Autobiographical Sketch*; see Orenstein, *A Ravel Reader*, 32.

7. Regarding the Straussian conception, see Ravel's letter to Jean Marnold of February 7, 1906, quoted in Orenstein, *A Ravel Reader*, 83. Ravel also emphasizes "not Richard, the other one, Johann" (Orenstein, *A Ravel Reader*, 80). The quotation comes from an interview with *De Telegraaf* on September 30, 1922; see Orenstein, *A Ravel Reader*, 345.

8. See Helbing *Choreografie und Distanz*, 283–89. The third example—the *fête polonaise* from Chabrier's *Le roi malgré lui* (1887)—can also be seen in more specifically musical sense as a precedent for *La Valse.*

9. Ravel greatly valued the piece's relation to the stage. See the letters to E. Ansermet of October 20, 1921 (Orenstein, *A Ravel Reader*, 212), and to Maurice Emmanuel of October 14, 1922 (Orenstein, *A Ravel Reader*, 230).

10. The use of the term "development" is justifiable insofar as measures 442–579 are differentiated in their tendency toward fragmentation, discontinuity, and metric complexity from the first two phases of the "recapitulatory stretta" (mm. 580–693); this part of the work, while indeed distorted, is more cohesive and possesses a "conclusive emphasis" in its reference to the seventh and eighth waltzes.

11. In example 7.1, the horizontal beams indicate hypermetric units, as opposed to melodic groupings (which, starting in the second period, are displaced from the two-measure hypermeter).

12. In contradistinction to its usage in the *musica poetica* tradition to refer to a melodic figuration, chiasmus is taken here to mean two motivically analogous phrases (here each of eight measures) with the harmonization I–V|V–I. The placement of the harmonic change in the seventh measure is conventional (cf. the opening phrases of Strauss's *Wiener Blut* op. 354 or the dance chorus from Chabrier's *Le roi malgré lui*).

13. The slight anticipation of the second beat—characteristic of the "guitar bass"—is a "typical Viennese mannerism." See Mosco Carner, "Walzer" in *Die Musik in Geschichte und Gegenwart I*, Vol. 14 (Kassel: Bärenreiter 1968), 227.

14. Cf. *An der schönen blauen Donau.* There the sixth above the tonic is resolved at the last moment. The suspension-laden stratification of ii^7 over V at the beginning of the second phrase (mm. 79–83) is a reference to Strauss and indeed the entire tendency of the Viennese waltz toward restrictive harmony.

15. The "Strauss formula" often occurs in connection with the melodic figure 6̂– 5̂– 1̂, usually scored for trumpet and timpani (or snare drum). See the concluding phrases of waltzes 1b, 2a, and 4b of *An der schönen blauen Donau.*

16. The falling seventh in measures 144–45 resumes that of measure 108.

17. Cf. *Wiener Blut*, no. 2b.

18. The division of the consequent phrase is based on the hypermeter; a division corresponding to the melodic grouping would be 2 + 2 + 1 + 1 + 1 (with m. 106 as an upbeat to the second waltz).

19. Measure 136 initiates the chromatic progression, resulting in a progressive increase in density of the foreground.

20. The measure groups are here counted in accordance with the eight-measure ideal schema, as opposed to the melodic groupings displaced from this schema by one measure.

21. This is true even more for the *Valses nobles et sentimentales*, especially nos. 2, 4, 5, and 8.

22. The second phrase of Ziehrer's waltz seems to serve as the model for the seventh waltz of *Valses nobles et sentimentales* as well as for the ninth waltz of *La valse*.

23. For the close relation between chromatic neighbor notes, rhythmic accentuation, and gesture, see *Wiener Blut*, op. 354, especially no. 1.

24. As carriers of a motion that is at times flowing, at other times seesawing, soaring up, or driving forward, running eighth notes play a significant role in *La valse*. (See for example mm. 154–55, 215–17, 244–74, and 293–95) In the development they take on a brutal character (e.g., mm. 485, 503–5, and 507–8).

25. Note the striking instrumentation—bass drum, tam-tam, tuba, string glissandi. By "centrifugal figure," I mean those moments in Ravel where one has the impression that a huge turning motion, traversing a large span of the registral space, entails the whole orchestra. Examples may be found at the end of the *Rapsodie espagnole* (32), in *Daphnis et Chloé* (3 mm. before 221), and in *L'heure espagnole*, when Ramiro plays with the grandfather clock containing Gonzalve (39). One may also think of Ravel's father's "Tourbillon de la mort"; see Hans Heinz Stuckenschmidt, *Maurice Ravel: Variationen über Person und Werk* (Frankfurt: Suhrkamp, 1976), 85–87.

26. The contrary minor-third cycles of measures 672–74 and 682–84 (only the triads of the brass are strictly octatonic) are representative of this drastic dramaturgy taken already by the development to this point.

27. See Helbing *Choreografie und Distanz*, 44–45. The technique is found in analogous passages (immediately before the climax) in almost all spirally-formed compositions.

28. As expected measure 688 should repeat measure 686.

29. F♯ does not appear before measure 753. It is remarkable that Ravel, generally dismissive of the whole-tone scale, reserves the moment of most extreme chaos for its use. (Annotation by Peter Kaminsky.)

30. The conductor and Ravel student Manuel Rosenthal justified his decision to slow down the tempo in the last bars along the following lines: "Il faut se dire: 'C'est terminé,' et ensuite Ravel nous dit posément: 'Et-voi-là-c'est-tout.' Ti-ta-ti-ta-ta. Plus lent. Alors là, oui, on sent que c'est l'affirmation (libératrice?) de celui qui a ordonné ce tumulte terrible et qui, maintenant, s'en écarte, sciemment." (We must say to ourselves: "It's over," and then Ravel says to us calmly: "Well, that's all." Ti-ta-ti-ta-ta. More slowly. At this moment we feel that this is the [liberating?] affirmation of the man who arranged this terrible tumult and who now deliberately steps aside.) Quoted in Marcel Marnat, *Ravel: Souvenirs de Manuel Rosenthal* (Paris: Hazan, 1995), 72.

Chapter Eight

Diatonic Expansion and Chromatic Compression in Maurice Ravel's Sonate pour violon et violoncelle

Elliott Antokoletz

At the first performance of Maurice Ravel's *Sonate pour violon et violoncelle* on April 6, 1922, some critics were shocked by what they referred to as a "massacre," because of its supposed abundance of "wrong notes." While this invective is incongruous with a work of such beauty and logic, the "wrong-note" conception nevertheless implies a certain "mischievous" quality that is manifested initially in the bimodal (minor/major) duality of the first movement. It is striking that the first movement of the Duo Sonata, published in *La Revue Musicale* on December 1, 1920, was followed by three more movements that were composed in the midst of Ravel's work in May of 1921 on his opera, *L'enfant et les sortilèges,* whose dramaturgy and music expressly invoke the mood of mischief.

The intention in this study is to show how Ravel's Duo Sonata exhibits what may be appropriately termed "mischievous" transformations between diatonic (i.e., symmetrical minor/major) constructions and a more abstract chromaticism.[1] These two conflicting spheres—modal and chromatic—are linked by means of intermediary intervallic stages. These stages include the octatonic scale especially, a symmetrical construction that represents a partial chromatic compression of pentatonic and diatonic intervallic content.[2] These stages include other symmetrical (cyclic-interval) pitch constructions, as well. Harmonic transformation in the Duo Sonata actually reflects some of the "sardonic" contrasts and interactions so important to the musico-dramatic character of *L'enfant et les sortilèges.* This seems to be more than mere coincidence, given the overlapping dates of composition. More broadly, a study of the Duo Sonata reveals, within the more general historical context of the principles outlined above, connections with other sources that include works by Béla Bartók, Igor Stravinsky, and other early-twentieth-century composers.

Excerpts from Maurice Ravel's *Sonate pour violon et violoncelle,* © 1922 Redfield B.V. / Nordice B.V., are reproduced with the kind authorization of Les Editions Durand.

As for the sources of Ravel's modality, Bartók states that

> pure folk music begins to exert an overwhelming influence on our higher
> art music only at the end of the nineteenth century and the beginning of the
> twentieth. The works of Debussy and Ravel should be considered the first
> ones on which the folk music of Eastern Europe and Eastern Asia exerted a
> permanent and, to some extent, leading influence.[3]

Bartók further asserts that he will not "speculate upon the sources of the pentatonic element in the work of Ravel,"[4] but he does invoke a significant association to the music of Mussorgsky and Russian folk music. Bartók also points
to the greater congeniality between his own Hungarian character and that of
the French culture rather than the German, thus further supporting the link
between the French composer and Eastern-European sources.[5]

In the evolution toward the breakdown of the traditional major/minor
scale system, the pentatonic/diatonic modalities of peasant music and the
ultra-chromaticism of German late-romantic music represent two main
opposing sources for the development of new principles of pitch organization in the early twentieth century. Many composers turned to the modalities
of folk music as the basis for composition,[6] but it was Bartók who transformed these modes most radically into a new kind of chromatic, twelve-tone
language. Bartók himself referred to the principle of diatonic "extension
in range" of chromatic themes and the reverse, chromatic "compression"
of diatonic themes, in his music;[7] this premise may also serve as a point of
departure for elucidating certain harmonic and structural notions of Ravel's
Duo Sonata. One of the primary differences between contrasting sections or
passages in the music of these composers lies in the relative position of the
musical materials between modal (diatonic) and chromatic (cyclic-interval or
symmetrical) extremes.[8]

It is precisely with regard to the unifying, organic interconnections between
opposing diatonic and chromatic (symmetrical) spheres in Ravel's Duo Sonata
(as exemplified most prominently in the first movement)—which has much in
common with certain basic principles of Bartók's musical language—that one
may discern important differences in the theoretic-analytical approaches of
various scholars. Mark DeVoto has made several astute observations in describing the traditional tonal relations that stem from the basic major/minor duality of the main accompanying motif. In assessing the structural functions of the
motif's basic components, DeVoto focuses on the individual tonal roles within
the sonata form of the first movement, rather than on the integration of these
elements within the broader pitch-set premise. He asserts that

> the way that A minor is defined in this Sonata has abundant echoes in Ravel's
> earlier works. . . . The natural-minor scale is preferred, the relative major

(C major) is a readily available alternative focus and the Dorian raised sixth
(F♯) appears frequently. . . . As if to compensate for the intensive use of the
major/minor pattern, the recapitulation brings back this first theme with a
new accompaniment consisting of the violin's open strings plus middle C,
directing the ear away from A minor and more towards C major, but still
effectively combining the two keys.[9]

In his tonal observations, DeVoto appropriately follows the path of traditional
functional logic:

> A transitional theme . . . effectively leads to G, the dominant of the second
> key. . . . The second theme . . . is easily recognized in C major, preceded by
> eight bars of dominant harmony. In the recapitulation, however, the strength
> of the expected C major is attenuated and varied by combination with the
> opening accompaniment pattern, freely moving among distantly related tri-
> ads in the bass, forming polychordal harmony with the well-established C
> major above.[10]

In his otherwise keen efforts to reveal the means by which Ravel creates
both tonal contrast and unification, DeVoto's focus on traditional functional
roles provides an incomplete picture of the principles of tonal contrast and
cohesion. As will be discussed below, these tonal relations acquire an expanded
meaning in a context based not so much on "C major . . . freely moving among
distantly related triads in the bass, forming polychordal harmony,"[11] but rather
on new harmonic entities as part of a modulatory process that moves from
diatonic modal (or bimodal) forms through a more compressed symmetrical
(i.e., octatonic) context toward completion of the chromatic continuum. The
issue here is not so much one's choice of analytical approach (that is, a more
traditional tonal perspective versus a more contemporary pitch-set interpretation), but rather a more complete understanding based on combined analytical interpretations of how traditional tonal principles can be absorbed into a
kind of twelve-tone language based on symmetrical, cyclic-interval construction that underlies the principle of intervallic expansion and compression. As
in Bartók's music, the new means of harmonic construction and progression
represent a synthesis of traditional and contemporary (modal, polymodal, and
symmetrical) principles, which expand and give new meaning to conventional
tonal, harmonic notions. Ravel's decision to write for two single-line instruments results in a lean contrapuntal texture, and the linearity of the writing
makes this work unusually recondite analytically in relation to his oeuvre. Its
linearity further encourages closer focus on pitch collections and their transformations—which in turn suggests looking to Bartók's words and music as a
point of departure.

In his structural analysis of the Duo Sonata, in which the "zyklisches Motiv" is shown to play a significant unifying role in the larger thematic interactions throughout the work, Walter Pfann appropriately explores the increasing complexity of structural levels, including modal (hexatonic and heptatonic) development from the basic pentatonic source of the main theme.[12] Appropriately disclaiming any connection with the free atonal or dodecaphonic idiom of the New Viennese School, Pfann does broach the issue of "dodecaphonic" sonority as part of a larger bimodal context.[13] His assertions insightfully reveal (1) the significance of consonance/dissonance structural functions in connection with bimodality;[14] and (2) the main theme and cyclic motive as part of a multiparametric developmental process. At the same time, a greater emphasis on principles affecting the highest level of pitch-set integration in this work—i.e., transformational relations that synthesize diatonic-modal and chromatic-octatonic spheres—would have added a significant dimension to his structural, thematic, modal, and tonal observations. Such transformational relations are essential to our understanding of cyclic-interval and symmetrical pitch strategies which underlie the melodic and harmonic organization of the Duo Sonata.

An important solution to the problem of total chromaticism for Bartók—and this is entirely relevant to Ravel's Duo Sonata as well—was the principle of "bimodal" or "polymodal chromaticism" on a common tonic.[15] As Bartók asserts,

> To point out the essential difference between atonality, polytonality, and polymodality . . . we may say that atonal music offers no fundamental tone at all, polytonality offers—or is supposed to offer—several of them, and polymodality offers a single one. Therefore our music, I mean the new Hungarian art music, is always based on a single fundamental tone, in its sections as well as in its whole. And the same is the case with Stravinsky's music. He lays stress on this circumstance even in the titles of some of his works. He says, for instance, "*Concerto in A.*" The designation "major" or "minor," however, is omitted; for the quality of the third degree is not fixed.[16]

As in the works of Bartók, polymodal chromaticism in Ravel's Duo Sonata belongs to a larger system of intervallic relations. The harmonic and melodic material of the Duo Sonata can be modeled according to a systematic interlocking of the interval cycles. As part of a twelve-tone language having little to do with Schoenberg's serial idea, interactions between interval cycles and the pentatonic and modal elements of Eastern European folk music are fundamental to the organic development of the first movement of Ravel's Duo Sonata. Figure 8.1 outlines a general principle underlying Ravel's transformational processes, wherein combined interval cycles provide the framework for a scheme of expanding *interval ratios.*[17] Accordingly, ratio 1:1 represents pairs of semitones separated by a semitone, ratio 1:2 pairs of semitones separated by a whole tone, ratio 1:3 pairs of semitones separated by a minor third, etc. Higher-level ratios include the pentatonic ratio 2:3, which represents pairs of whole tones separated by a minor third, and 3:2, which represents pairs of minor thirds separated by a whole tone. The organic process of the music itself is linked to the abstract expanding and contracting of interval ratios, which are illustrated here to model what are actually more irregular local processes in Ravel's Duo.

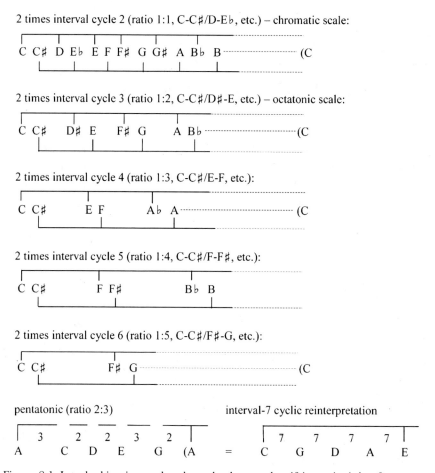

Figure 8.1. Interlocking interval cycles as background unifying principle of Ravel's Duo

Exposition

First-Theme Group, Measures 1–29: Diatonic Modal and Bimodal Unfolding

The exposition of the first movement divides as follows:

- Main cyclic motif, mm. 1–17
- Theme 1 in tonic key, mm. 6–17, 18–29
- First transition, part 1, mm. 30–47
- First transition, part 2, mm. 47–68
- Theme 2 in subordinate key, mm. 69–81
- Transition to development, mm. 81–105
- Truncated second statement of Theme 2, mm. 101–5[18]

The structural significance of increasing chromatic compression of the pentatonic intervals in figure 8.1 is evident from the outset of the Duo. The spare two-part counterpoint permits several levels of identity and distinction to be perceived between the main A-pentatonic cello theme (Theme 1) and the A-minor/major bimodal violin ostinato.[19] Both thematic ideas encircle the A-minor triadic substructure of the larger bimodal complex (ex. 8.1). However, while the ostinato generally remains fixed in shape and content for substantial stretches of time, the structure of the cello theme is an expanding, evolving entity. The cello theme (mm. 6–10) initially belongs exclusively to the anhemitonic pentatonic framework (A–C–D–E–G). This symmetrical pentatonic substructure serves as point of departure for larger modal and polymodal chromatic unfolding. The arithmetically expanding phrase structure of the first statement of Theme 1—antecedent phrase (three measures), middle phrase segment (four measures), consequent phrase (five measures)—is conceptually associated with the theme's expanding range and modal content. The middle phrase segment (mm. 9–12) expands the A-pentatonic content (A–C–D–E–G) to six notes of the A-Dorian mode by the addition of the major-sixth degree (F♯). This gives us A–[ ]–C–D–E–F♯–G and, finally, the complete seven-note mode (A–B–C–D–E–F♯–G) at the peak of the consequent phrase.[20]

The second statement of Theme 1 (mm. 18–29) is an exact repetition of the first, but given now to the violin and transposed up a perfect fourth from A to D. While the pentatonic/diatonic context is maintained, one note of the original A-Dorian mode is altered in the transposition to D-Dorian (D–E–F–G–A–B–C). This note (sixth degree, F♯)—the first element of modal expansion of the A-pentatonic content—is the first to be altered by means of diatonic transposition of Theme 1. For convenience, let us view the overall thematic diatonic content without regard for its modal tonality by interpreting the overall pitch-class content in neutral terms.[21] The A-Dorian modal content (A–B–C–D–E–F♯–G)

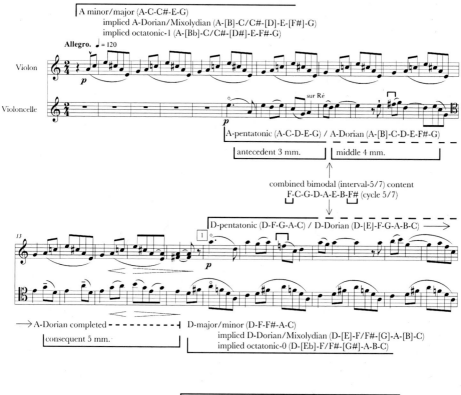

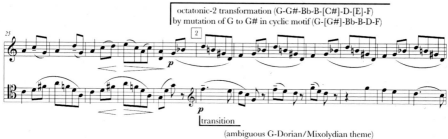

Example 8.1. Ravel, *Sonate pour violon et violoncelle*, I. Exposition, Theme 1, mm. 6–29

can be shown as a seven note segment of the interval 5/7 (perfect-fourth/perfect-fifth) cycle, C–G–D–A–E–B–F♯, the D-Dorian mode (D–E–F–G–A–B–C) as F–C–G–D–A–E–B.[22] Together these transformed modal collections form an eight-note segment (F–C–G–D–A–E–B–F♯), or two adjacent seven-note diatonic segments along the cycle of fifths (fig. 8.2). The boundary of this cyclic (bimodal) collection gives us the first semitone (F–F♯), precisely the difference between the two Dorian transpositions (D–E–F–G–A–B–C and A–B–C–D–E–F♯–G). Thus, transposition of the diatonic mode by its cyclic interval, the perfect fifth, foreshadows the larger progression toward chromatic transformation of the diatonic sphere.

D Dorian content, D–E–F–G–A–B–C (mm. 18-29, violin)

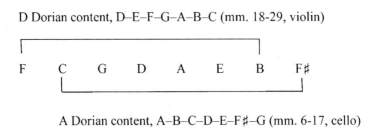

A Dorian content, A–B–C–D–E–F♯–G (mm. 6-17, cello)

Figure 8.2. Theme 1, first two statements (mm. 6–17, mm. 18–29)

First-Theme Group, Measures 1–29: Chromatic and Symmetrical Transformation of the Diatonic Sphere

While this background-level chromatic semitone (F–F♯) simply represents the difference between the two diatonic modal transpositions, its bimodal-chromatic significance is implied in the contrasting ostinato major/minor motif, especially its opening four notes, A–C–E–C♯. Bartók tells us how interesting it is

> to note that we can observe the simultaneous use of major and minor thirds even in instrumental folk music. Folk music is generally music in unison; there are areas, however, where two violins are used to perform dance music: one plays the melody and the other plays accompanying chords. And rather queer-sounding chords may appear in these pieces. We may say that music based on such principles can be labeled [as] bimodality, or polymodality.[23]

In Ravel's Duo, these bimodal thirds are absorbed into the linear ostinato motif, but collisions between major and minor thirds are also vertically projected into the contrapuntal harmony in the course of the work (as in m. 8 where the minor-third C of the cello theme clashes with the C♯ of the violin's ostinato). The opening A-minor/major ostinato is correspondingly transposed to D major/minor (at mm. 17–29), in counterpoint with the transposed (D-Dorian) main theme. In this reversed (i.e., D-major/minor) order of the original bimodal form on A, the respective modal sixth (F♯) and third (F) degrees of the two transposed Dorian thematic statements now appear in closer proximity as part of the symmetrical bimodal construction (D–F–F♯–A) of the ostinato motif.

This correlation between the combined diatonic content of the two Dorian transpositions (on D and A) of the main theme (in cycle-5/7 order, F–C–G–D–A–E–B–F♯) and the bimodal (D-major/minor) ostinato by way of the F–F♯ conflict implies a deeper-level transformational relation. The opening bimodal diatonic motif (A–C–C♯–E) also has octatonic potential. The entire content of the ostinato is A–C–C♯–E–G, plus the cadential F♯ (m. 17), which gives us A–C–C♯–E–F♯–G; this suggests not only A-Dorian and A-Mixolydian combined, but also octatonic-1, A–[B♭]–C–C♯–[D♯]–E–F♯–G.[24] Analogously, the D-major/minor transposition (D–F–F♯–A–C) of the ostinato motif (mm. 17ff.) implies not only D-Mixolydian/Dorian (D–[E]–F/F♯–[G]–A–[B]–C), but also octatonic-0 (D–[E♭]–F/F♯–[G♯]–A–[B]–C). Taken together, these octatonic implications of A minor/major and D major/minor point potentially to the entire chromatic complex on a more background level. This chromatic-octatonic combination contributes to a more general chromatic-versus-diatonic polarity in its contrapuntal opposition to the main pentatonic/diatonic theme. (This polarity, which is only partially fulfilled in the first-theme group [to m. 29], is outlined in appendix 8.1.)

Interpretation of ambiguous diatonic or octatonic modes, which are implied in the opening A-minor/major theme (A–[ ]–C–C♯–[ ]–E–[ ]–G), will tend toward one or the other of these two set types, depending on the modality of the accompanying counterpoint. For instance, in the opening measures where there is no counterpoint against the theme, modal incompleteness maximizes ambiguity. The two types of modal sets (diatonic and octatonic) are implied equally in the thematic pitch content. That is, A–[ ]–C–C♯–[ ]–E–[ ]–G can be completed either as A-Dorian/Mixolydian (A–[B]–C–C♯–[D]–E–[F♯]–G) or octatonic (A–[B♭]–C–C♯–[D♯]–E–[F♯]–G). Ambiguity due to modal incompleteness (A–[ ]–C–C♯–[ ]–E–[ ]–G) of the theme results in set-type fusion. Conversely, where a modally unambiguous contrapuntal line appears against a more complete, contrasting modal form in the theme, set-type polarity tends to prevail over the sense of fusion. Motion toward or away from polarity between diatonic (or bimodal) and more chromatic (octatonic) spheres in the counterpoint is essential to the overall formal shape.

The transposition of the main theme from A minor/major to D major/minor brings out the structural significance of their contrasting modal components (F and F♯), further emphasized by the major/minor thirds (F♯/F) of the transposed ostinato on D (see ex. 8.1). This convergence of the two contrapuntal thematic lines in terms of the common F–F♯ semitone rounds out the first-theme group. There are also deeper links between the contrasting bimodal main theme and the minor/major ostinato motif (as shown in appendix 8.1). While the minor/major "wrong-note" ambiguity suggests a certain irony from the outset, this irony quickly loses its impact of surprise because of the regularity of the ostinato and the logic of the common pitch-class links established between the contrasting thematic entities. In example 8.1 (and appendix 8.1), we see that the cyclic-interval 5/7 symmetrical reordering of the two successive Dorian transpositions (on A and D) *and* the D-Dorian/Mixolydian content of the transposed ostinato motif generate both the same F–F♯ polarized elements as well as the identical total pitch content (F–C–G–D–A–E–B–F♯).

Transition Part 1, Measures 30–47: Real Chromatic Mutation versus Polymodal Chromaticism

Thus far, all of the seemingly "wrong" notes fall logically into place within the larger polymodal context. The first real surprise within this context of incomplete, shifting modal figurations leaps out at us in the transition (anacrusis to m. 30). A new transposition of the ostinato motif at the next perfect fourth higher (on G) reveals the first intervallic mutation of the minor/major ostinato pattern. The previous transpositions of the ostinato were based on incomplete larger Dorian/Mixolydian or octatonic collections. But here, one intervallic mutation (G♯) in the new transposition on G, while distorting the motivic contour and pitch structure of the ostinato, realizes important basic pitch-collectional implications of the previous ostinato transpositions.

These implications point up the subtle but fundamental distinction between *real chromaticism* and *polymodal chromaticism*. About this Bartók writes:

> Just as the two types of the minor scale can be used simultaneously . . . two different modes can be used at the same time as well. . . . As the result of superposing [for instance] a Lydian and Phrygian pentachord with a common fundamental tone, we get a diatonic pentachord filled out with all the possible flat and sharp degrees. These seemingly chromatic degrees, however, are totally different in their function from the altered chord degrees of the chromatic styles of the previous periods. A chromatically-altered note of a chord is in strict relation to its non-altered form; it is a transition leading to the respective tone of the following chord. In our polymodal chromaticism, however, the flat and sharp tones are not altered degrees at all; they are diatonic ingredients of a diatonic modal scale.[25]

Set against the new cello theme of the transition (beginning in m. 30), now in the relative major (C) of A minor/major, the ostinato idea on G introduces the first *real* chromatic semitone of the piece by raising the minor/major triadic root from G to G♯ (see ex. 8.1). The dual third degrees (major/minor) of the successive ostinato transpositions (C–C♯/F–F♯/B♭–B)—each third degree representing Bartók's polymodal chromatic principle rather than real chromaticism—unfold in an interval-ratio of 1:4, or by transpositions of perfect fourths. The real chromatic mutation from the G to G♯ root in the violin ostinato (mm. 29–37.) breaks this pattern by introducing a new interval ratio in relation to the other nonanalogous semitones. That is, G–G♯ forms a 1:2 ratio with the B♭–B third degrees to produce G–G♯/B♭–B and a long-range 1:1 relation with the preceding F–F♯ to imply the presence of the most compressed chromatic combination, F–F♯/G–G♯. A sense of mischief is imparted by the G–to–G♯ mutation and its 1:2 combination with the B♭–B third degrees (i.e., G–G♯/B♭–B); structurally, this mutation is drawn into a complete octatonic context. While the 1:2 ratio (G–G♯/B♭–B) constitutes an octatonic tetrachord, in actuality the entire pitch collection (from the G–B♭ anacrusis of m. 29 through the first eighth-note value of m. 31) forms a complete octatonic collection for the first time. The first three notes (F–E–D) of the diatonic cello theme together with the mutated ostinato motif (G–G♯–B♭–B–D–F) outline a seven-note segment (G–G♯–B♭–B–[ ]–D–E–F) of octatonic-2. The remaining element (C♯) is supplied at the "cadence" (m. 38) to complete the collection.

It is striking that the only nonoctatonic element of the entire passage is the note C in the diatonic theme of the cello, in the key of C. This single note, the sole element to diatonicize the otherwise octatonic thematic content, also creates a chromatic cross-relation with the octatonic C♯ of the violin. These conflicting notes refer back to the original minor/major third degrees (C/C♯) of the opening ostinato motif on A. While the F–F♯ semitone of the second ostinato transposition (mm. 17–29, cello) had established itself as a connecting link in the alteration from A-Dorian to D-Dorian in the two statements of Theme 1, the original bimodal third degrees (C and C♯) are now drawn into the realm of common elements at the opening of the transition, in the conflict between diatonic and octatonic pitch collections. Thus mutation, surprise, and mischief, all invoking the critical notions of "wrong-note" intrusions mentioned earlier, become legitimized by the systematic relations between contrasting bimodal and octatonic spheres within which they play essential roles.

Exposition from Transition to Development, Measures 30–105: Complementary Octatonic Relations and Move toward Increasing Chromatic Density

In the transition, the explicit emergence of the octatonic sphere (especially in the ostinato motif at mm. 29–37 and mm. 43–47) is part of a broader pitch-organizational process. The opening A-minor/major ostinato (A–C–C♯–E–G) implied not only the larger A-Dorian/A-Mixolydian collection but also (potentially) octatonic-1. The analogous transposition to D–F–F♯–A–C (m. 17) implied D Dorian/D Mixolydian and octatonic-0. Here in the transition, we not only have a complete octatonic collection, but it is octatonic-2 (G–G♯–B♭–B–C♯–D–E–F), the remaining complement of octatonic-0 and octatonic-1. Hence it emerges in the context of progressively increasing chromatic density in juxtaposition with pentatonic/diatonic thematic passages.

A fundamental aspect of the mutated ostinato in the transition is the more distinct cyclic-interval construction. While the initial minor/major head motive (A–C–C♯–E) represents a symmetrical tetrachord, in Theme 1 the bimodal diatonic character predominated over the more implicit octatonic quality. Here with the G♯ mutation (at m. 30, the octatonic cyclic-interval construction becomes explicit by outlining one of its cyclic-interval 3 partitions, G♯–B–D–F (see ex. 8.1). Paradoxically, this symmetrical cyclic-interval unfolding occurs together with increasingly mischievous "wrong-note" intrusions. Even the contrasting diatonic themes are absorbed into, or contrapuntally juxtaposed with, the opposing ostinato motif.

As new themes unfold in the transition,[26] new levels of diatonic-chromatic interactions occur during modulation to the traditional relative major (C) of the sonata-form. This entails an increase in traditional harmonic implications (e.g., mm. 61–63 in C: V⁷–French sixth–V), which support one side of the widening polarity between diatonic and chromatic spheres. The transition unfolds two statements of its initial diatonic theme, the first statement (mm. 30–38) against the octatonic-2 ostinato motif of the violin (G–G♯–B♭–B–C♯–D–[ ]–F) (ex. 8.2a). This statement suggests the piano's "white-key" collection in an unresolved C major. The second statement (mm. 39–47) unfolds at the tritone transposition to suggest the complementary "black-key" collection in an unresolved F♯ major. Together, the statements imply the presence of the entire chromatic continuum. The consequent phrase (mm. 43–47), while still (enharmonically) unfolding the diatonic form in G♭ (= F♯) major, G♭–A♭–B♭–B–C♯–[ ]–F, is transformed by the new cello figure of E–D (in harmonics), into octatonic-2, [G♭]–G–A♭–B♭–B–C♯–[D]–E–F, with one "odd" note (G♭) from the diatonic thematic mode. Hence this passage repeats the process of the first-theme group, which moved from pentatonic/diatonic modality and ambiguous bimodal/octatonic construction to the more chromatic octatonic sphere.

In contrast to the tritone-motivated chromatic polarity between the two preceding diatonic thematic statements, a more angular theme in the cello (mm. 47ff.) now intercalates two pentatonic registral levels at interval-class 1/11 (ex. 8.2b). The upper accented line unfolds the descending pentatonic formation G–F–D–C–B♭, the lower line a secondary four-note pentatonic formation, A♭–F♯–[ ]–C♯–B a major seventh below. The result is a more local chromatic integration and compression of the two pentatonic transpositions, B♭–B–C–C♯–D–[ ]–[ ]–F–F♯–G–A♭–[ ], based on nine of the twelve pitch classes. However, the wide leaps minimize the sense of chromatic compression, a state that will be more expressly fulfilled in the development section.

Significantly, the transition ends with widely spaced triadic and cyclic-interval counterpoint underpinning the angular pentatonic/chromatic theme (ex. 8.2c). The dominant of C (m. 52) moves to the tonic harmony as represented by the cello's 5/7 cyclic segment C–G–D–A (mm. 53–54). This symmetrical formation serves not only as a focal point for the quasi-functional cadential harmonic progression, but also more broadly as a continuation of the successive fifth transpositions of the ostinato motif: on A (mm. 1–17), D (mm. 17–29), G (mm. 29–37), and C (mm. 105ff.). Although the tonality of C major is established in this transitional section (mm. 52ff.) and maintained throughout Theme 2 (beginning in m. 69) to the final cadence of the exposition (mm. 103–5), the actual thematic statement on C is withheld until the opening of the development section (beginning in m. 105).

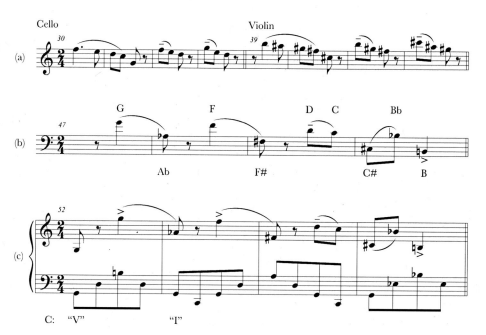

Example 8.2. Transition themes

Development

Development Section, Measures 105–75: Polarity and Fusion of Diatonic (Bimodal) and Chromatic (Octatonic) Spheres

Polarity and fusion of diatonic and chromatic spheres reach their peak in the development section. Real chromaticism is immediately suggested at the opening violin ostinato statement in C major/minor (mm. 105–10) by the contrapuntal juxtaposition of the cello fragments, B–B♭ and G–F♯–E (ex. 8.3, mm. 105–29). These fragments produce chromatic collisions against the bimodal ostinato (C–E♭–E–G–B♭) which also implies octatonic-1 (C–[D♭]–E♭–E–[F♯]–G–[A]–B♭). While G–F♯–E supports the octatonic implications of the C-major/minor content, pitch B of the first segment disrupts both the diatonic and octatonic interpretations. This interaction differs in general from those in the exposition, where such chromatic intrusions served as either octatonic or diatonic extensions of the bimodal (minor/major) ostinato or the diatonic main theme. It is striking that pitch B, which is the only nonoctatonic pitch, could be construed as a chromatic appoggiatura to the B♭, which keeps the passage in a prolonged C major/minor-plus-minor-seventh space. This further instantiates the "mischief" idea, as the actual appearance of C-as-tonic is delayed from its "proper" place in the second-theme zone to the juncture between the end of the exposition and beginning of the development. At the point where B is "released" from its resolution-as-appoggiatura duties—at the *En animant*—the development proper can begin by projecting B as tonal center.

This "new" exclusively diatonic theme of the development (beginning in m. 112, violin) parallels the role of Theme 1 in the exposition (beginning in m. 6.) in that it enters in counterpoint against the ostinato in approximately the same temporal relation. However, the A-Dorian Theme 1 only hinted at thematic similarities to the initial A-minor/major ostinato; in contrast the new development theme (in either B Dorian or B Aeolian, given the omission of the sixth modal degree) grows directly out of the arpeggiated contour of the ostinato.[27]

The antecedent segment—pentatonic B–D–E–F♯–A (violin, mm. 112–14, first beat)—of the development theme also differs from the C-major/minor violin ostinato (C–E♭–E–G–B♭) by the same intervallic mutation of its bimodal (major/minor) structure. The half-step (E♭–E), formed by the second and third elements of C–E♭–E–G–B♭, is expanded to a whole-step (D–E) at the analogous points of the new theme's antecedent content (B–D–E–F♯–A) to produce the latter pentatonic structure. However, unlike the exposition themes which are built on a common tonic (A), the development theme entails a shift downward from the ostinato by one semitone (from C to B). Together the antecedent segment of this nonliteral transposition (on B) and the C-major/minor ostinato produce a maximally chromatic linear succession in the violin, C–E♭–E–G–B♭ to B–D–E–F♯–A, with only one note (E) in common. (At mm. 109–12, the modification of the violin ostinato from C–E–G/E♭–C–G–B♭ to C–E–G/A–E–D–C♯–D prepares us, by means of its mutated tail end, for the new theme, B–D–F♯/A–E–D–C♯.)

Unlike the intervallic mutations that had produced single octatonic compressions of the bimodal diatonic materials in the exposition (cf. mm. 29–38.), the combined linear content (B–c–D–e♭–E–F♯–g–A–b♭) of the ostinato and antecedent segment of the development theme (mm. 109–10) can be reinterpreted as *two* implied octatonic segments: octatonic-0, B–C–D–E♭–[ ]–F♯–[ ]–A, and octatonic-1, C–[ ]–E♭–E–F♯–G–A–B♭. More broadly, the chromaticism of the

Example 8.3. Beginning of development, mm. 105–29

development section intensifies by means of increasing mutation of the ostinato in counterpoint against the development theme. While the ascending
arpeggiation of the cello ostinato (mm. 113–20, B–F♯–D–F♯) duplicates the
ascending B minor triadic content of the pentatonic/diatonic theme, the
descending arpeggiation, A♯–E♯–C♯–E♯, introduces two chromatic collisions
against the latter—A♯ versus A and E♯ versus E. Consequently the A♯–E♯
mutation of the theme's A–E expands the latter's content to B–C♯–D–E–E♯–
F♯–A–A♯. One new note (G♯) is added in the ostinato (at m. 119) to produce
the total content of B–C♯–D–E–E♯–F♯–G♯–A–A♯–[B] between theme and
ostinato. This nine-note collection, like that of mm. 109–10, also implies the
presence of two intersecting octatonic segments: octatonic-2, B–C♯–D–E–E♯–[
]–G♯–A♯, and octatonic-0, B–[ ]–D–[ ]–E♯–F♯–G♯–A (fig. 8.3).

At the next unmodified transposition of the ostinato to G in the violin (mm. 120–26), the cello simultaneously unfolds a variant of the development theme. This contrapuntal combination of violin ostinato rooted on G (G–B♭–B–D–F) and cello antecedent segment of the development theme rooted a tritone away on C♯ (C♯–E–G♯–B) produces the complete octatonic-2 collection, g–G♯–b♭–B–b–C♯–d–E–f, as a local foreground event. At the same time, the cello theme sounds against the bimodal/octatonic ostinato exclusively in the diatonic mode of C♯ Phrygian (as opposed to Aeolian, given the flat second-degree D coloring the violin ostinato: C♯–[ ]–E–F♯–G♯–A–B). This contrapuntal combination of the bimodal/octatonic ostinato, G–B♭–B–D–F, and modal-diatonic theme, C♯–[ ]–E–F♯–G♯–A–B, with their chromatic collisions, produces ten of the twelve pitch-classes, g–G♯–A–b♭–B–b–[ ]–C♯–d–[ ]–E–f–F♯.

octatonic-2: B–C♯–D–E–E♯–[ ]–G♯–A♯

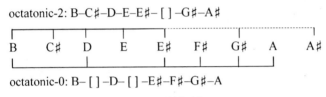

octatonic-0: B–[ ]–D–[ ]–E♯–F♯–G♯–A

Figure 8.3. Development, mm. 113–20

Climax of the Development, Measures 127–47: From Octatonic Chromaticism to Expanded Bimodal Diatonicism

A new hybrid combination of pitch sets appears at the next thematic violin statement on F♯ (beginning in m. 127), which introduces an intervallic mutation of the minor triad in the ascending antecedent segment: i.e., F♯–A–C♯–E is altered by a half-step lowering of the third element, from C♯ to C (ex. 8.4). This single mutation transforms the incomplete F♯-Dorian or F♯-Aeolian mode into an impure octatonic-0 segment, F♯–G♯–A–B–C/E, the seventh degree (E) partially maintaining the modal (diatonic) aspect and also preparing for a whole-tone mutation (anacrusis to m. 130 to m. 131, third eighth note) in the theme, G♯–F♯–E–C. The critical element here is pitch-class C, prepared in the diminished triad (F♯–A–C) of the ascending antecedent segment as the single mutated element of the consequent segment. This "odd" pitch-class (C) also anticipates the final climactic statement of the theme on C, precisely marking the center of the development (mm. 135–47, violin), counterpointed by the slightly disguised restatement of the exposition's Theme 2 (marked *très expressif*) in the cello. Furthermore, both the diatonic fifths (B–F♯/A–E) of the ostinato (m. 128) and the following whole-tone segment in the violin anticipate both the widening intervals (i.e., beyond the 1:2 interval ratio of the initial octatonic manifestations) and the expanded thematic and ostinato ranges at the approach to the climax.

Example 8.4. Development, mm. 120–51

This pitch-set hybridization permits the two perfect fifths (B–F♯ and A–E) of the thematic structure (as contained in the initial thematic statement on B at mm. 112–20 and in the thematic mutation on F♯ at mm. 127–35) to be projected into the structure of the modified accompanying cello ostinato. While these fifths together have diatonic significance, they also reveal a tendency in this section toward expanding intervals. The A–E fifth is soon projected into the triadic boundary (A–C–E) of the penultimate thematic statement (mm. 132–35, violin) of the development. With the transpositions of the violin theme exclusively within the piano's "white-key" collection at the climax (mm. 135–47), a sequence of local interval-5/7 dyads unfolds within the thematic descent: A–E (m. 136), G–D (138), C–G (141–42), and D–A (147). Within the otherwise scalar structure of the linear thematic design, these 5/7 dyads together imply the cyclic-interval reordering of the modal theme in C major as E–A–D–G–C, an explicit representation of the theme's entire cycle-5/7 content (F–C–G–D–A–E–B). From measures 136 to 147 (this specifies the "consonant" combination of instruments, which changes beginning with m. 148), the cello's introduction of Theme 2, which also articulates 5/7 dyads within the "white-key" descent, adds one "black key" (B♭) in place of B. This implies another (adjacent) seven-note segment (B♭–F–C–G–D–A–E) along the cycle of fifths with respect to the entire thematic pitch content. The content of both diatonic lines (F–C–G–D–A–E–B and B♭–F–C–G–D–A–E) together implies an eight-note (bimodal) segment along the cycle of fifths: B♭–F–C–G–D–A–E–B.

However, beginning in measure 148, the contrapuntal context changes abruptly from relatively consonant (C major/Mixolydian) to highly dissonant. The shift is signaled by the (truncated) migration of Theme 2 from the cello to the violin (marked *forte* and *soutenu*), accompanied by the cello's successive ascending arpeggiations rooted on C quintal (C–G–D), E major (E–B–G♯) and G♯^{7} (G♯–F♯–B♯). The passage is significant in two senses: first, the "vertical slices" at 148, 149, and 150 recall important pitch-collectional features of the development as violin/cello together imply C Mixolydian, octatonic-2, and octatonic-0, respectively, thereby recontextualizing the theme; second, the respective bass roots of the arpeggiated chords—of C, E and G♯—by "distorting" a C-major triad in favor of C-augmented, subtly anticipate the secondary emphasis on C (through the pedal G$_3$) at the outset of the recapitulation (m. 176).

Preparation for Recapitulation, Measures 152–75: Compression and Progression from Bimodal Diatonicism to Bimodal Octatonicism

Beginning in measure 152, another collectional shift takes place as the exposition's Theme 2 gives way to a retransition theme in G♯ minor in the violin (mm. 156–67; example 8.5). The tonal context is dominated by the cello's pronounced structural bass progression G♯–C♯–F♯ (mm. 154–56), a linearization of the 5/7 motif?), accompanying the progressive rhythmic augmentation of the theme's tail A♯–D♯–G♯. Formally, beginning in measure 164, the arrival on bass F♯ initiates the retransition proper to the recapitulation in three four-measure phrases. Specifically, measures 164–67 have the cello arpeggiation (F♯^{9} up, C^{M7} down) supporting the tail motive; the next phrase repeats the same but reverses the instruments (the cello's F♯ m. 168 providing the one note too low for the violin to reach); and the last phrase reverts to the cello's arpeggiation. The formal arrangement emphasizes the sense of the recapitulation as a true arrival point, reinforced by the voice-leading resolution from bass F♯$_3$ to G$_3$, not coincidentally the lowest note of the violin which can then take over the ostinato.

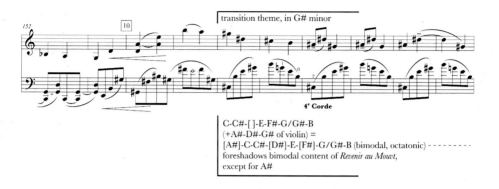

Example 8.5. Development, mm. 152–75

Beginning at measure 148, the cello has successive ascending arpeggiations rooted on C quintal (C–G–D), E major (E–B–G♯) and G♯⁷ (G♯–F♯–B♯). While measures 136–48 imply C major/Mixolydian, thereafter the situation becomes more complicated. Specifically, the forthcoming secondary emphasis on C major (along with the tonic A minor) at the beginning of the recapitulation (m. 176) appears in distorted form as C augmented (C–E–G♯ cello roots, mm. 148–54). Moreover, the "vertical slices" at measures 148, 149, and 150 "reformulate" some of the main structural features of the development as violin/cello together sound C Mixolydian, octatonic-2 (E–G–G♯–B–D) and octatonic-0 (G♯–B♯–F♯) segments.

At measure 168 (*Revenir au Mouvt*), a compounding of the original A-minor/major ostinato as two superposed major/minor (bimodal) constructions seems to compensate for the dissolution of the minor/major bimodality at the recapitulation of Theme 1. The upper elements of the arpeggiations form the bimodal figure, E–G–G♯–B, on the dominant, E; the lower elements form the bimodal figure, [ ]–C–C♯–E, on the implied tonic, A. This double bimodal combination is significant for more than simply preparing for the recapitulation by means of quasi-dominant/tonic simultaneity. The contrapuntal juxtaposition of F♯ and D♯ (mm. 168–71) against this special compounded form of the ostinato allows for an explicit interpretation of the original diatonic (minor/major) bimodality as a compound octatonic collection. The harmonic addition of these two notes (F♯ and D♯) expands the content of the arpeggiations to a six-note segment of octatonic-1, [ ]–C–C♯–D♯–E–F♯–G. The two remaining elements (G♯–B) outside this octatonic collection are part of an intersecting octatonic-2 segment, E–[ ]–G–G♯–[ ]–B–C♯–[ ].

The entire bimodal content of the ostinato violin arpeggiations (mm. 168–71), C–C♯–[ ]–E–[ ]–G/G♯–B (plus the F♯ and D♯ of the cello, which extends the collection to C–C♯–[D♯]–E–[F♯]–G/G♯–B), is already foreshadowed in the preceding cello arpeggiations, which accompany the transitional G♯-minor theme of the violin (see ex. 8.5, mm. 156–67).[28] Under the same upper arpeggiated cello notes (E–G–G♯–B), we have only the C♯ of the following violin ostinato ([ ]–C–C♯–E), while the long F♯ of the cello harmony is already part of the cello arpeggiations. At the same time, the long cello D♯ appears, conversely, in the violin harmony against the cello arpeggiations. The total content at the *Revenir au mouvt* is thereby identical to the preceding ostinato and transitional violin theme, except for one note, A♯, which first appears in the cadential interval-5/7 figure, A♯–D♯–G♯, of the G♯-minor violin theme. This note (A♯) expands the octatonic-1 content of the *Revenir au mouvt* to seven notes, [ ]–A♯–C–C♯–D♯–E–F♯–G, and the intersecting octatonic-2 content (E–[ ]–G–G♯–[ ]–B–C♯) to six notes, [ ]–E–[ ]–G–G♯–[A♯]–B–C♯.

Significantly, the pitch content of these two combined octatonic segments incorporates the entire modal (diatonic) content of the transitional G♯-minor violin theme (G♯–D♯–C♯–B–A♯–D♯–G♯). In other words, the G♯-minor theme serves as a diatonic link to the final, more intervallically compressed double-bimodal/double-octatonic phase of the development. The most significant element, which is missing from the violin-ostinato preparation ([ ]–C–C♯–E/E–G–G♯–B) for the recapitulation—indeed, missing from the entire retransitional passage (mm. 156–75)—is the tonic note, A. Its reassertion in the recapitulation in the new cyclic-interval-5/7 form of the ostinato and as the tonic of the main theme completes the A-minor/major ("tonic") segment ([A]–C–C♯–E) of the double bimodal combination ([A]–C–C♯–E/E–G–G♯–B), as well as the octatonic-1 portion ([A]–A♯–C–C♯–D♯–E–F♯–G/G♯–B) of the preceding passage.

Recapitulation

Recapitulation, Measures 176–265: Further Extensions of the Diatonic and Octatonic Spheres

Beginning in m. 176, the recapitulation introduces a significant modification of the ostinato. While Theme 1 returns unaltered in the cello, the original A-minor/major ostinato is replaced in the violin by the cyclic-interval 5/7 figuration that accompanied the transition theme (see C–G–D–A at mm. 53–54 and mm. 59–60). In the recapitulation, this cyclic-interval content is extended in the ostinato to C–G–D–A–E. This move summarizes the internal perfect-fifth "pillars" of the successive ostinato transpositions from the opening of the exposition to the beginning of the development: in descending form, E–A (mm. 1–16), A–D (17–28), D–G (29–36), and G–C (105–110), which together imply the interval-5/7 outline, as well as representing the A-minor/C-major pentatonic (E–A–D–G–C). In this way the opening of the recapitulation reinforces the symmetrical, cyclic-interval significance of the bimodal (minor/major) motif on both local and large-scale structural levels.

Equally important, the tonal-contextual changes at the recapitulation's opening further develops the polarity between the cycle-5/7 (diatonic) sphere and the cycle-3/9 (octatonic) sphere. The cycle-5/7 content (C–G–D–A–E) of the modified ostinato motif is extended by the addition of B and C♯ (m. 187, violin) to C–G–D–A–E–B–[ ]–C♯. While the basic A-Dorian cello theme maintains its original modal structure (A–B–C–D–E–F♯–G), its cyclic-interval content (C–G–D–A–E–B–F♯) is identical to that of the ostinato, except for its replacement of C♯ by F♯, which fills in the one cyclic-interval gap (between B and C♯) to generate C–G–D–A–E–B–F♯–C♯. This cyclic-interval construction, with its one conflicting semitone, C–C♯, implies the original A minor/major bimodal form. By extension, the following D-Dorian transposition, D–E–F–G–A–B–C, together with the more explicit cyclic-interval-5/7 form of the ostinato counterpoint, outlines F–C–G–D–A–E–B–F♯, plus one more 5/7 step (B♭) to form the nine-note interval-5/7 collection, B♭–F–C–G–D–A–E–B–F♯. In turn this expanded segment implies a larger polymodal collection, D Dorian (D–E–F–G–A–B–C), D-Mixolydian (D–E–F♯–G–A–B–C), and D Aeolian (D–E–F–G–A–B♭–C).

While polymodal chromaticism results from the cyclic-interval-5/7 extensions of the diatonic sphere, the transition becomes chromaticized by means of octatonic transformation of the diatonic transition theme (mm. 201–11). The "white-key" antecedent phrase is transformed in the consequent phrase into the seven-note octatonic-2 segment, B–B♭–A♭–G–F–E–D. The overlap in the preceding three measures of the cadential notes (E–D and G–F of the diatonic violin phrase by B♭–A♭ and B–D in harmonics of the cello) establishes the transformational elision between the diatonic (in descending scalar order, G–F/E–D) antecedent and octatonic-2 (B–B♭–A♭/G–F/E–D) consequent.

Theme 2 of Recapitulation and Coda, Measures 229–End: Polarization of the Diatonic and Octatonic Spheres and Culmination of the Structural Process

The ostinato form of the counterpoint against Theme 2 (mm. 229–41) intensifies the octatonic-diatonic polarity between them and, furthermore, transforms the cyclic-interval-5/7 construction of the preceding ostinato figuration (mm. 176–200) into the cyclic-interval-3/9 construction essential to the octatonic sphere. In contrast to the exclusively "white-key" content of Theme 2, the cello ostinato unfolds in several chromatic segments separated by pizzicato chords. The cello segments appear, respectively, as altered D-minor/major, G♯-minor/major, C♯-minor/major, D-minor/major, E-minor/major, and C-major/minor arpeggiations. The first bimodal segment (mm. 229–30) in D minor/major (D–F–A–F♯–D♯), mutates the D tonic degree to D♯ in the descending phase, which confirms the octatonic version of the bimodal construction (ex. 8.6). Correspondingly, the original minor/major form of the ostinato, which is constructed around the stable perfect fifth, now shifts its structural-interval priority to two interval-3 cyclic segments: ascending D–F and descending A–F♯–D♯. (The preceding F–G♯/C–A anticipates these respective interval-3/9 cyclic segments.) The F–G♯ is extended to D–F–G♯ by the D-minor/major ascent, the C–A to C–A–F♯–D♯ by the descent. Thus we have an explicit cyclic-interval-3/9 partitioning (D–F–G♯–[ ]/D♯–F♯–A–C) of the larger octatonic-0 collection, D–D♯–F–F♯–G♯–A–[ ]–C. The initial diatonic segment of the violin theme, F–E–D–A, has three of its four notes (D–F/A) in common with octatonic-0, the dissonant E establishing the diatonic polarity against the octatonic content. The following nonmutated G♯-minor/major segment (G♯–B–D♯–C(B♯)–G♯–D♯) is the tritone transposition of the segment on D. Hence it belongs to octatonic-0, and provides the missing B to complete the collection (D–D♯–F–F♯–G♯–A–B–C) in the two ostinato segments taken together.

Still in the same phrase, at the upbeat to measure 234 the C♯-minor/major segment (C♯–E–G♯–F(E♯)–C♯–G♯ implies a shift to octatonic-2. The contrapuntal alignment with G–F–E–B of the violin theme confirms the collection by extending the bimodal segment to C♯–[ ]–E–F–G–G♯–[ ]–B. With the new phrase at measure 235, the return to D minor/major reiterates octatonic-0 and the cyclic-interval-3 partitioning. This is followed by a return to octatonic-2, but now at the minor-third transposition of the C♯ bimodal segment to E minor/major (E–G–B–G♯–D–G♯), the bimodal segment here extended to E–F–G–G♯–[ ]–B–[ ]–D. The final, mutated C major/minor segment (C–E–G–D♯ (E♭)–B–A) implies the remaining octatonic-1 collection in its first four notes and last note (C–E♭–E–G/A); however, the contrapuntal alignment with E–A–B–D of the violin theme obscures the octatonic affinity of the ostinato by adding the dissonant diatonic notes D and B (the latter note doubling the "odd"

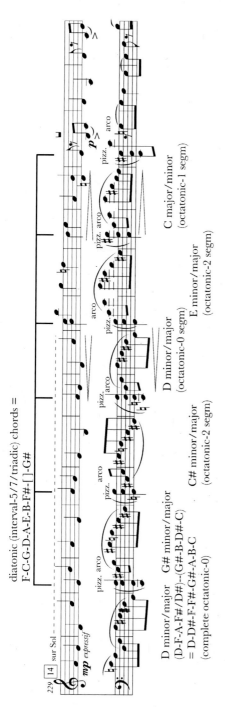

diatonic (interval-5/7/triadic) chords =
F-C-G-D-A-E-B-F#-[ ]-G#

D minor/major   G# minor/major
(D-F-A-F#/D#)--(G#-B-D#-C)
= D-D#-F-F#-G#-A-B-C
(complete octatonic-0)

C# minor/major
(octatonic-2 segm)

D minor/major
(octatonic-0 segm)

E minor/major
(octatonic-2 segm)

C major/minor
(octatonic-1 segm)

Example 8.6. Recapitulation, mm. 229–41

B of the ostinato segment). These two nonoctatonic-1 notes produce an intersection of an octatonic-0 segment (A–B–C–[ ]–D♯) with octatonic-1 (C–[ ]–D♯–E–[ ]–G–A–[ ]).

While all three octatonic collections are thereby represented in these ostinato segments against Theme 2, the last segment and the thematic elements together produce the more chromatic double-octatonic collection: octatonic-0, A–B–C–[ ]–D♯, and octatonic-1, C–[ ]–D♯–E–[ ]–G (together, A–B–C–D♯–E–G). Significantly, this entire passage both clarifies the bimodal/octatonic manifestations of the earlier retransition at the end of the development (mm. 156–75) and extends the octatonic sphere from two to all three octatonic collections. Furthermore, the passage establishes more explicitly the cyclic-interval-3/9 components in the bimodal segments on D and E, the latter partitioned into the ascending minor third (E–G) and descending 3/9 cyclic segment, B–G♯–D (plus F in the violin theme).

The intervening pizzicato chords heighten the diatonic versus octatonic polarity, as together they unfold C–G–D–A–E–B–F♯–[ ]–G♯, exclusively. The next "black-key" element to appear in the following diatonic lines (cello, at m. 249; violin, at m. 266) is C♯, the one element missing from the interval-5/7 content of the combined chords. The "black-key" elements then form an interval-5/7 cyclic segment (F♯–C♯–G♯) prior to the culminating octatonic realizations, again in the minor/major (bimodal) ostinato statements.

The concluding nine measures of the movement (ex. 8.7) release the chromatic octatonic tension by dissolution of the ostinato in the final cyclic-interval-5/7 collection, F–C–G–D–A–E–B–F♯. This cyclic-interval collection is an exact return to the combined pitch content of the first two statements of Theme 1 (mm. 6–17, mm. 18–29), as seen in the interval-5/7 reinterpretation of the modal (A Dorian and D Dorian) collections of the two thematic statements, respectively (cf. figure 8.2). This compression also occurs instrumentally as the cello and violin intersect in hocket and stretto (at mm. 281–84). Furthermore, the last six measures dissolve the chromatic tension and compress the tonal action of Theme 1 by movement through A–D–G–D–A. Thus, mutation, surprise, and "mischief," all invoking the critical notions of "wrong-note" intrusions, are legitimized by the logical, systematic relations between contrasting bimodal and octatonic spheres within which they play essential roles.

The cyclic recurrence of the main ostinato (minor/major) motif of the first movement is essential to the large-scale thematic integration of the entire work and, furthermore, to the development of systematic bimodal-octatonic relations. The fundamental principle of expanding/contracting intervallic ratios may be considered a primary integrative harmonic conception of all four movements. Perhaps more than any other multimovement work in Ravel's output, the four movements of the Duo Sonata are strongly linked to one another by these thematic and harmonic means.

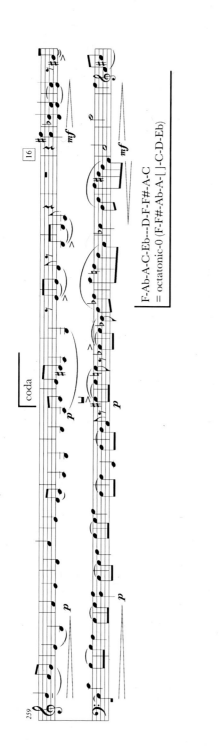

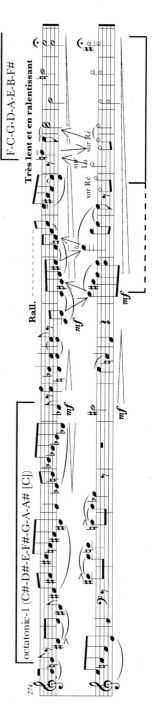

Example 8.7. Coda, mm. 265–end

While a thorough exploration of their interrelationships lies beyond the scope
of this chapter, I will choose the fourth and final movement to sketch some of
the more important connections, especially in relation to issues of polymodal
chromaticism in the opening movement.

Fourth Movement: Transformation of the Bimodal Half-Step

The function of the bimodal (minor/major third) half step, which pervaded
much of the first (and second) movement, is transformed in the fourth movement, in conjunction with the shift in tonic from A to C. In the first movement,
the half step appeared from the outset as a primary surface detail in the bimodal
ostinato theme (A–C–E–C♯–A), which served as a common pivot between the
latter and the more compressed octatonic transposition (G–B♭–D–B–G♯) in the
transition (beginning in m. 29, violin). In the rondo finale, the diatonic and
octatonic spheres tend to remain more separate from each other in the interactions between modal thematic statements and their respective counterpoint.
The initial A theme may be interpreted as a thematic transformation of the
bimodal ostinato of the first movement; it implies the incomplete single mode
of D Dorian (D–E–F–G–[ ]–[ ]–C), with a tonal shift to F at the first cadence
(m. 6). The transposition to implied A Dorian (A–B–C–D–[ ]–[ ]–G) brings the
D-Dorian seventh degree (C) back momentarily to its original minor-third position in A Dorian. In the following alternations between these two thematic transpositions (mm. 1–24), the "white-key" collection remains exclusive, while the
tonalities become increasingly unstable by the contrapuntal addition of V–I in C
major (bass line of cello pizzicato chords in mm. 13–24). This harmonic emphasis on C supports the tonal shift in the final statement of A′ from A Dorian to C
major (mm. 22–24). While this recalls the tonal duality between A and C in the
preceding movements, it also reprises the basic harmonic elements (A and C) of
A minor from the A-minor/major ostinato that opened the first two movements.
     In the first movement (mm. 29–38, violin), the mutated transposition of
the ostinato in G minor/major (G–B♭–D–B–G♯) reveals the dual pivotal function of the minor/major third (in this case, B♭/B) between the ambiguous
diatonic and octatonic spheres. A similar process of compression to the more
chromatic octatonic collection unfolds at Theme A2 of the finale (m. 25); here
however, the initial A′ theme is based on a single—but tonally more ambiguous—modal form of the "white-key" diatonic collection, in contrast with the
original bimodal ostinato theme. At the same time, the addition of the cello
line in counterpoint with A2 (mm. 25–30) alters the role of the half step in
the similar transformation of Theme A′ into a hybrid diatonic-octatonic
segment. The linear unfolding of A♯–G–F–B–G♯ in the cello, to which is
added C♯ (at m. 32), transforms the implied B-Aeolian mode (B–[ ]–D–E–
[ ]–G–A) of the violin's A2 variant into a complete—but impure—octatonic

collection, B–C♯–D–E–F–G–G♯–[A]–A♯. This area of compression features only the major-mode form (A–C♯–E) within the diatonic/octatonic collection, whereas only the minor-mode form (A–C–E) is implied in the exclusive "white-key" content of A1 and its "C-major" chordal addition prior to A2.

Thus the process of compression in the finale is analogous to that in the opening passages of the first movement. Note that pitches C and C♯ come into somewhat closer linear proximity (mm. 38, 40, and 42) as the cello unfolds toward the cadence. Nevertheless, although the transformation from diatonic to octatonic (as in the first three movements) still tends toward chromatic compression, the mischievous quality of the bimodal half step has now become obscured or hidden altogether.

Related to this chromatic compression is the octatonic transformation of diatonic modality. The second statement of A2 (mm. 44–56) presents one of the clearest moments of such transformation, while maintaining the distinction between the two spheres. In counterpoint against the gapped diatonic minor tetrachord (D–E–[ ]–G) of the violin, the cello unfolds the tritone transposition (G♯–A♯–[ ]–C♯). While the essential contour of each thematic segment is maintained, the combined linear cells form a six-note segment of octatonic 2, D–E–[ ]–G–G♯–A♯–[ ]–C♯. The original bimodal half step is no longer essential as a linear anchor in this transformational process from diatonic to octatonic spheres. At the phrase ending (mm. 55–56) the cadential scale reverses the process from diatonic and whole-tone to diatonic modality in A major (G–G♯–A♯–B–C♯/D–E–F♯–G♯–A♯/B–C♯–D–E–F♯–G♯–A). Thereafter, echoes of the half step are freely used against transpositions of the successive rondo themes and their counterpoint, though the bimodal clarity of the original ostinato theme is no longer explicitly manifested.

The original "mischievous" meaning of the bimodal half step seems to be invoked by its very absence. This conjecture is supported by the momentary cyclic return of the original bimodal ostinato in the middle of the finale (mm. 135–48). It is striking that this stretto return (mm. 135–37) is in D major/minor, which brings back the conflicting F and F♯, the two notes representing the first change of modal content in the first movement from the A-Dorian statement of Theme-1 (cello, mm. 6–17) to the D-Dorian statement (violin, mm. 18–29). Another stretto (mm. 145–48) then presents the basic ostinato theme in the original bimodal key of A minor/major, which represents the only significant recombination in this movement of the specific dual third half step C–C♯. Thus, this brief cyclic recurrence of the ostinato in A only faintly echoes the mischievous element.

Besides the primary intervallic clashes and dissonant chromatic juxtapositions, Ravel's special handling of instrumental devices within the changing textures also contributes to the mischievous, even sardonic quality manifested in many passages of the work. As DeVoto points out in the second movement, "Très vif,"

Ravel once again shows his fascination with exaggerated use of pizzicato in A minor, as in the String Quartet and the Piano Trio. . . . The B♭ minor melody over an ostinato of C, D . . . and A at bar 97 is very close to the combination of "bell chords" that Mussorgsky used in the Coronation Scene of *Boris Godunov*, but the mixture of instrumental colours, plucked *fortissimo* notes with lightly bowed harmonics, makes this relationship difficult to hear. (The pitches of the melody itself, though not the tempo, sound like an echo of two prominent melodies in Stravinsky's *Le Sacre du Printemps*.) The combination of major and minor triads differing by a semitone results in a harsh sound, familiar to Bartók but new for Ravel, as used later across bars 142–48.[29]

In conclusion, Ravel's Duo Sonata may give the impression of a free combination and recombination of themes, with transpositional and pitch-collectional strategies taking place within a conventional formal organization. However, the foregoing analysis has demonstrated the broad consistency of Ravel's complex but highly structured pitch organization from the perspective of polymodality and polymodal chromaticism as central to the tonal process. Given the prevalent linearity of the work, due to the absence of the piano, the texture naturally lends itself to such a manner of organization. Consequently, as we have seen, this most unusual work for Ravel interacts suggestively with certain of Bartók's compositional techniques and strategies. As one of only two instrumental chamber works composed by Ravel after World War I, the Duo Sonata at once represents his most elusive as well as his most sophisticated work in this vein.

(a) **THEME 1**, Two statements (on A, mm. 6-17, cello, and D, mm. 18-29, violin):
Combined D Dorian/A Dorian modes in eight-note segment of interval-5/7 cycle, i.e., two
adjacent seven-note segments along the cycle of fifths

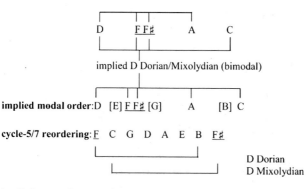

modal order: (2) D-Dorian content, D E F̲ G A B C (mm. 17-29, violin)

cycle-5/7 order: F̲ C G D A E B F♯   (background

                                          semitone, F̲-F♯,

                                          bimodal difference)

modal order: (1) A Dorian content, A B C D E F♯ G (mm. 1-17, cello)

---

versus

(b) **OCTATONIC MOTIF**: combined incomplete D Dorian/D Mixolydian modes

(2)   D major/minor (mm. 17-29, cello)

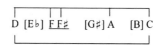

D   F F♯   A   C

implied D Dorian/Mixolydian (bimodal)

implied modal order: D [E] F F♯ [G]   A   [B] C

cycle-5/7 reordering: F   C   G   D   A   E   B   F♯

                                         D Dorian

                                         D Mixolydian

implied octatonic-0 transformation:

D [E♭] F F♯   [G♯] A   [B] C

Octatonic-1 chromatic complement of octatonic-0 to suggest all twelve tones in
combination of opening A minor/major ostinato (violin) and following D
major/minor ostinato (cello)

Appendix 8.1. Polarity of diatonic bimodality and chromatic octatonicism, linked
by common substructures

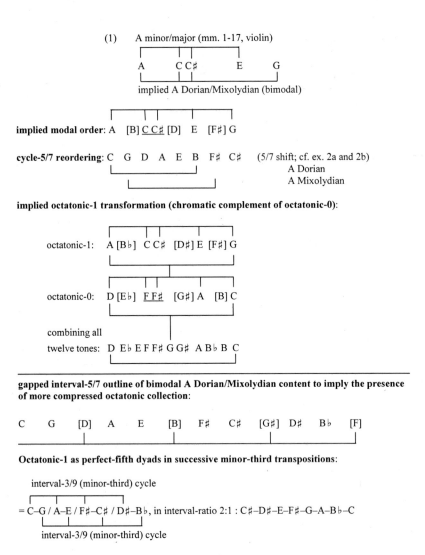

(1)   A minor/major (mm. 1-17, violin)

A   C C♯   E   G

implied A Dorian/Mixolydian (bimodal)

implied modal order: A   [B] C C♯ [D]   E   [F♯] G

cycle-5/7 reordering: C   G   D   A   E   B   F♯   C♯   (5/7 shift; cf. ex. 2a and 2b)
                                                               A Dorian
                                                               A Mixolydian

implied octatonic-1 transformation (chromatic complement of octatonic-0):

octatonic-1:   A [B♭] C C♯ [D♯] E [F♯] G

octatonic-0:   D [E♭] F F♯ [G♯] A [B] C

combining all
twelve tones: D E♭ E F F♯ G G♯ A B♭ B C

---

gapped interval-5/7 outline of bimodal A Dorian/Mixolydian content to imply the presence of more compressed octatonic collection:

C   G   [D]   A   E   [B]   F♯   C♯   [G♯]   D♯   B♭   [F]

Octatonic-1 as perfect-fifth dyads in successive minor-third transpositions:

interval-3/9 (minor-third) cycle

= C–G / A–E / F♯–C♯ / D♯–B♭, in interval-ratio 2:1 : C♯–D♯–E–F♯–G–A–B♭–C

interval-3/9 (minor-third) cycle

Appendix 8.1. Polarity of diatonic bimodality and chromatic octatonicism, linked by common substructures—*(concluded)*

Notes

1. Even though Ravel combines major and minor structures in the bimodal context of the Duo Sonata, producing a larger symmetrical formation (e.g., triads A–C–E and A–C♯–E together produce the four-note symmetry, A–C–C♯–E), I shall take the liberty of referring to the basic context as "diatonic."

2. The interval sequence of the octatonic scale (e.g., A–B–C–D–E♭–F–F♯–G♯), 2–1–2–1–2–1–2–1, reveals a partial chromatic compression of the diatonic interval sequence, e.g., in the A-Dorian mode (A–B–C–D–E–F♯–G–A), 2–1–2–2–2–1–2, and may therefore serve as an intermediary stage between diatonic-modal and chromatic extremes. We may note another angle to the chromatic compression point: that, thinking of both scales as comprising two 2–1–2 tetrachords, the Dorian transposes them by T7 (perfect fifth) while the octatonic *compresses* this to T6 (tritone).

3. In "The Influence of Folk Music on the Art Music of Today," in *Béla Bartók Essays*, ed. Benjamin Suchoff (New York: St. Martin's Press, 1976), 317.

4. In "The Relation of Folk Song to the Development of the Art Music of Our Time," *Béla Bartók Essays*, 325.

5. In "The Influence of Debussy and Ravel in Hungary (1938)," *Béla Bartók Essays*, 518.

6. See Bartók, "The Influence of Folk Music on the Art Music of Today," 317.

7. Béla Bartók, "Harvard Lectures," *Béla Bartók Essays*, 381–83.

8. An *interval cycle* is a series based on a single recurrent interval, for instance, the whole-tone scale or the cycle of fifths, the sequence completed by the return of the initial pitch class. The total complex of interval cycles consists of one cycle of minor seconds, two of whole tones, three of minor thirds, four of major thirds, only one of perfect fourths, and six of tritones. The entire set of uni-intervallic cycles is outlined in Elliott Antokoletz, *The Music of Béla Bartók: A Study of Tonality and Progression in Twentieth-Century Music* (Berkeley: University of California Press, 1984), ex. 70, p. 68; see chapter 8 ("Generation of the Interval Cycles"), especially. Furthermore, a collection of pitches is *symmetrical* if the intervallic structure of half of it can be mapped into the other half through mirroring, i.e., literal inversion. Symmetrical pitch formations are derived through operations upon the precompositional alignment of inversionally related interval cycles.

9. Mark DeVoto, "Harmony in the chamber music," in *The Cambridge Companion to Ravel*, ed. Deborah Mawer (Cambridge: Cambridge University Press, 2000), 108.

10. Ibid.

11. Ibid.

12. Walter Pfann, in *Zur Sonaten-gestaltung im Spätwerk Maurice Ravels (1920–1932)* (Regensburg: Gustav Bosse Verlag, 1991), 21.

13. Ibid., 23.

14. Ibid., 27.

15. In connection with Bartók's own writings, which bear this principle out in very definite terms (see Bartók, "Harvard Lectures," 365–75), see also Colin Mason, "An Essay in Analysis: Tonality, Symmetry, and Latent Serialism in Bartók's Fourth Quartet," *Music Review* 18, no. 7 (August 1957): 195, and Elliott Antokoletz, "Theories of Pitch Organization in Bartók's Music: A Critical Evaluation," *International Journal of Musicology* 7 (1998): 277–81.

16. See Bartók, "Harvard Lectures," 370–71.

17. The term "interval ratio" is used for convenience here to designate the relationship of two semitones to one another in terms of their intervallic separation. "Interval ratio 1:2," which indicates two semitones separated by a whole tone, for instance, is the ratio that indicates the octatonic scale or its segments.

18. Walter Pfann (pp. 17–18) identifies what he considers to be the first transition of the movement by the entry of the new cello theme at m. 30, and Theme 2 by the wide, angular cello theme in counterpoint with a new scalar idea at measure 47. In contrast, Mark DeVoto (pp. 108–9), identifies Pfann's Theme 2 as the transition. Pfann's Closing Theme (mm. 69–81) is, therefore, DeVoto's Theme 2. Although both formal thematic interpretations have their merits, they also evoke some structural and perceptual questions. The quasi-traditional tonal scheme, in which the relative major key (C major) of the opening A minor/major tonality first emerges at measure 52, i.e., in the middle of DeVoto's transitional theme, and is then established clearly at DeVoto's Theme 2 (m. 69), provides stronger support for DeVoto's formal conception. I shall therefore employ DeVoto's thematic-structural designations, but will adopt Pfann's designation of the transition as beginning at m. 30.

19. See Bartók's discussion, in "Harvard Lectures," 369–70, of this principle of minor and major thirds in instrumental folk music, as described below (n. 23; see also n. 16 and corresponding quote from Bartók).

20. Brackets [ ] are used to indicate a missing (or implied) element from a given mode or pitch collection.

21. Any diatonic collection can be shown as a symmetrical seven-note segment of the cycle of fifths.

22. Intervals imply their complements or harmonic inversions in the same interval class and may be specifically designated by double numbers, the number of each interval calculated in semitones: the perfect unison (or octave) will be interval 0/12; the minor second (or major seventh), interval 1/11; the major second (or minor seventh), interval 2/10; the minor third (or major sixth), interval 3/9; the major third (or minor sixth), interval 4/8; the perfect fourth (or perfect fifth), interval 5/7; and the tritone (which is equivalent in its harmonic inversion), interval 6/6.

23. Bartók, "Harvard Lectures," 369–70.

24. We shall arbitrarily assume a referential position for each of the three octatonic scales, beginning with the whole step. Any permutation of that scale that can begin with pitch-class C will be referred to as octatonic-0, that with pitch-class C♯ as octatonic-1, and that with pitch-class D as octatonic-2.

25. Bartók, "Harvard Lectures," 367.

26. See DeVoto, "Harmony in the chamber music," 108–9.

27. This contention is supported by the transformation of the ostinato to C–E–G/A–E (at mm. 108–9). At the entry of the new theme, C–E–G is moved down to B–D–F♯, while dyad A–E is retained as a common link (B–D–F♯/A–E). The "new" development theme is also prefigured by measures 57–59 of the transition, part 2, albeit in a different rhythm and metrical placement.

28. See Pfann, n. 12, above.

29. DeVoto, "Harmony in the chamber music," 109–10.

Part Three

Interdisciplinary Perspectives

Chapter Nine

Deception, Reality, and Changes of Perspective in Two Songs from Histoires naturelles

Lauri Suurpää

Introduction

This chapter analyzes two songs from *Histoires naturelles* ("Le paon" and "Le cygne"), focusing on the music, text, and musico-poetic associations. *Histoires naturelles* (1906), composed to poems by Jules Renard, provides a particularly interesting subject for an analysis of text-music relationships. Ravel's own comments shed light on both his views of Renard's poems and his ideals of text-music associations at the time of the cycle's composition. Of the poems Ravel said that "the direct, clear language and the profound, hidden poetry of Jules Renard's works tempted me for a long time."[1] According to Renard's journal, Ravel said that he had taken the poet's words as a direct starting point when composing the song cycle:

> M. Ravel, the composer of *Histoires naturelles,* dark, rich, and elegant, urges me to go and hear his songs tonight. I told him I knew nothing about music, and asked him what he had been able to add to *Histoires naturelles.* He replied: I did not intend to add anything, only to interpret them.
> But in what way?
> I have tried to say in music what you say with words, when you are in front of a tree, for example. I think and feel in music, and should like to think I feel the same things as you.[2]

The analyses of this chapter shed light on how Ravel set this "profound, hidden poetry" in two songs from *Histoires naturelles*—intending not, in his own words, "to add anything," but "only to interpret" the poems. I will argue that the songs' text-music associations do not stem only from direct and unequivocal associations, like imitation and tone painting or expressive similarities, as might be implied by Ravel's suggestion that he "tried to say in music what you [Renard] say with words." In addition to such direct connections, significant structural factors of the poems find their counterparts in Ravel's music, creating more abstract musico-poetic associations alongside the direct instances of tone painting and imitation. Such abstract, concealed connections help illuminate the musical counterparts of the "hidden poetry" that Ravel appreciated in Renard's texts.[3]

The five poems that Ravel set in his cycle do not form a unified narrative arch. Rather, they can be understood as a set of individual tableaux featuring animals, creatures often invested with human characteristics. In spite of their independence, there are some associations between the poems, and examining "Le paon" and "Le cygne" as a pair is justified by textual factors. Both feature irony and tragedy, the latter expressed in a comic disguise. Moreover, both include two kinds of oppositions: the juxtaposition of deception and reality; and the contrast between the perspectives, or beliefs, of the poems' respective protagonists (the peacock and the swan) and their narrators (the outside observers). In both poems the protagonists' and narrators' preceptions of reality differ: in "Le paon" the narrator is aware of reality while the bird deceives himself, whereas in "Le cygne" the it is the narrator who is deceived.

The examination of "Le paon" and "Le cygne" as a pair is also musically justified in that both songs are harmonically unified. In "Le paon" the foreground is saturated with extended tertian harmonies (mainly ninth chords), harmonies that provide the framework for the large-scale linear structure. In "Le cygne" tertian sonorities, often with added notes (mainly sixths) play a similar role. Thus in both songs the local vertical sonorities and the large-scale linear structure are based on similar harmonic units.

Theoretical Perspective

In the course of the analysis, I shall address musico-poetic associations from three perspectives: imitation, emotional tone, and structural relationships. Imitation refers to situations where the music mimics sounds of the external world. For vocal music I also use this term to describe gestural imitation of aspects mentioned in the text—an obvious instance being, for example, setting the word "descend" with a registrally descending musical progression.[4] For our purposes, the term "emotional tone," or expression, shall be limited to designating basic emotions related to the tragic and nontragic and their various shades and intensities.[5] The examination of structural relationships is more complex, in that one must be able to model the tensions of both the music and the text in order to enable their close comparison. Accordingly I apply modified Schenkerian theory for describing musical structure and certain concepts of Greimassian semiotics, based on the work of the linguist A. J.

Greimas, for examining the textual structure. The two theories provide analogous approaches to the analysis of music and text, in that they both delineate salient relationships at different structural levels. This methodology enables us to analyze abstract relations independently in the music and the text—issues like postponement of the resolution of tension or the quest for primacy within the elements of a binary opposition—and in turn to demonstrate significant correlations between their structural trajectories.

Since the songs are not strictly tonal, a Schenkerian approach has to be modified. My analysis adopts two principles fundamental to Schenkerian analysis, but modifies their application. First, I retain the notion of a referential sonority as the matrix of the musical structure. But, whereas the referential sonority in tonal music is a triad (specifically, the tonic triad), in Ravel's songs the referential sonority assumes other formations. These sonorities (or their subsets) function, then, as triads do in tonal music—they are stable elements and hence define the norms of consonance and dissonance. Second, I will argue that such referential sonorities (and their transpositions) form the basis for prolongation (*Auskomponierung*) at foreground and middleground levels.[6]

In "Le paon" and "Le cygne" the tonic triad has been replaced by harmonies that traditional Schenkerian theory would consider dissonant. In "Le paon" extended tertian harmonies (mainly ninth chords) assume the function of referential sonority, and in "Le cygne" tertian sonorities with added notes (mainly sixths) have a similar function.[7] In the two songs such referential sonorities function much as tonic triads do in tonality: at deeper levels they provide the basis for the large-scale harmonic and contrapuntal structure, while at local levels they appear transposed as vertical sonorities. (We will see, however, that the two songs also include significant differences: "Le paon" departs markedly from traditional major/minor tonal procedures while "Le cygne" retains them to a greater extent.)

Before discussing Renard's poems, a brief introduction to Greimassian semiotics is in order. His work—specifically the actantial theory—provides the basis for modeling the two sets of binary oppositions that we find in the poems: deception versus reality; and contrasting perspectives of the narrator and protagonist. According to Greimas, the text is interpreted as a set of relations between actants, roles abstracted from the text. Figure 9.1a shows two pairs of actants: subject versus object and sender versus receiver (the arrow shows that the pairs of the oppositions are structurally connected).[8] I will not attempt to give a thorough picture of actants, but will limit the discussion to those aspects that will be applied in analyzing the two poems. The pair of subject and object forms the primary actantial opposition. The subject can be understood as the protagonist, say a poor peasant in a fairy tale, while the object is something the subject wishes for, say a treasure in our tale. The second pair of actants, sender versus receiver, are related by the transmission of information—the sender is the source of information that the receiver then receives. In our tale we can think of an elf telling the peasant where the treasure is, where the elf functions as the sender and the peasant as the receiver, in addition to his function as the subject.[9] Figure 9.1b shows that subject and object can be either conjoined or disjoined—the peasant has either found the treasure or has not. Finally, figure 9.1c represents the transformation (indicated by the double-lined arrows) from one state to another. In the first state of our tale (the beginning) the peasant has not found the treasure; in the second state the elf tells him where it is; in the third and final state the peasant, having followed the elf's advice, has found the treasure. Even though Renard's poetic world is much more subtle than this imaginary tale, the same Greimassian principles can be used to describe the underlying tensions in both.

(a) Actants

$$S \rightarrow O$$
$$Sr \rightarrow R$$

S   = subject; the "protagonist"
O   = object; sought for by the subject
Sr = sender; sender of information—power that either allows the subject to reach the object or prevents it from doing so
R   = receiver; receives the information sent by the sender

(b) Conjunction and disjunction

$S \cap O$ = subject and object are conjoined
$S \cup O$ = subject and object are disjoined

(c) Narrative transformation

State 1   State 2   State 3

$(S \cup O) \Rightarrow (Sr \rightarrow R) \Rightarrow (S \cap O)$

Figure 9.1. Some basic concepts of Greimassian semiotics

Analyses

"Le paon"

The Peacock

He will surely get married today. It was to have been yesterday. He was in full dress and ready. He was only waiting for his bride. She didn't come. She won't be long now. In his conceit, he struts about with the air of an Indian prince and wears the customary rich presents. Love heightens the brightness of his colors and his aigrette trembles like a lyre. His bride doesn't show up. He ascends to the roof and looks toward the sun. He utters his diabolical cry: "Léon! Léon!" That's what he calls his bride. He sees nothing coming and no one answers. The chickens, who are used to it, don't even raise their heads. They are tired of admiring him. He comes down to the yard again, so sure of being handsome that he is incapable of bearing a grudge. His wedding will take place tomorrow. And, not knowing what to do with the rest of the day, he heads for the stairway to the house. He climbs the steps, as if they were temple steps, with an official gait. He lifts his robe, with its train that is so weighed down with eyes that were unable to tear themselves away from it. He repeats the ceremony once again.[10]

The poem is about a peacock that plans, or hopes, to get married. His wishes are in vain, however, which is evident to the reader almost from the outset of the poem. But the peacock refuses to admit this. After stating the bird's certainty of the forthcoming marriage, the poem recalls the preceding day, when the peacock expected to get married. But the bride did not arrive. The poem then returns to the present: the bird is still waiting for his bride, in vain. Yet the peacock is certain that she will arrive—if not yesterday or today, then tomorrow. Proud and sure of his magnificence, the peacock parades around, preparing for the wedding that will take place, he is convinced, tomorrow. In the poem the perspective of the bird represents illusion while that of the narrator (and reader) represents reality. The futile certainty of the peacock creates a comic contrast to the reality apparent to the reader. Yet there is also a tragic undertone: although one is amused by the bird's vanity, one also feels sympathy. The peacock is doomed to face disappointment over and over again, given the certainty that the bride will not arrive (if a bride exists at all).

Figure 9.2 analyzes significant structural aspects of the poem. Figure 9.2a shows the underlying binary opposition between reality and illusion. The peacock is interpreted as the subject and the marriage as the object. In the illusion (representing the bird's hopes) the subject and object are conjoined, whereas in reality (representing the reader's knowledge) they are disjoined. Figure 9.2b traces the narrative progression, explaining how the underlying opposition occurs in different parts of the poem. I have divided the narrative into four successive states. State 1 is already past and refers to the bride not arriving; hence the subject and object are disjoined. State 2 shows the tension prevailing at the beginning of the poem. The peacock waits for his bride, but it is not known if she will arrive, so it is uncertain whether the subject and object will be conjoined or disjoined. This uncertainty is resolved in State 3: the bride does not arrive, and the subject and object are disjoined; thus State 3 describes the situation in the latter part of the poem. State 4 refers to the future. The peacock hopes that his bride will arrive tomorrow and that he will then get married. Therefore the subject and object are here conjoined. But the reader knows that this hope is ultimately only illusion.

(a) Underlying opposition

illusion,	reality,
perspective	perspective
of the peacock	of the narrator

$(S \cap O)$ vs. $(S \cup O)$

S   = the peacock
O   = marriage

(b) Narrative aspects

State 1	State 2	State 3	State 4
past	present$_1$	present$_2$	future
reality	uncertainty	reality	hope (illusion)

$(S \cup O) \Rightarrow (S \cup O) \text{ or } (S \cap O) \Rightarrow (S \cup O) \Rightarrow (S \cap O)$

Figure 9.2. Ravel, "Le Paon," structural aspects of the poem

Formally the music can also be divided into four parts; see example 9.1. (The boxed numbers between the staves of example 9.1a designate formal divisions; there is no exact one-to-one correspondence between the textual and musical sections, however). The bass consists of ascending thirds: F in section 1, A in section 2, C and E♭ in section 3, and finally G in section 4. These pitches arpeggiate the opening sonority of the song (ex. 9.1b). A 9/7/5/3 sonority on F functions as the referential harmony of the song: this sonority both begins and ends the song, and is "composed out" (in traditional Schenkerian terms) in the bass part of measures 1–44.[11] The significance of extended tertian sonorities, in particular ninth chords like the referential harmony, is evident immediately in the opening measures of the song.

The first part of the song (mm. 1–15) divides into two phrases (mm. 1–8 and 9–15) that begin similarly but end in a different manner (ex. 9.2). The first phrase, almost entirely instrumental, captures the stately, ceremonial, and pompous nature of the peacock. Harmonically the opening tonic ninth leads at measure 5 to a sustained ninth chord on G, related to the opening sonority as a neighbor-note chord. Thereafter a hollow-sounding gesture, consisting of bare parallel fifths and octaves, is interpolated in measures 7–8. This gesture, which will hereafter be called the "fifth-gesture," would seem to be rooted on the bass note C, suggesting that this harmony serves as functional dominant

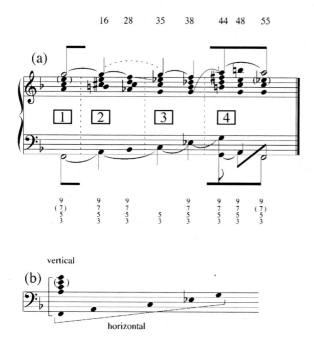

Example 9.1. Ravel, "Le Paon," an overview

to the opening F sonority. However, the remainder of the phrase denies this interpretation, as the G–F bass motion in measures 8–9 reintroduces the opening bass note emphatically in a stepwise manner. With the vocal entrance in measure 8 ("He will surely get married today"), the bird recalls vividly the disappointment of the preceding day, but is nevertheless convinced that the marriage will happen today. The fifth-gesture is subordinated as a prolongation of the bass note G arrived at in measure 5, which prevents the the bass note C from functioning as the dominant of F. The denial of the dominant function of C can be seen as the musical counterpart to the protagonist's choice to follow illusion and to deny reality. Additionally, the fifth-gesture has a significant expressive function: I propose that it represents a kind of threat that the marriage might not take place, after all. But the hollow and tragic atmosphere of the fifth-gesture vanishes, just as the tragedy of the nonappearance of the bride vanishes in the bird's mind. The character of the music following and preceding the fifth-gesture conveys the ever-hopeful attitude of the peacock.

The next phrase (mm. 9–15) recalls the failure of the marriage to take place the preceding day, and looks ahead to its taking place today. ("She didn't come. She won't be long now.") While the opening of the phrase remains intact (with added vocal part), the ends of the two sections, and subsequently their overall structural course, are different. Unlike the first section, which closes with a

Example 9.2. "Le Paon," mm. 1–16 (part 1), analytical sketch

deep-level neighboring motion, the second section remains open. The concluding D minor ninth chord (m. 13, transformed into a D dominant ninth in
m. 15) is closely associated with the F major ninth chord of measure 9: four of
the five pitches in the chords are the same.[12] The similarity between the two
chords and the surface figuration of measures 12–15 interacts suggestively with
the text. If the fifth-gesture in mm. 7–8 is associated with the peacock's refusal
to accept reality, then the return of the referential sonority of measure 9 represents the bird's belief in the forthcoming marriage; here the perspective is
that of the peacock, and the bird's belief constitutes the "reality" at the beginning of the poem. (The return to the opening material in m. 9 retrospectively suggests that the bird's belief also governs the instrumental mm. 1–6.)

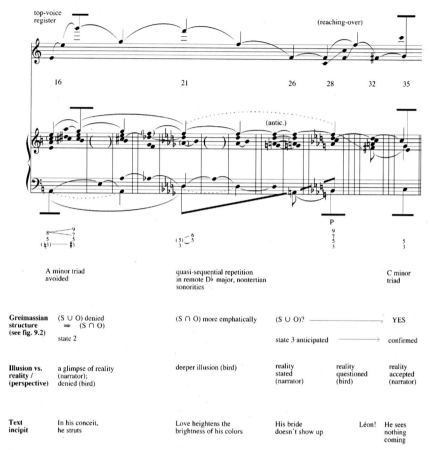

Example 9.3. "Le Paon," mm. 16–35 (part 2), analytical sketch

The unwillingness to abandon the sonic realm of the referential F major ninth chord in measures 13–15 corresponds to the bird's persistent belief in the marriage. In the music the diminuendo and decrease in rhythmic activity in measures 13–15 create an impression of expectancy: what is going to follow this calming down? By retaining the sonic profile of the referential sonority, the music implies that the peacock's hopes may be fulfilled.

But they are not. In measure 16 the character of the music changes drastically. The time signature changes from $\frac{4}{4}$ to $\frac{3}{4}$; a clearly contrasting harmony is heard after the F major and D minor ninth chords; the figuration changes; and new, appoggiatura-like dissonances are introduced. Example 9.3 presents an analytical sketch of measures 16–35, the second part of the song. As the thorough-bass numbers indicate, ninth chords (and other tertian sonorities) still appear prominently. The bass motion begins with an apparent arpeggiation of an ascending (enharmonic) major third from A to D♭ (m. 21) correspond-ing to the change of key signature. The latter is prolonged for the next five measures, until the return to A♮ in the bass in measure 26 leads to bass B♭ and eventually to C with the section change at measure 35. Thus the progression subordinates the initial ascending major third to the deep-level bass motion from A to C. As we shall see, the revelation of the incipient arpeggiation as illu-sory in the wake of the "real" bass motion at a deeper level is reflected precisely in the dramatic progression represented by the Greimassian structure.

The harmonic tension intensifies immediately at the beginning of mea-sure 16. After the D minor ninth chord in measures 13–15 (transformed into a major chord in m. 14), which emphasizes pitches E and C as the two uppermost voices, the bare fifth A–E that opens measure 16 sounds like an incomplete A minor triad. But the chord is immediately transformed into an A dominant ninth chord (the principal sonority governing mm. 16–20). This chord is a (near-) transposition of the referential harmony that opened the song, so the music manages to retain the chord quality while almost all other musical aspects change. Thereafter the material of measures 16–17 is treated in a freely sequential manner. In the text the peacock is certain of his mag-nificence: "In his conceit, he struts about with the air of an Indian prince and wears the customary rich presents. Love heightens the brightness of his colors and his aigrette trembles like a lyre."[13] The bird does not even consider the possibility that the bride will not come. Instead, he dwells on the thought of his own beauty, which his love increases. That is, of the two options shown in state 2 of figure 9.2b he considers only the first, the conjunction of subject and object, as a true possibility. Dramatically the transformation of the A minor triad into a dominant ninth chord conveys the notion of refusal: the music refuses to accept the A minor triad, just as the bird refuses to accept the pos-sibility that the bride will not come (see ex. 9.3). Yet the novel expression and the fleeting, implied A minor sonority create a new, more intensely emotional atmosphere, which questions the preceding nontragic emotion; the reader of the poem guesses by now that the hopes of the marriage are futile even though the peacock himself refuses to accept this. The narrator's perspective has become clear.

As the annotations of example 9.3 signify, after the bird has refused to accept the possibility of the negative option of state 2 (S ∪ O), represented musically at the beginning measure 16, he plunges deeper into his illusion; the perspec-tive of the narrator shifts to the background while that of the bird moves to the surface. Intensification of illusion occurs with the quasi-sequential repetition of measures 16–20 in measures 21–25. Moreover, in measure 21 with the turn to the apparently stable but ultimately illusory key of D♭ major, we lose all trace of the implied minor triad of measure 16. Poetically, the bird no longer even con-siders the negative option he refused to admit in measure 16.

But the reality soon becomes unequivocal when the narrative of the poem arrives at state 3 of figure 9.2b, where the subject and object are disjoined. This arrival occurs in two stages (see ex. 9.3). Reality is first reaffirmed at measure 26 ("His bride doesn't show up"). The bird continues to seek the bride, however, so state 3 arrives first in a somewhat anticipatory manner. Gesturally, the long chord and the staccato bass notes in measures 26–27 differ greatly from both the preceding and the following music. Poetically, the sudden change in the music's figuration at measure 26 relates to the return to present reality: the peacock, surprised by the fact that the bride has not come, realizes that there was a negative option, after all. Harmonically, measures 26–27 are related both to the preceding music (the peacock's dreaming in D♭ major) and to the following music (in which he tries, after noting the bride's absence, to find her). ("He ascends to the roof and looks toward the sun. He utters his diabolical cry: 'Léon! Léon!' That's what he calls his bride.") As the graph indicates, the anticipation in measure 25 of the right-hand harmony of measures 26–27 creates a link between the peacock's dreaming and the present reality: that is, the stable D♭ major with added sixth gives way to the unstable D♭ augmented triad with added augmented fourth, which leads to the B♭ major ninth harmony of measure 28. Thereafter measures 28–34 form the dramatic culmination of the song. The bass drops out as a long crescendo and the registral ascent of the top voice in measures 28–30 lead to the fast *tremolandi* in measure 31 and finally to the *fortissimo* of measure 32. The registral ascent directly imitates the bird's ascent in the poem, while the descending third F–D in measure 32 mimics the cry of the peacock.

Structurally, the outburst at measure 32, related to the peacock's cry, has a decorative role: the underlying harmony functions as an appoggiatura chord, similar to that of the harmony of measures 26–27. (This association is enhanced by the textural similarity between mm. 26–27 and 33–34.) These two harmonies also bear a similar poetic function: both are related to the waking up to reality, to the fact that the bride does not arrive—the former to the anticipatory arrival at state 3, the latter to its confirmation. An appoggiatura beautifully describes such a relationship between illusion and reality: as a decorative and subordinate element, an appoggiatura is resolved into a more stable element. By analogy, in the poem the dream or illusion is replaced by reality, and the expressive outburst in measure 32 represents resistance to the unequivocal arrival of state 3 in measure 35.

After this outburst the dynamic level of the music decreases immediately and the momentum seems to stop. In measure 35 the bass returns and an unexpected C minor triad arrives, revealing itself as the destination of the structural bass motion initiated in measure 16. Measures 16 and 35 are associated by similar texture and figuration, as well as the underlying voice leading. At the same time, their modality changes: as noted above, at measure 16 the implied A minor triad is replaced by an A dominant ninth chord, reflecting the peacock's refusal to accept the possibility that the bride might not arrive. At measure 35 however, with the turn to C minor, the bird no longer can avoid accepting this reality. Finally, the bass C at measure 35 represents the third step in the arpeggiation of the opening referential harmony (see ex. 9.1). In sum, the unfolding of the underlying middleground structure, along with the tragic modal shift, stresses the peacock's admission of reality and confirms the change of perspective from bird to narrator.

But the narrative structure of the poem, shown in figure 9.2b, does not close in the tragic state 3. Rather, there remains state 4, the hope of marriage in the future. Similarly, the music does not dwell in the tragic (ex. 9.4). Following the sequential move from C minor to Bb minor (mm. 35–38), a sudden forte reintroduces the opening ninth chord in the middle of measure 38, this time on the bass note Eb, the fourth note of the extended middleground bass arpeggiation (cf. example 9.1). Here the perspective changes once more in the poem from the narrator's reality ("He [the peacock] sees nothing coming and no one answers) back to the bird's illusion ("He comes down to the yard again, so sure of being handsome that he is incapable of bearing a grudge. His wedding will take place tomorrow."). Indeed, the peacock almost violently returns to his illusion: the Eb major ninth chord at measure 38 seems to arrive two eighth notes too early. The resultant syncopation and the *forte* dynamic together forcibly deny the minor mode and its tragic associations. Uncertainty still remains, however. With the return of the fifth-gesture in measures 42–43 comes the renewed threat to the marriage's taking place. But, as in measures 8–9, the fifth-gesture once more leads through a bass descent to the transposed reprise of the opening thematic material, thereby nullifying the threat and preserving the bird's illusion.

The song's fourth and final section, whose voice leading is shown in example 9.5, functions as a kind of a recapitulation—the opening thematic material returns on a bass-note G, the last element of the extended middleground bass arpeggiation. In measures 44–49 the return to the opening musical material appropriately conveys the return to the opening situation—the waiting for the bride. But since the repetition is in G rather than the tonic F, the musical context is not as stable as it was at the song's beginning. Similarly, the expectations of the bride's arrival are less secure at the end of the poem than at the beginning. Accordingly, the reprise of the opening material makes some telling changes. In measures 46–47 the chromatically altered pitches F♮ and G♯ depart from the diatonic environment of the song's beginning, thereby affecting the music's expression—the ceremonial quality of the music becomes invested with tragic undertones. It is as if the peacock admits, deep inside, that there is no foundation for his certainty of marriage. But the chromatic elements vanish, and the opening character of the music returns in measure 48.

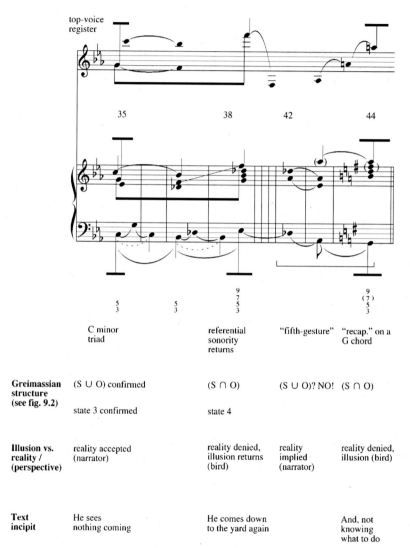

Example 9.4. "Le Paon," mm. 35–44 (part 3), analytical sketch

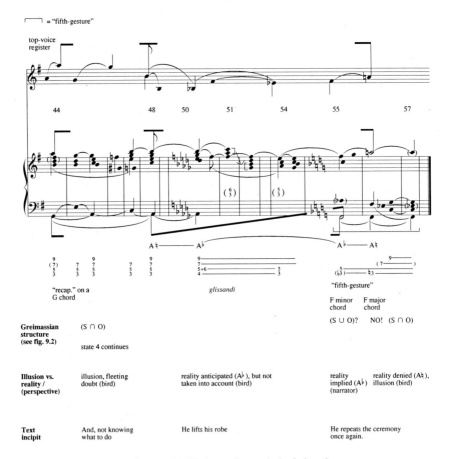

Example 9.5. "Le Paon," mm. 44–58 (part 4), analytical sketch

Thereafter measures 50–54 depart radically from the preceding music: the harmonies are mostly nontertian, the *glissandi* of measure 51 introduce a new textural element to imitate the spreading of the peacock's train, and there are no dotted rhythms. Both structurally and expressively, the most significant event is the half-step motion in the bass from A♮ to A♭ (more on its interpretation below). The dramatic move to A♭ and its prolongation colors the middleground unfolding of the bass from A to F (ex. 9.5); this supports the intricate voice leading and the resolution of the upper-voice sixth and fourth (F and D♭ respectively) to the fifth and third of the A♭ major triad in measure 54.

Upon its transformation from triad to the primary 9/7/5/3 sonority, the threatening fifth-gesture returns at measure 55 for the last time at the tonic pitch level. There is one significant difference between this fifth-gesture and its two preceding occurrences: at the end of measure 55 the last two eighth notes skip a fourth while in the corresponding measures 7 and 42, the skip has been a third. As a result, the last eighth note of the bass in measure 55 is A♭, a minor third above the F that opened the measure. Owing to this A♭ and the prolonged A♭ in measures 50–54, one clearly gets the impression that the chord of measure 55 is a minor harmony. Measure 56 cancels this impression, however, as the top voice ascends from F in measure 55 via a passing-tone G to A♮ in measure 56; the motion thereby *reverses* the bass motion from A♮ to A♭ of measures 49–50. These chromatic motions bring together the structural and poetic strands heard throughout the song. Specifically, the pitch A♭ and its relation to A♮ sum up the juxtaposition of illusion and reality, and by extension the perspectives of the peacock and the narrator. A♭ appears first in measures 50–54, where the bird concentrates on his magnificence; he does not notice the potential threat posed by this pitch, which could function as the minor third of the tonic chord. When the fifth-gesture returns in measure 55, the narrator's perspective becomes apparent—A♭ is now implied as the third of an F minor sonority. The final words of the poem convey the peacock's unshakeable faith: "He repeats the ceremony once again"; and the implied A♭ of the narrator's real perspective gives way to the A♮ of the peacock's illusion.

"Le cygne"

The Swan

He glides on the pond, like a white sleigh, from cloud to cloud. For his hunger is only for the fleecy clouds that he sees forming, moving and being lost in the water. It is one of them that he desires. He aims at it with his beak, and suddenly immerses his snow-clad neck. Then, just as a woman's arm emerges from a sleeve, he pulls it back. He has caught nothing. He looks: The startled clouds have disappeared. He remains disillusioned for only a moment, for the clouds return before very long, and, over there, where the ripples on the water are dying away, one cloud is already forming. Softly, on his light feather cushion, the swan paddles and approaches. . . . He exhausts himself fishing for empty reflections, and perhaps he will die, a victim to that illusion, before catching a single piece of cloud. But what am I talking about? Every time he dives, he burrows in the nourishing mud with his beak and comes back with a worm. He's fattening up like a goose.[14]

Like "Le paon," "Le cygne" juxtaposes reality and illusion, and the perspectives of animal and narrator. But, whereas in "Le paon," the bird's perspective represented illusion and the narrator's reality, in "Le cygne" the functions are reversed. Now the narrator, cast in the first person, has an active role, reporting what he or she sees and drawing conclusions about the swan's behavior. Observing the swan gliding on the pond, the narrator believes that the bird is trying to reach the reflections of clouds on the water, and that if it continues in this pursuit, it will surely die. Near the end of the poem the narrator is surprised to find that the bird is not trying to reach reflections of cloud; instead, he is picking up worms from the mud in the bottom of the pond—and of course has been doing so all along, unaware of the tragic interpretation that the narrator has attached to his actions.

Figure 9.3 presents a schematic chart of the poem's structure. Figure 9.3a shows the underlying opposition between illusion (the perspective of the narrator) and reality (that of the swan). The difference between the two perspectives results from the juxtaposition of two objects. The narrator thinks that the swan is trying to reach the cloud reflections (O_1), a futile task, while the bird actually is getting worms (O_2) and is highly successful in this undertaking. Figure 9.3b schematizes narrative tensions as an outcome of the information passed from the narrator to the reader. The swan does not participate in this exchange of information: he just keeps eating worms. I interpret the narrator as the sender of information and the reader as the receiver. In state 1, at the beginning of the poem, S and O_1 are disjoined; the bird cannot reach the clouds. The narrator, and consequently also the reader, believes that this first state represents reality. A transformation in the narrative, indicated by the double-lined arrow, leads to state 2, in which the swan's reality is perceived by the narrator. In state 2, S and O_2 are conjoined; the swan is able to get the worms he is trying to reach. This second state represents reality and the first state is understood, retrospectively, as illusion.

Example 9.6a provides an overview of the music. Cast in ternary form, the song's middle section (mm. 19–25) contrasts with the A sections in its slower tempo and tragic expression. As the thorough-bass numbers indicate, extended tertian sonorities, including added sixths, play a significant role as in "Le paon." Example 9.6b indicates that the opening sonority $(\frac{9}{5} + \frac{6}{3})$ unfolds as the middleground bass progression in the A^1 section. Extended tertian harmonies figure prominently in both "Le paon" and "Le cygne," but there are also significant differences in the tonal organization of the two songs. Most importantly, while "Le paon" is largely unconventional with respect to harmonic function, "Le cygne" makes extensive, albeit implicit, use of harmonic convention, as delineated by the roman-numeral analysis in example 9.6a.

The song opens by subtly introducing the song's referential harmony $\frac{9}{5} + 6$; example 9.7). The referential sonority, which includes all five pitches of a pentatonic scale, creates a distinctly pentatonic sonic quality at the song's beginning. Strikingly, the root of the harmony—the tonic B—does not appear in the bass; rather, the chord appears in the first inversion, with D♯ as the lowest note (ex. 9.7b). In addition, the added sixth G♯ receives a kind of dual treatment (ex. 9.7c). In the one-line octave it sounds like a neighbor note to F♯ and thus represents a contrapuntal as opposed to a harmonic element. In the two-line octave, on the other hand, G♯ forms part of the pictorial arpeggiating figure and hence has a harmonic function. (The arpeggiation itself obviously

(a) Underlying opposition

illusion,   reality,
perspective   perspective
of the narrator   of the swan

$(S \cup O_1)$ vs. $(S \cap O_2)$

S = the swan
O_1 = clouds, reflected on water
O_2 = worms

(b) Narrative aspects

State 1   State 2

initial state,   final state
expected reality (= illusion),   true reality,
perspective of the narrator   perspective of the bird

$$[(Sr \to O_1 \to R) \to (S \cup O_1)] \quad \Rightarrow \quad [(Sr \to O_2 \to R) \to (S \cap O_2)]$$

Sr = the narrator
R = the reader
O_1 = clouds, reflected on water
O_2 = worms
S = the swan

Figure 9.3. Ravel, "Le Cygne," structural aspects of the poem

plays on art-song and pianistic conventions of imitating the rippling of water; the use of the pentatonic helps further convey a sense of innocence and illusion.) This dual function is extended to the large-scale structure. With respect to middleground voice leading, the G♯ of measure 5 can be understood as an incomplete neighbor, a contrapuntal rather than a harmonic element; at the same time, it functions harmonically as part of the horizontalization of the referential sonority (see ex. 9.6a–b).[15]

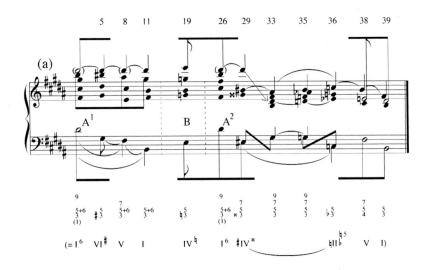

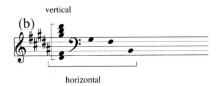

Example 9.6. Ravel, "Le Cygne," an overview

Example 9.6a shows that the deep-level structure consists of an auxiliary cadence beginning with a first-inversion tonic chord and reaching the root-position tonic only in the last measure.[16] The unusually high register at the beginning supports the fact that the root is not initially sounded in the bass. The opening sonority—the use of the high register coupled with the use of the third of the chord as the lowest note—gives rise to a central musico-dramatic duality for the song. As we shall see, register plays an important role in the song, and is directly related to Renard's text. In the poem the important juxtaposition of O_1 and O_2 also implies a juxtaposition of high and low; clouds in the sky (or their reflection on water) versus worms in the mud at the bottom of the pond. The former represents illusion, the latter reality. Similar use of registers is suggested in the music: the high register may be associated with illusion, the low with reality. (We will see, however, that Ravel's setting is subtler than this). Register is also related to issues of tonal stability, which in turn carry dramatic implications.

As example 9.8 indicates, measures 1–12 of the A^1 section articulate clear and stable vertical sonorities representing the tonal functions I^6, VI♯, V, and

Example 9.7. "Le Cygne," harmonic analysis of the beginning

I. Registrally the "bass" descends from $D\sharp_4$ to B_1, while the top voice gives up the high register. The descent is gradual; the bottom voice attains bass register in measure 5 while the top voice arrives at the lowest register only in measure 11. This registral descent leads to the song's first root-position tonic chord in measure 11. However, as the graph shows, at a deep level the low B does not displace the $D\sharp$ that opens the song. Despite the motion from $F\sharp$ as V to B as I, there is no clear cadential, closing gesture; therefore the root-position tonic does not sound like a strong goal of motion. Moreover, the brevity of the chord (only two measures compared to four measures of I^6 and three measures of $VI\sharp$ and V each) further weakens its structural primacy.

These musical events create subtle associations to the poem. The text set in measures 1–12 does not yet reveal the narrator's lament for the swan's futile attempts to reach the clouds—the narrator just states that the bird desires the clouds. Accordingly, measures 1–12 enact only the first part of the first state shown in figure 9.3 ($Sr \rightarrow O_1 \rightarrow R$) without yet including the second part ($S \cup O_1$). At the start of the poem O_1 in actuality represents illusion, reflected musically

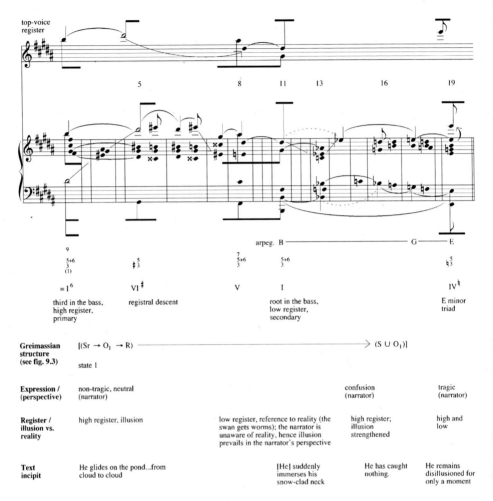

Example 9.8. "Le Cygne," mm. 1–19 (A[1] section), analytical sketch

by means of register and the use of an unstable form of the tonic. But the narrator and reader are not yet aware of the illusion; they think the swan truly fancies reflections of clouds. The musical structure conveys this precisely: measures 11–12 attain a root-position tonic and the low register that ultimately will displace the first inversion and high register opening the song. But the tonic at this point of the song is still subordinate to the opening chord. Thus the harmony of measures 11–12 represents a mere image of tonal stability, which will be achieved only at the end of the song, just as the gesture of the swan *as understood by the narrator* already looks ahead to the reality revealed at the poem's end.

At this point the poem starts to turn toward tragic. ("Then, just as a woman's arm emerges from a sleeve, he pulls it back. He has caught nothing. He looks: The startled clouds have disappeared.") The narrator's misinterpretation of the swan's gesture is reflected by the return to the high register of the opening in measures 13–15, while the disjunction of S and O_1 is suggested by the abandonment of the implied tonic. Moreover, the narrator imputes confusion to the bird: he thinks that the disruption of the clouds' reflection on the surface of the water surprises the swan. This confusion that the narrator assumes the bird is feeling finds its musical counterpart in the fragmentary musical gestures of measures 15–17. More broadly, the idea of confusion relates to the musical structure, in that measures 13–18 consist of passing events filling in the motion from the B major chord (m. 11) to E minor (m. 19). As in "Le paon," the details of structural function suggest at a deep level the relationship between Greimassian actants, illusion, and reality: here the tonic at measure 11, subordinate to the deep-middleground bass motion D♯–to–E, presents the illusion of structural depth, representing the narrator's perception of the swan immersing his "snow-clad neck" into the reflection of the cloud.

In the song's B section (19–25), the tragic tone now becomes explicit (ex. 9.9). The narrator tells us that the swan again prepares to reach the illusory cloud, set in the tragic E minor. Once more musical structure conveys the poem's undercurrents, as the E minor triad at the deep middleground represents a neighboring harmony that prolongs the opening referential sonority until its return at the beginning of the A^2 section (see ex. 9.6).

In example 9.9, the voice-leading reduction helps convey the highly ambiguous dramatic situation at this point of the poem. The figure of measure 19 is repeated in measure 22 a whole tone lower on a passing D minor triad, leading in measure 23 to a 9/7/5/3 sonority on G. The G chord creates a dual effect: on the one hand, at the middleground level it extends the E minor triad of measure 19; on the other hand, all of its pitches except the bass (B as well as D, F, and A♭ reinterpreted enharmonically) are related to the return of the referential sonority in measure 26, either as anticipations or as appoggiaturas (within a typically Ravelian octatonic context). Hence the dual function of the sonority of measures 23–25 represents an intermediate stage in the forming of the image: it looks backward to the E minor triad whose tragic expression marks the disappearance of the original images; and it looks ahead to the new image that is formed when the referential sonority returns, initiating the formal reprise.

Symbolically there is still more at stake in the bass motion of the B section. The emphatic arrival of G♮ at measure 23 represents the song's lowest note thus far, and it prolongs the E of measure 19. But thereafter, measures 25–26 abandon the bass register and abruptly break the continuation implied by the descending fifths motion (E–A–D–G, but not C). We have seen that high and low registers are clearly juxtaposed in the song, the former associated with the

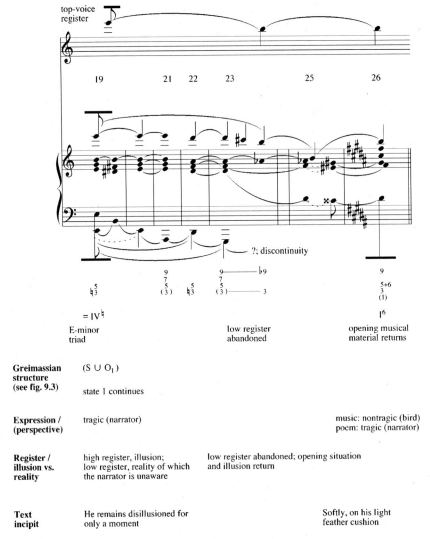

Example 9.9. "Le Cygne," mm. 19–26 (B section), analytical sketch

narrator's illusion and the latter with the swan and reality. In measures 19–23 both registers appear simultaneously, so the two perspectives are implied at once. That of the narrator is primary, however—neither the narrator nor the reader knows at this point that the swan has been successfully fishing worms. In sum, the low register is given up—the bass-note G of measure 23 disappears—when the music returns to the opening referential sonority. The time of reality has not yet arrived, and the high register of the narrator's illusion still prevails.

Example 9.10 details the dramatic transformation in the reprise from the narrator's perspective to that of the swan, and the corresponding process of musical closure. In Greimassian terms, at the outset of the reprise the original state 1 (Sr → O₁ → R) remains intact and indeed becomes intensified beginning in measure 29. Here the material derived from measures 5–10 is reharmonized over bass E♯ (♯IV) which initiates the predominant area. This passage further intensifies the tragic mode for the song ("He exhausts himself fishing for empty reflections, and perhaps he will die"). Here the music becomes slower and quieter, as if it were fading away like a dying swan. With the unfolding of E♯ to its upper third G♯ (m. 33), the state of tragic illusion reaches its apex ("[a victim to that illusion], before catching a single piece of cloud"); temporally the G♯ looks backward and relates to music already heard, just as the words of the narrator relate to his ongoing perspective of illusion. From measure 33 to 34, the transformation from B to B♯ and the resultant G♯ dominant ninth chord provide the first hint of a change of perspective.

With the bass motion from G♯ to G♮, everything changes: the harmony swings from sharp side to flat side (♯IV to V/♭II to ♭II); the lyrical texture shifts to comic, and tragic illusion gives way to comic reality. All this, together with the full cadence ♭II–V–I to the first true root-position tonic, unmistakably signals the revelation of the truth to the narrator ("But what am I talking about? Every time he dives, he burrows in the nourishing mud with his beak and comes back with a worm. He's fattening up like a goose"). Less obvious is the anticipation of the transformation in the preceding section. Recall that the bass line of the middle section established a strong sense of continuity via descending fifths motion before breaking off abruptly at G♮, thereby continuing the narrator's illusionary perspective. In the reprise, the reappearance of bass G♮ now has a proper continuation, leading to C♮, supporting the dominant of the Neapolitan and initiating the fifths progression to the end (V/♭II–♭II–V–I). In Greimassian terms, the initial state—the disjoining of swan and clouds under the illusion of the narrator—is preserved until measure 35. The conjoined state can occur only between the swan and worms, not between the swan and clouds. Hence the disjunction and discontinuity that characterize section B and the breaking off at G♮ become supplanted by the concluding continuation of the fifths progression that culminates in the reprise, in which the musical representations of the swan and worms are conjoined.

One final aspect of resolution concerns the symbolic aspect of register. After measure 33 the high register is given up (the upper staff of the piano part changes to bass clef from the middle of measure 33 to the end, and the bass of the cadential dominant of measure 38 is the song's lowest pitch). At the same time, the top voice drops into an inner voice (see the staff above the graph in example 9.10). Both registral shifts have musico-poetic significance. When the (high) clouds are described in the poem, the corresponding music has the structural top voice in the high three-line octave (see ex. 9.6). But when the

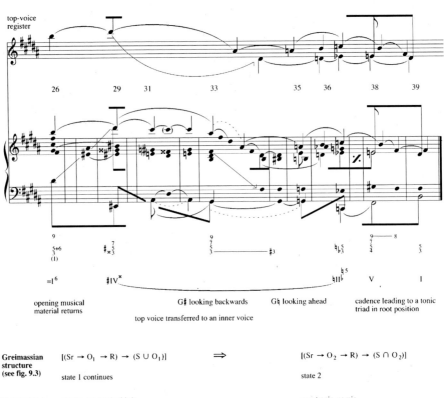

Example 9.10. "Le Cygne," mm. 26–39 (A² section), analytical sketch

worms (O_2) at the bottom of the pond are finally revealed as the reason for the the swan's dabbling, the structural top voice appears in the one-line octave and in an inner voice. At the song's end, the primary top voice appears below the highest notes—just as the worms are below the surface of the water.

Epilogue

Our investigation began by quoting Ravel's own comments concerning the composition of *Histoires naturelles*. He claimed that his intention was to not add anything to the poems, but merely to say in music what Renard says in words. Such a statement would appear to imply a literal imitative approach to the task of musical text-setting; but this would be at odds with his further comments on his attraction to the "profound, hidden poetry" of Renard's texts. Once profundity and hiding enter into the discussion, Ravel's claim to a "mere" transposition of poetry into musical terms becomes manifest as a self-conscious posture: his musical representations of illusion and reality reveal a sophisticated and complex understanding of the text that goes well beyond the literal.

In analyzing two representative songs from *Histoires naturelles,* I have applied concepts drawn from Greimas as a means of conceptualizing important oppositions within the respective texts. The Greimassian schema can be mapped onto a Schenkerian approach to musical structure: the oppositions and intersections of illusion and reality in the poems are interpreted structurally, through registral, scalar, and harmonic motion in the context of foreground and middleground voice leading within Ravel's expanded tonal practice. For the purposes of this chapter I have focused on the two songs that most strongly express the oppositions noted above. Further analysis along these lines could, for example, explore Ravel's musical means of realizing oppositions in other songs in the set. More generally, the methodology offered here provides a flexible analytical approach to the hidden poetry and deep structural connections inherent in Ravel's unique and masterful corpus of songs.

Notes

1. Quoted in Arbie Orenstein, ed., *A Ravel Reader: Correspondence, Articles, Interviews* (1990; repr., Mineola NY: Dover, 2003), 30–31.

2. Ibid., 36.

3. Since this chapter studies only two songs, I will not examine *Histoires naturelles* as a cycle or discuss its position in Ravel's output. Neither will I study musico-poetic aspects in his vocal music on a general level. For a thorough introduction to Ravel's vocal music, see Peter Kaminsky, "Vocal Music and the Lures of Exoticism and Irony" in *The Cambridge Companion to Ravel,* ed. Deborah Mawer (Cambridge: Cambridge University Press, 2000), 162–87.

4. This view on imitation draws on ideas by Roger Scruton, who makes a distinction between imitation and representation; see Roger Scruton, *The Aesthetics of Music* (Oxford: Oxford University Press, 1997), 118–39. Scruton examines instrumental music only, however, so the musico-poetic connections between musical gestures and the content of text are outside his theory.

5. Stephen Davies has discussed problems that arise if music is said to be expressive of "higher" emotions that require an object; see Davies, *Musical Meaning and Expression* (Ithaca: Cornell University Press, 1994), 201–40.

6. The most thorough—and in my view the most plausible—application of Schenkerian principles to posttonal repertory can be found in a series of three articles by Olli Väisälä, whose theoretical premises I follow in this chapter; see Olli Väisälä, "Concepts of Harmony and Prolongation in Schoenberg's Op. 19/2," *Music Theory Spectrum* 19, no.

2 (1999): 230–59; Väisälä, "Prolongation of Harmonies Related to the Harmonic Series in Early Post-TonalMusic," *Journal of Music Theory* 46, no. 2 (2002): 207–83; and Väisälä, "New Theories and Fantasies on the Music of Debussy: Post-Triadic Prolongation in *Ce qu'a vu le vent d'ouest* and Other Examples," in *Essays from the Third International Schenker Symposium*, ed. Allen Cadwallader (Hildesheim: Olms, 2006), 165–95. Väisälä considers the conditions for prolongation proposed by Joseph N. Straus ("The Problem of Prolongation in Post-Tonal Music," *Journal of Music Theory* 31, no. 1 [1987]: 1–22) but draws different conclusions. Whereas Straus argues that the conditions for prolongation cannot be fulfilled in posttonal, nontriadic repertory, Väisälä suggests that they can, under specific contextual conditions. Such specific contextual conditions can be found in the two Ravel songs.

7. The significance of extended tertian sonorities, occasionally with added pitches (specifically sixths), in Ravel's music has been frequently noted in the theoretical and analytical literature: to name but a few, see Eddy Kwong Mei Chong, *Extending Schenker's 'Neue musikalische Theorien und Phantasien': Towards a Schenkerian Model for the Analysis of Ravel's Music* (PhD diss., University of Rochester, 2002), 137–82; Roy Howat, "Ravel and the Piano," in Mawer, *The Cambridge Companion to Ravel*, 76; Philip Wade Russom, *A Theory of Pitch Organization for the Early Works of Maurice Ravel* (PhD diss., Yale University, 1985), 30–34 and 75–78; and Felix Salzer, *Structural Hearing: Tonal Coherence in Music.* (1952; repr. New York: Dover, 1962), 194.

8. I base this highly selective and simplified exposition of Greimas's theory on Algirdas Julien Greimas, *Structural Semantics: An Attempt at a Method*, trans. Daniele McDowell et al. (Lincoln: University of Nebraska Press 1983), 198–209; and Greimas, *On Meaning*, trans. Paul J. Perron and Frank H. Collins (Minneapolis: University of Minnesota Press, 1987), especially chapters 5, 6, and 7.

9. It is quite common that the same character (or actor, according to Greimassian terminology) functions both as the subject and as the receiver: see Greimas, *Structural Semantics*, 204.

10. Translation from Maurice Ravel, *Songs 1896–1914*, ed. Arbie Orenstein (Mineola NY: Dover, 1990), xxi.

11. In the opening and closing chords the seventh is implied rather than explicitly stated. In the opening sonority the implied seventh is E♮, in the closing sonority E♭. (The choice of the added note depends on the context: E♮ appears as a decorative element at the beginning, E♭ at the end.) In the large-scale bass arpeggiation the seventh, E♭, is clearly stated.

12. In example 9.2, which describes the musical structure from a modified Schenkerian perspective, I have interpreted the relationship between the chords of measures 9 and 13 as resulting, ultimately, from a 5–6 progression. The relationship between the two chords could be described in a more abstract manner, and without tonal implications, by applying neo-Riemannian transformational notions.

13. The change of the time signature from $\frac{4}{4}$ into $\frac{3}{4}$ creates an ironic effect: owing to the triple meter, the gait of the bird—an instance of gestural imitation—sounds somewhat limping.

14. Translation from Ravel, *Songs 1896–1914*, xxi.

15. This duality of function is clarified by a distinction, made by Joseph N. Straus, between two models of atonal voice leading: prolongational and associational; see Straus, "Voice Leading in Atonal Music," in *Music Theory in Concept and Practice*, ed. James M. Baker, David W. Beach, and Jonathan W. Bernard (Rochester, NY: University of Rochester Press, 1997), 237–42. The former refers to Schenkerian principles

of *Auskomponierung*. From this perspective the G♯ is a contrapuntal, decorative element. Since the stepwise G♯–F♯ bass motion suggests neighboring motion rather than arpeggiation, G♯ should not be taken as part of the prolonged harmony. The associational model, on the other hand, states that there are large-scale linear projections of harmonic units appearing as vertical sonorities on the musical surface. Thus there is no need to define the structural function of G♯ as either part of the prolonged harmony or as a contrapuntal element. For "Le cygne" this duality is part of the subtle effect of the music, which at the same time possesses a clear tonal framework and also steps outside of it.

16. The concept of "auxiliary cadence" refers to a harmonic progression that begins with a chord other than the root-position tonic and ends with a perfect cadence. Such a harmonic progression has a strongly goal-directed quality. For a thorough discussion on the auxiliary cadence, see L. Poundie Burstein, "Unraveling Schenker's Concept of the Auxiliary Cadence," *Music Theory Spectrum* 27, no. 2 (2005): 159–85.

Chapter Ten

Not Just a Pretty Surface

Ornament and Metric Complexity in Ravel's Piano Music

Gurminder K. Bhogal

By now it is a truism that Ravel's piano music is better known among performers than scholars. While pianists continue to astound audiences with their mastery of lightning-speed repeated notes in "Scarbo" or seamless double-third glissandi in "Alborada del Gracioso," the academic's aloof intellectual response mimics little more than a disinterested yawn. The same old conundrum that hindered a serious investigation of Liszt's piano works for several decades seems also to have haunted the critical reception of Ravel's piano compositions: how can a piece that is thoroughly obsessed with its surface communicate anything more meaningful than an attention-seeking display of human prowess? With the remarkable strides that have been made in the study of Liszt's pianistic achievements, the time seems right to reevaluate Ravel's role in defining a distinctly French school of virtuosity in the realms of performance and composition.

My choice of Liszt as an opening point of comparison might seem obvious, but it is also somewhat deliberate, given the aesthetic resemblances between the two composers. These overlaps are most compelling in Ravel's *Jeux d'eau* (1901), one of his first major works for piano, which emulates Liszt's "Les jeux d'eaux à la Villa d'Este" from the *Années de pèlerinage* (troisième année, 1877–82). Noticeable parallels are seen on the level of musical texture, since Ravel also chose to evoke the play of water through rapidly shifting motifs characterized by a varied configuration of short rhythmic values. However, what separates Ravel from Liszt—and what places him firmly within the early twentieth-century school of French piano music—is his tendency to focus on rhythmically intricate figuration *independently* of a melody and (decorative) accompaniment texture. Ravel's *Jeux d'eau*, in other words, reflects the cultural preoccupations of its milieu through a structural emphasis on ornament. In

Excerpts from Maurice Ravel's *Miroirs*, © 1995 by Hinrichsen Edition Ltd., and *Gaspard de la nuit*, © 1991 by Hinrichsen Edition Ltd., by permission of C. F. Peters Corporation.

this work, texture is achieved through rhythmic complexity, by which I refer to layers of motion that are faster (or more active) than those established as the norm within a given context. In a piece that uses predominantly quarter- and eighth-note values, for example, shorter values of sixteenths and thirty-seconds might be perceived as contributing complexity.

The opening measures of *Jeux d'eau* show how far Ravel has veered from his Lisztian correlate: melody—to the extent that we might consider the arpeggiated right hand motion as such—is now bound up with decorative figuration to the point of becoming inseparable from it. Further on in the piece, there are occasional lapses into a romantic "melody and intricate accompaniment texture," where submerged figuration provides support for a structurally superior event, such as the arrival of significant melodic material. These moments call attention to the fact that Ravel was working with two styles of ornament at this time: one that assumes a distinctly French avant-garde identity in its appearance as unbounded, surface-consuming figuration and another that takes a more traditional marginal role as accompaniment or transitional material. The former is often rhythmically irregular and metrically dissonant; its textural prominence also has (destabilizing) repercussions on aspects of form, texture, and musical continuity. The latter is more contained, in that it is texturally and formally under some sort of structural "control," even though the figuration itself might be rhythmically irregular and metrically unstable.

Jeux d'eau is a useful point of departure because it shows how Ravel was beginning to privilege one style of ornament over the other by the turn of the century. It also suggests how Ravel's pursuit of a modern, French vision of pianistic virtuosity necessitated a move away from Lisztian extensions of stylized ornament toward an expressive intensity marked by unlimited and virtually unregulated ornamental richness. I will examine Ravel's stylistic development in two compositions: "Noctuelles" (*Miroirs,* 1905) and "Ondine"(*Gaspard de la nuit,* 1908). My decision to use these pieces as case studies is motivated by several notable commonalities and differences between them that reveal Ravel's nuanced approach to creating luxurious surfaces.

Beginning with commonalities, it is worth noting that both "Noctuelles"and "Ondine" open multimovement works. And both are written in sonata form, although this might not be immediately apparent, because formal junctures are often obscured by highly elaborate surfaces. These pieces were composed just a few years apart, yet it is significant that "Noctuelles" is distinctly more avant-garde in spirit. This is reflected in its close alignment with techniques that define the contemporaneous visual arts movement, art nouveau, especially its use of *trompe l'oeil* as characterized by an ambiguous intertwining of figure and ground. Drawing on an analogous process of disorientation in "Noctuelles," Ravel deflects the listener's attention away from anticipated structural events by suddenly saturating the surface with ornament; the abrupt influx of intricate rhythmic patterns at formal junctures evokes fluid textural boundaries that create the effect of *trompe l'oreille*. In keeping with art nouveau's treatment of ornament, this technique is not without representational significance; in "Noctuelles," metrically irregular ornamental outbursts depict the whimsical flight of nocturnal moths.

Art nouveau's depiction of bejeweled *femmes fatales* seems to have influenced the structure and ornamentation of "Ondine," which uses an irregular thirty-second-note motif to portray the eponymous water nymph. Ravel's initial presentation of this motif as accompaniment reverts to a Lisztian ornament/structure opposition that complements his attempt to re-create the nineteenth-century aura of the poem on which this piece is based. However, his manipulation of this motif is hardly as innocuous as promised; while we are duped into hearing it as evocative, background filler at the opening, we soon become aware of its increasing structural and expressive significance as the setting moves to the heart of the narrative: Ondine's proposal of marriage and her subsequent rejection and subordination by the narrator. Whereas in "Noctuelles," a varied and changing configuration of short values was used to depict erratic moths, here the gradual transformation of a single motif from a state of metrical dissonance to consonance narrates Ondine's tragedy.

Inspired by the different manifestations of ornament, my methodology draws on current resources in metric theory to show how Ravel uses specific rhythmic and metric techniques to enact poetic narratives. Ravel's affinity for contrapuntal complexity accommodates an analytical methodology devised by Harald Krebs that focuses on the perception and schematization of metrical dissonance, mainly in the Austro-German repertoire.[1] Given the dearth of critical reflection on meter in *début-de-siècle* French music, my analyses will adapt the work of Krebs to a French context, and combine his influential ideas with recent insights offered by Richard Cohn, Justin London, Jonathan Kramer, and William Rothstein. This eclectic combination of theories and methodologies seeks to illuminate idiosyncratic features of Ravel's metric style, while demonstrating he powerful role that ornament assumes as a structural and expressive component of his repertoire.

Trompe l'oreille in "Noctuelles"

"Noctuelles" was the rebellious retort of a young Ravel to conservative, admonishing academics who did not understand his work. Five failed attempts to win the *Prix de Rome* followed by the scandalous "affaire Ravel" left him feeling determined to develop his compositional voice.[2] The result of this resolve was a period of intense creativity during which Ravel wrote *Miroirs*, a collection of pieces that he knew was different from anything he had written before. In his Autobiographical Sketch Ravel confessed, "the *Miroirs* form a collection of piano pieces which mark a rather considerable change in my harmonic evolution; this disconcerted musicians who until then had been thoroughly accustomed to my style."[3] While his harmonic writing certainly puzzled his contemporaries, Ravel's comments glide over what is surely one of the most striking stylistic aspects of *Miroirs:* his cultivation of metric complexity through profuse ornament. The dizzying, decorative flourishes that saturate the surface of "Noctuelles" correspond to the image in a prose poem by the dedicatee, Léon Paul Fargue: "The nocturnal moths in their barns launch themselves clumsily into the air, going from one perch to another."[4] In this piece, Ravel explores the Symbolist tones of Fargue's nocturnal fantasy through an aesthetically appropriate attention to objectified ornament.

A recent article by Volker Helbing hints at Ravel's preoccupation with the decorative in "Noctuelles."[5] His study of structural levels yields an unusual relationship between surface levels—with which we typically associate ornament—and middle-ground levels—from which we typically disassociate ornament. Helbing's extensive harmonic analysis serves to demonstrate how "the surface not only tends to veil, but also to change and partly to disintegrate the middleground."[6] His major observations indicate a central tension in Ravel's conceptualization of ornament and structure in "Noctuelles." First, Helbing's emphasis on the type of interaction between surface and middle-ground levels suggests a blurring, rather than a clear separation, of structural levels that is initiated by the (least-empowered) surface. Related to this is his attention to harmonic ambiguity between "ornamental" (surface) and "structural" (middle-ground) progressions, which indicates a lack of clear differentiation between the opposing states. We might characterize this state of confusion using visual metaphors of figure and ground, also implied by Helbing in his explanation of harmonic ambiguity: "There are no clues by which one could decide which frame of reference is the primary one, and which is secondary."[7]

Helbing's conclusions allude to the technique of *trompe l'oeil* and its "deception of the eye" through a manipulation of the viewer's perception of dimension. In the visual arts, *trompe l'oeil* takes advantage of a viewer's ambiguous perception of an object to blur the line between real life and still life. The term is also applied to contexts where the viewer is confronted by unstable relationships between opposing states of figure and ground, which lead to a similar state of uncertainty. A well-known example is Giuseppe Arcimboldo's *Four Seasons* (1563), which can be perceived both as the grotesque head of a man and as a pile of seasonal vegetables. Which is primary here, the profile of the man, or the constituent vegetables? *Trompe l'oeil* depends upon our hesitation to locate the primary frame of reference. Helbing's similar indecision in response to "Noctuelles" suggests an analogous process at work that I shall call *trompe l'oreille*, a "deception of the ear."

The following scenario enacts Ravel's evocation of *trompe l'oreille*. Through a series of conventional gestures, he leads the listener to establish expectations of melodic completion, tonal stability, and metric continuity at the anticipated moment of a cadence. Just when our expectations are about to be fulfilled, Ravel deceives us by suddenly saturating the texture with decorative flourishes, which thwart our anticipation of a structural event. Ravel's switch from a middleground or deep-level event (such as a cadence) to a surface-level event (such as fleeting decoration) shifts our attention too abruptly, even though we are conditioned to expect the peripheral participation of ornament in the guise of melodic embellishment and its constituent tonal dissonance at a cadence. Interruption by abundant ornament suggests a release from its restriction to the periphery; now, textural empowerment, coupled with Ravel's formation of fluid structural boundaries, facilitates the blurring of deep-level phenomena with surface-level ones.

As we continue to listen, we begin to realize that this strategy carries great expressive significance for Ravel, especially given his programmatic impulse. At the same time, we become aware of a more versatile mode of listening as we actively adjust between interpreting repeated incidences of ornamental influx as a disruption to an ongoing process and as a competing frame of reference. We experience two modes of listening: one that is guided by a continuously interrupted experience of musical continuity (thereby privileging figure); and another that takes sweeping flourishes as its primary point of orientation (thereby privileging ground).

There are several moments of blurring between figure and ground in "Noctuelles." At each instance, rhythmic values suddenly become shorter and irregularly grouped so that they no longer delineate a specific meter. The powerful destabilizing effect of these gestures is also intensified by their *accelerandi* toward (denied) cadences.[8] Since this is usually accompanied by a rapid descent or ascent in register, the meter appears to fragment under the dissipation of rhythmic energy notated in the form of short values. The volatility of these events stimulates comparison with processes of rapid vaporization, as noted by Helbing, who claims that "the piano texture evaporates."[9] Ravel's own term, "evanescence," captures the fleeting sensation of such passages.[10] In now undertaking a more focused analysis, I propose an alternative characterization of ornamental prominence as evoking metrically unmeasured units of (musical) time. I will use this slightly cumbersome label to consider how each unit intrudes to suspend the basic pulse, which in turn delays the establishment of a defined meter until a significant formal juncture. My study of metrically unmeasured units against a sonata-form framework will show how cadential denial upsets formal articulation and hypermetric regularity by permitting ornament to veil formal strategies through techniques of disorientation.

Let us begin by examining the first moment of cadential completion (see ex. 10.1). In measure 3, several factors suggest cadential rhetoric. First, measure 3 presents a point of tonal stability, since this is where the tonic, D♭ major, is first attained. Second, measure 3 resolves a grouping dissonance presented in measures 1–2; a G3/2 between quarter and dotted-quarter pulses resolves

G3/2 between quarter and dotted-quarter pulses

Example 10.1. Ravel, "Noctuelles," cadential completion, mm. 1–3

into a rhythmic grouping that articulates a dotted-quarter pulse by density accents on tonic and dominant pitches in the left hand. Third, the repetition of measure 1 in measure 2 suggests a bar form construction, which anticipates change in measure 3. This expectation is fulfilled in the emergence of a new melodic triplet figure, which migrates from the left hand (mm. 1–2) to the right hand in shorter rhythmic values (m. 3). Metric, rhythmic, melodic, and tonal tension of measures 1–2 thus dissipates through the metric and tonal stability of the tumbling triplet figuration at measure 3.

The completion of measures 1–2 by a stable consequent brings melodic, metric, and tonal stability to an antecedent-heavy, metrically and tonally dissonant unit. Still, two factors destabilize the cadential force of measure 3. First, the consequent is only one as opposed to two measures long. While this contraction means that the thematic lopsidedness of the opening repetition is not fully stabilized, it also suggests that a bar-form grouping has usurped the place of an anticipated sentence form. Second, the grouping dissonance of measures 1–2 is only partially resolved, since the G3/2 between triplet-eighth and eighth pulses continues through measure 3.[11] These measures encapsulate an integral feature of Ravel's metric style that is responsible for his creation of metric instability: the establishment of metric structures that are consonant on some levels and dissonant on others.[12]

As a point of comparison, let us now turn to the first moment of ornamental disruption at measures 6–9 (ex. 10.2). Since measures 4–5 parallel measures 1–2, we expect to hear a cadence in measure 6 to parallel that of measure 3. Instead of a cadence, however, we hear the intrusion of a metrically unmeasured unit conveyed by wisps of ascending scales that embody short values. The disruptive impact of this flourish is felt on two metric levels. First, periodicity on the level of the pulse is suddenly suspended. Second, discontinuity is experienced on hypermetric levels since the three-measure hypermeter established in measures 1–3 and begun in measures 4–5 does not reach its projected completion at measure 6. By fracturing metric stability on the highest and lowest levels, ornament destabilizes the entire metric hierarchy at a moment where we expect the highest degree of metric consonance: hypermetric and cadential completion.

Hypermetric upheaval caused by this metrically unmeasured unit may also be explored through the pervasive grouping dissonance, G3/2. Since measures 1–3 suggest a three-measure hypermeter and measures 4–5 project the same pattern of continuation, then it is possible to hear metrical conflict against this three-measure hypermetric pattern. Conflict emerges when the right hand projects a pulse that is equivalent to a notated half measure. This dotted-quarter pulse suggests a grouping in $\frac{9}{8}$ that conflicts against the notated $\frac{3}{4}$ meter projected by the left hand. A $\frac{9}{8}$ grouping in the right hand may also go against our tendency to privilege melodic parallelism between measures 1–2. Instead, this grouping allows us to hear (in conjunction with the density marking of a crescendo) the G_5 at the first beat of the second $\frac{9}{8}$ measure as initiating a "drive to the cadence."[13] In the parallel instance (mm. 4–6), this metric reinterpretation reveals that the metrically unmeasured unit occurs *exactly* where the second and third beats of the second $\frac{9}{8}$ pattern are to achieve completion. The "drive to the cadence" implicit in the first $\frac{9}{8}$ grouping is thus yearned for on a deeper level where the absence of hypermetric completion affects the continuation of G3/2 and renders the metric background unstable.[14] This process of deep-level destabilization exacerbates the effect of surface-level rupture (and vice versa).

We have seen how the first metrically unmeasured unit articulates high and low-level instability by saturating the surface, suspending the pulse level, preventing cadential closure, and disrupting hypermetric continuity. Ravel disorients his listener by investing flourishes of the metrically unmeasured unit with the capacity to actively (re)organize events typically understood as deep-level processes. The swift change in our attention from deep-level processes to surface-level gestures in measures 6–9 reflects ornament's ability to mediate between surface and deep levels, and subsequently weakens the conceptual boundary that separates ground from figure. In so doing, it disorients our notion of structure and ornament to such an extent that we begin to wonder whether ornament comes to *replace* rather than *delay* anticipated structural

G3/2 between quarter and dotted-quarter pulses

Example 10.2. Ornamental disruption and G3/2, mm. 1–9

events altogether. The disorienting effect associated with *trompe l'oreille* urges Ravel's listener to consider whether the metrically unmeasured unit functions as structure or embellishment. The fact that we ask this question implies that the swirling figurations of "Noctuelles" extend an influence far beyond their traditional restriction to the surface.

Other Instances of *Trompe l'oreille*

The intensity of blurring between figure and ground that we experience at measure 6 defines a singular moment. Subsequent metrically unmeasured units create an intense experience of *trompe l'oreille*, as we will now study. Although short values continue to saturate the surface to prevent metric continuity and cadential completion, their interaction with hypermetric levels does not project the same degree of deep-level rupture. Nonetheless, the fact that ornament subsumes the surface, and in so doing, replaces other musical processes to become the sole object of our aural experience means that we are still dealing with figure/ground blurring, albeit one of an altered potency. As in the opening, a sustained emphasis on metric dissonance precedes metrically unmeasured units in the remainder of this piece. We will see how these units continue to work in conjunction with a variety of grouping and displacement dissonances to characterize "Noctuelles" as a work of considerable conflict and instability.

Our focus in this section will be oriented around how metric procedures identified in the first nine measures obscure points of formal articulation at structural levels of sonata-form design. Figure 10.1 outlines formal junctures and metrically unmeasured units in "Noctuelles"; the thickness of the shaded bars indicates the relative duration of the units. This figure suggests that idiosyncratically weak, nonmetric ornaments occur at significant formal points; their appearance blurs the formal boundaries that indicate the end of a section or subsection. Just as a sudden ornamental flourish at measures 6–9 closes the presentation of the first theme, so also an ascending arpeggio-like figuration at measures 19–20 signals the end of the bridge, and a descending arpeggio-like pattern at measure 36 indicates the end of the exposition.

The duration and degree of disruption varies from unit to unit, depending on the intensity of figure/ground play created by the influx of ornament in relation to the surrounding metric and formal environment. In measures 19–20, for example, the abrupt dissipation of short values also undermines our perception of a cadence—this time, one that marks the closing of the bridge theme. While this metrically unmeasured unit creates instability by suspending the pulse, Ravel draws on several metric techniques to heighten the effect of this interruption. First, we hear metric irregularity through the addition of a 3/8 measure at measure 13. Second, the sudden diminution of triplet sixteenths into quintuplet thirty-seconds at the ends of measure 14 and measure 15 creates unstable *accelerandi* surges that drive toward the upcoming flourish. Third, a G3/2 between quarter and dotted-quarter pulses suggests metric fluctuation from $\frac{6}{8}$ to $\frac{3}{4}$ (mm. 14–18). The destabilizing effect of these dissonances is intensified rather than resolved by the nonmetric flourish of measures 19–20. Although ornament does not participate in deep-level hypermetric processes here, it still performs an element of figure/ground blurring by forcing

	Subsections	Metrically unmeasured units
Exposition	First theme: mm. 1-13	mm. 6-9
	Bridge: mm. 14-20	mm. 19-20
	Second theme: mm. 21-36	m. 31 m. 36
Development	mm. 37-62	m. 52 m. 54
	mm. 63-84	
Recapitulation	First theme mm. 84-97	mm. 90-93
	Bridge mm. 98-104	mm. 103-104
	Second theme: mm. 105-120	m. 115 m. 120
Coda	mm. 121-131	

Figure 10.1. Sonata form in "Noctuelles"

us to change our expectation from melodic closure in a tonally stable cadence to the perception of irregular decoration.

Metric instability also prepares the ornamental outburst of measure 36. From measure 21, the notated meter fluctuations between $\frac{2}{4}$ and $\frac{3}{8}$, and the abrupt appearance of thirty-seconds in conjunction with a rapid crescendo in 3/8 measures create the effect of *accelerandi*. The energetic impulse of these *accelerandi* is met not by (anticipated) cadential resolution, but by a sudden switch to 5/8 meter (m. 27). Despite the metric change to $\frac{2}{4}$ at measure 30 and the following ornamental gesture on the downbeat of measure 31, we still perceive five eighth-note pulses that prepare a notational return to $\frac{5}{8}$. However, the following metric shift to 6/8 is highly destabilizing (ex. 10.3): we hear G3/2 between quarter and dotted-quarter pulses in measure 33 and D4–2 (where 1=sixteenth) in measure 34, which also creates G3/2 between quarter and dotted-quarter pulses (mm. 34–35). As in measure 6 and measure 19, short values at measure 36 replace emphatic, boundary-affirming cadential rhetoric. Ornamental profusion deteriorates formal boundaries and prevents continuity to open up additional temporal space for the listener to enjoy the rippling sensation of a descending flourish.

Decorative gestures reflect Ravel's concern to soften formal divisions so that the piece evolves as a continuous whole with the improvisatory character created by unmeasured units. His unique articulation of sonata form is seen in the way that irregular interspersions create metric instability at formal junctures that also become destabilized as a result of this metric condition. In keeping with our experience of *trompe l'oreille*, it is of course possible that we might perceive metric disintegration at formal boundaries as *highlighting* the transition into a new section rather than veiling it; while we experience discontinuity on a metric level, these disruptions might serve as points of orientation on a formal level. Either way, it is clear that Ravel's manipulation of our expectations concerning meter and form pursues an ambiguous musical experience that plays on our disorientation as created by abundant ornament.

From Formal Ambiguity to Formal Affirmation

Even though metrically unmeasured units play a crucial role in both obscuring and highlighting formal boundaries, their changing appearance in the development section alters our understanding of these units' relationship to the formal framework. Through a subtle process of rhythmic and metric transformation, the *unmeasured* unit is now transformed into a *measured* unit in anticipation of metric consonance at the recapitulation. In contrast to their previous behavior, we will see how metrically measured units come to facilitate formal affirmation and tonal stability.

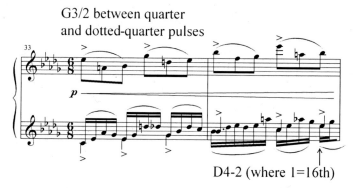

Example 10.3. Grouping and displacement dissonance at mm. 33–34

Turning now to the development section (mm. 37–84/1), let us consider the first half (until m. 62). Here, another change of meter to $\frac{5}{4}$ introduces a displaced bass ostinato on F (D2 + 1 where 1=eighth) that underlies a number of shifting rhythmic groupings. Although briefly suspended by unmeasured units at measure 52 and measure 54, this syncopation subsequently emerges on the pitch B♭ at measure 55, and is aligned with metric downbeats so that it articulates a regular quarter pulse by measure 61. This metric resolution facilitates the transformation of unmeasured units into measured units as we draw nearer to the most consonant moment of "Noctuelles," the recapitulation. We will first examine Ravel's approach to the recapitulation where metric instability is heightened, and then focus on the discharge of accumulating dissonance into the opening of the recapitulation.

In the second part of the development section (mm. 63–84/1), Ravel places a metrically measured version of units above the regular quarter pulse of a B♭ pedal. In this way, he displaces the entire section forward by a quarter (D3 + 1, where 1=quarter). These insertions can be seen at measure 64/1 and measure 68/1 where they destabilize the regular quarter pulse of the left hand (ex. 10.4). At these points, their function to prevent the emergence of $\frac{3}{4}$ meter is clear from the otherwise conjunct, metrically consonant juxtaposition of melodic ideas heard in their absence.

The return of the first theme above a regular pulse (m. 63) and the measured appearance of decorative units embody two metric transformations that hint at a moment of future metric alignment. To heighten our expectations of impending metric consonance, Ravel gradually increases metric instability during this passage (ex. 10.5). This process is initiated in measure 73 by a displacement of the right hand (D2 + 1 where 1=eighth), which threatens the regular quarter pulse established by the B♭ pedal at measure 61. This displacement dissonance is mitigated at measure 75 where $\frac{3}{4}$ meter is reinforced by the left hand grouping. Stability is short lived, however, since a

Example 10.4. Metrically measured units prevent consonant articulation of $\frac{3}{4}$, mm. 63–68

quarter pulse displacement is introduced in the right hand at measure 76/3 (D3–1 where 1=quarter) and remains until measure 79/2. Furthermore, an extra quarter pulse at the end of measure 79 leads into a section where the conflict between $\frac{6}{8}$ and $\frac{3}{4}$ is played out to create G3/2 between quarter and dotted-quarter pulses. Within this texture, chromatic motion of the inner right hand voice articulates a clear dotted-quarter pulse to reinforce $\frac{6}{8}$ meter. It is only at measure 84/2–3 that conflict between the two meters comes to a head as the accent on the last quarter pulse of the left hand impels the meter toward a resolution in $\frac{3}{4}$ at measure 85.

The victory of $\frac{3}{4}$ is suggested primarily by the emergence of a melody that defines $\frac{3}{4}$ meter at a crucial moment of formal articulation, the recapitulation. This moment is marked as both tonally and metrically strong by a V–I cadence (mm. 84–85), and the presentation of melodic material in a clear $\frac{3}{4}$ meter. In order to accentuate the consonance of this moment, Ravel does not bring back the opening melodic material in its initial form, which, as we remember, enacted a resolution to a dotted-quarter pulse in measure 3. Instead, he provides an ostinato-like repetition of the second half of measure 1–2 (right hand, beginning m. 80). Upon the ninth and tenth iteration of this gesture, the bass finally enters with V–I on the downbeat of measure 85, supporting the original thematic segment from measure 3. At the same time, the double stem on D$\flat_5$ in measure 85 and the complex slurring show a thematic combination of this part of Theme 1 and the transposition of the development theme whose impetus is measures 38–39, but which is more directly a transposition of measures

50–51. In conjunction with the contrapuntal synthesis, the melody at the recapitulation projects a stable $\frac{3}{4}$ meter for the longest duration thus far. A return
of the opening tonality without a clear statement of the first theme suggests an
unconventional treatment of sonata form that favors indistinct formal seams
and their projection of a continuously evolving form, a characteristic that was
also evident in Ravel's treatment of metrically unmeasured units at the end of
the first subject and exposition.

Nonetheless, an underlying element of tension is implied in the conflict
between quarter and dotted-quarter pulses in measures 85–86. Whereas this
G3/2 was associated with a new melodic surface in measure 3, it is here relegated to an accompanimental role and thus subsumed by the clear quarter
pulses of the $\frac{3}{4}$ melody. Since triplet sixteenths are no longer prominent in
articulating a dotted-quarter pulse, their chief defining dissonance also loses
its identity because it is submerged beneath the $\frac{3}{4}$ melody and is discontinuous
(it is absent in m. 87 and m. 89). A temporary, latent G3/2 allows the $\frac{3}{4}$ melody
to be privileged as directing the momentum of this passage. We consequently
perceive accumulated metric dissonance as discharging into a relatively stable
resolution at this point.

The resolution of large-scale conflict between a dotted-quarter and quarter pulse creates a structural downbeat at the moment of tonal and metric
resolution (m. 85).[15] The impact of this downbeat is most apparent on subsequent metrically unmeasured units, which seem to lose their ability to disorient and fragment. Consequently, when the unit heard initially in measure
36 is extended to form a minicadenza in measure 120, it appears to lead away
from the structural downbeat into the coda of the *Presque lent* (mm. 121–25).
The emergence of an unmetered sixteenth pulse from the G3/2 between triplet and duple thirty-second pulses (m. 120) also characterizes the cadenza as
stable in comparison to earlier, irregular flourishes. Moreover, even though
the dazzling final measures fail to articulate $\frac{3}{4}$, a repetitive chromatic motion in
the inner voice (G–Ab–A–Bb, mm. 128–30) articulates a regular quarter pulse
before the final fleeting gesture. Closing gestures of the cadenza and coda suggest a close relationship to metrically unmeasured units in their tendency to
dissipate. Unlike the opening however, these ornamental flourishes are somewhat tamed by the regularizing reverberation of the structural downbeat at
measure 85.

Despite the gradual and subtle transformation of unmeasured units into
measured units, ornament still creates a general effect of disorientation
throughout the piece. This is especially so given Ravel's use of ornament first
to subvert conventional oppositions between structural and decorative gestures; only later does he weaken its tendency to unsettle metrical and formal
structures. The opportunity for musical expression as afforded by a fluctuating
musical progression is clear: constant shifts from states of metric dissonance
to consonance, and vice versa, create a fluid context that enhances Ravel's

preference for bravura figuration. Together, metric instability and ornament work in parallel to evoke the disoriented movement of the fluttering moths.

The avant-garde nature of Ravel's metric techniques is evident in a contemporaneous concert review by Edouard Schneider, who criticized the piece's incoherence and exclusion of all musicality.[16] Ornament emerges as the victim in his criticism of "Noctuelles": "It is always the same and unintelligible babble of notes, the same stuttering without end, which becomes exasperating in the long run."[17] On the other hand, M. D. Calvocoressi embraced Ravel's rhythmically rich, ornamental conception: "The rhythms [are] so diverse, so supple which . . . 'celebrate their orgy' above all in Noctuelles."[18] A critic writing for *Le Monde Musical* also enjoyed Ravel's decorative approach to composition. "A. M." wrote:

> [Ravel] never wants to evoke a sentiment that penetrates the depth of a thing or being. In taking the fragile, delicate, light, diaphanous envelope he prefers to decorate it with the thousand tones of his palette. He totally abandons the *architecture* for the benefit of the *exterior covering*, without seeking to draw lines in forming an edifice, which has a base, a centre, a summit. One could, without inconvenience, perform these pieces beginning at any place and stopping where one wanted.[19]

He goes on to claim that "the pieces produced the effect of spiritual intoxication on the audience and gave them [the audience] the elation that one experiences when smoking opium or hashish."[20]

In subtle ways, Ravel's critics seem to support our observation of *trompe l'oreille;* like us, they noticed how Ravel's dissolution of formal boundaries disguised the normative strategies of sonata form to suggest formlessness. They also perceived how ornamental surplus at crucial moments of formal articulation served to conceal the "architecture" through emphasis on the decorative surface (the "exterior covering"). Critics such as A. M. embraced the improvisatory quality of the musical form, which is also a consequence of evaded cadences and fluid formal boundaries. Most of all, the analogy with drug-induced states comes closest to approximating our feeling of disorientation. The rhythmic, metric, and formal innovation, and flamboyant figurations of "Noctuelles" reflect the Symbolist penchant for sensation and ambiguity over reason and order.

Ornament, Tragedy, and the *Femme fatale* in "Ondine"

A return to Symbolist ideals at the close of our analysis serves as a fitting transition to a discussion of "Ondine." By the *fin-de-siècle,* the water nymph of Baron Friedrich de la Motte Fouqué's novella had evolved into a Symbolist *femme fatale.*[21] This figure was especially well known in her guise as Salomé, as Gustave Moreau's oil painting *Salomé tatouée* (1876), attests. Here, the seductress drips with ornament from head to toe; her prominent display of finery appears at first glance to reflect self-empowerment. Like most turn-of-the-century depictions of Salomé, however, Moreau's portrayal hardly affirms gender equality. He exposes Salomé's aspiration toward masculinity and power as nothing but an illusion; her jewels do not bolster her bodily outlines; instead, transparent layers of tattooed ornament obscure Salomé's naked body to give her a ghostly appearance.

Ravel's "Ondine" is based on a prose poem by Aloysius Bertrand from his collection *Gaspard de la nuit* (1838). Several aspects of Ondine's fate may be aligned with that of Salomé; both women express desire and a sense of empowerment through ornament, and both are admonished for their transgressions. Ravel portrays Ondine's hypnotic allure through a prevalent thirty-second neighbor-note motif, whose short values suggest ornament. This profusion of ornament both obliterates and gives shape to her musical representation, as her veils both reveal and conceal her body in Moreau's painting. In the prose poem on which the music is based, the narrator imagines a disembodied voice adorned by the intricate movement of water, a Freudian symbol of sexual desire. Other similarities between these *femmes fatales* are seen in their association with death (Salomé, through her demands; Ondine, through her fatal kiss), and in the punishments meted out to them for their boldness; the narrator's rejection of Ondine's marriage proposal tames her *irregular* thirty-second-note motif—symbolic of her desire and material being—into a *regular* motif. Analogous to the subordination of Salomé to Herod's realm of repression and cruelty is the subordination of Ondine to the narrator's realm of order and stability.

By endowing the thirty-second-note motif with structural and expressive value, Ravel participated in a widespread cultural movement that privileged detail and its allusions to feminine sexuality. Ornament's emerging status unsettled long-held aesthetic beliefs and allowed artists to confront Western philosophy's previous warnings against the feminine lure of reckless embellishment. Like their predecessors, French artists perceived destabilized boundaries between structure and ornament as perverse. But rather than condemn this imbalance, they exploited its inversions and ambiguities to expose marginalized associations that became synonymous with conceptions of female hysteria in the contemporaneous *psychologie nouvelle*. At this historical moment, artists expressed their simultaneous arousal and repulsion by unrestrained ornament through depictions of bejeweled women as physically and morally degenerate, yet dangerously alluring—a pungent cocktail that culminated in the enduring figure of the extravagant temptress.

It is against this cultural backdrop that we will examine how Ravel reconceives Bertrand's poem through a subtle metric and rhythmic development of the thirty-second-note motif. In an attempt to understand integral aspects of Ravel's metric style, we will see how the motif's metric transformation from a state of instability to stability traces a similar progression of metrically unmeasured units in "Noctuelles"; this recurring process reveals Ravel's underlying interest in exploring metric evolution between opposed metric states. Significantly, this transformation is paralleled by another musical process that emphasizes ornament in "Ondine": while this motif re-creates a Lisztian background accompaniment for much of the opening, its gradually increasing textural prominence reflects the narrator's rising uneasiness. Eventually, the motif's deliberate emergence at an important formal juncture breaks the textural frame to which it had been relegated as accompaniment.[22] This powerful textural schism ties ornament's struggle for audibility in the piece with Ondine's struggle for visibility in the mind of the narrator.

*   *   *

Each piece from Ravel's *Gaspard de la nuit* is prefaced with the corresponding poem from Bertrand's collection. I have reproduced below Roger Nichols's translation of Bertrand's "Ondine."[23] Three narrative voices claim our attention here: that of Bertrand's narrator; that of Ondine (set off by double quotation marks); and that of the narrator of Brugnot's epigraph. Even though Ondine's song seems to be structured as a ternary form (ABA), her narration thwarts this possibility because of an unpredictable development of ideas. For instance, the arresting effect of Ondine's opening cry, "Écoute!–Écoute!" gains our attention and leads us to believe that she is about to embark on a mysterious tale. While her song is indeed captivating, we receive "irrelevant" snippets of information about her home and domestic life that eventually lead to a comical description of her sisters and their mocking behavior toward the "bearded willow." Instead of leading us directly toward the central goal of her narrative—her marriage proposal—she subtly skirts this issue to create a series of loosely connected impressions.

Ondine

    I thought I heard
a vague harmony casting a spell over my slumber, and
near me a murmuring break out like the interrupted song
of a sad and tender voice.
                Charles Brugnot—*Les deux Génies*

"Listen!–Listen!–It is I, it is Ondine who brushes with these
crops of water the vibrant panes of your window, lit by the
melancholy rays of the moon; and here, in a robe of watered
silk, is the lady of the castle who, from her balcony, gazes at
the beautiful, starry night and the beautiful sleeping lake.

Each wave is a water-sprite swimming in the current, each
current is a path that winds towards my palace, and my palace
is built of water, in the depths of the like, in the triangle of
fire, earth and air.

Listen!–Listen!–My father beats the croaking water with a
green alder branch, and my sisters caress with their arms of
spray the cool islands of grass, of water-lilies and gladioli, or
mock the weeping willow as he dips his fishing-line in the lake."

She finished her murmured song and begged me to put her
ring on my finger, to be the husband of a water-nymph, and
to come down with her to the palace as king of the lakes.

And when I told her that I was in love with a mortal woman,
she began to sulk in annoyance, shed a few tears, gave a
burst of laughter, and vanished in a shower of spray which ran
in pale drops down my blue window-panes.

On one level, Ravel's treatment of the thirty-second-note motif suggests a
tentative formal correspondence to Bertrand's poem as outlined in figure 10.2.
At the same time, however, tension gradually mounts as the music moves away
from the tonic at measure 42 into the climax, resolution, and returns toward
the tonic at measure 66. This scheme reflects a large-scale sense of struggle
that is reminiscent of a sonata form development section; the formal schema
becomes particularly charged because of the modifications that Ravel makes
in response to Bertrand (see fig. 10.3). Of course, Ravel's "deformations"—
including a reversed subdominant recapitulation and delayed tonic return—
have historical precedence. But their expressive effect is unique in "Ondine"
because of the way that he integrates the narrative capability of the thirty-second-note motif into a sonata-form template.

Just as Brugnot's epigraph and Bertrand's narrator suggest a narrative frame for
Ondine's directionless song, her thirty-second-note motif similarly forms a frame:
it is conspicuous at the opening and closing of the piece, and recedes into the
background once Ondine begins to sing (as evoked by the opening left-hand melody). Although the thirty-second-note motif is prominent in articulating irregular groupings during the exposition and development, it is eventually unable to
project dissonance as a result of gradual changes in grouping patterns during the
recapitulation. Against a fluid metric environment that constantly sways between
states of stability and instability, irregularity and regularity, Ravel alters the irregular grouping of the motif in three ways. First, he *juxtaposes* the motif against other
groupings to create indirect dissonance; then he *superimposes* the motif above
different groupings to create direct dissonance that is at its most intense at the
recapitulation; finally he *transforms* the irregular motif into a regular grouping

Neighbor-note motif			No neighbor-note motif
mm. 0-29	mm. 30-41	mm. 41-83	mm. 84-91
Stanza 1	Stanza 2	Stanza 3	Stanza 4 and 5

Figure 10.2. Possible correlations between musical form of Ravel's "Ondine" and Bertrand's poem

	Theme	Measure nos.	Formal-harmonic cues
Exposition	First Theme	1–15	C♯: V⁹/iv, I
	Bridge Theme	16–21, 22–29	
	Second Theme	30–41	V⁹
Development		42–61	Begins in V⁹/V
	Re-transition	62–65	V/IV
Recapitulation	Second Theme	66–71	iv/IV
	Second Bridge Theme	72–79	Tritone ♭V/IV, I (F♯)
	First Theme	80–83	V⁹
Coda	Narrator's Reply	84–87	Tritone v/V (D minor)
	Ondine's laugh	88	Octatonic
	Ondine's exit	89–91	I

Figure 10.3. Sonata form in "Ondine"

at the coda to create metric consonance. We will now see how this seemingly superficial flourish, by gradually losing its identity as a destabilizing metric force, narrates Ondine's failed seduction even as she fails to mention her central encounter.

A Decorative Motif and a Broken Frame

As a figure that represents not only the lake water but also Ondine's desire and the narrator's gaze, the neighbor-note motif mesmerizes the listener using two techniques idiosyncratic to ornament: repetition and irregular, ambiguous rhythmic patterns. Several features contribute to the listener's complex perception of this motif. In example 10.6a, the pitch oscillation from G♯ to A suggests two conflicting grouping possibilities. If G♯ (the fifth scale degree of the sustained triad) is perceived as a central pitch and A (the flattened sixth) functions as a neighbor-note, then a 3 + 3 + 2 pattern is established across each group of eight thirty-seconds.[24] This pattern also emerges from the pitch A's occurrence at irregular intervals: on the second, fifth, and eighth thirty-second pulse. Alternatively, the return to G♯ after the first A creates a tonal accent which stresses the pitch of return, G♯, and emphasizes melodic parallelism between the last six thirty-second notes (ex. 10.6b). In this case, the emerging 2 + 3 + 3 pattern exists in a subliminally dissonant relationship to the 3 + 3 + 2 pattern.

Irregular groupings of this motif have repercussions on higher metric levels (ex. 10.7). If the eighth-note pulse is grouped into two, then we hear one regular alternation from G♯ to A. If, however, this motif is grouped into three eighths where A functions as an upper neighbor to G♯, then the progression G♯–A–G♯ is heard as one complete oscillation. Tension is thus established between grouping the G♯–A oscillation as a "parallel scheme" according to a duple-eighth grouping (G♯A–G♯A–G♯A–) or a "switchback scheme" according to a triple-eighth grouping (G♯AG♯–AG♯A–G♯A♯G♯–).[25] Conflict between what Richard Cohn describes as "parallel" and "switchback" interpretations penetrates higher levels of the metric hierarchy where the "switchback" triple eighth grouping creates a "parallel scheme" on the dotted-quarter level, which may also be perceived as a "switchback scheme." Ravel's decision to open "Ondine" with six quarter beats as opposed to four or two relates more readily to the time-signature: six is equally divisible by a duple-eighth grouping (a "parallel scheme") and a triple-eighth grouping (a "switchback scheme").

With the repetition of the opening melody at measure 14, Ravel makes the first significant modification to the neighbor-note motif. Example 10.8 shows how he fractures the 3 + 3 + 2 pattern across three registers to articulate a new irregular grouping through accents of registral change on weak beats. Overlapping registers between the neighbor-note motif and arpeggiated melody displace the metric downbeat to create a blurred perception of Ondine's song (mm. 14–15). The instability of this moment is momentarily overcome by the bridge theme (m. 16), which reinstates segregation between song and accompaniment at an instance where the neighbor-note motif is abandoned in favor of consonant 4-groupings of thirty-seconds. However, Ravel destabilizes these regular groupings by juxtaposing them against irregular quasi-thirty-second-note groups (m. 17, m. 19) that coexist with shifting meters ($\frac{3}{4}$ to $\frac{2}{4}$ in mm. 16–17, and mm. 18–19).[26] Metric stability of consonant thirty-second-note groupings is further destabilized by a jolting accent on the second eighth of every $\frac{2}{4}$ measure (D2 + 1 where 1=eighth, m. 17 and m. 19, example 10.9).

With the return of the neighbor-note motif at the second bridge theme in measure 23, Ravel subtly manipulates our expectations by transforming the original 3 + 3 + 2 pattern into 1 + 2 + 1 + 1 + 2 + 1 (ex. 10.10). Whereas the original grouping had an uneven number of attacks on G♯ and A, the transformed motif has four attacks on each pitch so that each pattern is modulo-8 equivalent. Overall, we experience a deterioration of the thirty-second-note motif begun first in its expansion across three registers (mm. 14–15), then in its disassociation from the $\hat{5}$-♭$\hat{6}$ oscillation (mm. 16–21), and finally, in its

Example 10.6a. 3 + 3 + 2 grouping of the neighbor-note motif in m. 1

Example 10.6b. 2 + 3 + 3 grouping of the neighbor-note motif in m. 1

Example 10.7. Switchback and parallel interpretations of the neighbor-note motif

Example 10.8. Irregular registral changes of the neighbor-note motif in m. 14

D2+1 (where 1=eighth)

Example 10.9. 4-groupings of thirty-seconds are juxtaposed against irregular thirty-second groups, which coexist with displacement dissonance, mm. 16–17

regular articulation of rhythmic attacks (mm. 23–25). Motivic transformation is accompanied by increasing levels of instability that include indirect dissonance between quarter and dotted-quarter pulses (mm. 23–25); a return of the elongated upbeat of measure 22 in measure 26; and abundant displacement dissonances. The reemergence of the thirty-second-note motif as we approach the second theme overcomes this momentary lapse of periodicity and brings about relative stability.

Example 10.10. Ravel transforms the original 3 + 3 + 2 pattern into 1 + 2 + 1 + 1 + 2 + 1, m. 23

As we well know by now, metric stability is rarely a normative, durable state for Ravel. The stability associated with the second theme is gradually eroded by his destabilizing treatment of thirty-second-note groupings alongside increasing levels of dissonance. Whereas motivic groupings were previously juxtaposed, Ravel now *superimposes* different groupings to heighten our awareness of the changing thirty-second-note motif (ex. 10.11). At measure 37/3, the 3 + 3 + 2 grouping is superimposed above a 4 + 4 grouping before irregular groupings of quasi-thirty-seconds burst through at the ends of phrases (m. 39, m. 40). Although, following Rothstein, we may interpret this rhythmic surge as creating forward momentum, it also speaks of a malleable musical frame, given the rising textural prominence of thirty-second-note values in general. As we approach the moment where textural distance between the neighbor-note motif and Ondine's song is reduced, we witness a growing obfuscation of the surface by thirty-second-note values. For instance, the increasing presence of quasi-thirty-second-note values in irregular groupings at the ends of phrases undermines the stabilized return of the neighbor-note motif at the development section; here, the addition of $F\times_5$ and $D\sharp_6$ projects a temporary eighth-note pulse (ex. 10.12). Ravel's increasing emphasis on ornament is further manifested in his replacement of thirty-second-note groupings with end-accented sixty-fourths (mm. 47–48).

Throughout the development section, metric stability is constantly undermined by the neighbor-note motif's juxtaposition against quasi-thirty-seconds or sixty-fourths. These short values are inevitably experienced as cadenza-like figurations similar to the evanescent flourishes of "Noctuelles." In the first half of the development (mm. 42–51), however, they possess only a mildly destabilizing effect despite their increasing length; florid gestures (ranging from groupings of five, six, and seven thirty-seconds) do not interfere with the clear

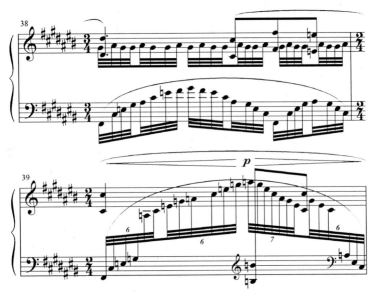

Example 10.11. 3 + 3 + 2 pattern is superimposed above a 4 + 4 grouping and juxtaposed against irregular thirty-second groupings, mm. 38–39

Example 10.12. Increasing presence of irregular thirty-seconds at ends of phrases destabilizes the eighth-note pulse projected by F$\times_5$ and D$\sharp_6$

metric articulation conveyed by quarter-, eighth-, sixteenth-, and thirty-second-note pulses of the melody and accompaniment.

The situation changes in the second half of the development, where assertive short values contribute to rising levels of dissonance in anticipation of the recapitulation (m. 66). Example 10.13 shows how a 9-grouping of thirty-seconds displaces the first beat at measure 55. This arpeggio is experienced as an upbeat to beat 2, which is subsequently reinterpreted as beat 1. We perceive a complete measure of $\frac{4}{4}$ from measures 55/2–56/2, and the subsequent arpeggiation of short values between measures 56–57 as an elongated upbeat to measure 57/1. Consecutive strong accents between the density accent of the arpeggiation in measure 56 and the downbeat of measure 57 create momentary irregularity that is overcome by the relative stability of measure 57. Here, the development of melodic material from measure 45 establishes a consonant relationship between eighth-, thirty-second-, and sixty-fourth-note pulses. Nonetheless, agogic emphasis on beat 2 and a density accent on beat 4 create an uneven articulation of $\frac{4}{4}$ that treats beat 1 as an anacrusis. As a result, the squeezed-in arpeggio of measure 56 together with the first beat of measure 57 create an elongated upbeat toward the agogically accented second beat of measure 57. This displacement moves the entire progression from measure 57 to measure 61 forward by one quarter (D2 + 1) in a projected articulation of $\frac{2}{4}$. Displacement dissonance between notated and perceived meters only ends at measure 62, where it coincides with the density accent on the first beat of $\frac{3}{4}$. Although the displacement dissonance beginning at measure 55 is resolved here, the move to $\frac{3}{4}$ at measure 62 is not entirely consonant, since we hear indirect dissonance between duple and triplet sixteenths (G3/2).

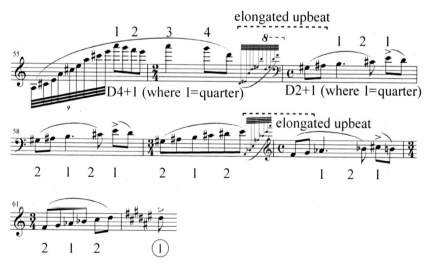

Example 10.13. Rising levels of dissonance in the development section, mm. 55–62

Taken together, the downbeat emphasis, the regular eighth pulse, and the lack of thirty-second-note values in measures 62–65 mark the retransition as the most consonant passage of the piece. Metric consonance resolves large-scale dissonance initiated at measure 55 and enhances our experience of intense instability at the recapitulation (ex. 10.14). This is prepared by the absence of thirty-second-note values, which drop out of the texture in the ascent toward measure 66. Consequently, when dissonant thirty-second-note groupings fully *merge* with the melody at measure 66, we, like Ondine, are overwhelmed by the intense breakthrough of short values that fill the soundscape. By dissolving the frame, direct conflict between thirty-second-note pulses positions measure 66 as a strong moment of structural inversion; short values now saturate the surface, and in so doing, foreground previously submerged dissonance. Even as we experience consonance on an eighth-note level—the eighth pulse of each left-hand thirty-second group supports the eighth pulse of the right-hand melody—this passage projects intense dissonance on a thirty-second-note level. For the first time, two classes of quasi-thirty-second-note pulses are superimposed to create direct grouping dissonance. Irregular thirty-second-note groupings of seven against six and seven against five create a series of dissonances, which threaten to overpower the eighth pulses of the melody and implied quarter pulses of the left-hand bass articulation. As we saw in "Noctuelles," a conflicted relationship between consonance and dissonance is a basic feature of Ravel's metric style; in this context, consonance as conveyed on eighth and quarter levels subsumes dissonance on thirty-second levels of the hierarchy.[27]

It is not by chance that the recapitulation forms a fragile turning point for the piece. Metric instability of this moment highlights a latent tension between Ondine's voice, the narrator's fantasy, and her body. We might read the material essence of water here as evoking the narrator's gaze, his imagination of Ondine's presence. This becomes even more compelling, given that it is the meandering thirty-second-note motif that gives shape to Ondine's imagined song. While the narrator's gaze provides Ondine with a physical presence, tensions between reality and illusion, vision and voice, create ambiguous relationships between the narrator and Ondine. Consequently, the increasing volatility of water as exemplified by rising prominence of the thirty-second motif represents two tensions: Ondine's longing for the narrator, and the narrator's desire to see Ondine, who is present to him only as a disembodied voice. In confusing the relationship between the background thirty-second-note motif and the foreground melody—Ondine's frame and her song—Ravel collapses the boundary between narrator and protagonist to create, momentarily, a single voice. The turbulence with which Ondine's motif breaks the frame at measure 66 signifies the rising tension of Ondine's increasing desire. From the perspective of the narrator, the conflation of frame and the enframed indicates a different union, one in which aural illusion—Ondine's song—and visual hallucination—her physical appearance as water—fuse.

Example 10.14. From metric consonance in the re-transition (m. 62) to extreme dissonance at the recapitulation (m. 66)

By measure 70, the narrator's hallucination subsides to create balance between the accompanimental thirty-second-note figuration and the longer values of Ondine's song. When the neighbor-note motif eventually returns at measure 70, the irregular pattern of registral accents from measure 14 and measure 37 is replaced by four thirty-seconds grouped in the same register, with no link to the original 3 + 3 + 2 grouping. Gradually, increasingly *regular* registral accents alter Ondine's murmuring motif in measure 83 (4 + 2 + 2) in anticipation of the narrator's intrusion. Before Ondine has had a chance to even broach the issue of marriage, the narrator is compelled to end the fantasy and reinstate patriarchal order; his monophonic resistance thus severs her intricately woven music to restore the stable regularity of his rational world. The trauma of this confrontation is manifest in Ondine's sarcastic laugh and melodramatic exit beginning at measure 88. These now emphasize *regular* thirty-second groupings that prepare the tragic transformation of her motif in the coda, in which we glimpse the repercussions of severe formal imbalance as created by the destructive frame.

A Tragic Consonance

By repeating the exposition in reverse, Ravel traces an unusual metric trajectory; the music unfolds from the relatively unstable character of the second theme through the instabilities of the second bridge theme until it reaches the relative stability of the first theme, and finally, the stability of the transformed neighbor-note motif. To enhance the metric impact of this motivic transformation, Ravel precedes the coda with several passages that explore the potential for metric ambiguity and dissonance.

Beginning with the return of the second bridge theme at measure 72, Ravel extends the nonmetric triplet quarter grouping above a glissando through an extra measure in order to suspend the metric pulse for a longer period. Although these glissandi are notated in $\frac{4}{4}$, they do not reinforce the melodic grouping to articulate $\frac{4}{4}$ meter. Instead, we hear the momentary suspension of a regular pulse, similar to the experience of a cadenza passage, but different in that the return fails to reinstate a stable meter.[28] It is only when the first theme returns in measure 80 that a relatively stable pulse is restored on higher metric levels, while the registrally changing neighbor-note motif creates irregular accents on lower levels (as in mm. 14–15). The 'unstable stability' of this hierarchic grouping is eventually undermined by the metric expansion of measure 82 from $\frac{4}{4}$ into $\frac{5}{4}$, which alters the thirty-second grouping and facilitates the breakdown of thirty-second activity to mark the dramatic turning point: the narrator's confession. Although this monophonic intrusion creates deep textural contrast against the contrapuntal rhythmic complexity of earlier sections, it also serves to tame subsequent activity. Consequently, Ondine's outburst at measure 88 is perceived as an intricate web of thirty-second-note groupings, organized initially into nonmetric 12-groupings that nonetheless articulate a regular eighth pulse as they descend.

Most significant is the transformation of the neighbor-note motif in the coda. Example 10.15 shows that the 3 + 3 + 2 grouping is now fractured across three registers, obliterated through octave displacement, and distorted by being divided between two hands. Several factors contribute to the transformation of this motif. First, since pitches of the thirty-second-note grouping are no longer confined to a single register as in the opening, it is difficult to perceive a 3 + 3 + 2 pattern. One could argue, however, that their

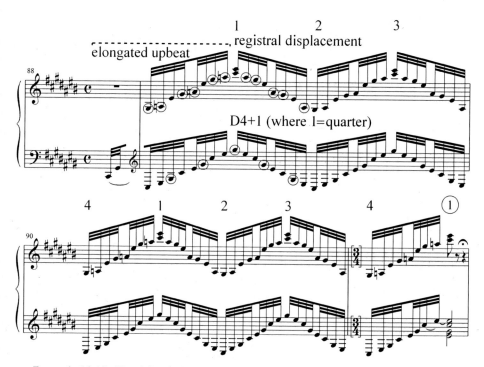

Example 10.15. 'Tragic' transformation of Ondine's thirty-second-note motif in the coda, mm. 89–91

organization into specific registers projects a 3 + 3 + 2 grouping: G♯–A–G♯ confined to the lowest register, G♯–A–G♯ to the middle register, and G♯–A to the highest. However, Ravel's performance indication *bien égal de sonorité*, along with the strong quarter pulse, eradicates any remnant of the 3 + 3 + 2 pattern; the neighbor-note motif is truly disfigured at this point.

For the first time, a regular 4-grouping of the thirty-second-note motif projects a regular quarter pulse, albeit one that is notated in the form of a displacement dissonance; the anacrusis and downbeat of measure 89 convey an elongated upbeat for displaced registral accents on the second and fourth beats of $\frac{4}{4}$. Although Ravel notates a displacement dissonance throughout these measures, our experience of this passage is mostly consonant; instead of resolving this dissonance, Ravel simply rewrites the final measure in $\frac{3}{4}$ so that we perceive two full measures in $\frac{4}{4}$ before the music ends on the downbeat of a third measure. Our equivocal experience of metric stability alludes to the ambiguity of the narrator's encounter; just as Ondine is poised between the realms of fantasy and reality, Ravel's listener is caught between the dissonance of her song and the troubled consonance of the narrator's response.

In Ondine's song, tragedy is portrayed through the narrator's violent distortion of her vibrant motif. As his fantasy threatens to spin out of control, the narrator takes charge by stifling Ondine's song, dismembering her murmuring motif across several registers, and finally, subordinating its metric instability. Ravel's treatment of sonata form also spells out Ondine's fate: by beginning the recapitulation in reverse (with the second theme), Ravel's formal strategy subverts the traditional trope of heroism associated with double return at the recapitulation. Timothy Jackson explains, "In the repertoire of works in the tragic reversed sonata form, there is no rescue, no *Deus ex machina*, no song of rejoicing."[29] By transforming Ondine's motif in the coda-space with a delayed return of the tonic, Ravel opposes the strife-to-victory sonata-form model. In this way, we witness the tragic disempowerment of a *femme fatale* who, as punishment for her audacious behavior, is rendered incapable of eternal song.

Epilogue

In this analysis, we have seen how Ravel evokes Bertrand's poem through the unlikely figure of a decorative thirty-second-note motif. By unleashing the expressive force of marginalized detail, Ravel unsettles conventions of formal balance. Fluctuating tension between center and frame also brings into focus other competing dichotomies within this piece. Against the penetrating monophony of the narrator, Ondine's music is highly textured; she invites the narrator into a realm of excess saturated with repetitive, fluid contours. As an imaginary object, she inhabits his subconscious, an interior world that thrives on sensation and nervous tension. While traditional oppositions characterize "Ondine," they are certainly not limited to this piece or to Ravel's compositional style.

Recent scholarship by art historian Debora Silverman encourages us to perceive these contrasts in relation to a broader modernist discourse on luxury and interiority.[30] In her book on art nouveau, Silverman explores how artists rejected the Third Republic's emphasis on industry and science by embracing a nostalgic return to rococo ideals. Influential figures such as Émile Zola and the Goncourt brothers spoke openly of their desire to escape the fatigue of urban life and "retreat to an ornamental fantasy in the organicized private interior," an inner space that was "feminine and intimate."[31] Luxurious interiors promised comfort and solace, but these sanctuaries rarely served as utopian sites of rest and regeneration; Symbolist aesthetics continued to focus on the wounded interior as seen in the preference to depict states of agitation, anxiety, hysteria, and apathy. Heavily ornamented interiors exacerbated these sensations rather than assuaged them; excessive ornament tended to disorient rather than soothe and pacify.

Despite a tendency by some authors to dismiss "Ondine" as mere "ear candy," I am tempted to read Ravel's provocative portrayal against this backdrop of social and political upheaval. In this setting, "Ondine" might emerge as the tale of a fatigued neurasthenic urban dweller who seeks refuge in a realm of imaginary freedom. At first, Ondine's soothing voice forms a comforting alternative for him. But her increasing agitation and his gradual loss of consciousness as he succumbs to her spell suddenly compel him to exert control. By putting a stop to fantasy, the narrator's actions prompt another reading, one that serves as an allegory of Ravel's troubled emergence as an independent, avant-garde composer. As an artist who identified with Symbolist aesthetics during a period of rejection by the Conservatoire and the Société Nationale de Musique, we might understand Ravel's focus on luxurious interiors as havens from the bitter criticism of conservative authorities. Ravel's cultivation of lavish surfaces is highly suggestive; as we have seen in "Noctuelles," ornament became the impetus behind an innovative technique that was denigrated as incoherent by some critics, and praised as "la musique ultra-moderne" by others.[32] At the same time, decorative interiors might have intensified Ravel's feelings of disillusionment and anxiety, while offering a private, hidden space in which he could create uninhibited and unchecked.

Even as "Ondine" might pose as a metaphor for professional angst, this piece challenges the image of Ravel as the persecuted modernist in significant ways. For example, we cannot overlook the work's regressive turn to a traditional melody and accompaniment texture. Equally detrimental, in this respect, is Ravel's reinstatement of a relatively conventional harmonic language, which mutes the modernistic edge of his experiments in *Miroirs*. Part of Ravel's conservatism can be attributed to the subject matter. The quintessentially romantic tale of Ondine appears to have shaped Ravel's Janus-faced conception of the *femme fatale;* she emerges as capricious fantasy in one respect, and prophetic metaphor in another. My musings find a certain level of resonance in an anecdote by Henriette Faure, Ravel's piano student. She explains:

> One single time I happened to force the barrier. We had to work on *Gaspard de la nuit,* and I said to him, "These three poems of Aloysius Bertrand are attractive!" He responded immediately with an enthusiasm that was badly hidden, "Read the entire collection, it is marvellous, all the Romanticism of the nineteenth century is contained in this little book." And, as if I had forced open the door of Barbe Bleue, I exclaimed with vivacity, "Ah! Are you therefore sometimes a Romantic?"
>
> Then he produced something surprising and sad. Ravel looked at me without seeing me, and a vague, distant, troubled air occupied his face. One would have said that he had lost his tongue. This lasted a long time, and as we were at the table I saw him turning his little fork tirelessly in his jam . . . and the discomfort persisted. Fortunately, the governess burst into the dining room to give dessert and she cried, "But Monsieur you have put jam into your saucer!" "Ah yes," said Ravel, "Excuse me." He refound his vivacity and his sense of humour.[33]

Whether this episode represents a moment of Bloomian anxiety or Ravel's horror at his inability to conceal underlying romantic sentiments, it certainly exposes the insecurity that pervaded Ravel's perception of his professional identity. At a time when his avant-garde status depended solely on his ability to experiment and innovate, Ravel was aware of the damage that could be inflicted by characterizations of his style, thought, or aesthetic as "romantic." In an attempt to reconcile his conflicting interests, Ravel might have looked to his compositional heritage to nurture a modern style inspired by ornament, just as other *début-de-siècle* artists looked to the rococo to help them forge a new aesthetic based on the decorative. If we are to give credence to the ornamental fantasies that swept through *début-de-siècle* Paris, then "Ondine" stands as much more than an addition to the *femme fatale* trope, and to romantic traditions of pianistic bravura. Together with "Noctuelles," "Ondine" becomes an emblem of a vivid and complex, innovative French virtuosity that places various manifestations of ornament at the core of its modernity.

Notes

1. To briefly summarize, Harald Krebs defines metrical consonance as aligned (or nested) interpretive layers whose cardinalities are multiples or other factors of each other. He identifies two types of metrical dissonance: (1) grouping dissonance (G), which occurs when nonaligned layers have different cardinalities and are not multiples or factors of each other; and (2) displacement dissonance (D), which arises when two or more layers of the same cardinality are nonaligned to create syncopation. In grouping dissonance, the label G3/2 denotes the dissonant combination of conflicting 3-layers and 2-layers. In displacement dissonance, the label D4 + 1 (1=quarter) informs us of a displacement dissonance where the initiation of a 4-layer is delayed by a quarter pulse. D4−1(1=quarter) would suggest that the 4-layer is anticipated by a quarter pulse. Krebs differentiates further between dissonance created through superposition (direct dissonance) and through juxtaposition (indirect dissonance). For a fuller explanation see "Metrical Consonance and Dissonance: Definitions and Taxonomy," in *Fantasy Pieces: Metrical Dissonance in the Music of Robert Schumann* (Oxford: Oxford University Press, 1999), 22–61.

2. See Arbie Orenstein, *Ravel: Man and Musician* (New York: Columbia University Press, 1991). Orenstein documents Ravel's attempts at the *Prix de Rome* competition in 1900, 1901, 1902, 1903, and 1905 (pp. 13–46). He also discusses the *affaire Ravel* that followed the 1905 competition (p. 42).

3. Roland-Manuel, "Une esquisse autobiographique de Maurice Ravel," *La Revue Musicale* (1938): 20. Translation from *A Ravel Reader: Correspondence, Articles, Interviews,* ed. Arbie Orenstein (Mineola, New York: Dover Publications, Inc.), 30.

4. Maurice Ravel, *Miroirs,* ed. Roger Nichols (London: Urtext Peters Edition, 1995), 6. The Symbolist aura of this phrase inspired subsequent characterisations of this piece. Consider the following description by Ravel's student, Henriette Faure: "Noctuelles dit la présence immatérielle de minuscules papillons de nuit, bruissement d'ailes, poussières de sons, atmosphère irréelle de la nuit, moiteurs, mystère." Henriette Faure, *Mon Maître Maurice Ravel* (Paris: Les Éditions A.T.P., 1978), 72.

5. Volker Helbing, "'Noctuelles' by Ravel: An essay on the morphology of sound," *Tijdschrift voor Muziektheorie* 8 (2003): 142–51. To summarize, Helbing mentions how at measure 17, "ornamental" chords such as the diminished seventh are heard "isolated from any context suggestive of an ornamental character"; the harmonic emphasis shifts from a "structural" dominant seventh to an "ornamental" diminished seventh. In measures 16–17, unresolved neighbor notes are prolonged for so long that "a differentiation between 'substance' and 'embellishment' is no longer possible." Delayed or suppressed harmonic resolution results in "the perforation of the harmonic texture just at the moments when, according to tonal logic, it should prove intact: at the moment of resolution" (p. 145). Finally, Helbing discusses Ravel's ambiguous use of octatonic collections. He notes that "it seems impossible to decide whether they function as ornaments or if they must be considered as part of the harmonic framework" (p. 147).

6. Ibid., 142.

7. Ibid., 151.

8. William Rothstein explains the perception of *accelerandi* in the following way: "[When] the melody and bass . . . begin moving in much faster note values than before . . . we might call it a 'drive to the cadence.'" See Rothstein, *Phrase Rhythm in Tonal Music* (New York: Schirmer, 1989), 22.

9. Helbing, "'Noctuelles' by Ravel: An essay on the morphology of sound," 143.

10. "Ravel aimait beaucoup les grands arpèges défilant de l'extrême aigu dans une diminuendo spectaculaire qu'il appelait l'évanescence." H. Faure, *Mon Maître Maurice Ravel*, 66.

11. Vladimir Jankélévitch interprets the unsettling effect of these evocative grouping dissonances as follows: "The polyrhythm of expression . . . expresses the frenzied zig-zag flight of the big moths which come blindly against the walls, flutter round the lights and, drunk with sleep and wandering, come flying limply to alight somewhere on the edge of darkness." See Jankélévitch, *Ravel*, trans. Margaret Crosland (Westport, CT: Greenwood Press, 1976), 98.

12. See Gurminder K. Bhogal, "Breaking the Frame: Arabesque and Metric Complexity in Ravel's Sunrise Scene," *Zeitschrift der Gesellschaft für Musiktheorie* 5, no. 1 (2008).

13. By accommodating a greater number of pitches toward the ends of phrases, Ravel achieves the equivalent of William Rothstein's "drive to the cadence." See Rothstein, *Phrase Rhythm in Tonal Music*, 22.

14. Following Justin London, I suggest that cyclic repetition of a dissonance (in this case, G3/2 on a hypermetric level) may create metric regularity. See London "Some Examples of Complex Meters and Their Implications for Models of Metric Perception," *Music Perception* 13 (1995): 59–77.

15. My interpretation here is inspired by Jonathan Kramer's discussion of deep-level meter in *The Time of Music: New Meanings, New Temporalities, New Listening Strategies* (New York: Schirmer, 1988), 112–20.

16. Edouard Schneider, "Quatuor Parent," *Le Courrier Musical* (March 1, 1906): 211. "Aucune des qualités du quatuor de M. Ravel ne se retrouve dans ces pièces incohérentes d'où semble exclue toute musicalité. . . . Qu'il s'agisse de *Noctuelles* . . . c'est toujours le même et inintelligible balbutiement de notes, le même bégaiement sans fin qui, à la longue devient exaspérant."

17. Ibid.

18. M D. Calvocoressi, "Société Nationale," *Le Courrier Musical* (January 1, 1906): 63.

19. A. M., "Salles Erard," *Le Monde Musical* (January 15, 1906): 13. Italics mine. "Jamais il ne veut évoquer un sentiment, pénétrer au fond d'une chose où d'un être. Il

préfère en prendre l'enveloppe frêle, délicate, légère, diaphane et la décorer des mille tons de sa palette. Il abandonne totalement l'architecture au profit du revêtement extérieur, sans chercher à dessiner les lignes, à former un édifice qui ait une base, un milieu, un sommet. On pourrait, sans inconvénient, commencer l'exécution de ces petites pièces à n'importe quel endroit et l'arrêter où l'on voudrait."

20. Ibid.

21. As we shall see, Ravel's "Ondine" diverges considerably from Friedrich de la Motte Fouqué's 1811 version of the story. In Motte Fouqué's tale, Huldbrand, the knight-errant, is on an adventure to prove himself worthy of his love, Lady Bertalda. He gets lost and finds himself near the home of a fisherman, who has a wife and an adopted daughter, Ondine. Huldbrand falls in love with Ondine, and she reciprocates, although she is warned by the King of the Ondines not to become involved with humans. Ondine's disobedience means that she is subjected to a harsh condition: if Huldbrand is unfaithful to her, or repudiates her on or near water, he will lose her and die. Rejecting Bertalda, Huldbrand marries Ondine and takes her to his court. Her lack of social graces embarrasses Huldbrand, who soon disowns her in favour of "civilised" Bertalda. To end Bertalda's taunting, Ondine unmasks her as the fisherman's natural daughter. She then returns to the lake. A year later, Huldbrand and Bertalda are preparing for their marriage; Ondine emerges on Huldbrand's wedding day to give him the kiss of death.

22. I explore another instance of this technique in Ravel's ballet, *Daphnis et Chloé* (1912). See "Breaking the Frame: Arabesque and Metric Complexity in Ravel's Sunrise Scene," *Zeitschrift der Gesellschaft für Musiktheorie* 5, no. 1 (2008).

23. See Maurice Ravel, *Gaspard de la nuit*, ed. Roger Nichols (London: Peters Edition, 1991).

24. Peter Schatt also notes the 3 + 3 + 2 pattern of this motif in "Undine lebt: Verkörperte Ästhetik in der Musik." *Musik und Bildung* 27 (1995): 47.

25. Richard Cohn coins the concept of "parallel" and "switchback" schemes in his analysis of the Scherzo from Beethoven's Ninth Symphony. He discusses the conflict between an "Odyssean" journey that involves the return to (a) after having completed a motion from (a) to (b), and a "Sindbadian reflex" that urges a movement back to (b) after having reached (a). The former suggests a triple interpretation (a "switchback scheme") while the latter suggests a duple interpretation (a "parallel scheme"). See Cohn, "The Dramatization of Hypermetric Conflicts in the Scherzo of Beethoven's Ninth Symphony," *19th-Century Music* 15 (1992): 191–93.

26. Rothstein's observations of how a melody and bass move "in faster note values . . . as they approach their goals" are relevant for "Ondine" where a large number of short values drive toward the consequent portions of phrases. In contrast to traditional cadential drives, which move toward points of rest, Ravel's treatment of such 'drives' bypasses anticipated cadential resolution. Instead, he pushes forward in measure 17, measure 19, and measure 20, dividing each eighth pulse into six then five thirty-seconds before signalling a 'weak' cadential gesture through the local plagal progression of a glissando in measures 22–23.

27. Also see Jonathan Kramer's discussion of how "irregularity may be subsumed into regularity on still deeper levels," in *The Time of Music*, 100.

28. See Rothstein, *Phrase Rhythm in Tonal Music*, 41–42.

29. Timothy L. Jackson, "The Tragic Reversed Recapitulation in the German Classical Tradition," *Journal of Music Theory* 40 (1996): 65.

30. Debora Silverman, *Art Nouveau in Fin-de-Siècle France: Politics, Psychology and Style* (Berkeley: University of California Press, 1989).

31. Ibid., 4 and 9.

32. "A. R.," *Le Courrier Musicale* (May 1, 1909): 318.

33. Henriette Faure, *Mon maître Maurice Ravel: Son œuvre, son enseignement, souvenirs et légendes* (Paris: Les Editions A.T.P., 1978), 24. My translation.

Chapter Eleven

The Child on the Couch; or, Toward a (Psycho)Analysis of Ravel's L'enfant et les sortilèges

Peter Kaminsky

During World War I, Colette wrote a ballet scenario on a commission from Jacques Rouché, director of the Paris Opéra, who suggested Ravel as an appropriate composer.[1] A copy of the scenario was sent to the front, but Ravel neither received nor saw it until he returned from his service as an ambulance driver in 1918. Colette's story, with its vivid depiction of the joys and especially the terrors of childhood, brimming with potent psychological overtones, dovetailed beautifully with Ravel's lifelong attraction to themes of childhood, toys, machines, automata, and magic. With the rise of Les Six, a new generation of French composers seeking to move beyond the heritage of Debussy and Ravel, *L'enfant et les sortilèges* presented Ravel with an opportunity to remain artistically relevant by revitalizing his musical language; hence the assimilation of American jazz and blues, polytonality, and an increased emphasis on linear counterpoint in *L'enfant* and his works of the 1920s. The resulting ballet-opera, which premiered in Monte Carlo in March of 1925, may be unique in the opera literature in telling its story from the point of view of a six-year-old child.

My study of *L'enfant et les sortilèges* will proceed in three parts. Part 1 summarizes Colette's story and goes on to trace the origin of its psychoanalytic interpretation and briefly assess the influence of this interpretation on subsequent commentary on the opera. I then propose a mapping between Ravel's music and the psychological overtones of the story, as viewed through a selective psychoanalytic lens. Part 2 examines several excerpts in tracing the parallel transformations of the Child and the music, focusing on the artful change of structural contexts for reiterated passages, consistent with the methodology of part 1. Part 3 provides a close reading of a single number,

---

Excerpts from Colette and Maurice Ravel, *L'enfant et les sortilèges*, © 1925–32 Redfield B.V. / Nordice B.V., are reproduced with the kind authorization of Les Editions Durand.

the central duet between the Child and the Princess, which brings together issues of musical and psychoanalytic mapping in music of surpassing depth and emotional charge.

Part 1: Mapping Story, Music, and Psychoanalysis

From the time of its premiere in 1925, Ravel's second and last completed opera, *L'enfant et les sortilèges,* has garnered as much attention for the psychological and symbolic qualities of its libretto as for its music. This is understandable, as the opera was premiered on the heels of the introduction of Freud's theories and a surge of artistic and public interest in them. Further, the fantastic subject matter of Colette's libretto—a naughty young boy and his mother; the boy's love for a storybook princess; sentient and talking flora, fauna, household furniture, bric-a-brac, and so on—naturally invite a reading of the opera sensitive to its psychological overtones. If we accept that the dramatic unfolding of the libretto and the progress of the musical structure are inseparable from one another (even if they are not always congruent), then the primary goal of analysis of *L'enfant* appears inevitable: to discover the musical means through which Ravel represents crucial dramatic events and themes that emerge from an interpretation of the story attuned to its psychological implications.

To date, no study has successfully achieved this goal. There are several reasons why this is so. First, the psychoanalytic interpretations have focused almost completely on Colette's libretto to the virtual exclusion of Ravel's music; these interpretations have consistently failed to take into account what is *musically representable.* The problem begins only a few years after the premier of the opera with psychoanalyst Melanie Klein's interpretation of Colette's libretto in light of (her take on) Freudian principles.[2] The story of a young boy who, in an epic temper tantrum, breaks furniture, tortures animals, and takes a knife to trees in the garden naturally was an attractive subject to Klein, given her interest in children's (sometimes sadistic) impulses. In her essay, first published in 1929, she writes:

> I will now examine more closely the details in which the child's pleasure in destruction expresses itself. They seem to me to recall the early infantile situation which in my most recent writings I have described as being of fundamental importance both for neurosis in boys and for their normal development. I refer to the attack on the mother's body and on the father's penis in it. [In Colette's libretto] the squirrel in the cage and the pendulum wrenched out of the clock are plain symbols of the penis in the mother's body. The fact that it is the *father's* penis and that it is in the act of coitus with the mother is indicated by the rent in the wallpaper.[3]

As a psychoanalyst Klein cannot make a valid *musical* case for her interpretive claims. Nonetheless, this does not mean that her views necessarily should be dismissed out of hand; rather, they offer a challenge and a test case for musical commentators to demonstrate whether Klein provides a useful path into the psychological overtones of Ravel's opera.[4]

More recently, Richard Langham Smith attempts to recuperate Klein, bolstering her reading with selected musical details. A sensitive analyst, Smith attends to a number of important dramatic-musical aspects of the opera. In particular, he cites the central duet between the storybook Princess and the Child as an emotional turning point. Paraphrasing Smith's discussion of the number, he addresses

- the bitonality of the opening (E major over F) conveying the magical aura of the beloved Princess;
- the representation of the Princess by a diatonic heterophonic texture (accompanied only by flute);
- the tonal shift to the sharp mediant signaling the beginning of the Princess's rejection of the Child;
- the phallic symbolism of the sword—"Colette cannot resist the humour of the Child 'wishing he had a sword like that of her cavalier,' knowingly unemphasised by Ravel, the more to make its effect."[5]

As will be seen in my analysis of the same number in part 3, Smith's observations provide a fruitful point of departure. My reading will consider the duet—including the above details—from a broadened structural, psychoanalytic, and dramatic context, taking into account

- the tonal and dramatic significance of the harmony and voice leading of the opening progression beyond the initial bitonal chord;
- the dramatic and structural implications of the Princess's texture in contrast to that of the Child;
- precisely where and how the Princess's rejection takes place in relation to the unique tonal/formal trajectory of the duet;
- the phallic sword as not only emphasized musically by Ravel, but as the tonal, formal and dramatic premise for the unfolding of the duet as a whole. (This will interact, but only slightly, with Klein's phallocentric views.)

Another problem with previous accounts of the opera is the mirror image of the first: an overly narrow focus on musical structure to the exclusion of the psychological. For example, while Christine Prost offers a mostly accurate formal exegesis of every number in the opera, her interpretation is both limited in scope and lacking in depth for not probing the psychological motivation for Ravel's musical choices.[6]

In seeking to address the problems outlined above, the issue of *mapping* necessarily arises: here, the mapping of significant points of correspondence between the domains of psychoanalytic interpretation and music analysis as they relate to Colette's story and Ravel's music. Figure 11.1 proposes a general schema for how the mapping process takes place for *L'enfant.*[7] Three large-scale structural correspondences underlie the interaction of the music and drama: (1) Mother's authority: tonality; (2) the Child's immaturity: tonal ambiguity; and (3) the Child's emotional development: musical development from relatively chaotic or ambiguous to ordered and consonant.

These general mappings take place alongside a purely musical one, in which the Child is linked with the opening theme and the Mother with her own leitmotif-as-cadence. These general mappings are pursued in more specific terms in the remainder of the example, with psychoanalytic inputs on the left and their music-structural analogues on the right. The subsequent analysis will reference these mappings throughout.

GENERAL
1. Human authority : Musical tonality
2. Mother's authority : Child :: Tonality : Themes (including the Child's)
3. Child's self-centered destructiveness : "chaotic" (often polymodal/polytonal) or tonally ambiguous passages ::
    development of *empathy* : their *transformed repetition* clarifying tonal context

CHARACTEROLOGICAL
Child : opening theme :: Mother : *leitmotif as cadence*

Basis for mappings: Convention-based rules governing human and musical behavior

Psychoanalytic inputs:

- Human authority: power to make and enforce rules

- Role of parents in articulating rules for Child's behavior

- Child's rejection of parental authority and self-centered
  destructiveness

- Gradual development of empathy in Child

- Child's acceptance of parental authority

- Emergence of Child's superego; internalization of
  moral code

Music-structural inputs:

- Musical tonality: power to articulate logical and conventionally
  understood musical context

- Role of tonal harmony and syntax in articulating logical and
  proper structural context for Child's theme—including *binding
  power of cadence*

- Tonal ambiguity; "chaotic" (often polymodal/polytonal) passages

- Transformed repetition of passages from relatively chaotic and
  broken to more ordered and tonal contexts

- Child's theme as harmonized by "global" tonic key

- Child sings Mother's cadence

Figure 11.1. Psychoanalytic-Musical Structural Mappings in Ravel's *L'enfant et les sortilèges*

Let us now turn to the story of the opera. Briefly, the opera opens with a young Child disobeying his Mother's wishes for him to do his homework. She expresses her disappointment and leaves him with sugarless tea and dry bread for his meal. The Child then goes on a destructive rampage against the pets, furniture, wallpaper, books, and bric-a-brac of the house. All these animals and objects come to life and reveal to the Child the consequences of his behavior. At the turning point of the opera, when the animals rise up against him, a Squirrel is injured in the mêlée, and the Child binds its paw before falling into a swoon. Now the animals recognize that the Child is good. Upon waking, the Child holds out his arms and sings "Maman."

Figure 11.2 provides a synoptic view of the story and delineates what I shall term the superego- and the empathy-paths to moral development (more on these below). The story is framed by the Child's initial repudiation of the Mother's authority and his concluding acceptance of it. This symmetrical frame is elaborated by specified musical and dramatic actions suggesting an arch form. Thus the pentatonic music of the opening returns to conclude the opera, transformed by its setting in the key of G major associated with the Mother; the Child's disobedience is balanced by the action of binding the Squirrel's paw; and the Child's destructive tantrum is matched by the animals' collective and equally destructive riot against the Child. In the box are selected scenes and actions from Parts I and II of the opera that take place in the Child's house and in the garden, respectively; together the boxed scenes represent preliminary steps leading to the empathic act of the Child's coming to the Squirrel's aid. In Part I the Child first experiences loss when he breaks his favorite Chinese teacup; he feels an intensified sense of remorse when the storybook Princess "rejects" him, and an intensification of fear when he perceives the Cats' size and their demonstrably sexual behavior. With the change of scene from the house to the garden, the Child begins to move toward recognition of the feelings of others and, correspondingly, of his place in the world. He recognizes the he has inflicted injury on the Tree by carving his initials in its bark; that he has deprived the Squirrel of its freedom by caging it; and that the Cats' behavior shows not only their lust but also their love for each other.

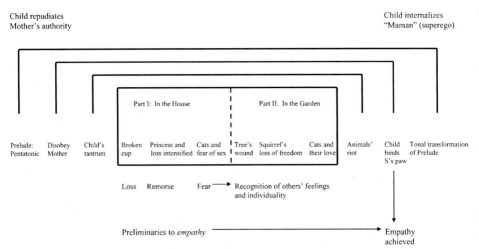

Figure 11.2. Formal symmetry and stages of moral development in *L'enfant et les sortilèges*

In wading into deeper psychoanalytic waters, I shall focus on only those ideas directly relevant to my musical analysis of the opera. In Freudian theory, the development of morality in children centers on the concept of the superego. The superego serves to modify the ego, enabling it in its complicated path toward independent judgment and ongoing emotional and behavioral maturation. The first step in the process of a child's developing a superego is the recognition of and simple obedience to parental authority. In time the child *internalizes* this authority, which constitutes a first step toward emergence of the superego. In Freud's words, "As the child was once under a compulsion to obey its parents, so the ego submits to the categorical imperative of its super-ego."[8]

An alternative perspective on childhood morality pioneered by Piaget constitutes more of an empirical model—as opposed to Freud's fundamentally theoretical model—based on observation of children in interactions with both caregivers and peers. Here the emphasis is on "ages and stages" of development. Notwithstanding their respective differences in perspective and emphasis, several researchers note the essential complementarity of approaches. Martin Nass (1966) writes, "Psychoanalysis conceives of the superego as greatly influenced by cognitive factors, and to postulate stages in the development of any function or structure is not to deny the existence of an overall broad process."[9] Writing some twenty-one years later, Robert Emde, William Johnson and Ann Easterbrooks, starting from the cognitive-empirical side, espouse a similar point of view, focusing on events leading up to the emergence of superego-like self-regulatory behavior. Significantly, they point to the emergence of empathy as a critical positive factor in the development of morality. They write:

> The first stream [of early moral development centered on emotions] . . . may have to do with the emergence of empathy. . . . The emergence of comforting responses during the middle of the second year, along with helping and sharing behaviors, has been demonstrated in the studies of Radke-Yarrow [and others], and has provided considerable evidence for empathy as a normative developmental acquisition.[10]

Returning to figure 11.2, the dramatic trajectory of the story may be readily construed along these lines; that is, the agency of the superego emerges as the end of a process through which the Child develops the capacity for empathy.

Part 2: How Child and Music Become Transformed

Since the Child's transformation stands as the central theme of the story, the focal point of the musical analysis shall be the manner and means of musical transformations enacting the Child's journey. For *L'enfant,* the primary music-structural elements enabling the process of transformation are

(1) tonality—both the framing global tonality of G major and the local tonal trajectories of the individual scenes; (2) the employment of a single leitmotif—the Mother—and its status as a metonym for tonal authority; and (3) the canny use of transformed contexts for reiterated material, or, more simply, *transformed repetition,* which is applied not only to the Mother's leitmotif and the opening melody of the Prelude, but also to much of the material within the individual scenes. These musical means take place within the broader context of Ravel's aesthetic and compositional predilections, especially his emphasis on economy of means.

Transformed repetition provides the musical means for enacting the initial conflict between Mother and Child and its resolution through the Child's transformation. Example 11.1 shows seven musical excerpts representing distinct stages in the above process; each is annotated in line with the mappings of figure 11.1. The Prelude opens with two oboes sounding an organum-like succession of perfect fifths and fourths; the pentatonic pitch collection G–A–B–D–E, together with the lack of a bass line, precludes the establishment of a clear tonal center. Dramatically, the pentatonic pitch collection, along with the timbre, texture, and open intervals, convey on the one hand a sense of perfect but fragile equilibrium for the "natural order" of the household and its inhabitants; and on the other, the "premoral" Child before the "Fall" of his world-shaking tantrum.[11] The first break in this natural order comes with the entrance of the double bass in harmonics, whose initial F♮ clashes harshly with the oboes' E. While the Child enters singing "I do not want to learn my lesson" (ex. 11.1b) in consonance with the pentatonic collection, the presence of the clashing double bass already suggests a sense of "before and after"—the perfect world before the Child's arrival on the scene, and its corruption thereafter.

With the entrance of the Mother (ex. 11.1c) and the introduction of her cadential leitmotif (labeled MC for "Maman cadence"), Ravel sets in motion the dramatic and psychological narrative. Significantly, given the lack of tonal definition leading up to its introduction, MC does not confirm a key or provide any sense of even temporary tonal arrival. More specifically, it does not articulate a conventional tonal function—e.g., predominant-to-dominant or dominant-to-tonic—in the intimated key of G major. Hence the tonal authority of MC remains latent, its latency a precise analogue to the Child's lack of acceptance of his Mother's authority at the outset of the story.

Toward the opera's end, example 11.1d illustrates the moment following the Child's binding of the Squirrel's paw. After the animals attempt to revive the unconscious Child, they recall the last word he said before their riotous uprising: "Maman." They cannot understand what the word "Maman" means; nevertheless they sense that it has magical powers. Thus they call her name and she appears via her leitmotif. Her thrice-stated cadence realizes its heretofore latent tonal authority by functioning as II–V in G major, melting into the tonic with the animals' fugal setting of "Il est bon, l'Enfant, il est sage" (ex. 11.1e).

(a) Opening of Prelude: "Natural order" and "pre-moral" Child

(b) Child enters, 2/2/4: Break in the natural order

(c) Maman enters with her cadential leitmotif, 3/3/1: latent authority

Example 11.1. Transformed repetition leading to Child's internalization of "Maman" in Ravel's *L'enfant et les sortilèges*

(d) "Maman Cadence" (MC) returns as II–V in Maman's key of G major, 97/2/4

(e) The animals recognize the Child's empathy and goodness and resolve MC to tonic, 98/1/4: MC "melts" into resolution to tonic

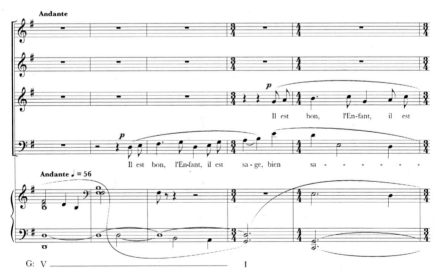

Example 11.1. Transformed repetition leading to Child's internalization of "Maman" in Ravel's *L'enfant et les sortilèges*—*(continued)*

(f) Penultimate contrapuntal combination of animals' "He is good," opening of
   Prelude, and G major tonal context, 100/2/2: natural order restored,
   underpinned by Mother's "tonal" authority

(g) Final gesture: Child sings MC at pitch to "Maman" in her key, reharmonized as
   V-I; Child *internalizes* Mother's authority

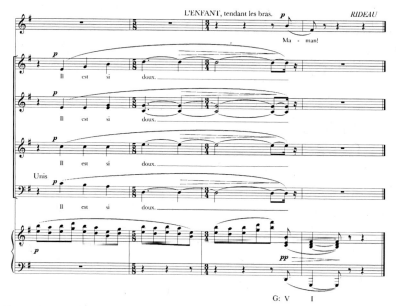

Example 11.1. Transformed repetition leading to Child's internalization of
"Maman" in Ravel's *L'enfant et les sortilèges*—*(concluded)*

In example 11.1f, Ravel shows off his contrapuntal dexterity by combining the pentatonic gesture from the opening of the opera with the fugue subject. Symbolically, the fragile equilibrium of the world before the Child's destructive tantrum is now grounded by the acceptance of Mother's authority in its musical form: the tonal context of G major.

In the final gesture of the opera (ex. 11.1g), the Child's transformation culminates in the process of musical and dramatic *internalization*. In her gloss on Freud's approach to moral development entitled "Morality and the Internalized Other," Jennifer Church writes:

> Acknowledging the superego—that is, becoming conscious of it without actually identifying oneself with it—thus depends on acknowledging its role as an overseer of the ego. Initially, of course, it is other people—parents in particular—who "oversee" our actions and decisions; and when they are internalized, it is precisely in their role as overseers that they retain the independence from the self that is necessary for a superego, or a moral "conscience."[12]

In musical terms, the Child literally internalizes his Mother's cadence. Thus he sings the treble line (the perfect fourth descent B–F$\sharp$), heretofore sounded only by instruments, which is supported by the MC. In contrast to the previous II–V progression of example 11.1d, the figure is now reharmonized as V–I in G. The isomorphism between bass and treble, Mother and Child, and superego and ego is now complete. The Mother's leitmotif becomes the structural cadence for the entire opera as the bass V–I progression supports the treble line. Consequently the latent moral and musical authority invested in the Mother not only becomes actualized, but is enacted through the Child's willing participation by holding out his arms and singing "Maman."

Using the boxed portion of figure 11.2 as a guide, the next three examples explore the role of transformed repetition in conveying the preliminary steps to empathy in Parts I and II of the opera. (The Princess will be taken up in the final section of the essay.)[13]

Example 11.2 excerpts the duet between the Wedgwood teapot and the Chinese teacup. Following the pot's foxtrot in the "black" key of A♭ minor, the cup has an F-pentatonic vocal line and pentatonic obbligato line in parallel perfect fourths within the tonal context of F major. Following their wild polytonal clash and eventual resolution to the cup's key, the Child, accompanied only by celeste, expresses his sadness upon breaking his favorite cup. Note that the same pentatonic material sets the parodistic orientalism of the cup and the serious feelings of the Child, albeit with two musical transformations: the celeste part is in rhythmic augmentation; and there is no bass. For the Child, the absence of the bass connotes the lack of any basis for transformation of his character: he experiences loss for a material possession but nothing else in his self-centered universe at this point in the story.

Entrance of the Child's beloved Chinese teacup, set to "parody" pentatonic, 20/4/1

The Child's first recognition of loss, set to rhythmic augmentation of parody pentatonic, 25/1/1

Example 11.2. The Child's first recognition of loss and the consequences of his actions

Example 11.3 presents the opening of Part II of the opera and its trans-formation. Like the Prelude, Part II opens with a gesture of perfect parallel intervals in organum-like texture, the muted strings accompanying first the slide whistle and then the solo piccolo. Thereafter, following the cacophonous chorus of frogs, the Child enters over the organum strings, singing "Ah— quelle joie de te retrouver, Jardin" [Oh, what joy to be in my garden again]"; the opening sounds suspiciously like another opera beginning out-of-doors— Debussy's *Pelléas et Mélisande*. Immediately thereafter, the Tree enters singing "Ma blessure [My wound]" (the dramatic association with Wagner's Amfortas is not reinforced by overt musical quotation). It is accompanied by the strings, which transform the linear motion in near-Wagnerian fashion from major seconds and thirds accompanying the Child to appropriately painful tritones. Besides the obvious text painting, the scene aligns itself with the opening of the opera in conveying in musical terms the state of the Child's world before and after his rampage. The difference here is that the Child actually talks to the Tree and experiences for the first time a profound sense of guilt: he real-izes that his action has defaced the unspoiled natural beauty of his beloved garden and inflicted pain.

Example 11.4a presents the last of the preliminary steps to empathy in the Child: the Cats' duet concluding Part I and its truncated reprise in Part II immediately preceding the animals' uprising against the Child. The upper portion of the example shows a schematic comparison of the respective scenes; the lower provides a harmonic reduction of the concluding cadences. Har-monically there are virtually no pure triads or seventh chords throughout: this is sexy slinky Cat music, arguably the most explicitly erotic writing in all Ravel's works. Musically and dramatically, the most significant detail is the aborting of the expected cadence and the structural resolution at the end of the scene concluding Part I (62/2/2ff.). Following the subdominant reprise, the sound-ing of $F\sharp^9$ initiating section B_2 strongly suggests a functional II chord in the tonic E major and implies continuation to V–I (see bottom left of example). Instead, the chord becomes transformed to $F\sharp^{\varnothing7}$ which is prolonged to the end of the scene and simply gives way without resolution to the F major triad that initiates the change of scene to the garden. (The notation $P_{2,0}$ uses Douthett and Steinbach's parsimonious voice-leading convention to show the motion of two pitches by semitone and none by whole step, along with the preservation of two common tones.)[14] This transformation of the F♯ chord accompanies a huge dynamic, registral, and textual crescendo depicting the increasingly intense and wild sexual behavior of the Cats. In their overt sexuality, the Cats likely stand in for the Child's parents, and their behavior is overwhelming, cha-otic, and frightening to him; no wonder the Child seeks to get out of the house and take refuge in the garden.

The reprise of the Cats' music in Part II tells a much different story. This first becomes apparent through the motivic link (denoted by square brackets)

Opening of Part II: the Child's beloved Garden and parallel perfect gesture, 64/1/1

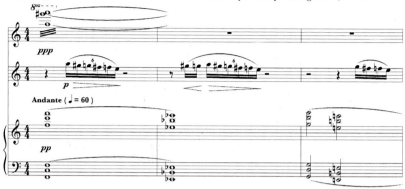

Tree's wound distorts the opening Garden music by tritone motion − Child experiences guilt, 67/1/1

Example 11.3. The Garden before and after the Child's rampage

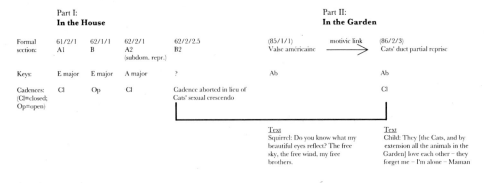

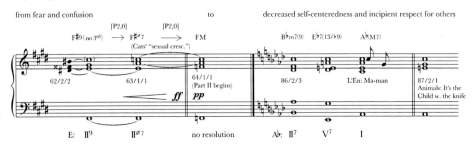

Example 11.4a. The Cats' duet and its partial reprise

between the theme from the "Valse américaine" immediately preceding and the Cats' music (both ascend a step followed by a perfect fifth; example 11.4b). As a consequence the respective texts of the two passages become linked as well. In the Valse, the Squirrel responds to the Child's rationalization for imprisoning him in a cage with: "Do you know what my beautiful eyes reflect? The free sky, the free wind, my free brothers." In the Cats' music, the Child sings: "They [the Cats, and by extension all the animals in the garden] love each other—they forget me—I'm alone." The admonitions of the Tree, Dragonfly, Bat, and Squirrel are beginning to take effect. And, in a real sense, the actual behavior of the Cats has not changed; rather, it is the Child who has changed in recognizing their love and the feelings of the other denizens of the garden. This change is registered in the reprise of the Cats' duet: their music decreases in slinky chromaticism and now leads to a full cadence concluding on a pure tonic triad, accompanying the Child's involuntary "Maman," sung to the perfect-fourth descent of Mother's leitmotif. These elements—the II–V–I motion, the Child's internalized "Maman," and a close approximation of her cadence—together foreshadow the concluding scene of the opera (although the key of A♭ major is still a half step away from that of Maman's key of G major). The Child is ready, both morally and musically, to rescue the Squirrel.

Example 11.4b. The Child's growing empathy

Part 3: The Duet between the Princess and the Child

In approaching this duet, we turn our attention away from developmental morality per se, in favor of a central Freudian concept attendant to the development of the superego—the Oedipus complex. I shall focus narrowly on the most basic tenets of the Oedipus complex as they apply to the unfolding of the story in the duet, and in turn to Ravel's musical setting.

In his well-known study *The Uses of Enchantment: The Meaning and Importance of Fairy Tales,* psychoanalyst Bruno Bettelheim applies Freud's theory to a classic type of fairy tale in a chapter entitled "Oedipal Conflicts and Resolutions: The Knight in Shining Armor and the Damsel in Distress."[15] Bettelheim begins by reviewing the basic premise of the Oedipus complex for boys and, more problematically, for girls. (We will stick with boys since the Child is male.) In brief, a young boy's first love interest naturally is his mother, given her role in addressing his needs from the moment of birth. As the baby grows into a little boy, his feelings of love for his mother come into conflict with the presence of the father: he cannot have the mother to himself for fear of retribution from the father. For Bettelheim, the story of the knight and the damsel in distress has an important adaptive function for the boy in resolving the Oedipal conflict: the beautiful princess provides a substitute outlet for his love for his mother. The boy casts himself as the knight and the only one who can save the damsel. This task may involve slaying a dragon or other dangerous creature, a creative substitution for dealing with the father.

In Colette's libretto and Ravel's musical setting, this account of the Oedipal conflict takes on a radical twist. At the end of the previous scene, the pastoral chorus of shepherds and shepherdesses has receded back to the wallpaper from whence it came. In its place, there emerges a beautiful blond princess from the scattered pages of the book of fairy tales that the Child has torn apart. The Princess is held captive by an evil enchanter, and she awaits a Knight with the crest the color of dawn to rescue her. The trappings of the classic tale in all its Oedipal overtones as described by Bettelheim are present; the Child is ready to claim his place as Knight and come to the rescue. There is only one flaw, and it is fatal: in his rampage, the Child has destroyed the pages that reveal the ending of the story. Without the certainty of a happy ending, no matter how hard he tries to rescue his Princess, he is doomed to failure.

This paradoxical scenario provided a distinct challenge to a composer as concerned with representation of story and text as Ravel. For in order to realize in musical terms this particular dramatic situation, he must simultaneously empower and disable the Child: on the one hand, to give him the strength and magical power of the Knight with the *potential* to rescue the Princess; on the other, to nullify this potential as a painful consequence of his having torn the book. For the Child, this state of affairs transforms the adaptive power of the fairy tale into an Oedipal conundrum with only one possible outcome: the Princess's unwilling return to a purgatory of the imagination, eternally waiting for a rescue never to be fulfilled.

The ensuing analysis explores how Ravel realizes in musical terms this Oedipal conundrum. For clarity's sake, the discussion shall make four passes through the music, each focusing on a different parameter. Pass 1 concentrates on form and text; pass 2 on texture, in particular the opposition of contrapuntal versus harmonic textures and their ramifications for representing the characters of the Princess and the Child; pass 3 on the melodic and motivic structure of the vocal lines; and pass 4 on tonal organization—in particular, the Child's desire for cadential resolution in the tonic E♭ major as an analogue to his desire to dictate the ending of the story.

Pass 1: Form and Text

Example 11.5a presents a formal overview for the duet. An outwardly conventional ternary form, the duet unfolds in highly symmetrical fashion. (The example aligns the A sections, while the brief B section is set off middle-right; measures are numbered from 1 coinciding with 41/1/1 of the vocal score.) Following the introduction, which conjures up the Princess from the book's torn leaves, section A_1 divides into 3 + 3 vocal phrases sung by the Princess; these are designated P_1Pr for phrase 1 Princess, P_2Pr, and so on. Following P_6Pr, an additional phrase marks the reentrance of the Child and serves as a transition to the B section; this divides symmetrically into two parts of approximately equal length coinciding with the change of key signature. The following reprise takes a surprising turn: the first three vocal phrases sung by the Princess in the opening section are now taken over by the Child; these are designated P_1E for phrase 1 *Enfant* and so on.[16] Thereafter the Princess reprises her next three phrases, after which there is a concluding section that combines a return of the introduction accompanying the disappearance of the Princess, and a transition to the Child's touching solo aria "Toi, le Cœur de la Rose."

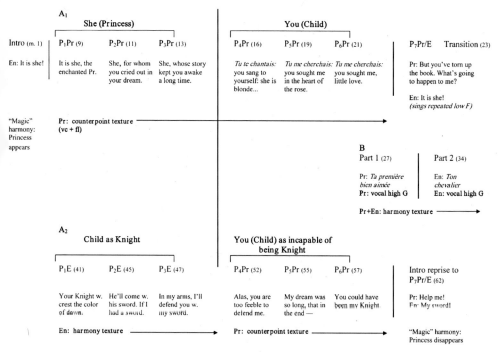

Example 11.5a. Form and text overview, Princess-Child duet

Let us now consider the summary of the text in translation, displayed according to the form. Like the musical design, Colette's text is strikingly symmetrical. In the first three phrases of A_1, the Princess conveys her magical aura by speaking of herself in the third person ("C'est Elle"—It is she). The next three phrases turn to the Child ("Tu te chantais"—You sang to yourself). With the seventh phrase, the Princess gives voice to the turning point of the duet: "But you've torn up the book. What's going to happen to me?" Section B hinges on two key rhyming phrases: the Princess's "ta première bien aimée" (your first and best love [whose fate you'll never know]) and the Child's "Ton chevalier" (your Knight), each phrase culminating on a climactic high G. This is the moment where the Child makes his claim to be the knight in shining armor, sung to the Princess's music. In the first three phrases of the reprise, the Child begins by naming the storybook Knight, then turns repeatedly to his sword (He'll come with his sword / If I had a sword / I'll defend you with my sword). More important than the aforementioned phallic symbolism is that for the Child, the sword represents a metonym for knighthood in all its power to rescue the Princess and thereby resolve the Oedipal dilemma. (Conveniently, "chevalier" (Knight) and "épée" (sword) rhyme, as well.) Sadly, the Princess tells the Child that he could have been her Knight if he had not destroyed the ending. The duet concludes with the Princess crying "Help me!" and the Child obsessing over his sword, singing "Mon épée" over and over.

Pass 2: Texture

Throughout the duet, the Princess is represented by two-voice counterpoint, her vocal line in duet with the flute, which shares approximately the same tessitura. By contrast, the Child is represented by the full harmonic texture of melody and accompaniment. Their textural opposition is as obvious as it is appropriate: the Child is real in a way that the Princess is not; hence her texture is ethereal and his is not. Perhaps less obvious but equally important are the consequences of this opposition. While the Princess's counterpoint is relatively conventional with respect to consonance and dissonance, the lack of a bass line significantly limits its ability to establish E♭ as a definitive tonic. Naturally the Child wants to reconstitute her as real and complete in his imagination. His way of doing that is to control the tonal progression: specifically, armed with a functional bass and harmonic progression, he can establish and resolve to tonic. As a necessary precondition, this means establishing *his texture* as the predominating one. This miniature drama of power and control first becomes explicit in the B section. Here the Princess and Child sing in duet in the Child's harmonic texture; in turn this leads to the reprise in which he sings *her* vocal part in *his* harmonic texture, reharmonizing it with the goal of cadencing in tonic. His failure is signaled by the Princess's resumption of her duet with the flute.

Pass 3: Melodic and Motivic Organization

Example 11.5b provides a melodic and harmonic reduction of the duet; the formal divisions are shown above the staff and aligned as in the previous example (measure numbers are once more indicated in parentheses). Following the Child's "Ah, c'est Elle" in the introduction, the Princess enters on a sustained high G_5. This high G becomes a touchstone throughout the duet, its iteration always marking a formal and dramatic arrival. The Princess's fourth, fifth, and sixth phrases make this explicit. Each phrase begins with the same musical gesture (labeled x), a neighbor figure followed by an ascending leap of a perfect fourth (the inversion of the Maman cadence motive), successively transposed up by step. The sequence follows Colette's rhyming text: "tu te chantais" is sung to B♭–E♭, "tu me cherchais" to C–F, and a rhythmically augmented "tu me cherchais" to D–G, thereby allowing the Princess to regain her initial G5. In the ensuing transitional P_7Pr/E, the Princess leads to her highest note thus far on B♭$_5$, once again on the rhyming "première bien aimée," while the Child makes his entrance singing "Ah, c'est Elle" as he did in the introduction. Unlike in the introduction, and perhaps unexpectedly, he intones his line on a single pitch in his lowest register, F_4. The repeated low pitch serves as a textural transition from the linear counterpoint of two treble voices to a fully harmonic texture with a real bass. (We shall consider the harmonic significance of this gesture in the next pass.)

Like section A_1, B divides into two parts on the basis of the voice leading of the Princess's vocal line. In the first part, her line rises by step from B_4 to the landmark G_5, again on the words "première bien aimée." Strikingly, this high point is treated in parallel fashion to the earlier passage: in Part 2 (beginning m. 34) the Princess, this time in duet with the Child, sings three loosely sequential phrases that rise by step from E to F, culminating in the regaining of G_5, which coincides with the formal reprise. This time, however, the Child, not the Princess, sings the high G on the words "ton chevalier"—your Knight. Hereafter, the vocal phrases proceed as they did in the opening section, albeit with a radical change of meaning engendered by the Child's takeover and reharmonization of the Princess's part.

Pass 4: Tonal Organization; or, His Chord Is His Sword

The opening of the duet in which the swirling harp conjures the fairy-tale Princess is perhaps the most evocative moment in the opera. It may also be the most structurally prescient, as Ravel condenses the subsequent course of the entire duet into the opening two chords. The introduction begins where the previous pastoral chorus left off. The chorus ended with an open fifth A/E in the bass, supporting the dominant E-major triad in the upper voices. With

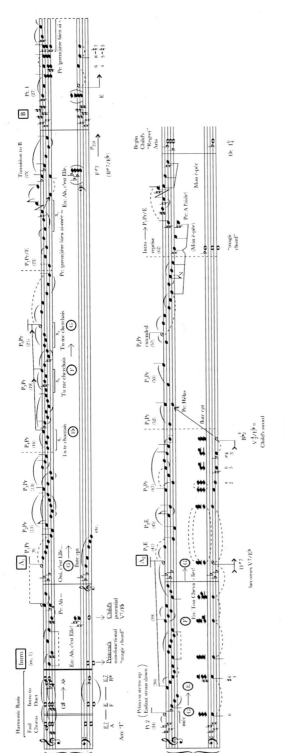

Example 11.5b. Melodic-harmonic reduction, Princess-Child duet

the bass shift down to the fifth F/C and suspension of E major above, the harmony perfectly conveys the magical aura surrounding the Princess. Significantly, this nonfunctional magic chord gives way to a hypothetically functional, albeit chromatically altered and extended, dominant seventh of E♭. An apparently trivial detail is the enharmonic shift from G♯ in the first chord as third of the upper-voice E-major triad to A♭ as chordal seventh of the dominant; its importance is revealed later. In light of the progress of the duet, this two-chord succession may be construed as follows: the movement from tonal ambiguity, suggested by the first chord, to potential functionality, suggested by the second chord, represents the unattainability of the Princess and the Child's attempt to realize his love for her.

Following the Princess's contrapuntal texture, the first hint of a real chord comes just before the B section. Specifically, the Child's repeated pitch F_4 on "c'est Elle" provides the bass and root for the Princess's plaintive cry, "But you have torn the book. What's going to happen to me?" The implied harmony is $F^{ø7}$; following the functional implications of the introduction, it presents itself as a potential $II^{ø7}$ in the Princess's implied key of E♭. Symbolically, we needn't stretch too far to read the Child's singing the functional root of the II chord as part of his desire to take control of the musical narrative and, eventually, to resolve it according to his wishes. The Princess, however, has other ideas, as $F^{ø7}$ leads not to V/E♭, but rather to E major via the voice leading $P_{2,0}$. (Both the harmony and its resolution are of course none other than the Tristan chord at pitch and its initial resolution; unlike his parody of Wagner's leitmotifs in *L'heure espagnole*, here Ravel's intent is hardly comic in nature.)

With the arrival on E major in first inversion, the duet for the first time has a bass line and a corresponding sense of tonal direction. The course of the bass follows the formal divisions precisely: G♯ leads first to E, coinciding with the arrival of the Princess's G_5 on "première bien aimée" and then to D on the Child's "ton chevalier" which overlaps with the reprise. This D supplies the root of another half-diminished seventh chord (m. 41); unlike the implied predominant function of $F^{ø7}$, $D^{ø7}$ unmistakably asserts dominant function. Thus the bass descends by step to A♭ supporting B♭$^4_2$. Here the Child is flush with youthful heroism as he sings "Come! With my sword, I will know how to defend you!" His final phrase arrives climactically on the long-awaited V^7 of E♭. He has wrested away the Princess's vocal line and reharmonized it to get to this point. In short, his chord is his sword: with his V^7 as his sword, he can resolve to tonic and thereby write the end of the story and rescue the Princess. He can even settle the enharmonic problem of the opening G♯/A♭: by transforming the Princess's bass G♯ at the beginning the B section to his bass A♭ an octave lower and resolving it, he turns uncertainty into reality, triadic atonality into tonality. Of course, there is one flaw in his thinking, and once again it is fatal: as any freshman theory student knows, a dominant seventh in four-two inversion cannot serve as a cadence; it can resolve locally, but it can't even provide a phrase ending, much less a formal point of articulation. When the Princess returns to her contrapuntal texture singing, "Alas, my little friend who is too feeble, what can you do for me?" she also conveys a metaphorical music-structural message: "Your dominant seventh could have been your sword; but it is inverted and therefore too feeble to rescue me."

To summarize, it is not only possible but fruitful to interpret the duet not only in light of Freud's Oedipus complex and Bettelheim's appropriation of it to the fairy tale, but also in terms of Colette's and Ravel's radical modification. Ravel had a rare ability to capture the world of a child in its extremes of joy and terror. In this, the central number of *L'enfant,* he uses this ability to represent the Child's deepest desires with remarkable psychological insight by means of form, texture, melody, harmony, and counterpoint.

To conclude, for Ravel's *L'enfant,* the early exegesis of Melanie Klein and its adaptation by Langham Smith have provided a useful point of departure for further analysis by suggesting the dovetailing of psycho- and music-analytic perspectives. My analysis began by placing Klein and selections from the succeeding psychoanalytic commentary on the opera within a broader context of approaches to developmental morality, including Bettelheim's work on the adaptive power of fairy tales for children. This critical contextualization enabled the mapping between musical and psychoanalytic concepts and processes on the structural scale of the opera as a whole, as well as for the central duet. This mapping helps reveal the issues of power and control underlying much of the opera as well as the moral growth of the Child into a kinder and gentler being. Both aspects are expressed in musical terms primarily through the technique of transformed repetition. Ravel employs the same music to represent different and even diametrically opposed things: Princess and Child; the Child's fear of the Cats' sexual behavior and recognition of their love; the ridiculous caricature of orientalism in the Chinese cup and the Child's remorse; and finally, self-centeredness and empathy. Transformed repetition has also expressed the orderly world in the house and in the garden and its corruption by the actions of the Child; the failed rescue of the Princess and the successful rescue of the Squirrel; and the Mother's disapproval and approval. In the best of all possible worlds, at the end of the opera the older but wiser Child would go back to his house, back to the library, and save the Princess. At least now his sword would have a better chance of being in root position.

Notes

1. Roger Nichols, *Ravel* (London: J. M. Dent, 1977), 109.

2. Melanie Klein, "Infantile Anxiety-Situations Reflected in a Work of Art and in the Creative Impulse," *International Journal of Psychoanalysis* 10 (1929): 436–43; reprinted in Melanie Klein, *Contributions to Psycho-Analysis 1921–1945* (London: Hogarth Press, 1950), 227–35. It is worth noting that the conflation of Kleinian and Freudian principles

is by no means universally accepted in psychoanalytic circles. In an earlier version of this essay, given at the annual meeting of the American Psychoanalysis Association (January 2007, New York), the audience of mostly Freudian psychoanalysts was roundly dismissive of Klein's work, including her interpretation of *L'enfant.*

3. Ibid., 228.

4. A related problem crops up in more recent psychoanalytic work on *L'enfant.* In "L'enfant et les Sortilèges Revisited," *International Journal of Psycho-Analysis* 81 (2000): 1195, Debbie Hindle writes "In thinking about this opera, I was struck by Ravel's ability to convey complex and changing states of mind and to elicit emotional responses in the listener. His use of abstract musical structures replicated feelings of conflict, ambivalence and anger, while his use of more conventional and lyrical modes allowed more tender, regretful or loving feelings to be expressed." While Hindle's distinction between dramatic modes is evident, her attempt at a musical parallel is problematic, since all musical structures are abstract, lyrical or otherwise. In "Outside Ravel's Tomb," *Journal of the American Musicological Society* 52, no. 3 (Autumn 1999): 465–530, Carolyn Abbate offers a sweeping and provocative slant on aspects of Ravel's music for *L'enfant* in relation to a number of related notions including *tombeau* as a musical and historiographical topic, automata, and early twentieth-century modernism. She does not, however, engage issues concerning musical structure with the exception of orchestration.

5. Richard Langham Smith, "Ravel's operatic spectacles: *L'heure* and *L'enfant*," in *The Cambridge Companion to Ravel*, ed. Deborah Mawer (Cambridge: Cambridge University Press, 2000), 205.

6. Christine Prost, "Ravel: L'enfant et les sortilèges: l'infidélité aux modèles," *Analyse Musicale* 21 (November 1990): 65–82.

7. My thinking on mapping has been inspired by Lawrence M. Zbikowski, *Conceptualizing Music: Cognitive Structure, Theory, and Analysis* (New York: Oxford University Press, 2002), and his ideas on "cross-domain mapping." I have modified this idea for purposes of this analysis in addressing psychoanalytic implications and their possibilities for musical enactment.

8. Sigmund Freud, "The Ego and the Id," in *The Freud Reader*, ed. Peter Gay (New York: Norton, 1989), 651.

9. Martin L. Nass, "The Superego and Moral Development in the Theories of Freud and Piaget," *The Psychoanalytic Study of the Child* 21 (1966): 60.

10. Robert N. Emde, William F. Johnson, and M. Ann Easterbrooks, "The Do's and Don'ts of Early Moral Development: Psychoanalytic Tradition and Current Research," in *The Emergence of Morality in Young Children*, ed. Jerome Kagan and Sharon Lamb (Chicago: University of Chicago Press, 1987), 259.

11. It goes without saying that virtually every commentator has a different dramatic interpretation for this stark and idiosyncratic opening. Mine attempts to take into account the varying contexts in which the passage recurs throughout the opera.

12. Jennifer Church, "Morality and the Internalized Other," in *The Cambridge Companion to Freud*, ed. Jerome Neu (Cambridge: Cambridge University Press, 1991), 215–16.

13. In Part II, the encounter between the Squirrel and the Frog (beginning 81/4/1 of the vocal score) is analyzed in detail in Peter Kaminsky, "Ravel's Late Music and the Problem of 'Polytonality,'" *Music Theory Spectrum* 26, no. 2 (Fall 2004): 248–51.

14. Jack Douthett and Peter Steinbach, "Parsimonious graphs: A study in parsimony, contextual transformations, and modes of limited transposition," *Journal of Music Theory* 42, no. 2 (Fall 1998): 241–63.

15. Bruno Bettelheim, *The Uses of Enchantment: the Meaning and Importance of Fairy Tales* (New York: Knopf, 1976), 111–16.

16. It should be noted that all other analytical accounts of this duet that I have encountered fail to note that the reprise takes place as still another transformed repetition: the Child sings the Princess's material. Rather, in these accounts the point of reprise is placed at what I am calling P_4Pr on the basis of the return of the Princess and her accompaniment by the flute.

Contributors

ELLIOTT ANTOKOLETZ is professor of musicology at the University of Texas at Austin, where he has held the Tacquard Endowed Centennial Chair and E. W. Doty Professorship in Fine Arts. He is the author of *The Music of Béla Bartók* (1984); *Béla Bartók: A Guide to Research* (1988, 1997); *Twentieth-Century Music* (1992); and *Musical Symbolism in the Operas of Debussy and Bartók* (2004), which was nominated for the Kinkeldey Award by the AMS Awards Committee (2005); and coauthor of Manuel de Falla's *Cuatro Piezas Españolas: Combinations and Transformations of the Spanish Folk Modes* (2009). He is a contributing editor of *Bartók Perspectives* (2000), *Georg von Albrecht: From Musical Folklore to Twelve-Tone Technique* (2004), and the *International Journal of Musicology*. He is a contributing coeditor of *Rethinking Debussy* (in press). Antokoletz received the Béla Bartók Memorial Plaque and Diploma from the Hungarian Government in 1981. After majoring in violin under Delay and Galamian at Juilliard (1960–65), he received his PhD in Musicology from the City University of New York (1975).

GURMINDER KAUR BHOGAL is assistant professor of music at Wellesley College. Recent publications include "Breaking the Frame: Arabesque and Metric Complexity in Ravel's Sunrise Scene," *Zeitschrift der Gesellschaft für Musiktheorie* 5, no. 1 (2008); and "Debussy's Arabesque in Ravel's Daphnis et Chloé (1912)," *Twentieth-Century Music* 3, no. 2 (2007). She is currently preparing a monograph that explores the significance of ornament in early twentieth-century French music and culture.

SIGRUN B. HEINZELMANN is assistant professor of music theory at the Oberlin College Conservatory. She holds a PhD in music theory from the Graduate Center of the City University of New York, a Master of Music in music theory and piano accompanying from the University of Massachusetts–Amherst, and the German State Diploma in piano from the Musikhochschule Stuttgart. Her essay, "Ravel and the Problem(s) of Prolongation," forthcoming in *Essays from the Fourth International Schenker Symposium*, vol. 2, offers a Schenkerian approach to the music of Ravel. She is a contributor to the *Schenker Documents Online* and has published in the *Zeitschrift der Gesellschaft für Musiktheorie*.

VOLKER HELBING teaches music theory at the University of Arts Berlin, the University of the Arts Bremen, and the Frankfurt University of Music and

Performing Arts. Following studies in flute, music theory, musicology, and German studies in Hamburg, Freiburg, and Berlin, he received his PhD in musicology in 2005. His dissertation entitled *Choreography and Distance: Studies in Ravel Analysis* (Olms Hildesheim) was published in 2008. Helbing recently contributed to and edited the special Ravel issue of *Zeitschrift der Gesellschaft für Musiktheorie*. Besides Ravel, his main research is the analysis of late-twentieth-century music (including Ligeti and Kurtág).

STEVEN HUEBNER is the author of *The Operas of Charles Gounod* (1990) and *French Opera at the Fin de Siècle: Wagnerism, Nationalism, and Style* (1999; winner of the Prix Opus 2000). His many articles and reviews have appeared in such journals as *19th-Century Music, Journal of the American Musicological Society, Cambridge Opera Journal, Music and Letters, Journal of the Royal Musical Association,* and *Revue de musicology,* as well as in several collections of essays in English, French, and Italian. His article "Zola the Sower" was winner of the 2002 Westrup Prize. Recent essays include "Ravel's Child: Magic and Moral Development," "Maurice Ravel: Private Life, Public Works," "*Laughter:* In Ravel's Time," and "Molière 'librettist': Gounod, Georgina Weldon, and *George Dandin.*" Huebner currently serves as coeditor of *Cambridge Opera Journal*. His PhD was granted by Princeton University in 1985; since then he has taught at McGill University.

PETER KAMINSKY is widely recognized for his research on the music of Maurice Ravel. His articles and essays on Ravel have appeared in *Music Theory Spectrum, Music Analysis, College Music Symposium, Zeitschrift der Gesellschaft für Musiktheorie,* and *The Cambridge Companion to Ravel;* other scholarly interests include the music of Schumann, popular music, text-music relations, and currently, issues in performance and analysis. He received his PhD from the Eastman School of Music of the University of Rochester in 1989. He has served on the faculty at the University of California–Santa Barbara, Louisiana State University, and since 1993 at the University of Connecticut–Storrs, where he is professor of music and associate head for the Department of Music.

BARBARA L. KELLY is professor of musicology at Keele University, England, UK. She researches on late-nineteenth and twentieth-century French music. She is the author of *Tradition and Style in the Works of Darius Milhaud (1912–1939)* (2003) and editor of *French Music, Culture, and National Identity, 1870–1939* (2008), and *Berlioz and Debussy: Sources, Context and Legacies* (2007, with Kerry Murphy). She has published several articles and chapters on Ravel, Debussy, Milhaud, Honegger, and Les Six, and has contributed many articles to *The New Grove Dictionary* (2001 edition), including entries on Ravel and Jolivet. In 2008 she received a British Academy award to work on the Léon Vallas Archive. She is currently completing a book on French music between the wars.

DAVID KOREVAAR, associate professor of piano at the University of Colorado–Boulder, received his BM, MM, and DMA degrees from The Juilliard School, where his teachers included Earl Wild and Abbey Simon. David Korevaar performs a wide range of solo and chamber music with a special interest in French repertoire. Honors and awards include top prizes in the University of Maryland William Kapell International Piano Competition and from the Peabody-Mason Music Foundation, as well as the Richard French award from The Juilliard School honoring his doctoral document on Ravel's *Miroirs*. Recordings include CDs of Ravel, Dohnányi, Liszt, Bach's complete *Well-Tempered Clavier* and *Goldberg Variations*, Lowell Liebermann, Brahms, Beethoven, Hindemith, and French music from the University of Colorado's Ricardo Viñes Collection. He has published on Dohnányi, Ravel, and the music in the Ricardo Viñes Collection.

DAPHNE LEONG is associate professor of music theory at the University of Colorado–Boulder. Her research interests include analysis and performance, rhythm, and the music of Béla Bartók. Her publications appear in *Journal of Music Theory, Intégral, Theory and Practice, Music Theory Online, Gamut,* and *Acta Musicologica,* as well as in edited collections. On the topic of Ravel, she has previously published (with David Korevaar) on the *Concerto pour la main gauche.* Leong is also an active pianist and chamber musician, performing in recent years in the United States, Canada, England, Romania, and Hong Kong. She holds a PhD (music theory), MA (music theory), and MMus (piano performance) from the Eastman School of Music.

MICHAEL J. PURI, associate professor of music theory at the University of Virginia, devotes his research to opening up new critical-theoretical perspectives on nineteenth- and twentieth-century French and German music, with special emphasis on Ravel and Wagner. His articles appear in the *Journal of the American Musicological Society, Music Analysis,* and *19th-Century Music,* and he has contributed to three essay collections on Ravel, including this one. Winner of the 2008 Alfred Einstein award from the American Musicological Society, he is currently finishing a book entitled *Decadent Dialectics: Memory, Sublimation, and Desire in the Music of Maurice Ravel* (Oxford University Press).

LAURI SUURPÄÄ is professor of music theory at the Sibelius Academy in Helsinki, Finland. His research concentrates on analysis of tonal music, combining technical analysis with more dramatic aspects including programmatic tensions and narrativity. His articles have been published in *Journal of Music Theory, Music Theory Spectrum, Dutch Journal of Music Theory, Intégral, Theoria,* and *Theory and Practice,* as well as in many anthologies. He is also the author of *Music and Drama in Six Beethoven Overtures: Interaction between Programmatic Tensions and Tonal Structure* (1997). Currently he is writing a book on musico-poetic aspects in Schubert's *Winterreise.*

Index

Page numbers in *italics* indicate figures.

memory, 27, 53, 70, 76; and nostalgia, 64, 66, 75; "prosthetics" of, 4, 64, 78n6

Menuet antique (Ravel), 28–30

Menuet sur le nom d'Haydn (Ravel): and Debussy's *Hommage à Haydn*, 90–96

Messiaen, Olivier, 52

Messing, Scott, 36n16, 56n8

Milhaud, Darius, 44, 45, 50, 57n25

Miroirs (Ravel), 117, 137, 274–75; and Fargue, 20–22, 275; Roland-Manuel on, 42. *See also* "Noctuelles"

Mixolydian mode, 94; in Ravel's Duo Sonata, 219–21, 228, 229, 231, *240*

Moreau, Gustave, 287

Mother Goose tales, 24–25. *See also Ma mère l'oye*

motion, 111–38; dance-like, 113–14, 117–18, 124, 134, 137, 180–82; mechanical, 113–19, 196. *See also* spiral forms

motivic transformation, 156–59, 289–90

Mozart, Wolfgang Amadeus, 11, 12, 34; Ravel on, 174n3; sonatas of, 143, 169

musical objects, 113–15, 137, 144, 156–59

Mussorgsky, Modest, 212, 238

Nass, Martin, 311

neoclassicism. *See* classicism

New Viennese School, 214

Nichols, Roger, 288

Nicholsen, Shierry Weber, 82n54

Nietzsche, Friedrich, 86

"Noctuelles" (Ravel), 20, 117–18, 139n22; Bhogal on, 273–86, *281*, 301–2; Helbing on, 275, 276, 303n5; Jankélévitch on, 303n11; motives of, 114; ornament in, 273–74, 293; Schneider on, 286, 303n16; sonata form in, 280, *281*. *See also Miroirs*

"Oiseaux tristes" (Ravel), 20, 21, 38n56, 115

"Ondine" (Ravel), 98, 110n29, 208n2, 286–302; *femme fatale* in, 274, 286–87, 300, 301; ornament in, 273–74;

sonata form in, 289, *290*, 300. *See also Gaspard de la nuit*

Orenstein, Arbie, 31, 82n48, 108n2, 138n1

ornament, in Ravel's piano music, 272–302

Paddison, Max, 79n21, 80n28, 81n44

Panofsky, Erwin, 77n3

pantoum form, 160, 169, 176n33, 177n34, 178n54

"Le paon," 245–59, *250*, 268–69. *See also Histoires naturelles*

"parallel scheme," 291, 292, 304n25

Parks, Richard S., 174n10

"Pavane de la belle au bois dormant" (Ravel), 86–90, 108

Pavane pour une infante défunte (Ravel), 4, 86–90

Pensky, Max, 81n35

Pfann, Walter, 214, 242n18

Phrygian mode, 156, 169, 220, 226

Piaget, Jean, 311

Piano Concerto in G Major (Ravel), 114, 116, 119–24, 137

Piano Concerto for the Left Hand (Ravel), 3, 116, 137

Piano Trio (Ravel), 137; and Chopin's Piano Sonata op. 4, 177n42; and *Ma mère l'oye*, 177n39; musical form of, 143–44, 154, 160–74, *164, 170*; Roland-Manuel on, 171

Plato, 78n6

Poe, Edgar Allan, 4, 13–18, 46; and Baudelaire, 13–15, 37n24, 45, 97; and Mallarmé, 13, 15–16, 37n22, 97; on melancholy, 17; Ravel on, 15–16; and Ravel's "Le gibet," 97, 107–8

Poe, Edgar Allan, works of: "The Masque of the Red Death," 14; "The Philosophy of Composition," 9–10, 14–18, 45, 48, 97, 107–8; "The Raven," 9, 14, 16, 18, 48, 109n22

poètes maudits, 13

poetic-choreographic idea, 181–84, *182–83*

polymodal chromaticism, 214, 220–21